MORE PRAISE FOR FEAR'S JUSTICE

PRAISE FOR MARC OLDEN'S
FEAR'S JUSTICE

"A tense and muscular crime adventure. Olden lays down a hard-as-nails story that rings with savvy appraisal of halls of power and mean streets."
—*Publishers Weekly*

"A nonstop nail-biter and terrific read."
—Richard Givan, *Lexington Herald-Leader*

"Tough, gritty, and compelling. . . . A cop to the core, the hero of Marc Olden's new thriller is politically incorrect and proud of it as he bulldozes his way through a blue wall of corruption and death."
—W.E.B. Griffin, author of the bestselling Badge of Honor series

"Refreshingly realistic. . . . The first book I've read that tells it like it is. . . . Top of the line for pure reading enjoyment."
—Bob Steel, *Chattanooga Free Press*

"Piano-wire writing: razor-sharp but oh-so lyrical in a leather-tough sort of way. Dirty Harry with a heart of gold."
—*Kirkus Reviews*

D1329272

MORE PRAISE FOR *FEAR'S JUSTICE* AND MARC OLDEN

"Olden's thriller is unfailingly readable and terrifically well-written, a guilty pleasure of the highest order."

—Booklist

"Marc Olden comes out with his .9mm cocked and ready to fire in *FEAR'S JUSTICE,* a taut, gripping thriller that easily hurdles the restrictions of its genre. Olden has etched his characters with detailed precision and skill, bringing them to life, making them feel and sound as real as a front-page headline. The plot hits overdrive from the first sentence, the pacing is *French Connection* nonstop, and the story never stalls, always picking up speed until it slams face first into its final chilling resolution. With *FEAR'S JUSTICE,* Marc Olden has composed a dynamic and original novel, one bound to resonate long after publication. Just like Fear Meagher, this one can't miss."

—Lorenzo Carcaterra, author of Sleepers

"Marc Olden is as good a crime writer as we have, and in *FEAR'S JUSTICE* he outdoes himself to produce a tense, dramatic novel. . . . This is a powerful, gripping tale of cops and crime, one that puts the reader dead center in the power politics of NYC's criminal justice system. . . . A first-rate suspense thriller that will keep readers on the edge of their seats."

—Richard Langford, The Observer

Books by Marc Olden

Dai-Sho
Gaijin
Giri
Oni
Te
Kisaeng
Krait
Gossip
Poe Must Die
A Dangerous Glamour
The Book of Shadows
Cocaine
The Informant
Narc
Black Samurai
Choices (as Lesley Crafford)
The Harker File
Fear's Justice*

*Published by POCKET BOOKS

FEAR'S JUSTICE

MARC OLDEN

POCKET BOOKS

New York London Toronto Sydney Tokyo Singapore

This book is a work of fiction. Names, characters, places and inci-
dents are products of the author's imagination or are used ficti-
tiously. Any resemblance to actual events or locales or persons,
living or dead, is entirely coincidental.

 POCKET BOOKS, a division of Simon & Schuster Inc.
1230 Avenue of the Americas, New York, NY 10020

Copyright © 1996 by Marc Olden

Published by arrangement with Villard Books

All rights reserved, including the right to reproduce
this book or portions thereof in any form whatsoever.
For information address Villard Books, a division of
Random House, Inc., 201 East 50th Street, New York,
NY 10022

ISBN: 0-671-00379-8

First Pocket Books printing January 1999

10 9 8 7 6 5 4 3 2 1

POCKET and colophon are registered trademarks of
Simon & Schuster Inc.

Cover photo by Tony Stone Images

Printed in the U.S.A.

For Joe Quarequio,
who is the best of
Fear Meagher

Acknowledgments

I'd like to thank my mother, COURTENAYE, for her love and unwavering faith and for putting me in touch with the soul of this book; RICHARD PINE, who did everything right and without whom the book would never have happened; and, finally, DIANE CRAFFORD, who gave me the title and who made me believe that Camus was right, that women are all we know of paradise on this earth.

"Every society gets the kind of criminal it deserves. What is equally true is that every community gets the kind of law enforcement it insists on."

    —ROBERT F. KENNEDY,
      Free Enterprise in Organized Crime

I
The Game

On an icy Sunday in March shortly after 10:30 P.M., the black vagrant agreed to help the chubby white man unload his van, with whitey coming through when the job was done.

One hundred dollars for ten minutes' work.

"Dodge minivan at the entrance to the parking lot," the white man said. "Bitter cold out. If you don't want to do it, I'll understand."

"Cold won't bother me," Maurice said. "I'll be there."

"Like I said, ten minutes at the most."

They were in the steel-and-glass lobby of the International Arrivals Building at Kennedy Airport, in front of the main currency exchange, now closed for the night. Hotel-reservation desks, ticket counters, and baggage check-ins had short lines or no customers at all.

A hundred dollars for ten minutes' work. Maurice blew on fingers chilled by a hawkish north wind. For that kind of money, he would soak his drawers in gasoline and run through hell.

He was in his late thirties, a slim, dark-skinned man with fleshy lips, black mustache and goatee. His forehead was covered by dreadlocks that hid a scar he'd received when a cop had clubbed him with a police radio hard enough to break the batteries.

His top front teeth were missing. His remaining teeth were discolored or broken; his cheeks were bumpy with ingrown hairs. He was wrapped in a filthy green quilt and wore a seedy fur hat. Instead of shoes he wore several pairs of dirt-encrusted socks. For protection he carried a linoleum knife in the pocket of his sweatpants.

1

He said to the white man, "We best be getting over to the parking lot."

"You go ahead," the white man said. "I have to make a phone call. I'll meet you there. Remember: Dodge minivan near the entrance."

Maurice wiped his runny nose on the quilt. "Dodge minivan. Got it."

The white man watched Maurice walk away, quilt mopping the floor in his wake. His sourish smell hung in the air. When Maurice exited through the automatic doors, the white man welcomed the cold draft. Damn nigger stank to high heaven.

Kennedy Airport was full of homeless blacks panhandling, thieving, and scaring passengers; they were living illegally in hangars, heating plants, cargo complexes, chapels, and office buildings. The white man spotted a black derelict sleeping on the terminal's observation deck, wrapped in a dirty army blanket, head resting on beat-up sneakers to prevent them from being stolen. Where the hell was security?

He pulled on a pair of black leather gloves, covering the detective's gold ring on his right hand. His wristwatch had a silver-link bracelet and a jeweled face that gave the time in major cities around the world. He stared at Maurice through dark glasses, watching him cross the access road between the terminal and the parking lot. Twice the vagrant tripped over the quilt, dropping to his knees and rolling around like a sleeper having a nightmare.

The white man couldn't be seen entering the parking lot with Maurice. He'd go in from another direction. He had to play the game right.

Outside under a moonless sky the white man stood alone in an empty taxi rank, blowing warm air into his cupped hands. Cold as a bitch out here. He turned up his coat collar and watched Maurice drag his sorry ass into the parking lot.

Finally.

Grinning, the white man jogged across the road. Ready to play the game.

* * *

Queens Homicide Task Force/Detective's Report (DD5 No. 238)

INTERVIEW WITH MAURICE ROBICHAUX AKA DWAYNE MUSTAPHA, TYRELL CLIFFORD, TONY MONTANA

CASE: *Schiafino Murder*

Subject interviewed March 22, 0145 hours, at borough headquarters. Subject is male black, 38, 5'7", 140 pounds, with dreadlocks, black beard and mustache. He states he is homeless and lives at Kennedy Airport. Subject states that around 10:30 p.m. on 3/21 he walked from the International Arrivals Building to the parking lot opposite the terminal. He arrived minutes later, where he met a male white who had hired him to unload a Dodge minivan.

Subject states he and m/w were alone. He further states the m/w, whose name he never knew, handed him a bottle of wine. Subject drank from the bottle and immediately passed out. He states he awoke in the parking lot to find himself in the custody of homicide detectives, who arrested him at 0200 hours for the murder of Det. Schiafino. Airport security guards had summoned homicide detectives after discovering the subject lying beside Det. Schiafino's body.

Subject states he met the m/w, described as thirtyish, chubby, bearded, and wearing dark glasses, a week ago in the International Arrivals Building. Subject states the m/w gave him a hundred-dollar bill every day during this time.

Subject stated he was set up, that he believes the m/w murdered Det. Schiafino and arranged for him to take the blame.

Maurice Robichaux's version

"Tonight I come to the terminal round 10:30. I was meeting this white man because every day he give me a new hundred-dollar bill. He do that for a week. He don't tell me his name, he just give me money. I didn't tell nobody because niggers at the airport always robbing people. At first I thought the hundreds were counterfeit, but they turned out to be real.

"Tonight we meet, and this white man say he like

3

to help people down on their luck like me. He say he would give me another hundred if I help him unload a minivan in the parking lot. Hundred dollars for ten minutes' work. Since he always give me money, I say I help him out. I wait for him in the parking lot. He show up and he give me some wine. I drink it, and next thing I know I wake up in handcuffs, and cops say I killed some policewoman. I never kill nobody."

Case Information

Subject is a known EDP with a history of drugs and violence. He has served time on Rikers Island for criminal trespass, criminal possession of stolen property, and possession of burglary tools. Subject was discovered 3/22, 0100 hours, drunk and unconscious in parking lot opposite International Arrivals Building at Kennedy. He was lying beside Det. Lynda Schiafino, who had been hacked to death with a linoleum knife found in subject's hand.

II

Dead Women

I had fallen asleep at my desk, and when I awoke the dead girl was standing in my office doorway. A violent-crimes cop is always haunted by ghosts.

She was a Hispanic female, fifteen at most, slim-hipped, small-bosomed, in green spandex pants, Phillies Blunt T-shirt, and silver high heels with pink anklets. Her black hair was short, the sides streaked purple and green. Delicate gold bracelets brightened her skin-and-bones wrists. She stepped from the doorway, turned her back, and pointed to the bullet holes at the bloodstained base of her skull. Smiling, she motioned for me to touch her wounds.

I'd worked violent crimes in Manhattan for fifteen years,

half with homicide before switching to OCCB, the Organized Crime Control Bureau. I saw the victims' faces in my sleep and wondered why the women haunted me most of all, and decided it was because I'd failed to protect them.

The dead girl crossed to the window and pointed to an airliner silhouetted against a full moon. Then she stepped through the glass.

Outside, she turned her small face to me and tapped the glass twice. The sound was barely audible. I shivered, and I don't scare easily.

Seeing ghosts was nothing new for me. But I'd never heard one until now. *Never.*

A sudden burst of wind rattled the window frame, puffing up the curtains. I smelled the perfume the dead girl was wearing when she'd been murdered. I left my chair and started toward her, but before I took a step, she vanished.

She had been Lourdes Balera, a former sophomore at the Bronx High School of Science and the daughter of a Manhattan hospital administrator. It was as a teenage prostitute that she, along with her boyfriend, had been shot to death this afternoon in a Times Square hotel opposite the Port Authority Bus Terminal.

The boyfriend had been twenty-two-year-old Tonino Cuevas, a chunky Ecuadoran who should have gone south when he had the chance. In the past month, seven Ecuadoran males had been murdered in New York. Tonino was number eight.

The Ecuadorans had been whacked by professionals. Two shots in the back of the head at point-blank range, no witnesses, no clues, and the shooter always took time to pick up his shell casings. Care and diligence bring luck, they say.

The vics had been young males, late teens, early twenties—illegal aliens who'd banded together under Tonino to hijack trucks from the city's largest department store. The swag, everything from furs to juicers, was being sent back to Ecuador for sale on the black market.

Tonino's boys had kept themselves in rice and beans through the serious use of knives on hijacked truck drivers. One unfortunate driver, slashed in the face, had lost an eye; another had a hand nearly severed from his wrist. The Ecuadorans were ball busters, hard-nosed greasers who resisted arrest and slashed their fingertips to avoid identification.

But the winds of change were blowing. Tonino's home-boys were being murdered, their bodies left in plain sight. You might say someone was sending a message.

I had thought the Ecuadorans were being smoked by Italians. Hijacking is a wop specialty, and they discourage competition. I checked with a Gambino capo, who assured me these particular beaners were not being iced by anyone in New York's five families.

Which didn't mean the wops were sorry to see them go. When you're alone in the race, you win every time.

OCCB is based in police headquarters, with branch offices throughout the city. I worked out of the Park Avenue office, in a penthouse built for a lunatic millionaire who'd had a concrete frame poured to hold three thousand tons of dirt for a vegetable garden before deciding he really didn't want to live there.

We were up to our armpits in work. Immigrants were pouring into the city, bringing new criminal syndicates with them. Organized crime wasn't just Italian anymore. It was Israeli diamond thieves, Nigerian credit card scams, Korean white slavers, Chinese heroin importers, and Russian gun smugglers—alien trash staining New York like snails leaving a shine.

As a white, meat-eating, heterosexual male, I didn't like it. As a cop I liked it even less.

A third of the city's seven million people were now foreign born. Korean beauty salons, Indian spice shops, Colombian travel agencies, Lebanese bakeries, Chinese real estate agencies, African sidewalk peddlers—New York wasn't America anymore. Not my America.

What the hell had Lourdes Balera been trying to tell me?

I used my fists to rub tired eyes and decided on a final look at the crime-scene photographs before packing it in. Something in them bothered me.

I'd taken the first drag on a cigarette when I heard a knock on my open door. Until now I'd thought I was alone, the only person on either floor.

A detective entered my office, holding two cups of steaming coffee and frowning at my messy desk. He was a thirty-two-year-old black man, ten years younger than me, with almond-shaped eyes and a pigeon-toed walk. He was dressy, in a black leather shirt, white bow tie, and gray flannel trousers with knifelike creases.

I put both feet on the desk and faced him. "Detective Antoine Hardaway, who refused to become just another conk-headed, jive-ass spade preacher and instead joined the police force, where he became a credit to his race."

"Detective Feargal Meagher. A fat white Mick with a bucket head. If I saw something as ugly as you in the forest, I'd shoot it, then run back to the car."

"Two-ten isn't fat. Fat's when you step on your dog's tail and it dies."

"Two-ten. On the left side of your ass maybe." Antoine handed me the coffee as he sat on my desk. "Two-thirty in the morning. Don't you have a home? When it's time to go, you leave even if you got nowhere to go."

Antoine was married to a Jew and spoke Yiddish, which helped him make cases against the Russian mobs, whose members were mostly Jews.

He'd just arrested a Long Island rabbi for importing counterfeit American hundred-dollar bills from Iran and passing them through Jewish charities and diamond shops. Jews were protesting the bust, calling it discrimination and a frame-up. Antoine's wife was a protest leader, so he wasn't in any hurry to get home.

"I understand you got lucky again," he said, taking one of my cigarettes. "I thought your sorry *tochis* was gone for sure this time."

"You live right, and good things come to you."

On a recent drug bust a Jamaican dealer had shot and killed an OCCB detective, then wounded me in the hand. I responded by picking him up and dropping him on a fire hydrant six times. A brutality complaint—blacks had filed three against me this year—had just been dismissed.

"Fear Meagher," Antoine said. "A dark moment in black history."

"True, but that's just a small part of my work. Anyway, you're not black, you're a cop." I pointed to the crime-scene photographs. "Do me a favor and check them out. I'm beat. Can't see straight anymore."

"The Ecuadorans?"

"*Sí, sí.* This is an election year, as you know, and I have to stay up late because the mayor wants to keep his job. One of his biggest fund-raisers is Jonathan Munro, the same Mr. Munro who owns the store Tonino's greaseballs are ripping off. Or, should I say, were ripping off."

"I see. Well, the mayor's a brother. Let's keep his black ass right where it is."

"The mayor's an asshole," I said. "We need a new asshole to take his place."

Antoine picked up the photographs, a dozen five-by-seven color shots, and sang in a gravelly whisper, "Love will make you go home early / love will make you stay out all night long."

He looked at me. I looked at him. A gust shook the window, sending cold air into the room and turning pages of a magazine lying on the windowsill. I said, "Maybe some other time."

He said, "Up to you. You talk, I listen."

I warmed my hands around the coffee cup. The mayor wasn't my only reason for putting in an eighteen-hour day. I had to do something to keep from thinking about Lynda, the woman I loved more than any I'd ever known.

Yesterday I'd walked out on her; I'd had no choice, not after what she'd done. I wondered if she knew how deeply I felt about her. If she did, things might have been different.

She was a thirty-four-year-old detective assigned to a Queens precinct just blocks away from the house I shared with my father. She was married to a cop, a psycho who was making her life miserable. If he ever learned we were seeing each other, he'd kill us both.

Antoine held a magnifying glass to a photograph and squinted, sending frown lines across his forehead. He said, "Contact wounds. The shooter wanted to make sure."

"He used a twenty-two Magnum," I said. "The weapon of choice for discriminating hit men."

Antoine moved nearer the desk lamp. "No signs of forced entry. They let the killer in. Man, I don't believe it."

"Maybe he had a key. Or pretended to be a john. The Ecuadorans kept moving around to avoid this guy. One night in Brooklyn, the next in the Bronx, then over to New Jersey, Connecticut, wherever. They grew beards, wore dark glasses, tried to lose themselves in the Hispanic community. Tried passing as Cubans, Mexicans, Dominicans, Puerto Ricans. Forget it. The shooter found them every time."

Antoine nodded in admiration. "He's good. Wish I knew where he gets his information." He tapped one photograph with a long, manicured finger. "Tonino had an arsenal with him: Uzi, Tech-9, Browning automatic, ammo clips. The man was ready. Guess a blade wasn't good enough, not with his ass on the line."

"We found that stuff in the closet."

"Tonino sees his friends dropping like flies. He knows he's next. He gets himself some serious firepower, but he's not holding it when the shooter comes through the door. Am I missing something here?"

I rubbed my stiff neck. "The shooter outfoxed Tonino. And just when the spic found true love, too. Lourdes's name was carved on Tonino's guitar. We came across a copy of a song he'd written for her in Spanish. She's why he hung around New York."

"Pussy will get you every time." Antoine shook his shaved head. "Guy on the run always heads for a woman when he should be heading for the border."

I stood up. Suddenly, I was awake. "That's it. That's what's been bothering me. *The girl.* She wasn't in the wrong place at the wrong time. She was a target. Just like Tonino."

Antoine's slanted eyes were slits notched in brown wood. "A contract on a runaway? You serious?"

"She knew too much. She had to go."

"What the hell could she know? She was living at home till a month ago. Probably split when she got tired of being raped by her father. She wasn't a thief. She was Tonino's girlfriend, period."

"For sure," I said. "She had no criminal record and no known criminal associates other than Tonino. But she did have something of value. Something worth killing her for."

"I'm listening."

"She knew where Tonino was."

Antoine closed his eyes. "Shit, you're right."

"She led the shooter to Tonino. The one thing Tonino and the shooter have in common is little Miss Baiera."

I turned toward the window, half-expecting to see Lourdes nodding her head in approval. I said, "The shooter doesn't make mistakes. He knew Tonino had company. He knew what he'd find at the hotel."

"I'll buy that." Antoine studied another photograph. "Our boy could have isolated Tonino. Gotten him alone, then taken him out. *If he'd wanted to.*"

"Not this time." I swallowed some coffee. "This time somebody booked a party of two. Could be our first break. I'm betting there's a connection between Lourdes and the shooter. Has to be. Otherwise why kill her?"

The phone rang. I gave Antoine a thumbs up for his help, then grabbed the receiver. "Yeah?"

A woman said, "Fear?" Her voice trembled. She'd been crying.

"This is Detective Meagher," I said. "Who is this?"

"Detective Lisa Watts. Has anyone told you?"

I knew Lisa only slightly and didn't like her. She was Lynda's partner, a chain-smoking little woman with a tremendous need to criticize. Had she been present at Creation, she'd have offered some useful hints. Lynda liked her, but I found the lady hard to take.

"Has anyone told me what?" I said.

"Lynda's dead," Lisa said. "She was murdered a few hours ago, at Kennedy Airport."

I stumbled into my desk and gripped it to keep from going down. Until Lynda, I had doubted my capacity to love anyone. She was the last thing I had to lose. From now on I knew the future would hold nothing, leaving me angry and frightened.

I said, "How did she die?"

"Stabbed to death. It was horrible."

Lisa went quiet. She tried to speak but couldn't. My hands were cold and sweaty. I listened to her whimper, then finally said, "Who did it?"

"A homeless guy who hangs out at the airport. They got him."

"She positively identified? You sure it's her?"

"The guy had her gun, badge, and ID. Oh God, I don't know how I'm going to get through the funeral. It's tomorrow afternoon. She was Jewish. She has to be buried within twenty-four hours."

"Thanks for calling." I hung up and walked to the window, unable to concentrate. My vision was blurred.

Two dead women. That's what Lourdes Balera had tapped on my window. And the plane she'd pointed at had been heading to Kennedy, where Lynda had been killed.

I pressed my forehead against the cold glass and wept, and I thought about the guilt that would follow me forever.

III

The Cemetery

Brooklyn's Green-Wood Cemetery is 150 years old and has 480 acres of landscaped hills, quaint lakes, and winding trails with names like Twilight Dell and Hemlock Path. Buried here are Lola Montez, Samuel F. B. Morse, and John Matthews, the inventor of soda pop. Here also are the remains of Albert "Mad Hatter" Anastasia, head assassin for Murder, Inc., and Joey "Crazy Joe" Gallo, who killed Anastasia and was later gunned down while eating pasta in a Manhattan restaurant.

To discourage sightseers, the graves of Anastasia and Gallo have been left off cemetery maps.

The reverse is true of dead cops. Their graves, while a poor remembrance, are never secret.

It was three-thirty in the afternoon. My father and I were in Green-Wood with Lynda's family and friends at the graveside service. Reporters and photographers eyed us the way hyenas regard crippled zebras.

I had spent last night in the cold darkness of my bedroom,

drinking Irish whiskey, thinking about Lynda, and hating myself for having walked out on her. I fell into a troubled sleep just as the sun crept into the backyard. My dreams had been full of violence, and I'd raced through them like a hunted man, waking up exhausted and heartbroken.

I'd never had much use for funerals. All they did was entertain the living, hold up traffic, and make undertakers rich.

The graveside service is the most useless part of the farce. I couldn't bear watching sniveling relatives collapse as the departed was lowered into the ground. I usually picked this time to head for the exit.

Not today. There'd be no walking away from Lynda's grave. The guilt inside me was her. And she was a heavy burden.

My father, Dion Meagher, clutched a rose and watched a hard north wind tear at the flag covering Lynda's coffin. A plump, fiftyish rabbi, skullcap clipped with bobby pins to graying hair, conducted the service. Unbeknownst to him, the rabbi topped my father's shit list. He had stopped Dion from placing the rose on Lynda's grave, saying Jews don't allow flowers or markers on graves for a year.

"They use that year to shop around for the best deal," Dion whispered.

Dion Patrick Gavin Meagher was a small sixty-two-year-old retired Irish cop who worked as a security guard. He had a drinker's red-veined nose, and his right shoulder was partially numb from nerve damage. Before leaving the force, he'd been hacked with a meat cleaver by a fifteen-year-old black girl he had been trying to arrest, the young woman having killed her month-old son by airmailing the little bastard from a ten-story Harlem window when he wouldn't stop crying. These days he worked as a bank guard on Staten Island, where he spent weekends with a forty-year-old red-haired loan officer who walked nude on his bare back in high heels.

We were alike, Dion and me. Quiet, reserved, and not good at communicating with other people. We took risks and were bad losers.

I admired him and had imitated his example, making us

12

both politically incorrect. Reporters, civil libertarians, and racial activists viewed me as a bigot, homophobe, and sexist porker. Apparently, I'd failed to catch that great train of human-rights advances rolling across our land these past thirty years.

Since the thirst for brotherhood didn't run all that deep in me, being condemned by the PC crowd wasn't too agonizing. Straight up, I didn't give a shit about the oneness of mankind.

In Harlem, I'd once arrested a black man for slicing the arms and legs off a five-year-old girl with an electric saw. While I was escorting this raisin to a squad car, one of his black neighbors threw lye on me, burning my hands. In Washington Heights, I was putting the cuffs on a fifteen-year-old boy, a hit man for a Dominican drug mob, when his loving mother broke my elbow with a baseball bat. To me, brotherhood was a bad dream.

Lynda's funeral preceded the graveside service. It was held in a hundred-year-old synagogue located among the old brownstones and private clubs in Brooklyn's Park Slope. Outside, the governor, mayor, police commissioner, and ten city-council members had stood with thirteen thousand cops in a formation stretching fifteen blocks. I stood beside Lisa Watts, who told me Lynda had been the first woman detective killed in NYPD history.

New York rarely becomes excited over violent death. The city's indifference to corpses and mortal remains is immense, to put it mildly. Lynda's death, however, was different. It stirred up more commotion than anything I'd seen in some time.

Newspapers ran front-page editorials denouncing politicians opposed to the death penalty. The police department demanded more-powerful handguns for cops. Television interrupted its regular programming to announce the arraignment of Lynda's killer. Her congressman called for an investigation of airport security nationwide.

The *Times* received a letter from a psycho who vowed to blow up the courthouse during the trial of Lynda's killer. *That jungle bunny's going to get what's coming to him.* This was New York. Full of free spirits ready to share their secret wishes with you.

Black militants, civil libertarians, and homeless advocates refused to see Lynda's murder as a crime. Instead they chose to blame her death on four hundred years of slavery in America. To my knowledge, Maurice Robichaux was living in a free country. He wasn't a slave anymore. So there went his right to kill cops.

Our black mayor did what I expected him to do. He was running for reelection and had a stranglehold on the black vote. Lynda's murder presented him with an opportunity to tighten that grip. I looked for him to choose racial politics over being rational and wise, and the schmuck didn't disappoint me. He wasn't about to criticize his black brothers. Not even when they were shoveling shit.

He held a press conference that morning, at which he refused to condemn blacks and liberals who support cop killers. He said, "Do not let this vile crime tear apart the wonderful, varicolored tapestry that is New York." He also said we were all in this together. That's when I had trouble holding on to my breakfast.

Cops are in it alone. Alone on mean streets with the freakiest bunch of drug-damaged psychos since Charles Manson and his fun seekers roamed the California countryside looking for strangers to play with.

The time for linking arms and singing "We Are the World" was past.

Five police helicopters had roared over the synagogue in tribute. Police bagpipers played their death song. There were muffled drums, and a police bugler blew taps. CNN and six local channels had televised the funeral live.

Hearing a British accent in the crowd, I turned and saw a slight, thirty-something Englishman, a reporter with teeth that couldn't be cleaned by sandpaper. Speaking into a tape recorder, he was describing the grim faces of white-gloved officers in dress blues as they escorted the hearse from the synagogue.

"To understand New York's high crime rate," he said, "one must first understand urban demographics."

Translation: blacks are committing most of the city's violent crimes.

Which is why whites are moving to the suburbs, leaving New York to the brothers and whoever wanders into their sights.

At Lynda's grave I watched family members huddle around her ailing father, Oz Lesnevitch. He was a dwarfish seventy-year-old Polish Jew, a retired shoe manufacturer suffering from glaucoma, stomach cancer, and a bad heart. He blinked away tears and clung to his nurse, a flat-faced black woman at least as wide as a barn door. Like my father, he'd been both widowed and divorced.

Clutching his arm was Judith Lesnevitch, his redheaded eighteen-year-old daughter and Lynda's half sister. Earlier, when I'd offered my condolences, her response had been a bit testy. "My name is not Judith," she said, looking at me as though I were describing the first time I'd ever masturbated.

I attributed her snot-nosed attitude to her being upset over Lynda's murder. Then I remembered Lynda had said her half sister wanted to be an actress and had renamed herself. Judith was now Jullee Vulnavia. The name Jullee was her own concoction. Vulnavia came from her favorite movie, a Vincent Price flick, *The Abominable Dr. Phibes*. Jullee Vulnavia lived with her father in Queens, in a house near the ruins of the 1964 World's Fair, and pretty much did as she pleased.

The service ended with Fred Estevez, the pop-eyed thirty-nine-year-old Cuban who ran Lynda's precinct, handing the folded coffin flag to Detective Robert Schiafino, Lynda's husband. Schiafino held the flag to his chest—a thirtyish, beefy man, hatless in the March chill.

Say the name Robert Schiafino, and a picture formed. He had a reputation as a conniving son of a bitch, a man who was not merciful. He was known as Bobby Schemes, king of the mind fuckers. He was also a stud muffin with the ladies.

I knew Schiafino only slightly, enough to realize I was better off keeping my distance. He was violent and slick and had pulled some frightening shit in his time. Word was he had recently shoved the owner of a gay escort service into a closet with a pit bull, a reminder to keep those payoffs coming.

We'd worked together once, three months on a task force investigating Russians and dagos skimming gasoline taxes, then hiding the money in offshore banks. That's when I'd watched him take a running leap and jump on the face of a fat, bald-headed Russian suspect who'd called him a faggot.

"Fuck him if he can't take a joke," Schiafino said.

Now and then we ran into each other at police seminars, picnics, and a bar on Manhattan's West Side. Our relationship was hello–good-bye, nothing more. This seemed advisable since he was a known head case and I was fooling around with his wife.

I wasn't afraid of him, but why look for trouble. Bobby Schemes had a reputation for getting even. You never saw him strike, and he didn't leave fingerprints.

A cold afternoon sun was casting long shadows across cemetery headstones as I left my father and walked toward Detective Schiafino. I intended to shake his hand and offer my condolences. I needed a drink and I needed to be alone, but the commiseration thing had to be done.

Schiafino wore dark glasses and held a handkerchief to his face. Just the thing for those heartwarming, prize-winning press photos. See the flag-toting, grieving detective being comforted by grim-faced fellow officers. See him struggle to carry on after having lost his beloved wife.

What we had here was an Oscar-winning performance, shuck and jive in the cold March air, because Bobby Schemes didn't give a rat's ass about Lynda. He'd broken her jaw and he'd knocked her unconscious. He'd treated her like dirt. He'd also pointed a loaded gun at her. They had recently agreed to a divorce.

Yesterday, at our last meeting, Lynda showed up scared shitless. I had never seen her so afraid.

I asked if Schiafino had hit her again. She dug her nails into my forearm and said her husband was into something very scary. Something involving a secret group of cops from New York and Washington. Working with him was Eugene Elder, the former Manhattan prosecutor who was now Schiafino's attorney. While telling me this, Lynda either chain-smoked or chewed a corner of her mouth. I'd never seen her so jumpy.

I knew Eugene Elder and didn't like him. He was a tall, long-faced black man in his late thirties with a bass voice, large teeth, and a tendency to be vicious and unscrupulous when seriously inconvenienced or upset. He was called Daddy Duke because of his elegant wardrobe and a readiness to advance the careers of young women willing to succumb to his animal magnetism. He was a man of odds and angles, good at taking credit and avoiding failure, and he got along with cops, provided they listened to him with admiration and took his advice on working cases. I found him to be a self-serving prick who made more promises than he could keep.

We'd worked together two years ago, chasing Albanian immigrants who were burglarizing Manhattan jewelry stores and selling the stones in Eastern Europe and Russia. As Elder saw it, my mission in life was to push him to the top of the mountain, to bust my hump making him famous. Blacks need positive role models, he'd said. Consequently, white cops like myself had a responsibility to make him look good. I wanted to be as sensitive about this as possible, so I told him every district attorney in America would have to die before he became my hero. After that we didn't have much to say to each other.

Meanwhile it was the same old shit. I made the Albanian case, and Daddy Duke ended up hogging the credit.

We had one final run-in last year, when I was tipped that confiscated cash and drugs were disappearing from his office. The tip came from a female coworker who'd gone to bed with him in hopes of receiving a promotion. Instead she'd been fired and now wanted my help in making Daddy Duke's life one sad song.

I set about collecting evidence tying Elder to these thefts. Within a week I had enough to send him to prison. I saw him going down faster than a frozen turkey carrying an anvil. I was enjoying paradise in this world. It isn't every day you send a prosecutor away to college.

Unfortunately, they didn't make them any slicker than Daddy Duke. He began with a con job on his superiors. He portrayed my informant as an incompetent worker who wanted revenge for having been fired. A lady like that shouldn't be taken seriously.

His next move was to threaten the DA's office with exposure. He knew where the bodies were buried, and if he went down, so would a few others. Before you could say *kiss my entire black ass,* criminal charges were dropped, and he was allowed to resign without being disbarred. Daddy Duke was still large and in charge.

I asked Lynda what these special cops did for Schiafino and got no answer. Instead, she opened the motel-room door and looked outside, as though checking to see if she had been followed. I noticed she kept a hand in her purse. I was sure the hand was on her gun.

I asked if she'd spoken to her partner. Lynda said yes, but she'd gotten nowhere. Schiafino's reputation as a psycho had scared Lisa off. He was also known for having big ears, for maintaining a pipeline into every corner of the department. Lisa Watts wasn't about to bring charges against Bobby Schemes. Lynda was on her own.

Which left me as the only one she could turn to.

Later, I would see there had never been a more important time for us to trust each other. But before she could say more about Schiafino, something went wrong between us, and I left feeling angry and hurt, and now I was standing beside Lynda's grave, thinking how things might have turned out differently and wondering if the rest of my life was going to be one long regret.

"I'm sorry about what happened," I said to Schiafino. "Lynda was a good cop and a good lady."

I offered my hand. He ignored it. I thought, Do we have a problem here, or what? We eyed each other in silence for long seconds, our breath steaming in the cold air. I had no idea what his game was. I tensed as you do when you can't avoid an oncoming punch.

Finally, Schiafino removed his sunglasses and stared at an overcast sky. Then he lowered his blue eyes to me, eyes as icy as the weather. Leaning forward, he whispered, "Life is short but long enough for you to get what's coming to you. See you around, *detective.*"

Aloud he said, " 'Preciate your showing up." Bobby

Schemes was putting on a show. Laying it on thick for the benefit of his audience. A second later he backed into a protective huddle of cops, family, and in-laws.

I told myself I was imagining things, that I had nothing to worry about. It would have been a relief to believe Schiafino didn't know about Lynda and me.

The truth is he did.

IV
The Letter

I drove south on the Van Wyck Expressway, toward Kennedy Airport. It was nearly sundown. My father's eyes were closed, and Lynda's rose stood upright in his small hands.

I wanted to stand where Lynda had last been alive, to feel her presence as I'd felt that of Lourdes Balera in my office. Dion understood. When you're a cop, the dead stay with you a long time.

We passed white clapboard houses where lawns were spotted with patches of blackened snow. Enormous icicles hung from streetlights. Ahead a frozen lake glowed orange under the setting sun. Spring was a day old.

I reached into my overcoat pocket and took out a miniature replica of Lynda's gold detective's shield, which hung on a small gold chain. Cops gave them to wives or sweethearts. Lynda was the only woman I'd ever known who'd given one to a male cop.

I hung the tiny badge from the rearview mirror. It was a reminder of how much I had lost. A reminder that my pain was going to be permanent. Without Lynda the world seemed quieter and more threatening.

My father pointed to the chain. "What's that?" His eyes still appeared to be closed.

"A copy of Lynda's shield. The last thing she gave me before she died."

"And Schiafino knows you were seeing her."

"Yesterday she's telling me about this crew of cops he and Eugene Elder have from New York and Washington. Today she's dead."

"Schiafino's an asswipe," Dion said. "But he had nothing to do with Lynda's death. She was killed by a butt-ugly shine who is now under arrest. Case closed. Schiafino has an alibi, not that he needs one. When Lynda was being murdered, he was at the Garden watching a hockey game. Him and three friends, all cops."

"I know Robichaux's the perp. I've just got Schiafino on the brain is all."

"Fooling around with a psycho's wife will do that to you."

"Detectives found Lynda's badge and panties in Robichaux's pocket. And he was holding the knife that killed her. They should all be this easy."

"The man was lying unconscious beside her corpse. He's a crackhead, a wino, *and* a nutcase. Six to five he doesn't remember killing her."

"Probably tried panhandling Lynda. She says no and he goes ballistic."

"Not according to him," Dion said. "He claims he was framed by a white man who gave him a hundred-dollar bill every day for a week. Says this same white man lured him to the parking lot with a promise of another hundred. We got ourselves a mental giant here."

"I'd like to know why Lynda was at the airport."

"Meeting an informant, according to one reporter."

"Lynda and I talked the job all the time. She had nothing going at Kennedy."

Dion massaged his stiff shoulder. "Some homeless spook murders a white policewoman, thereby presenting the police commissioner with a racial nightmare he would like to see disappear forthwith. Pay attention. The department don't care why Lynda went to the airport. Her killer's been arrested. *That's* what they care about."

He looked at me. "I understand how you feel. But don't rock the boat on this one. It ain't smart, believe me."

"Hop on the steamroller, or be part of the road. Is that what you're saying?"

"Whites think the jig killed her. Cops agree. Way I see it, nobody else's opinion counts."

"Steamroller or no steamroller, Lynda had no reason for being at the airport."

I saw her face in the windshield. Spiky black hair starting to gray. Snub nose, brown eyes, lopsided grin. Long-legged and knock-kneed. Looking ten years younger than her age, thirty-four. A chain-smoker who loved hoop earrings. A giving woman.

I collect fight films. I like the old silents best, the soundless black-and-white prints showing the great boxers in their prime. I also collect fight photographs, some of them more than a hundred years old. I have films and photographs of John L. Sullivan, Battling Siki, Kid McCoy, Tiger Flowers, and a young Jack Dempsey when they called him Man Killer.

What I didn't have, and wanted badly, was the 1909 fight between Jack Johnson and Stanley Ketchel, the Michigan Assassin. The black Johnson versus the white Ketchel. Johnson, the greatest heavyweight of all time, against Ketchel, the greatest middleweight who ever lived.

A racial grudge match. A classic.

Dion told Lynda about my wanting this film. A week later she presented me with a copy and refused to take anything for it.

Dion collected piano jazz records. He had hundreds of seventy-eights, LPs, piano rolls from the 1920s, transcription discs from 1930s radio shows. They included autographed recordings by Tatum, Garner, Basie, Ellington, Thelonious Monk—stuff worth a fortune. He'd known all of these guys personally. He'd hung with them in Harlem, at Small's Paradise and the Red Rooster, and downtown, at jazz clubs on Fifty-second Street.

Lynda gave him a rare 1923 piano roll of Fats Waller's "Low Down Papa"—and put a lump in his throat.

We passed South Ozone Park and Howard Beach, where small boats were anchored in the backyards of row after row of modest houses. I wondered if anyone in those houses had lost something important in his life. In losing Lynda, I'd been forced to confront some unpleasant things about myself. Such as the shield I had built between me and the rest of the world. If they were lucky, the people in those houses were as ignorant today as they'd been a year ago.

We drove past Aqueduct Race Track, the last raceway left in the city. New York's racetracks had been wiped out by Jewish lightning, real estate developers who found racing less profitable than shopping malls. Just beyond the Aqueduct turnoff stood an oversize cardboard figure, a tacky drawing of a woman in G-string and stiletto heels, with platinum hair, a goofy smile, and big boobs. Some half-wit had poked out her nipples, replacing them with empty beer cans. The figure was a promotion for Club Libido, a local topless joint offering nude dancers, a two-girl lesbian show, and slow touch dancing.

The sign reminded me of another topless club, one owned by Bobby Schemes. Department rules prohibit cops from involvement with any business selling alcohol. Nevertheless, Schiafino had himself a titty bar. Over drinks one night at Farel O'Toole's in Woodside, Lynda had given me the details.

Schiafino's club, called Shares, was opposite the UN General Assembly Building on Manhattan's East Side. He had two partners, Lynda said. One was Jesus Bauza, a skinny thirty-five-year-old Puerto Rican detective working out of the South Bronx. The other was Eugene Elder, old Daddy Duke himself. Elder had put the deal together, Lynda said. He hid Schiafino's interest in the name of a seventy-five-year-old uncle in a Brooklyn nursing home and Bauza's in the name of his thirty-year-old wife. Elder's interest was concealed in holding companies registered in Panama and Luxembourg.

Shares was six months old, with a branch in Washington. Lynda assumed the clubs were making money; Schiafino was bringing cash home and hiding it. He had gotten the name from a Bible verse engraved at UN Plaza. Something about beating swords into plowshares. It was his revenge on the nuns who had smacked him around when he was a kid in

Brooklyn, beating his palms with a leather strap coated with maple syrup so that the strap pulled at his skin.

Schiafino was a control freak, Lynda said. He insisted that Shares be upscale, the better to attract big spenders and couples. Which is why the club had a stock ticker, safe-to-eat food, and a boutique. All floor managers wore tuxedos. Lap dancing, also called zipper polishing, was out. So was nude touch dancing and turning tricks on the premises. Schiafino didn't want to risk a prostitution bust that could close down the club and cost him money.

He also laid down the law to his dancers, Lynda said. A girl couldn't finger her crotch. Couldn't lick her tits. Couldn't dip her G-string in a customer's drink and wring it out in his mouth. This from a man whose idea of humor was to visit coffee shops, stick a tampon in a ketchup bottle, and leave it on the counter.

Lynda stayed away from Shares. She couldn't tolerate Elder's arrogance or watching her husband hit on the dancers. Schiafino had never been able to keep his dick in his pants. And he didn't use condoms. Bobby Schemes's idea of safe sex was a padded headboard.

He was pinning his hopes on Shares, Lynda said. He hated New York. Hated its cold weather, welfare cheats, high taxes, and fag politicians. When he had the money, he was moving to sunny California. Los Angeles was his dream town, Lynda said. Elder and Jesus Bauza preferred life in the East. Daddy Duke still wanted a shot at New York politics, while the married Bauza was thinking about moving to Puerto Rico with his new girlfriend.

In L.A., Schiafino was going to live on a houseboat in Marina del Rey and French-kiss the ass of every blonde in Hollywood. Since Lynda wasn't going with him, she didn't care what he did. He'd finally agreed to a divorce, minus any alimony or cash settlement. Moving to California was expensive, he told her. Fortunately, Shares wasn't the only thing he had going. Lynda knew nothing about his business affairs and did not want to know. Anything he was into, Shares or this other thing, had to be illegal.

I wasn't talkative or demonstrative and usually kept my problems to myself. Now I needed to unwind. I told Dion how afraid Lynda had been at our last meeting and how it seemed to be tied in with a secret crew of cops put together by Schiafino and Elder. I told him we'd argued and I'd walked before she could say more about these cops.

A motorcyclist roared past the car. I watched him weave in and out of the traffic, envying his freedom to go wherever he pleased.

Dion patted my arm. "Want to tell me about the argument?"

I wasn't comfortable showing affection or having people touch me. My raw-meat persona, Lynda called it.

I screwed my cigarette into the car ashtray. "It was over a letter she'd written. She was putting her life in my hands, she said. So she wanted to show how much she trusted me. That's when she told me about the letter."

A hard, shaking chill came over me. My throat became hoarse. I blinked away tears.

Dion waited.

Lynda and I had met two years ago, on a drug task force working Cubans in New York and New Jersey. We argued constantly. I thought she was too touchy-feely to be a cop. She thought I was crazy, a certified looney tune. There had been nothing in our relationship to indicate we would ever get together. Life surprises the hell out of you sometimes.

"She wrote the letter after our last case," I said. "But she never mailed it. She hid it, probably in a safe-deposit box somewhere. Yesterday she told me she intended to destroy it. She trusted me, so she didn't need it anymore. The letter had been her protection."

"Protection?" Dion said. "From what?"

"From me."

"You're kidding."

"She thought I might kill her. That's why she wrote it."

Dion shook his head. "Was she crazy or what?"

"Things did get a little hyper on our last case. Anyway, if I killed her, this letter was to go to Internal Affairs. But now she trusted me. The letter wasn't necessary, she said. Yesterday, as she's telling me this, I'm thinking, why the fuck should I trust *her?* Didn't she write a letter that could hang me?"

"Hang you? What kind of letter we talking about?"

"I got loud," I said. "I accused her of stabbing me in the back. I walked. She begged me to stay, but I wouldn't listen."

Dion looked down at his lap. "What's in it?"

"What's in it can send me to prison for twenty years."

V
Crime Scene

The airport's glass terminals gleamed red in the last sun of the day. Lynda had been murdered in a parking lot facing the International Arrivals Building. Guarding the lot entrance was a sizable cop with a harelip and a manner suggesting he was in a mood that went beyond cranky.

Maybe he hated cold weather. Maybe he hated being over forty and still in uniform.

Maybe he hated having people stare at him. Harelip was being eyed by locals stacked behind a police barricade, some in woolen scarves long enough to wrap around trees.

I figured most were here out of curiosity. A headline murder doesn't happen in your backyard every day.

A couple of sightseers in hunting caps struck me as nutcases. Both looked like toothless people from trailer camps and carried camcorders, and you had the feeling they wanted the killer to show up and do it again so they could catch it on tape this time.

The parking lot was a vast stretch of black asphalt ringed by chain-link fencing. I'd spent last summer at the airport, working Nigerian heroin traffickers, when the lot had wall-to-wall cars, trucks, and just about anything on wheels. Now it was almost empty. Closed until further notice by order of the Queens DA.

Only two vehicles remained on the lot. One was a red

Jeep Cherokee, and the other an orange bus from a Nassau County school for the blind. Security guards with Dobermans now patrolled the area's perimeter. They hadn't been here when Lynda was murdered. The airport had brought them in today to discourage ghouls from hopping the fence and messing up the crime scene.

I showed Harelip my shield. We didn't engage in conversation. He eyed my tin and assumed I was here on official business. I didn't correct him. To keep warm, he was stamping his feet. Without interrupting his little dance, he waved me inside.

The murder site was five yards away and to the right. The homicide guys had it cordoned off with police tape attached to empty oil drums. I kept my hands in my pockets. Crime-scene evidence isn't to be touched until it has been photographed and recorded in notes.

Just being here was violating department rules. Only essential or authorized personnel are allowed on a crime scene. Access is restricted to prevent evidence from being destroyed or misplaced. Given the politics surrounding this case, if I stepped on a matchstick, I could end up selling dinner jackets in Ethiopia.

I ordered Dion to remain with the guard. Keep Harelip busy. And give me time alone. I wanted him to find out a couple of things. Such as who had processed the crime scene. And what evidence had been turned up.

Homicide detectives and evidence technicians were finished for the day. But they would be back tomorrow. And the next day. They'd tear the lot apart for days to come. The hunt for evidence in a cop killing is furious. The more evidence, the more likely a conviction.

Lynda's 1990 blue Ford wasn't here. I figured it had been impounded for fingerprinting and a detailed inspection. Robichaux had grabbed Lynda's ankles, and yanked hard. She hit the ground headfirst. The official medical report wouldn't be ready for another twenty-four hours, but I'd talked to the coroner's office and learned Lynda had suffered a fractured skull before Robichaux had gone to work with his knife.

I stared at the yellow chalk outlines on the ground. I felt

worn down. My mouth was dry and my heartbeat speeded up. Suddenly, the air seemed much too cold.

Only one outline was smeared with blood. *Lynda's.*

I blinked away tears brought on by wind and regret. Robichaux had killed Lynda, then passed out, landing between her corpse and her car. He'd been doing drugs and drinking cheap wine. At some point he had dropped the wine bottle, which had shattered on impact. Near his outline, glass bits still glittered on the ground.

I thought of mistakes cops make that increase their chances of being killed. They trust people. They fail to take control of the perp. They drop their guard or don't follow the rules.

They also die because they're too sloppy. I wondered if Lynda had been sloppy. She was careful, as a rule. But a single mistake is enough to ground you for good.

I read a lot, Irish writers mostly. Reading has taught me things about myself. Sometimes writers do my thinking for me. I remembered a verse by Yeats. That's where I'd gotten the nickname *Rose* for Lynda. She had liked the name. She'd also liked the verse that I'd written out for her on a small card. The card was still in my pocket.

Red Rose, proud Rose, sad Rose of all my days! / Come near me, while I sing the ancient ways.

Dion tapped me on the shoulder. "Anything?"

"Zip." I rubbed my watery eyes. "What's with Homey the Clown?"

"The guard? Name's Pearlberg. Says he's got a bad back. Shouldn't be out here in all this cold. Says this place has been a madhouse—politicians, press, you name it. At one point two dozen people were walking through the crime scene."

"Jesus. Who let that happen?"

"Footman. Who else?"

Ray Nathan Footman was a gap-toothed forty-five-year-old Jew, and the first deputy mayor. He was also running the mayor's reelection campaign. When it came to the power game, only the mayor had more clout than Footman. Cops hated him. He was a liberal schmuck intent on improving the department. His improvements were usually a disaster.

Footman's latest brainstorm was to pull cops from clerical jobs and replace them with civilians. These replacements were women, minorities, and the physically challenged. The people least likely to strike oil. To call this an embarrassment was an understatement.

"Footman showed up with two deputy police commissioners," Dion said. "Neither of these dildos said word one about people parading through the crime scene."

"Who else showed?" I said.

"His Holiness."

"Be still, my heart."

His Holiness was Carmine Lacovara, a lard-assed fiftyish ginzo who had been Queens district attorney for the past eight years. Lacovara attended Mass seven mornings a week. He spoke in tongues and claimed to have seen a vision of the weeping Virgin Mary in the gazebo in his backyard. The man was one strong Christian.

He had announced plans to personally try the Robichaux case. Lacovara was not out to prove himself virtuous and worthy. He had 211 assistant district attorneys working for him, each of whom would have clubbed a baby seal for a shot at this case.

Trying a cop killer is instant glory. It's the front page of the *Times* and invitations to speak before the Knights of Columbus. It's talk-show heaven. That's why His Holiness had grabbed this case for himself. He would sooner have had his balls pounded with a wooden mallet than share the glory on this one.

Ray Footman was no high-toned humanitarian either. He had come to the parking lot to show the world that his boss, Mayor Roger L. Tucker, cared about white crime victims as much as he cared about black ones. It was, after all, an election year.

Tucker was in Washington, appearing before a congressional panel investigating drug use by young people. He had some experience in this area. Six months ago his sixteen-year-old daughter had died of a heroin overdose.

Sympathy for the family junkie aside, Tucker's four years as mayor had been a disaster. He'd done nothing for fear of doing something wrong. He'd divided his time between playing on the golf course, being photographed in his tuxedo, and cheating on his wife. I saw him as just one more sorry-ass spade blaming other people for what he couldn't change in life.

I watched a helicopter rise from behind the old TWA Terminal, hang in midair, then drift toward Jamaica Bay. Lacovara and Footman were following their own agendas. But this could not alter the fact that Robichaux's prints had been found on the murder weapon and on Lynda's badge.

Give me prints over a confession any day. A perp can deny his confession. He can deny eyewitness accounts and even deny the victim's story. But if his prints are on the scene, *he's* been on the scene, and denying it won't change a thing.

I said to Dion, "They find anything else?"

"No hundred-dollar bills if that's what you mean."

I jerked my head toward Lynda's outline. "She never had a chance."

Dion nodded, his mind somewhere else.

We were probably both thinking the same thing: if Lynda had known the truth, she wouldn't have written a letter detailing how I'd stolen drug money. Money I needed to prevent Dion from being murdered.

I watched the wind tear at the police tape and thought how much I owed Dion. And why I'd risked going to prison in order to repay him.

Dion is my father. Then again, he isn't.

I don't know my natural parents and don't care to. What would I say to them now anyway?

When I was two, someone dumped me on the steps of a Queens foundling home run by nuns. Dion, the beat cop, was allowed to name me. Feargal was for a grandfather hanged by the British for fighting in the 1916 Easter Rebellion. Thomas Francis was chosen for an Irish revolutionary he claimed as an ancestor.

I hated the foundling home. Hated the secondhand clothes and the shit food. The forced attendance at Mass. I hated the priests who molested the boys and those nuns who pretended it wasn't happening. On top of everything else, I was a handful. Big for my age. Defiant. Disobedient. Only Dion could reach me.

He took me to ball games, westerns, gave me my first cigarette, and told me about sex. He promised to get me on the cops. We were born friends. I had his help, and I had the confidence it would be there when I needed it.

At thirteen I punched out a bony priest who'd raped a Puerto Rican kid. When a dozen nuns came after me with mop handles, I hightailed it to Manhattan. I spent that night in the Village, hungry and afraid, rummaging through garbage cans for food. At dawn in Washington Square Park, I was surrounded by four black kids. They wanted money. If I didn't give it up, I was one dead white boy, they said. I didn't have a dime.

I was scared shitless, but Dion always said get your licks in first, so I jumped the blacks, screaming like a crazy man, swinging wildly, and dropping two before feeling an awful pain in my chest. I had taken a bullet to the heart. The spades ran, leaving me for dead.

To the amazement of doctors and the regret of the nuns, I lived. How, I don't know. I only know I was holding aces that day.

The nuns made sympathetic noises, but it was all an act. They wanted me out of their lives. According to Dion, they had no use for a boy who had punched out a priest. My presence in the orphanage might give the other kids wrong ideas. When I was discharged from the hospital, it was Dion who took me in. He became my family.

Since that shooting, death hasn't frightened me. I feared loneliness and failure and being disgraced. But I didn't fear death. I also wasn't too fond of blacks.

I had died once, and it hadn't been a problem. Why worry about it happening again? So I took chances without a moment's hesitation. My wild ways gave fellow cops the shakes, and many refused to work with me. Word was I did not have a heart. It had been shot out years ago, they said.

I was the Tin Man. Helter-Skelter with a badge.

* * *

Nearly thirty years had passed since that night in the Village. I wasn't alone anymore. And I wasn't scared. But I owed Dion.

"I need a cigarette," I said. "Let's walk."

We headed toward the school bus.

To stay out of prison, I had to find Lynda's letter before the department did. Otherwise I was looking at hard time upstate.

Dion said, "Think Schiafino knows about the letter?"

"Shit. I forgot him. He gets that letter, I'm fucked."

"Schiafino didn't create your problem. I did."

The Irish Catholic mind makes a career out of guilt. Contrition and remorse pollute it in ways that make an oil spill seem healing. Apart from Lynda, I carried no burdens on my conscience. I forgave myself everything. I didn't believe in God, in the unforeseen, in the miraculous or the extraordinary. Eleven years with the nuns had killed any desire I had to go to heaven. I would get my consolation in this world or not at all.

Dion was different. He went to Mass now and then. He feared the invisible power. What I thought was make-believe he found significant. He was tearing himself apart over Lynda's letter.

At the school bus I lit a cigarette. Dion stared down at his shoes. He appeared runty and sad—and a lot older.

It was a day for looking back and kicking yourself.

VI
Another Enemy

Two years ago Dion lost a security job when a building contractor went out of business. The company folded just after the contractor, a fifty-year-old Israeli, beat his spouse to death with a hammer. He'd caught AIDS from a male prostitute and, certain of death, had killed his wife to spare her a widow's life.

Between security jobs Dion usually tended bar. This time he hooked up with an Irish pub on Bainbridge Avenue in the Bronx. The area wasn't crime free, but it was safer than the kill-crazy black and Hispanic areas to the south. Bainbridge was immigrants from Cork, Kerry, and Dundalk, and delicatessens with black pudding, and dance halls where musicians played flutes, pipes, and whistles and singers sang of love's longing and Ireland's sad history.

I avoided Irish saloons, having grown tired of moth-eaten Micks talking about the good old times. To me it was like talking about funerals. Besides, once the past was gone, it didn't belong to you anymore.

Dion loved these slop shops. A week on Bainbridge and he was more Irish than corned beef and cabbage. He signed petitions backing amnesty for Irish illegals in America. He insisted the Irish had been the best politicians in New York history. And he wanted the English out of Northern Ireland forthwith.

I refused to sign Dion's amnesty petition. The city's fabric didn't need to be enriched by more illegals. It had enough. As for Irish politicians, they were like all party hacks. They believed their own lies, stole until they were caught, and then wrote a book about it.

However, I was with Dion on the English. I found them

32

deceitful little maggots. Violent and spiteful and without the good sense to leave when the going was bad. They had been in Ireland eight hundred years. Eight hundred years too long.

But they weren't going to be driven out by old men talking tough in Bronx gin mills. Or by dick-brain psychos in Belfast who dynamited shopping centers and killed English women and children. Like stupid people everywhere, these clowns expected things to happen that never could happen.

Maybe it was Dion's age. Or maybe he was looking for kicks. Whatever the reason, Bainbridge Avenue did a number on his head. He started ignoring me and his record collection and began spending his time getting drunk in the Bronx and shouting *Up the rebels*. The old fart was acting hard-nosed and wicked. I should have seen it coming.

He gave me the news over the phone. When I heard it, I cleared my desk with one sweep of my arm. He was going to be a courier for the *cause*, he said. He would be carrying money from America to Belfast. Gun money for the Irish Republican Army.

To avoid an argument, I kept quiet and let Dion ramble on about doing his duty for Ireland. *Duty?* He'd never been to Ireland in his life. Nor had most of the saloon soldiers he was hanging with. Didn't they know the English treated the IRA as terrorists and shot them on sight? Trash-talking in the Bronx was one thing. Messing with British paratroopers who gave Micks a warning shot through the forehead was another.

Dion was being jerked around by drunken barflies stumbling from dream to dream. And there was nothing I could do about it. He was never more stubborn than when he was wrong. He might have doubts before a decision, but none afterward. I told him to expect a royal fucking.

He made two trips to Belfast without a hitch. The third nearly got him killed. And put me on a road that could lead to prison.

It began with Dion taking an evening flight to Boston, then checking in to a Boylston Street hotel. Within minutes the money was hand-delivered to his room. He was to leave for Dublin at noon the next day.

An hour later in the hotel restaurant he noticed an attractive woman alone at a nearby table. She seemed upset.

They struck up a conversation. She called herself Perrin Dowd and was a red-haired thirty-three-year-old Irish schoolteacher who'd come in from the suburbs for dinner with an old friend, a Harvard physics professor. The professor was an hour late. Perrin wondered if she'd been stood up. Dion, the patron saint of redheads, invited her to join him.

They hit it off instantly. She laughed at his jokes, and when he told her about his daring deeds as a cop, she batted her lashes in all the right places. Dion was always ready to be flattered by a woman. Give him one who hung on his every word, and he was a happy man.

After dinner and two bottles of white wine, they went walking. In time Miss Dowd noted she had missed the last train home. The next one wasn't until six that morning. Dion invited her back to his room and, being true kindness itself, helped Miss Dowd out of her clothes, and together they did a few laps around the track until falling asleep sweaty and satisfied.

He awoke the next morning with one hell of a hangover. Miss Dowd was gone. So was Dion's money belt containing twenty-five thousand dollars of IRA money.

He'd have to wait for God's mercy because the IRA gave him nothing but jack shit. They didn't intend to limp because he'd gotten hurt. Twenty-five thousand dollars had gone south. Somebody had to take the weight. The IRA ordered Dion's execution.

All this had been behind us until Lynda's letter. I had enough problems without it; I didn't need more. But until I found that letter, I wasn't going to get much sleep. And neither would Dion.

In the airport parking lot Dion and I shivered behind the school bus. The evening had grown darker and colder. Our shadows merged into a coal-black path stretching across the asphalt. I lit a cigarette and watched the wind play games with pages of an abandoned newspaper. Taxis and buses had switched on their headlights.

Dion's Boston trip had been a setup. He'd walked into a trap with little Miss Redhead as bait. It had been embarrassing for him to get suckered. So we never spoke about Boston. Or the money I'd stolen to save his life. Don't ask, don't tell.

However, Lynda's death had changed things. If Internal Affairs were to discover her letter, I'd go to prison, and I'd be doing hard time. Dion might also be sent away. I'd known two detectives who had gone inside; both had been murdered by cons. One had his throat cut in the barber's chair. The other was set on fire while he was asleep in his cell. It was time I told Dion the full story.

I put a hand on my head to keep the wind from stealing my hat. "When you told me the IRA planned to kill you, I looked up Tom McNulty. I asked him to call off the dogs. Give me time to raise the money. He said forget it. The IRA executed thieves. You were a dead man."

McNulty was the club-footed sixty-four-year-old Irish American who owned the Bainbridge Avenue gin mill where Dion had gotten the urge to play commando. It was McNulty who had talked him into being a courier, then promised him a bullet in the head for having lost the money.

Dion turned up his coat collar. "Something changed McNulty's mind. What was it?"

"I said the day the IRA killed you, I'd kill him."

Dion grinned. "Bet he liked that."

"McNulty first, then his friends. You should have seen his face. The IRA would get me, I told him. But not before I emptied a few barstools." I began walking toward the parking-lot entrance. Dion fell in step. "I was ready to die. I didn't think McNulty or his friends were."

At McNulty's bar, cops would hear the name Meagher and ask Dion if he was related to Fear Meagher. The detective they called Home Alone because nobody wanted to work with him.

I said, "McNulty made a phone call, then told me the shooters had been temporarily called off. I had five days to come up with the money. Otherwise the hit was back on."

"I could have helped."

"You'd have been an accessory. If I went down, I wasn't taking you with me."

"Accessory? What the hell did you do?"

I finished my cigarette and dropped the butt into my overcoat pocket. Two years ago in East Harlem, Lynda and I had arrested a Cuban fag named Baby Cabrera, a midlevel cocaine distributor operating in New York and Florida. We caught Baby alone with an open safe. The rules of evidence say you can't enter a safe without a warrant. We didn't have one.

I told Dion about the arrest and the safe. "We tossed the safe," I said. "We found false passports, the names of dealers Baby was supplying, and records of his wire transfers. He was taking in a million bucks a week. We also found two keys of Bolivian flake, Polaroids of Baby in full drag, and eighty-five thousand dollars in cash. I sent Lynda out to get a warrant."

"Get them over the phone nowadays," Dion said. "One hour. In my day it took forever."

"She comes back with the warrant. And with two uniformed cops as witnesses. Everything by the book. The cops counted the money."

"Twenty-five thousand dollars of which is now missing."

"Lynda is angry as hell but doesn't say a word. Not a word."

"Where's Baby all this time?"

"Bedroom closet," I said. "Locked in with his cork wedgies. He never saw me take the money."

"And Lynda's on the warpath."

"The cops leave, and right away she starts in about the missing twenty-five thousand. I told her to back off, that what happened was none of her business. I said she should back her partner, not make waves. She hadn't seen me take anything, so why get excited?"

"You probably scared the shit out of her." Dion wiped his runny nose with the back of his hand. "Shame it had to happen."

"She'd watched me do a number on a Jamaican who had dozens of crack dealers working for him. I dropped him on a Brooklyn street corner, in an all-white neighborhood. Told him if he didn't give me his people, I'd leave him there. He gave me his people."

"And what about Jimmy Yip?"

Jimmy Yip was a Chinese perp who used Chinese illegals to run heroin from Hong Kong to New York. He promised five thousand a key to each mule but never paid up. When his mules arrived in America, Jimmy killed them, then buried the corpses in quicklime. I got him to talk by handcuffing him to my car bumper and gunning the motor. He literally shit his pants. I nailed him for eight murders, maybe a third of the actual total.

Lynda had heard the Jimmy Yip story and thought I was crazy. I was missing a few dots on my dice is how she put it.

"Still don't see how you and she got together," Dion said.

It happened because she needed to talk. Just after she transferred near my home, we bumped into each other on the street. She told me two detectives were giving her a hard time. They didn't want a woman on the squad. I knew everyone at the station house, so I promised I would look into the problem.

I saw the detectives, told them Lynda and I had worked together and that she was a good cop. I asked them to give her a chance. They did. She made a couple of big cases, earned three citations, and detectives fought to work with her because she made them look good. Watching everyone want her made me want her. I fell in love hard enough to break my ankles.

I lit another cigarette. I had distanced myself from people all my life and done the same with Lynda. Loved her yet distanced myself from her. And I had gained nothing by it. Years later I would look back and see this day as the day I began to die. As the day my fear of loneliness began to consume me.

Dion sensed my pain and changed the subject. "Anything new on the Ecuadorans?"

"Nothing." I shook my head. "The shooter, whoever he is, is making me look like I'm not cut out for this line of work. I ain't too thrilled with that."

I wanted to crack this one for Lourdes Balera. For a kid who had lost a game she hadn't even known she was playing.

So far I hadn't done right by her. Then again I hadn't done right by Lynda either. Time to go home and drink myself to sleep, the best way I knew to escape a growing sense of failure.

Sundown was giving way to darkness. The parking lot was becoming colder and more dismal. Lynda's murder site was the darkest spot; the lights here had burned out or been vandalized. I found myself wondering if better lighting might have kept Lynda alive.

What happened next caught me off guard. I was dog tired and wandering around in a fog. But Dion was on his toes. He saw the problem before I did.

He placed a hand on my forearm, stopping me in place. Then he pointed to the entrance, several yards away. I looked to see Officer Pearlberg arguing with a black woman. The two were screaming at each other, putting on a show for the handful of dimwits still behind the police barricade. I hadn't smiled all day, but I found myself smiling now, my happy face inspired by Pearlberg's misery. He was arguing with a twofer, a citizen who was black *and* female. Two kinds of trouble. Better him than me.

Black women are a problem for cops. They're not shy about mouthing off, and they know their rights. An angry black woman can leave a cop feeling like a horse's ass. She can abuse you to her heart's content, and you can't do a thing about it. Not unless you want to look like a trigger-happy bigot whose only delight is in beating the shit out of innocent citizens like herself.

One wrong move and Pearlberg could face suspension or a lawsuit. Black preachers would hit the streets to demand his head on a pole. Women's groups would insist he apologize to every female born this century. The brass would be more interested in calming the media and appeasing racial activists than in hearing his story.

I wasn't supposed to be in the parking lot. What's more, the black woman probably disliked cops. By becoming involved, I'd only be stepping in shit. Pearlberg would have to fight his own battles.

Life, however, has its little ironies. Pearlberg's problem suddenly became mine. I recognized the woman's voice and realized what Dion was trying to do. He wanted to keep us apart.

The woman was Carlyle Taylor, and she was a reporter for the city's largest tabloid. Tall and brown-skinned, she was in her mid-thirties, with a hawklike face and a fondness for suedes and leather. She was politically correct, deeply liberal, and deaf to anything she didn't want to hear. The best way to read what she wrote was to divide everything in half, then refuse to believe any of it.

The lady's contempt for cops was breathtaking. She despised white cops most of all and me in particular. In her book I was the lowest dirtbag on the planet. A one-of-a-kind asshole who shouldn't be a cop.

She was putting me through red hell.

VII

Not Enough Blood

If love is blind, so is hate.

When I forced Eugene Elder to resign from the prosecutor's office, he'd just started an affair with Carlyle Taylor. Neither a wife nor his reputation as a player seemed to bother her. Daddy Duke had entered her life, and it was time for dreams to come true.

She used her paper to polish Elder's political future, predicting he would become everything from senator to New York's first black governor. If you believed her, the man was the greatest force for good since Moses. Daddy Duke heard things about himself he wished were true, and he swallowed every line. When I took him down, Carlyle Taylor became my sworn enemy.

The day Elder resigned from the district attorney's office, she telephoned to say I was a goddamn hillbilly, a redneck bastard who couldn't stomach a black man in a white man's job. I was unfit to shine Elder's shoes. The sooner I caught AIDS and died, the better. Since then she had written a few articles about me, none favorable.

I wasn't chewing my nails down to the cuticles worrying about Miss Taylor. On the other hand, underestimating her would have been dumb. Her stories on police corruption and brutality had drawn a lot of attention, winning several awards in the process. Along the way she'd also ended a few police careers. White cops called her Schwarzenigger. As in *The Terminator*.

I watched her hammer away at Pearlberg, demanding entrance to the parking lot. She wanted a closer look at the murder site. Pearlberg told her, Forget about it. Get behind the police barricade, he said. Fingering the press pass hanging from her neck, Carlyle Taylor repeated her demand. She sounded as flexible as steel.

"You read what she wrote about Lynda?" Dion said.

"Every word."

Carlyle Taylor's racial views were at best simpleminded. I wasn't surprised when she blamed Lynda's death on "the city's failure to deal with the poor and the destitute." As if that wasn't enough, she went on to write, "The lost souls who live on the margins of American society will view this crime as the heroic act of a victimized black man rising against injustice." In other words, Lynda had it coming.

Reading this garbage made me want to start taking hostages. It was hard to reconcile the existence of a merciful, loving God with the existence of people like Carlyle Taylor. I should have left the parking lot without going near her. But guilt isn't rational. Someone had to speak up for Lynda. I walked toward the entrance.

Dion hung back. He would sooner have his lips removed than confront a pugnacious black woman. I was on my own. At the entrance I said to Pearlberg, "What's the problem, officer?" I kept my eyes on Carlyle Taylor.

"The lady wants to see the crime scene." Pearlberg shook his big head. "You know I can't allow that."

"She knows it, too," I said to Carlyle Taylor. "Crime scenes are closed to the public. That includes reporters."

"My, my," said Carlyle Taylor. "If it isn't New York's

foremost racial healer. When did you take over this case?"
She was chic in gray flannels, brown leather jacket, and a
mannish brown felt hat.

I looked at her through half-closed eyes. Staring people
down came easy to me. Dion once said I had a look that
could chill a gorilla. Carlyle Taylor held my gaze without
blinking. Her flared nostrils and sullen attitude indicated she
still had no use for me.

"I'm not assigned to this homicide," I said.

"In other words, you have no business here." She smiled
at me. The smile never reached her eyes. She wore orange
leather gloves drawn tight at the wrist by small gold chains.
One hand held a manila envelope.

"Civilians are not allowed in a crime scene," I said.
"You've been around long enough to know that."

"I'm not here as a sightseer, *detective*. Last night some
white cops, not unlike yourself, nearly murdered Maurice
Robichaux in this parking lot. That's the crime scene I came
here to see."

I pointed to the police tape. "Allow me to explain. That's
where Detective Schiafino was slashed to death by Maurice
Robichaux. It's the only crime scene around here. Try reading the official report."

"Like you say, I have been around," she said. "And I
know bullshit when I smell it, and I can smell your report
from here. I doubt if there's any mention of Maurice Robichaux being beaten by racist cops."

"Kind of shakes your faith, doesn't it."

"Racist cops leave a bad smell wherever they go. Don't
they, detective?"

I spat on the ground. "When words aren't enough," I said.
She headed in my direction.

I thought, *fuck me, here it comes*. From behind the police
barricade a man yelled, "Hey, Kojak, you going to do a
Rodney King on her?" I looked to see a stumpy twentyish
white male in a Raiders jacket aiming a camcorder at me.
His lunatic grin said he had just found happiness on earth.
*White detective videotaped during altercation with black re-
porter and is suspended pending an investigation.*

Waiting for Carlyle Taylor to close in left me antsy. The

advantage was hers. She could slap my face and call me everything but a child of God, and I couldn't lay a finger on her. Not with a camcorder on me, and not if I wanted to continue being a cop. All I could do was leave the set. I was about to do that when Carlyle Taylor stopped a foot away, pulled something from the envelope she carried, and thrust it in my face.

I stared at a large color photograph of Maurice Robichaux. He lay in a hospital bed, a bandaged wrist handcuffed to the bed railing. His eyes, swollen shut, were the size of tennis balls. Most of his nose was hidden beneath strips of adhesive. His face was lumpy and misshapen. Somebody had given him one hell of a tune-up. Fuck him. He had it coming.

"The police broke Maurice's jaw," Carlyle Taylor said to me. "His ribs, wrist, and God knows what else. His hands are so swollen he can't be fingerprinted."

I said Robichaux had resisted arrest. I was lying, and Carlyle Taylor knew it. Robichaux had killed a cop, and the arresting officers had held court here in the parking lot. Mr. Maurice had been presumed guilty because he was guilty.

"Excuse me, but Maurice did not resist arrest," Carlyle Taylor said. "He was unconscious when police found him. Unconscious and defenseless. Speaking of police brutality, weren't you recently charged with assaulting a black suspect? The fifth time in two years, I believe."

"The new charges have been dismissed. Like the others."

"Beat the nigger, then beat the rap. Sounds like a video game the Klan would love. One day your luck's going to run out, detective, and when it does, I'll be there to write your obituary. Wasn't Lynda Schiafino your partner at one time?"

"At one time." It suddenly occurred to me the less said about my relationship with Lynda, the better. Miss Taylor may have been a lot of things, but she was not stupid. It was never a good idea to become too distracted around her.

I watched her inspect Robichaux's photograph in the growing darkness, angling it to catch the lights ringing the parking lot. Her face turned somber, and her fingers gently touched the picture, as though offering him consolation. Her mouth was a thin, hard line. The wind tugged at a small white feather in her hat band and ruffled the knit scarf around her neck.

"You recently did Mrs. Schiafino a favor." Carlyle Taylor never took her eyes from the photograph. Her voice sounded relaxed. Too relaxed. "Apparently she was having trouble at her new precinct until you stepped in."

There's a story about the best way to cook a frog. You don't put the frog in hot water, because it will jump out. You put it in cold water and turn the heat up slow. Very, very slow. Each time Carlyle Taylor mentioned Lynda and me, I felt the water getting warmer.

Miss Taylor could be nasty in print and wasn't especially sensitive to the delicate feelings of cops. If she learned about my affair with Lynda, I could look forward to reading her juicy account of a love triangle between Lynda, Bobby Schemes, and me. This would not go over big with department brass or Bobby Schemes.

"You're not assigned to this case," Carlyle Taylor said. "So why are you here?" She held up a gloved hand. "Let me guess. You're planting evidence to make sure Maurice gets convicted."

"I'd only plant evidence if it meant *you'd* go to jail."

I watched the seagulls rise from Jamaica Bay, then disappear against the darkening sky. I was tired of standing around in ball-freezing cold and catching attitude from the liberal left. It was time to go home and hit the sauce. "This conversation's over," I said to Carlyle Taylor. "Step behind the barricade or leave the area."

I expected her to show me her claws. To get uppity, as it were. I forgot how unpredictable Miss Taylor could be. She said nothing. Instead she tossed Maurice Robichaux's photograph overhead, into the wind.

If Carlyle Taylor wanted to play the fool, who was I to stop her. I watched the wind carry the photograph toward the crime scene, and then the wind stopped, dropping the picture just outside the police tape. A second later a gentle breeze pushed Robichaux's photograph forward until it was inside Lynda's chalk outline. That's when the wind stopped.

"A black man was victimized here," Carlyle Taylor said. She pointed to the photograph. "There's the evidence."

I clenched my fists and tried to think clearly. I'd had a bad day, and seeing Robichaux's photograph in Lynda's blood didn't make me feel any better. All it did was make me want to slap Carlyle Taylor silly. I thought about arresting her for tampering with a crime scene. But confronting her was like standing behind a mule when it kicks. I knew the department didn't want trouble with her. And I didn't want trouble with the department.

I also didn't want Robichaux touching Lynda again.

"I'm going to get that picture," I said to Pearlberg. I jogged into the parking lot, one hand clamping my hat to my head. Running after Robichaux's photograph did not increase my love for him or Miss Megabitch.

I ducked under the police tape. As I reached down for the photograph, something caught my eye. I'd missed it the first time because I hadn't come here to look for evidence in a closed case. I was here as a man who had no choice but to feel guilty.

This time I saw it.

Lynda had died from multiple knife wounds. The worst cuts, according to Lisa Watts, had been to the carotid arteries. They had been viciously slashed, a wound that sends the blood flying in all directions. It speeds from the cut like a geyser, spraying everything and everybody. The crime scene looks like a butcher shop.

This one wasn't messy at all. In fact, it was neat. Too neat. Lynda's outline had blood near the shoulders and head but nowhere else. And there was no blood in the outlines marking Robichaux's body, his wine bottle, and Lynda's car.

I looked at the lights encircling the parking lot. Most were working. Four weren't. Whether they had burned out or been vandalized, I couldn't tell. I did notice one thing. The four missing lights overlooked the murder site.

An investigator is expected to work a homicide by making observations, not assumptions. He can't accept the obvious because that's the easiest way to blow a case. He must remember that evidence can be arranged to lead him up a blind alley. He must look for inconsistencies. Such as the way things appear as opposed to the way they should be.

The lack of blood at the murder site was a huge inconsistency. I'd known few cops more security conscious than Lynda. Day or night she never entered her car without first looking inside. Her home was protected by the best alarms money could buy. Alone on the street at night, she carried her gun in a jacket or coat pocket, hand on the grip. Yet last night she had parked her car in the dark, in the most dangerous spot on the lot. That wasn't the Lynda I knew.

I called to Dion and told him to bring Pearlberg's flashlight. When he'd given it to me, I aimed the beam at Lynda's bloodstains. I said there should be more blood. Much more. Dion shook his head and said if Lynda had been stabbed in the heart, that might account for it. He was right. A stab wound to the heart would have stopped the flow of blood immediately. Still, I knew what I'd heard from Lisa Watts. She'd said nothing about a heart wound. She'd said Lynda's neck arteries had been slashed.

"Lynda wasn't killed here," I said.

"What the hell are you talking about?"

I switched off the flashlight. "She was killed somewhere else, then brought here. That's why there's so little blood."

"This case is closed." Dion was unbending, as if his own reputation were at stake. He still believed cops could do no wrong. "Robichaux's the killer."

"I didn't say he wasn't. I'd just like to know where he did it, because he damn sure didn't do it here."

"Grabbing Robichaux so quick makes the brass look good. They ain't going to like nobody spitting in their soup, you understand?"

I said the brass was the problem.

Dion closed one eye. "What's that supposed to mean?"

"It means the mayor and the department want a quick end to this case. It means they're willing to sanction a sloppy investigation to make themselves look competent. Wouldn't be the first time." I looked at Lynda's blood. "The killer's been caught, so we can all go home. Leave the scene to those assholes who dig photo opportunities. And if this prevents investigators from doing their job, well, that's life in the big city."

I pointed to the missing lights. "I'd also like to know how long they've been out. And I'd like to know why Lynda didn't see Maurice before she left the car. Her car was alone in this area, and she was killed right after leaving it. That means Maurice had to be in the open. Lynda should have seen him."

"Maybe she did see him," Dion said. "Could be she didn't react fast enough."

He looked at me for a long time. Then, "Screw with the department on this, and you can die without getting buried, understand?"

I said I had to know the truth, then Dion and I left the lot. We drove home without speaking.

VIII
A Friend of the Family

I spent the next morning in Times Square, looking for anything that might connect Lourdes Balera with the killer of eight illegal immigrants. I had no problem with her boyfriend, Tonino Cuevas, getting bagged. He'd been on the killer's list.

Lourdes Balera was a different story. Until now Mr. Clean, the shooter who left no clues, had only iced male Ecuadorans. Lourdes Balera had been his first female. Mr. Clean's first detour. Maybe his first mistake.

Lourdes and Tonino had died in the Hotel Langham, a six-story fleabag on Eighth Avenue and Forty-first Street. The hotel faced the Port Authority Bus Terminal, two city blocks long and a passing home to some 250,000 commuters each day. The terminal was also home to a fair number of drug dealers, panhandlers, crazies, and muggers, all going after commuters like party guests attacking a cheese wheel. Prostitutes turned tricks in stairwells, doorways, and in cars parked on the terminal roof. The terminal, in Poe's words, was *"Hell, rising from a thousand thrones."*

The Langham was a single-room-occupancy hotel on a block of triple-X bookshops, peep shows, pawnshops, and fast-food joints. Adjacent to it was a shop selling fake police badges and empty crack vials. Two doors away a sign in a pool-hall window read LADIES INVITED TO PLAY WITH OUR BALLS. I'd heard that cops working down here boiled their handcuffs after every arrest.

Guarding the hotel entrance was a lone policewoman, black, young, and dwarfish. The sight of this munchkin was supposed to send johns home to their wives. With the exception of Lynda, I didn't think much of female cops. Too many were incompetent, frightened, or both. In a fight or a shooting they came apart in a hurry. They also suffered from CRS syndrome—can't remember shit. I showed the policewoman my badge and walked past her without a word.

The hotel lobby was small and dark with pitted walls and a flickering fluorescent light in the ceiling. A water pipe had burst, leaving puddles on a black linoleum floor. The sole piece of furniture was a green leather sofa, which sagged in the middle. A cigarette machine was chalky with plaster dust, and the elevator was broken. I'd have to walk up two flights to the crime scene.

At the front desk an argument was in progress between a male black in plaid pants and a black hooker in pink spandex. The male was Walter Moody, a shiny-faced, forty-ish Jamaican who managed the hotel. We'd met two days ago, on my first visit to this flea pit. It was Moody who'd discovered the bodies of Lourdes and Tonino, then telephoned detectives at Midtown South. Knowing of my interest in dead Ecuadorans, Midtown had reached out for me.

Up close the hooker turned out to be a transvestite with bird legs and a gold ring through her lower lip. She also knew a cop when she saw one. She made me immediately and became fidgety. Too fidgety, I thought.

I looked back at the policewoman, who was studying the ceiling with intensity. She wanted no part of Mr. Moody and Miss Thing, the reason being that if the situation turned physical, she'd have to do something about it. I doubt if she was smart enough to talk these clowns into keeping the peace. And she damn sure wasn't big enough to kick ass.

If things heated up, I figured her to react like most female cops. She'd panic. Then she would draw her gun and commence firing. The outcome would be one more needless shooting by a terrified policewoman. This was the department's dirty little secret, these trigger-happy ladies in blue. Why was it being kept out of the papers and off the tube? Because the department didn't want a fight with feminists and the PC crowd.

This mess was the result of ethnic hiring quotas, words destined to overheat my oven until the day I died. A liberal-minded judge, bless him, had ruled that one in three new police recruits must come from a minority. This included women, though how 50 percent of the population qualified as a minority escaped me. But his honor's word was law. The floodgates were open, and the department was now up to its ass in losers.

As it turned out, minorities and women weren't able to pass the tests. In response, the city had lowered recruiting standards. And that's why so many New York City cops were doing cocaine, taking payoffs, or killing themselves.

I walked over to Walter Moody, who kept his back to me. I remembered he had been less than cordial at our first meeting. Today this coconut was positively ornery. I tapped him on the shoulder. Without turning around, he angrily brushed my hand aside.

Compared with what I'd gone through lately, this wasn't even on the meter. I was having trouble accepting Lynda's death and I was having trouble with my supervisor, Lieutenant Jack Hayden—Jack the Ripper to those of us on his shit list. Jack needed to feel secure, and the more power he had, the more secure he felt. He was up for captain, and if I did my job, which was to find Mr. Clean, he could take the credit. Jack and I weren't having fun together. He was capable of behaving very stupidly when carried away by ambition, which usually happened whenever I told him I had nothing on the Ecuadorans.

I'd recently been outfoxed by a Chinese perp, a sociopath who scooped out his victims' eyes with a spoon, then gnawed through their throats with his teeth. A court interpreter had read him his rights in Chinese, in the Mandarin dialect. The perp, however, claimed to understand only Cantonese.

Whereupon a judge had thrown out his confession to four murders, then cut him loose.

I'd also arrested some Dominican crazies, killer cowboys who had been knocking over bodegas and other small businesses in upper Manhattan and the Bronx. Their specialty was robbing people who hid cash from the IRS or who feared banks. They dressed up as telephone or postal workers and conned their way inside, grabbing money, jewelry, and other valuables, racking up twenty-two homicides along the way. Unhappy at being arrested, their leader had vowed on his dead mother's eyes to have me killed.

Moody had gotten physical with me, and he had done it in front of a policewoman, and I couldn't let that pass. Word would get around, and before I knew it, cops would be asking if I wore lace around my drawers and used maxipads. Mr. Moody needed an attitude adjustment.

I gripped the Jamaican's ear between my thumb and forefinger, then twisted. He squealed and tugged at my hand. To give him something else to think about, I stepped on his foot. His knees buckled.

The hooker went bug-eyed, then backed up. She was on the verge of losing it. I assumed she was upset at seeing homeboy suffer. I was wrong.

What changed my mind was hearing Moody tell her to keep quiet or they would both end up with shit. These two had something going, and cops weren't supposed to know about it.

I wasn't too fond of chicks with dicks. I jerked my head toward the entrance, a signal for Miss Thing to take a hike. She started to say something to Moody, then changed her mind. Instead she gave him a look that said It ain't over till it's over, then minced her way around the puddles, stiletto heels clicking on the linoleum.

I released the Jamaican's ear and pointed to the ceiling. "Lead the way."

Moody gave me a dirty look. "You know where the room is," he said in a Caribbean singsong.

"You don't hear so good. I said lead the way."

"I know my rights, mon. You can't push me around. This is the nineties, you dig?"

"I know what year it is. I have a calendar. How'd you like to spend time on Rikers for assaulting a police officer?"

"You're a slicky boy, aren't you?"

"Upstairs. While we're still young."

I followed Moody up a squeaky staircase reeking of urine and lit by a naked lightbulb. On the second floor we entered an empty hallway carpeted in faded brown and smelling of marijuana, cheap wine, and years of human stink. Two boom boxes were tuned to competing salsa stations, and somewhere down the hall a dice game was in full flower. I kept one eye on the floor, not wanting to step in anything soft.

A door opened, and a fat, bearded Hasid stepped into the corridor. Spotting us, he faced the wall and scurried sideways like a crab. Behind him came a thick-lipped Puerto Rican boy in pump Reeboks, the boy no older than fifteen and smelling of perfume—and not caring who saw him. He stopped to give me a Times Square sales pitch, which consisted of grabbing his crotch and licking his lips.

Before I could respond, Walter Moody yelled, "Julio." The word was a warning and a threat, and young Julio got the point forthwith. They exchanged looks, Julio and the Jamaican, then the kid's eyes flicked to me, and a second later he was gone, sprinting downstairs, bouncing off staircase walls. The policewoman was doing a great job keeping out the riffraff.

Lourdes and Tonino's room was at the far end of the hall, near a window that overlooked a fire escape. There was no glass in the window, and a metal gate installed to keep out intruders had been bent to one side. Intruders and cold air could now enter freely.

The patrolman guarding the crime scene was a big-boned Italian with heavily lidded eyes and a nose flattened by too many punches. I identified myself, and together we peeled the police tape from the room door. When we finished, I told him to take a break. Grab some coffee, I said, and come back in a half hour or so. I didn't have to tell him twice.

I ordered Walter Moody to wait in the hall. He immediately started bitching about the cold, asking if he could go downstairs for a jacket. I ordered him to stay put. At ten in the morning, he smelled of liquor, and if I let him out of my sight, he just might find a bottle and not return.

Moody said he wasn't being paid to freeze. I could shoot him in the back if I wanted to, he said, but he was going across the hall for a blanket. I asked him how long that particular room had been empty. Moody said a week, then used a passkey to unlock the door.

Minutes later he was back in the hallway, wrapped in a red blanket and looking like a squeegee guy who spits on your windshield, then charges you to wipe it off. The sight of him set me to thinking about Lynda's killer and what I would like to do to that maggot. Something must have shown on my face because Moody flinched.

The crime-scene door was unlocked. I opened it with a gloved hand and stared inside. I saw a cubbyhole, ten by twelve feet, with flamingos and palm trees on the wallpaper. Two stained mattresses lay on the floor. A single window faced an air shaft. No furniture, no bathroom, no heat. I touched the lock, remembering there had been no forced entry. A runaway teenager and Mr. Clean. They had to be connected. Had to be.

Investigations begin with the elimination of as many suspects as possible. The search isn't about finding the right guy but about eliminating everyone else. I didn't have suspects to eliminate just yet, but I did have theories to get rid of, starting with the idea that Lourdes Balera had been murdered by a stranger. She'd known Mr. Clean. That's why she'd opened the door to him willingly.

I also didn't believe Tonino's people were the victims of a drug war. A couple of reporters were pushing this one real hard. Reporters knew shit about the city, being white, affluent, and out of touch. Any schoolkid knew the drug trade was controlled by blacks, Dominicans, and Colombians, each of whom would have chopped up Tonino's people in slaughterhouse fashion. Mr. Clean had his faults, but being messy wasn't one of them. Blacks would have hit the Ecuadorans with drive-by shootings, not caring who got caught in the cross fire. Latinos sodomized male victims before killing them, and so far Mr. Clean hadn't butt-fucked anybody.

I watched Walter Moody shiver under his blanket. I hadn't brought him along for his expertise as a guide. I wanted information, and to get it I would have to shake him up. I ordered him inside Lourdes's room, closed the door, and leaned against it, arms folded. I stared at Moody, who tried holding my gaze. When he couldn't, he looked down at his shoes.

Finally, I said, "Where's the stuff you stole from the victims?"

Moody nearly jumped out of his skin. He pulled the blanket tighter and coughed until he was red in the face. Eventually, he found his voice. He said, "You crazy, mon."

I looked at my watch. "The guard should be back soon. He makes an arrest, he gets a promotion. Want to talk about the penalty for interfering with a crime scene?"

I loosened my scarf. "Correct me if I'm wrong, but that is why you and Miss Thing were arguing. Who gets what, right?"

Moody opened his mouth to say something, then changed his mind. Instead he closed his eyes.

I said, "After you reported the murders, you helped yourself to whatever wasn't nailed down. Now Miss Thing wants her share. If I pressed her, I think she'd rat you out rather than spend the night in a cell with four guys who'll come at her without Vaseline."

Walter Moody went back to looking at his shoes.

Being a cop is about having power over people. I'd gotten hooked on that power from the beginning. Every cop does. A week of it and you never want to let go. I had power over Walter Moody because I could take everything from him. But why do that when I could use him.

"Here's the deal," I said. "Buy two, get one free."

Moody's head snapped up.

I said, "I'd take it if I were you."

"What kind of deal?"

"There's no bargaining," I said, and after telling him to listen up, I opened the door to see if the guard was coming back. He wasn't.

I shut the door and told Moody what I wanted and what was in it for him.

I said I wanted him to hand over everything he'd stolen. I also wanted to know if anyone had been around asking about Lourdes before she died. In return he got to keep his freedom.

Moody said the stuff was in his office.

"Let's go get it," I said, and after resealing the room, we went downstairs.

The small office was to the right of the lobby entrance. Inside I watched him take a suitcase from the closet, remove the loot, and spread it across his desk. He had stolen Lourdes's jewelry—a Mickey Mouse watch, cheap bracelets, earrings, and a bamboo choker. He had also taken Tonino's leather jacket and digital watch, a color TV, and two hundred in cash.

I told him to split the money with his she-male friend, then to call Midtown South and tell them he'd forgotten he'd been holding some stuff for the vics and for detectives to pick it up. If his lovely colleague didn't like this arrangement, she could complain to Midtown and hand over her share of the money.

Then I ordered Moody to repeat his story about discovering the bodies. I also wanted the names of anyone who had been asking about Lourdes prior to her murder.

Moody said around the time the killings occurred, he and LaShawna, Miss Thing, had been across the hall having sex, which is how she paid her rent. They hadn't heard any gunfire, but at one point Moody could have sworn he'd heard someone running down the fire escape. After finishing up with LaShawna, he had gone to collect Lourdes's rent. Her pimp used to take care of everything, but he wasn't around anymore, and she was late in paying.

The pimp was Reggie Cleveland, Moody said. Pretty Reggie, they called him. Nice-looking young brother in his early twenties. Except he wasn't all that nice-looking anymore, not after going up against Tonino. Moody said Tonino was Spanish and didn't want his woman selling her booty, so he had stopped Lourdes from turning tricks. Since this meant Pretty Reggie would lose money, there had to be a fight between him and Tonino. Moody had witnessed Tonino cutting Pretty Reggie up, down, and sideways, sending him off to the emergency ward bleeding like a stuck pig.

Two days ago, when Moody saw blood coming from under

Lourdes's door, the first thing he thought of was payback. Pretty Reggie had gotten even. That's what he had told police, who now considered Reggie their prime suspect. Detectives believed he was hiding out in South Carolina with relatives or an old girlfriend.

Moody's problem with LaShawna was that the bitch was greedy. She wanted all the jewelry, the color TV, plus half the money. If he didn't give in to her demands, she was going to report him to the police.

I said once LaShawna took her share of the money, she was an accessory and couldn't implicate him in any crime without implicating herself. Just make sure he turned everything over to Midtown before giving her the money. I didn't say he'd also be my now and future snitch.

I said, "Anybody been around asking about Lourdes?"

"Cops want Reggie. They don't want to hear about nobody else."

"I want to hear."

Moody said a week before the murder someone had been around asking for the girl. Fact is Moody had forgotten all about him until now. The guy was a detective and had been all over the neighborhood looking for Lourdes. Eventually, he'd ended up here at the hotel, claiming to be a friend of the family sent by Lourdes's father to bring her home.

Moody hadn't wanted any trouble with cops, so he'd cooperated, telling the detective about Lourdes and even mentioning Tonino. But a strange thing happened. The detective had left right away. Didn't even bother going up to Lourdes's room. Next morning, Moody said, the detective was back, asking if Lourdes and Tonino were still there. When Moody said she was, the detective again left without approaching her.

"You remember this detective's name?" I said.

Moody said no, he didn't, but he remembered the guy was Puerto Rican and his card was in the desk somewhere. The Jamaican found the card folded under a porn video and handed it to me. I unfolded the card and read the name of the detective who was a friend of the Balera family and had located the missing daughter but refused to return her to her family. The card belonged to Detective Sergeant Jesus Bauza.

IX
First Strike

I arrived at my office that afternoon to find a handwritten note from Jack Hayden Scotch-taped to my telephone. The Ripper wanted to see me immediately. *Immediately* had been underlined four times. Hayden had never really been calm. When his cork popped, which happened often, it made one hell of a noise.

I crushed his note and dropped it in the wastebasket. As I started to hang my coat up, the phone rang. I returned to my desk and lit a cigarette. The caller was probably Hayden. I decided to check the rest of my messages before seeing anybody.

An FBI agent, Lon Zajac, had called for the name of a judge I was investigating on corruption charges. Yeah, right. Nobody trusted the FBI. The Feebs took the credit and left you holding an empty bag. They refused to share intelligence but gladly took anything you had. I didn't know how Zajac learned about my judge, but I wasn't giving him squat.

A guy from the Jade Squad called. These were Asian American cops familiar enough with the language and customs to go after Asian criminals. I was working with Detective Tim Hong on a Chinese youth gang doing home invasions of wealthy Asians. The gang's specialty was pouring gasoline on a kid to force his family to give up money and valuables. Tim had called to say our chief informant, the gang leader's fifteen-year-old girlfriend, had skipped to China and was hiding out somewhere in Canton. Our case against the gang was in the toilet.

I had a fax from the Quito police. I'd asked them for a check on the whereabouts of Tonino's younger brother and a male cousin, both known to be traveling with the late

Señor Cuevas. I wanted to know if these two had returned to Ecuador. If so, Mr. Clean and I could quit looking for them.

The phone stopped. The Ripper had temporarily turned his attention from me and gone off to stick it to somebody else.

According to the fax, eighteen-year-old Marcos Cuevas, Tonino's baby brother, and Paco Nieves, his twenty-year-old cousin, hadn't returned to Ecuador. Both, apparently, were still in New York. I'd also asked whether any of the dead Ecuadorans had been involved in hometown vendettas. Negative on that. No past blood feuds for any of the deceased.

The Department of Corrections had sent over a copy of Maurice Robichaux's rap sheet, a list of arrests and convictions some forty-eight pages long. I was looking for a connection between Lynda and her murderer. Something to explain why Robichaux might have killed her. I dropped the rap sheet in a desk drawer, planning to plow through it later.

I looked at the other messages. Nothing from Lisa Watts, Lynda's partner. I'd called her twice today. Each time I'd been told she was tied up and would get back to me. I wanted to know if she'd spoken to Lynda the day of the murder. Also if Lynda had been meeting an informant that night. If so, where.

Also on my desk was the English translation of a magazine article found among Tonino's effects. The article, from a year-old Ecuadoran newsmagazine, offered advice to would-be illegal immigrants to the U.S. Helpful hints for the unauthorized.

An Ecuadoran illegal was advised to pass himself off as Mexican, taking care to learn Mexican slang and the Mexican national anthem. This way, if caught by immigration officials, the Ecuadoran would be deported only as far as the nearest Mexican border town. From there it would be easier to enter the U.S. again, as opposed to trying it a second time from Ecuador. Unfortunately, Tonino's next trip would be made from that great border town in the sky, increasing his travel time somewhat.

My phone rang again. I put out my cigarette and picked up the Quito fax. Time to see the Ripper.

Hayden had a fifteenth-floor corner office with three windows overlooking Park Avenue and a nonworking fireplace where he kept a set of golf clubs. A crystal chandelier installed by the former millionaire owner looked down from a blue-and-silver ceiling. The original green-and-white marble floor had been left untouched. The walls were scratch-coat plaster, dark brown and peeling, with the sad elegance of good taste going to ruin.

I sat in front of his desk, in a copy of an eighteenth-century Italian chair that looked pretty much like the real thing. Folding my hands in my lap, I waited for Hayden to tell me of his unhappiness with my latest efforts. He sat reading a report, a slim, baby-faced man of forty-eight with dyed brown hair, slits for eyes, and a fondness for pinstriped vests; an arrogant man who was paranoid about other cops getting ahead of him and whose nagging wife had turned him into a pussy-whipped social climber.

I had worked under him for less than a year. He tolerated me because I was doing the kind of job that increased his chances of making captain before his next birthday. When I stopped being useful, I was gone. Hayden had a sharp tongue and was unaware how blunt and insulting he could be. You either loved him or hated his guts. We worked reasonably well together but weren't friends.

He pretended to read a few minutes longer, his way of punishing me for not getting back to him sooner. I stared at the chandelier, wondering why the owner hadn't taken it with him. Finally, Hayden closed the folder and slid it to one side. Then he picked up the phone and told his secretary to hold all calls. Show time.

He said, "I have two pieces of news for you, and both of them are bad. Here's the first. Carlyle Taylor is digging into your relationship with the late Detective Lynda Schiafino. If you'd stayed away from the airport, this shit wouldn't be happening. She doesn't like you, so I suspect her story will make you, and possibly me, unhappy. Should I be worried? Is there anything you want to tell me?"

I said there wasn't and gave him a rundown of my airport meeting with Carlyle Taylor, mentioning her attempt to depict Maurice Robichaux as a victim. I wanted a cigarette but decided to forgo the weed for now. Light up, and I would look shaky. Instead I watched Hayden use a black crayon to doodle a flower on a memo pad and reminded myself that if Carlyle Taylor found Lynda's letter, I was on my way to the big cage.

"Your partnership with Lynda Schiafino is history," Hayden said. "And her homicide's been cleared. The only other reason for going to the airport is if you're a Hare Krishna, which you ain't. So why did you go?"

"To say good-bye to Lynda."

Hayden lengthened the stem on his flower. "Seems you two were close."

"We got along."

"Were you fucking her?"

"Is that what Carlyle Taylor called to ask?"

"In your position I'd lie, so I won't press you for an answer. Speaking of which, I was forced to lie to the commissioner's office on your behalf. They wanted to know what you were doing at the airport. I said you were touching base with customs on some Israeli diamond smugglers."

"The commissioner's office?" Now I needed that cigarette.

Hayden pointed to me with his crayon. "Excuse me, but did you really think your appearance at the scene of a major homicide would go unobserved, said appearance being unwanted, unwelcomed, and uninvited? Which brings me to my second piece of bad news. Seems the brass has received a complaint about you. Not that you're the type to alienate anybody."

"It's the furthest thing from my mind."

"I keep telling people that."

"Carlyle Taylor's had a beef with me ever since I—"

"Chill out, Turbo," Hayden said.

He told me the complaint had nothing to do with Schwarzenigger and Daddy Duke. It had come from Detective Robert Schiafino, who'd said I was bad-mouthing his dead wife. I was telling anyone who would listen that she should never have been a cop. What's more, she'd been a lousy partner who once or twice had nearly gotten me killed. I was blaming her murder on her own incompetence. Schiafino claimed he'd asked me not to attend the funeral. Being hell-bent on trashing Lynda, I'd shown up anyway.

Hayden smiled at his flower. "Schiafino says you came to the funeral just so you could dump on his wife in front of the press. He doesn't want you near her grave again. Or near her partner. He also wants you to stay away from the crime site. Sounds like a man with a grudge. But you got no problem with that. I mean, you weren't pumping his wife, right? By the way, I heard about that little scene between you and him at the cemetery yesterday."

I said nothing while Hayden darkened his petals. Now I knew why Lisa Watts wasn't returning my calls. Bobby Schemes had gotten to her.

"Is he lying about you and his wife?" he said.

I thought about it, then said, "He is."

"Thought so. People here say you took her death pretty hard."

I said, "Yes, I did."

"Then what is it between you and Schiafino?" Hayden said, wanting to know all and at the same time unwilling to accept more problems.

Outside the window, pigeons cooed and strutted in the icy sun, pecking at the cement ledge beneath their feet. Suddenly, the cooing erupted into an outcry; birds leaped into the air and hovered within sight of the window, wings flapping wildly. A fight had broken out between two pigeons still on the ledge. They fought like boxers in the last round of a close fight, both working hard to impress the judges. Their attacks—beak jabs and quick wing slaps—were violent and nonstop.

The fight, however, was a mismatch; one bird was bulky, the other a little guy with more heart than sense. He had speed and he used combinations, throwing two pecks to his opponent's one. But his opponent had size and weight and was using them to make the little guy back up. Just like Bobby Schemes was doing to me.

Schiafino may have been an asswipe, but he'd clearly won the first round. He'd hurt me with the commissioner's office. He'd put ideas in Hayden's head. And he had maneuvered me into a position where I couldn't fight back without hurting myself. As frames go, this one was top-drawer. Solid gold.

From now on I'd have to be extra careful around Hayden. One wrong word about Lynda and I'd be transferred on the spot, with rumors following me around like a bad smell. The Ripper had his eyes fixed on the prize. He had zero tolerance for any scandal that might come between him and his captain's bars.

The Turks were right. *To whom can you complain when the judge is fucking your mother?*

Schiafino's strategy was no surprise. He was the absolute best at messing with your head. He would push my buttons, and then one day while I was out strolling in the sun and bagging some rays, a piano would drop from the sky and land on my head, and when they scraped me off the sidewalk, Bobby Schemes would be standing around, grinning and holding up a sign reading I NEVER TOUCHED THE GUY. He'd be hard to fight. He had balls, he had clout. And he wasn't shy about using either one.

I had done the lowest thing one cop could do to another, namely, screw his wife. Schiafino was Sicilian; he couldn't live under the same sky with a man who had put the horns on his head. He'd jerk me around until he thought the time was right. Then he'd do something really ugly. Like pull out my heart and show it to me before I died.

Forget that Lynda and I had loved each other, that Schiafino had cheated on her and beat her, that he was a prick who would lie until a new world was born. I had played hide the wienie with his wife, making me a shit and assuring him the sympathy of every cop on the force. No matter what he did to me, cops would approve.

I couldn't even file a complaint with the Internal Affairs Division. IAD was a joke. The division was a dumping ground for incompetents and eight balls, for losers marking time until retirement. Those turkeys weren't interested in punishing bad cops. Not when it might lead to wider investigations that could harm the careers of police brass.

The average cop was too smart to be caught by IAD. And Bobby Schemes was smarter than the average cop. A lot smarter. He could outfox IAD with half his brain tied behind his back. He was slick enough to trick those idiots into investigating me on some bogus charge, the last thing I needed. I didn't want anyone poking into my life. Not as long as Lynda's letter was still out there somewhere.

Like the little pigeon, I was on the ledge and backing up. Except I couldn't fly, and it was a long way down.

X
Reading Material

"How high did Schiafino's complaint go?" I said to Hayden, who continued working on his flower.

Some flower. I hadn't seen anything that ugly in years. If this had been a test to determine mental stability, any shrink in the country would have ordered Hayden confined for observation.

He switched crayons, exchanging black for dark purple, then said, "How high? Try deputy commissioner. Which brings me to the following. The commissioner's office also wants to know what's shaking regarding certain dead illegals. Specifically, the ones who've been ripping off the mayor's friend and favorite campaign contributor, Jonathan Munro. Maybe I should say *were,* since they're no longer with us."

"At least two are still alive." I handed Hayden the Quito fax.

Hayden put on a pair of bifocals and read in silence. Finished, he said, "What's the point?"

"If we can get to Tonino's brother and cousin fast enough, they could help us ID the shooter."

"*Fast?* Did someone say the word *fast?* Coming from you, that's fucking hilarious."

I let that go by. Hayden was under pressure. Mayor Tucker wanted his friends taken care of, and he didn't want excuses. Especially during an election year. He wanted a second term in office, and to achieve that, he needed fat cats like Jonathan Munro and their checkbooks. But if Munro and other biggies felt they weren't getting enough protection, those checkbooks might remain inactive. What Munro had in mind was protection from greaseballs who hijacked his trucks and sent his insurance rates soaring.

I pointed to the fax. "Something else we can ask those guys if we catch up to them."

"Such as?" Hayden said.

"Such as did Tonino pull a double cross? Let's say he stopped sending loot back to Ecuador as agreed. Suppose he made a better deal with the Russians or the Nigerians. They're also into illegal exports, American goods preferred. Suppose Tonino changed fences, and someone back home didn't like it."

"So they send a shooter here to remind him to be true to his school."

I shook my head. I told him the shooter was local, that he knew his way around. No matter where Tonino's people tried to hide, the shooter was waiting for them. I reminded Hayden that Latinos played hardball; if Tonino had problems in Ecuador, his relatives would be dead by now. The fax said they were alive. Yes, Tonino was on someone's hit list. But that someone was in this country.

Hayden looked thoughtful. Or as thoughtful as a grown man could look holding a purple crayon. "Munro's worried," he said. "He doesn't think the hijackings are over. He thinks the thieves are having a falling-out, nothing more. When the fallout ends, he believes the hijackings will start again. He's talked to the mayor. The mayor's talked to the commissioner, and the commissioner's flunky has talked to me. In turn I am now talking to you. Give me something. Anything."

Give me something. Coming from your superior, it meant lie if you have to. But help me cover my ass.

I told Hayden that tomorrow I intended to talk to the father of Lourdes Balera. I might learn why the killer had made Lourdes his first female vic.

I didn't tell Hayden about Detective Jesus Bauza's appearance at the Langham just prior to Lourdes's murder.

That could be coincidence. Or it could be more. I certainly didn't like Bauza finding the kid, then refusing to return her to her father.

I wasn't protecting Bauza. I just wanted more proof before including him as a player. I was also being careful because going after Bauza meant taking on Bobby Schemes, his business partner. Schiafino was too much of a control freak not to know what his people were up to. Anything Bauza was doing, he was doing with Schiafino's knowledge and permission.

Department politics also figured in my decision to go slow. Jack Hayden didn't like going after cops. And neither did I. But if I had to, I could.

I had two loyalties. Green and blue: Irish and cops.

But loyalty had its limits. Some years back I'd helped send a partner, Danny Baldazano, to prison. He'd wanted me dead before I could testify that he was passing along court records and sealed indictments to his cocaine-dealing Colombian friends. After the trial, Danny's cousin, also a cop, accused me of betraying the brotherhood. I decked him with one punch. No one ever mentioned Danny Baldazano to me again.

I didn't go out of my way to challenge corrupt cops. No one in the department did. If a cop approached me with something dirty, I blew him off and kept my mouth shut. Turn in another cop, and you got a reputation for being a rat. It was a reputation that lasted a lifetime.

Over the years I had been offered big bucks to destroy evidence, give up witnesses, or protect drug shipments. I'd walked away each time. Turning your back on that kind of money was never easy. But it became easier the night I watched a mob capo spit in the face of a cop to whom he was paying five grand a week. The incident taught me that a bought cop had better be prepared to eat shit.

It also reminded me why I had joined the department. Being a cop was my life; it had given me power, respect, and, in Nietzsche's words, a corresponding degree of freedom from good and evil. I wasn't going to lose that by selling my badge. At the same time I didn't want trouble with other cops.

For now I decided to keep quiet about Bauza's appearance at the Langham. I would mention it to Hayden only when I had proof that Bauza had been looking for Lourdes.

Walter Moody's word wasn't proof enough. The guy wasn't your most upright citizen. Nor did he move in the most elevated social circles. He was a scuzzy coconut, and Bauza was a cop. Guess who had the advantage in court.

I also kept quiet about Lynda's murder. About the contamination of her crime scene and my feeling that she hadn't been murdered at the airport. I kept quiet about the sloppy evidence gathering, the racial politics surrounding this case, the missing lights in the parking lot. The Ripper had no interest in hearing about my side trips. Especially the ones that brought flak from the commissioner's office.

"A suggestion," Hayden said. "Two suggestions, actually. The first is, stay away from airports."

"Keep away from the Lynda Schiafino homicide, you mean."

"I mean if you want to amuse yourself, get a deck of Rodney King playing cards."

"A what?"

"Rodney King playing cards. Fifty-one clubs, one spade."

I smiled for the first time in days. Life wasn't all purple crayons around here.

"Second suggestion," he said. "Get your ass up to the Bronx. And I do mean now."

I said, "Want to tell me why?"

"Lourdes Balera. They're holding a vigil for her at a funeral home on the Grand Concourse. Get up there and schmooze with her family. See what you can pick up."

"I was planning on doing that tomorrow. Right now I've got a shitload of paperwork to catch up on."

Hayden's face became the color of his crayon. He slammed both palms down on the desk, shaking a desk lamp. Not being a big guy, his anger made him look like a jockey choking on a piece of meat.

He said, "You got a fart in your brain, Meagher, or what? I said *now*. I want you to move your fat butt out of that chair, walk through the door, and keep on walking until you hit the fucking Bronx. Do you grasp the meaning of my words?"

I said, "You're getting through."

"Let's have a show of hands," he said. "How many around here remember when Jack Hayden used to run this fucking squad?"

As I reached for the fax, Hayden shifted one palm and pinned it to his desk. His mood changed. He seemed pleased about something. He said, *Your girlfriend Carlyle Taylor's asking around about Baby Cabrera, some fag coke dealer doing a bit in Atlanta. Miss Taylor is interested in the last case you and Detective Lynda Schiafino worked, so she's dug up a copy of Baby's trial transcript.* Being somewhat curious, Hayden had obtained a copy, too. Nothing to worry about, he told me. But something had caught his eye, namely, the part where Detective Feargal Meagher had denied Baby's claim he'd stolen twenty-five thousand dollars from him. Hayden wasn't concerned, you understand, but one just had to wonder what Miss Taylor would make of that.

XI
Bingo

The Grand Concourse in the Bronx runs four lanes in each direction and is the widest street in New York. In the early 1900s it had been the borough's most exclusive address, the Bronx's answer to Park Avenue. Leon Trotsky had once lived here, and so had Babe Ruth.

In the 1970s drugs and arson took over the South Bronx. The area turned into a wasteland of heroin addicts and burned-out tenements and stray bullets looking for vital organs. Whites fled to the suburbs, taking a good chunk of the tax base with them. Today the Concourse is mostly nonwhite and largely run-down.

Yet it retains some degree of normality. The old houses still stand, and people live in them. If you're on foot, stay on the Concourse. Go east or west, and you've got a problem.

It was nearly six in the evening. I was in the small gray lobby of a funeral home on the Grand Concourse and 161st Street, standing at the front window, where unmarked gravestones faced the street like giant chess pieces. A blimp of a black security guard, 250 pounds of fat and unspecified muscle, guarded the front door. His job was to keep out the walking dead—junkies, crackheads, and those who spoke to God while pissing on the sidewalk.

I was the only white man in the building. Everyone else, mourners and staff, was black or Hispanic. All were long-faced and subdued, and nobody made jokes.

With me was Carlos Humez, a small-faced fortyish Puerto Rican who managed the funeral home. He was a friend of the Balera family, part of which was upstairs keeping a vigil by Lourdes's coffin. I'd seen her corpse at the Langham Hotel and didn't want to see it again. In the past forty-eight hours I'd been to two funeral homes and it was starting to wear on me. The last thing I needed was more cold, sad memories.

The only person I wanted to see was Nelson Balera, Lourdes's father. I wanted to know if he'd asked Detective Bauza's help in finding his daughter. Balera wasn't just any witness. He could exonerate Bauza or link him to nine homicides. You don't pursue that information over the phone. You interview the witness in person.

Humez said that Nelson Balera had been here but left over an hour ago. Some friends had taken him to dinner. Humez expected them back momentarily.

He had known Balera for years. They had attended Fordham University together, played on the soccer team, and graduated within six months of each other. Both were fellow Masons and ushered at the same Catholic church on Fordham Road. So much sadness for one man, Humez said. Three years ago Balera had lost his wife, Irma, when she committed suicide by swallowing sleeping pills, then tying a plastic bag around her head. Now Lourdes, the only child, had been murdered. *Muy triste,* Humez said. Very sad.

I remembered Nelson Balera from television newscasts reporting his daughter's murder. He was a light-skinned Puerto Rican, around the same age as Humez and nearly six feet tall, with a square-shaped head, thick lower lip, and receding blue-black hair. He lived on Boston Road in the Bronx, worked as a hospital administrator, and was on his local school board.

In the eyes of his community, Balera was as righteous as High Mass on Easter Sunday. But Lourdes had told Walter Moody about her father's dark side. She'd run away because Nelson Balera had raped her repeatedly. Afterward he'd get drunk and beat her with a wire coat hanger for being, as he put it, lewd and immodest.

Balera hadn't fired the gun that killed his daughter, but in my book he was an accomplice to her murder.

Moody claimed that Lourdes's mother had known what was going on. But she'd been unstable and high-strung, unable to help herself let alone anyone else. In the end she'd washed down a bottle of sleeping pills with a pint of vodka, wrapped her head in plastic, and taken off for what Shakespeare called the undiscovered country.

Nelson Balera's drink of choice wasn't vodka; it was his daughter's urine. He considered it an aphrodisiac and drank a small glass every day. The man was a sweetheart. Lourdes should have shot his balls off before running away.

If I told Humez the truth about his friend Balera, the guy would mark me down as some kind of culturally insensitive butthole. A man who viewed all Latinos as perverts.

He had that right. Incest is no big deal with these people, most of whom have names than they have underwear. When a Hispanic boy is born, the first thing Mom does is suck the kid's dick to make sure he'll be well hung. Then there's the old joke: a Puerto Rican virgin is any twelve-year-old girl who can run faster than her father and brothers. Except Lourdes Balera might not have seen it as a joke.

If I wanted Humez's cooperation, I had to cool it on the subject of Balera family values. At the same time I needed to know if Bauza figured in the equation.

This meant I had to run a game on Señor Humez.

So I told him that Nelson Balera should have hired a private detective to look for his daughter. Spend the money for an experienced investigator.

Humez said, "That's exactly what he did. Except he didn't have to pay him. He went to Lourdes's godfather for help."

"I'd like to talk to him. Is he here?"

"No. He's having dinner with Nelson. He'll be back soon. He's a cop who works here in the Bronx. His name is Bauza. Detective Jesus Bauza."

Bingo. Bing. Fucking. Go.

I said, "Could you spell that name for me, please?"

Like I didn't already know.

Humez gave Jesus the Spanish pronunciation. *Hay-soos.* And he spelled out Bauza.

I said, "Bauza," and wrote the name in my notebook. To calm myself, I printed it twice and never looked at Humez. I was keyed up. Positively wired. My first break in the Mr. Clean killings. And it was a biggie. I wanted to share my excitement with Lynda. To hear her say, *you got it going on, big guy.*

Moments like this only reminded me that I didn't have her anymore. I had never before lost anything this important in my life.

Bauza *had* been looking for Lourdes Balera. I had the confirmation I needed. When Nelson Balera showed up, I'd have more. Even Walter Moody was starting to look good. The spics had given him credibility.

Haysoos had been searching for Lourdes and Tonino, with Tonino the primary objective. Lucky Haysoos. He'd found both targets at once.

I saw it this way: Lourdes had trusted her godfather and had probably confided in him. She told him where she was staying in Times Square, maybe even why she'd run away. One thing was certain—the minute she mentioned Tonino, she was dead. Haysoos wasn't going to allow any weepy reunion with Daddy. Not while Lourdes could still blow the lid off the volcano. *Gee, Godfather, isn't it strange how Tonino got iced just after I told you about him?*

Now I knew why Lourdes's room had shown no signs of forced entry. She'd opened the door to her godfather.

Which didn't mean Bauza was the killer. Maybe he'd only set up the hit. But if he wasn't Mr. Clean, he knew who was.

I was about to rock Jack Hayden's world. Exacerbate that little fuck and convolute my own life as well.

"Jesus looked for her on his own time," Humez said. "He

went all over Times Square, the East Village, the West Side docks. He went up and down Eighth Avenue. Always he kept in touch with Nelson, keeping him informed of what he was doing. Unfortunately, nothing came of all his hard work."

"He did go to Times Square."

"Twice. Couldn't find Lourdes anywhere. He cried like a baby when he heard she'd been murdered."

"Did you hear Detective Bauza tell Mr. Balera he'd been unable to find Lourdes?"

"As a matter of fact, yes. After Lourdes ran away, Nelson became depressed. He couldn't stand to be alone, so I invited him to stay with me and my wife for a little while. Jesus came by the house to tell us he'd been in Times Square and couldn't find Lourdes. Why do you ask?"

Cops lie with a purpose. And that purpose is to make arrests. No lies, no arrests. Under these circumstances lying is not only excusable. It is necessary and unavoidable.

I looked Humez in the eye. "You know Lourdes's murder is somehow connected to the killing of several Hispanic males."

"There was something about that on the news last night. Very frightening."

"I want Lourdes's killer. I want him off the streets."

Humez nodded his little head. I'd just said what he wanted to hear.

Time to talk trash.

I said, "Just before his murder, the illegal who was with Lourdes had been spotted in Times Square in the company of two male Hispanics believed to be his relatives. I have their photographs with me." I tapped the left side of my chest, suggesting there was something in my inside pocket. There was. Cigarettes and an extra notebook.

"I'd like Detective Bauza to look at these photographs. It's possible he could have spotted these men while searching for Lourdes."

Humez nodded. "I understand." He was talking to me but looking through the window at a black Jaguar about to park in front of the building. "That's Jesus's car. I'm sure he'd like to see those photographs."

XII
Meet the Family

The Jag was a beauty, glittering in front of the funeral home like a huge pile of cracked ice. It was sleek and low to the ground, with vanity plates reading JEBAU 1. Haysoos's topless club had to be paying off. You didn't drive a Jag on detective's pay.

I followed Humez to the entrance, where the beefy black security guard opened the door for us. Outside, Humez stretched both arms overhead, enjoying the chilly weather. He wasn't wearing a topcoat and didn't seem to need one. I wondered if working with cold meat had affected his mind.

The funeral home was on a block of discount stores, bodegas, and porn theaters. A blood-orange sun was about to vanish behind art deco apartment buildings lining the Grand Concourse. Few people were outdoors. You had to be a fool to walk around the South Bronx after dark.

I watched a young boy quickly leave the Jag. He was a Latino, thirteen or so, with large ears, a short neck, and a thick waistline, the kind of kid other children call dorky. Dumb-looking. He wore a Yankee warm-up jacket, a flannel shirt, a black woolen cap, and baggy jeans that drooped around his ankles. He held one hand against his cheekbone. When he took the hand away, there was blood on it.

The kid eyed his bloodstained palm, then glared at the Jag. At whoever had just struck him in the face. He seemed more angered than scared. I liked his style. No sniveling or whining. Just give 'em a don't-fuck-with-me attitude.

A kid after my own heart. The kind who would bite a dog because the dog had bitten him.

Having been there, I knew what was going through his mind. He was having one of those moments when he wished

70

every adult around him was dead. I used to feel that way after the nuns had beaten the crap out of me.

Next to leave the Jag were two adult Latinos, a man and a woman. The woman raced to the boy and hugged him. She was younger than me, thirtyish, with broad shoulders, dyed blond hair, and a strong jaw. She wore gold hoops, a blue head scarf, and a brown fur jacket over a pink pantsuit. Her shoes were little more than five-inch heels, thin soles, and the tiniest of straps. She was coarse-looking and sexually attractive, the kind who didn't seem all that interested in foreplay.

The man with her was a puffy and wet-eyed Nelson Balera. His soft, mushy-looking mouth was open, and he needed a shave. A tan trench coat, yellow scarf, and tan, pointy-toed shoes gave him the appearance of an over-the-hill gigolo. He looked exhausted, ready to collapse at any minute.

I asked Humez about the woman, and he said she was Damaris Bauza, Jesus Bauza's wife. The boy was Gavilan, her son by a previous marriage. Covering his mouth with one hand, Humez whispered that Bauza and his stepson didn't get along.

Guess who had punched the kid.

Jesus Bauza was alone in the car, behind the wheel and shaking his head as though weighed down by life's strife and contention. I'd seen him with Bobby Schemes's crew at Lynda's funeral, a scrawny dude around thirty-five with wide nostrils and a forehead too big for the rest of his face. Lynda had described him as the original macho man, headstrong with a hair-trigger temper and hell to be around when he didn't get his way.

I said I'd like to talk to Nelson Balera, and Humez motioned him over.

Meanwhile Bauza leaned through the open window and told his wife he was tired of her fat-assed son showing him no respect, and that the next time the little bastard acted up, Bauza was going to present him with some serious pain. A New York City cop, Bauza said, didn't take no shit from some kid who was so stupid his teachers had to burn down the school to get him out of third grade.

Damaris Bauza aimed her square chin at her husband and said, You hit my boy again, I make you sorry for the rest of your life. Stay downtown, she said, and tell lies to your cop friends, your nightclub full of naked women, and your young whore. Downtown was where he belonged, not here in the Bronx with her and Gavilan.

Bauza had been drinking. He wasn't shit-faced yet, but he was well on the way. I watched him flash a goofy smile and continue playing the dozens with his stepson, zinging the kid with a passion.

He slammed the boy's weight, made fun of his dyslexia, and called him a retard. He also trashed the kid's looks. If ugly was a crime, Bauza said, Gavilan would get the electric chair.

Mrs. Bauza screamed at her husband in Spanish, and while I couldn't understand what she said I knew she wasn't offering him a slice of her onion quiche.

At that point a young male black in a beat-up cowboy hat, mangy red bathrobe, and dark glasses came strolling out of the shadows. His footwear was also funky—one tennis shoe, one orange high-top sneaker, both falling apart. His face was covered with scabs, and both hands were swollen. A junkie. And stoned out of his mind.

At the sight of the Bauzas, he came to a stop. I watched him stand in absolute quiet, openmouthed and half-asleep, taking in the action before finally saying to Haysoos, "Yo, brother man. Don't be lettin' no bitch rag on you like that. Whip her entire ass, understand what I'm saying? Whip her *entire ass.*"

Husband and wife ignored the dope fiend, who responded by scratching his head while thinking of something more to say. When you're on the needle, thinking doesn't come easy.

Then, without warning, the junkie clamped a hand over his mouth. He shook his head as if to say *You did something wrong, fool.* He backed off, waving to the Bauzas as though seeing them off on a trip. My guess was, the doper had made Haysoos as a cop.

Nelson Balera was standing in front of me, partially blocking my view of Bauza and his wife. Humez introduced us, saying I was a detective assigned to investigate Lourdes's murder. This wasn't quite true, but I didn't bother correcting him. There wasn't time. Sooner or later Bauza would notice I was on the set. Then he'd want to know why.

Balera gave me a dopey smile. His idea of shaking hands was to offer me his fingertips, which were soft and moist. He asked if I was from Manhattan South, and I said no. I showed him my ID, explaining that I wanted to catch Lourdes's killer but my main interest was in finding a connection between Balera's daughter and Tonino Cuevas.

Balera's eyes were red-rimmed, and he couldn't stop sniffling. He started to speak, lost his voice, and swallowed hard before talking again. He apologized for his vocal problems and asked me to please bear with him. Underneath the tears and whining I saw a man living in a dreamworld, where everything was beautiful and the sun never stopped shining. Present him with problems, and he'd still cling to his fantasies, refusing to leave never-never land.

Once he started talking, he couldn't stop. I figured the weight of guilt was on him. It had to be. He was Chester the molester, a child-rapist, and he had betrayed everything he could betray. It made no difference what he told other people. He had to feel guilt about sexually assaulting his own daughter.

He told me how wonderful she had been. How much I missed her. How they might still be together today had he only cut back on his hours at the hospital. Every minute with Lourdes, he said, had been quality time. He shed a few tears.

He wanted sympathy. Some kind of condolence. What I felt was a strong desire to be somewhere else.

I asked about Detective Bauza and Lourdes. Balera's story matched Humez's almost word for word. Yes, Bauza had gone looking for Lourdes. No, he hadn't found her.

I now had three people who could tie Bauza to the runaway girl. One—Walter Moody—could put him in her hotel room just prior to the double homicide. I was still missing something important, namely, a motive for the Ecuadoran killings. Without one my case was in the crapper.

I watched Balera give Bauza a sappy look, which went

unnoticed since he was still arguing with his wife. The detective, Balera said, was a great man. A very great man.

"Know what he did?" Balera said.

"No, I don't."

"He spent his own money trying to find my daughter. *His own money.*"

"Is that right?"

"A thousand dollars. That's how much he loved Lourdes."

"This thousand dollars. How did he spend it?"

"Information. He went to the street. Talked to junkies, pimps, whores, delivery boys. People who could tell him about runaways."

I turned to a new page in my notebook. "What did he find out?"

"Not a thing. They tricked him. Lied to him. Fucking bastards."

"He told you that, did he?"

"Detective Bauza's got a big heart. Maybe he trusts people too much."

"He sounds just as kind as a man can be."

"You better believe it." Balera dabbed at his eyes with a handkerchief. "I blame those animals for Lourdes's murder."

"Why's that?"

"Because they lied to get the money, the thousand dollars. They snatched it out of his hand, then sent Detective Bauza on one wild-goose chase after another. Bastards. They stopped him from reaching my daughter in time. Yes, I blame them. Every damn one of them. They put the bullet in her head."

I stopped writing and looked at Balera, wondering if I'd missed a turn somewhere. The Haysoos he'd just described was a man brimming with dedication. A man driving straight along the twisted road of life.

I knew cops who would dig into their own pocket to help a child, and Bauza wasn't one of them. Watching him this evening with his stepson told me the man didn't give a shit about kids, his or anyone else's. The real Detective Bauza was a half-sauced numskull who cheated on his wife, punched kids, and drove a car far beyond the salary of an honest cop.

He was also involved in a few murders. Nine, to be exact.

Balera said, "Detective, do you have any idea who might have murdered my daughter?" He placed a hand on my forearm. I didn't want this puke touching me and pulled my arm away. He was too wrapped up in himself to notice.

I said, "We're working on a couple of leads. Nothing I can go into right now."

"Never got a chance to say good-bye to her. I'd give anything to see Lourdes alive again. Just for a minute. That is all I ask of God. Bring my daughter to me for one minute, no more." Tears trickled down either side of Balera's nose.

I jerked my head toward the funeral home. "You have people waiting for you inside. If I need anything further, I'll be in touch."

I had what I'd come here for. And Balera was getting on my nerves. I couldn't have helped him with his guilt even if I'd wanted to.

I had just put away my notebook when Bauza yelled, "Bitch, you don't *ever* threaten me!" I watched as he shoved the passenger door into his wife, sending her staggering backward. One of her heels snapped, and she twisted her ankle. Screaming, she fell to the pavement, landing on her hip. Her pink trousers split in the rear, and her purse went flying under the Jag.

The collision with the car door hadn't been accidental. Bauza leaped from the Jag and raised his foot, preparing to stomp his wife. I was too far away to do anything, but Gavilan wasn't. The kid tackled his stepfather around the waist and drove him into the side of the Jag. Head down, Gavilan held on to his stepfather. Bauza had his hands free and punched the kid behind the neck, on the shoulder. When Gavilan let go, Jesus kneed him in the gut. Gavilan doubled over, and this put a craziness in my head. Bauza had his back to me and never saw me coming. I walked over to him and hooked a left into his kidneys and a right to his rib cage, and he dropped to his knees, sucking in air through his mouth. He put a hand on his rib cage and took a deep breath. Then he looked over his shoulder at me while massaging his rib cage and inhaling through clenched teeth.

He said, "Meagher." He closed his eyes and did some more deep breathing. Then he said, "You goddamn crazy, you know that? The hell you doing here?" He sat down on the sidewalk. His hand went inside his overcoat. He was reaching for his piece.

I carried two guns, a Glock nine millimeter with a fifteen-round magazine and a five-shot Taurus with a two-inch barrel. The nine was in the small of my back, rubber bands around the grip to keep it from slipping. The Taurus was in an ankle holster.

I didn't reach for either piece. Instead I leaned over Bauza until our noses nearly touched. I heard his raspy breathing, smelled his booze breath, and saw him nervously bite his lower lip. I also saw his eyes, and he saw mine. When he leaned away, I knew he had seen the madness that was a mystery even to me.

"From this distance you can easily get off a couple of shots," I said. "You'll hit me, no question about it. Hell, Stevie Wonder could hit me from here. The bad news is you're still going to die. You can empty your gun, but there's no guarantee you'll stop me. Meanwhile, you ever been gut-shot with a nine? Want to know what it feels like?"

A frowning Bauza shook his head. "Man, they're right. You're one twisted son of a bitch."

His hand came out of the coat. It was empty.

He rose, staggered over to the Jag, and sat in the passenger seat. Hand on his rib cage, he stared through the windshield, and he shot me a look hinting he might be having second thoughts about not having whacked me when he'd had the chance. I held his gaze until he looked away.

Haysoos was a weak sister. Yellow and gutless. No one but a candy-ass would smack his wife with a car door, then play groin soccer with his stepson. However, I wasn't dumb enough to underestimate someone who had filled so many body bags. Haysoos was dangerous. Next time he wouldn't meet me head-on. He'd Jap me. Come at me from behind.

I looked at Bauza's wife. Her mascara was running, but the hysteria had eased off. Her bad ankle forced her to lean on Humez, who'd also offered Mrs. Bauza his handkerchief. Her son was on his feet, wobbly-legged and rubbing his stomach. Nelson Balera was gently feeling the back of the kid's neck, where he'd been punched.

I said, "Mrs. Bauza, I'm Detective Meagher." I showed her my ID. "That's my car in front of the hearse. I'll drive you and your son home."

Bauza closed the passenger door, slid behind the wheel, and reached for the ignition key. Before turning it, he said to me, "You got a clear field, Meagher."

"What's that supposed to mean?"

He turned the key. The Jag purred. "Means I'm not coming home tonight. Means you can pork my wife. Like you did Schiafino's old lady."

He looked into the rearview mirror, started turning the wheel, then shot me a quick look. "Man, has Bobby Schemes got plans for you. He's always going to be one step ahead of your ass. Ain't nothing you can do he don't know about. I'm outta here. Later for you, Jack."

Bauza gunned the motor, made an illegal U-turn, and headed downtown.

He was right about one thing. I *was* interested in his wife. But I had no plans to jump her.

There's no one tougher to bring down than a rogue cop. His toughness lies in his ability to manipulate the justice system. He can hide evidence, intimidate witnesses, and spot surveillance in the dark. He can obtain court documents and reach out for jurors' relatives. He knows how to hide money. And the very tactics used to investigate him are the ones he's spent his career perfecting. Fellow cops will protect him even when he's charged with murder.

Forget wiretaps. A rogue cop is too smart to say anything over the phone.

There is, however, a way to get to him. A way that never fails.

You use his enemies.

I smiled at Bauza's wife and stepson. "Where's home?" I said.

XIII
Traveling Man

Riverdale is a well-to-do suburb in the West Bronx, between the Hudson River and Van Cortlandt Park. It has old mansions and lawns without sidewalks, reminders of a time when the area was once very exclusive. Apartment high-rises make Riverdale less select these days, but the area remains the Gold Coast of the Bronx, with some residents refusing to add the borough's name to their address.

The Bauzas lived in one of these high-rises. Their building was well kept and had a doorman whose neck was bigger than his head. A self-service elevator came with a mirrored ceiling and a lame version of "Eleanor Rigby."

I held Damaris Bauza's arm as she limped into her tenth-floor apartment. I expected to see a pigsty, with cockroaches and spray-painted walls and pictures of Christ painted on black velvet. Instead I saw a nice-size living room with a view of the Hudson, frozen over and gleaming under a white moon. The decor was strictly high-tech, with everything in black and white or chrome and silver. A couch and two armchairs were made of molded plastic, and the floor was sanded wood. Three wire chairs and a glass-topped table occupied a corner near an open kitchen, where utensils were displayed on hooks or racks. A mobile storage unit, the kind used in hospitals, held a TV, stereo, and VCR. Wall mirrors enhanced the lighting, and there wasn't a speck of dust in sight. A telephone, message light blinking, sat on a low black wooden table. There was a small corridor leading to what I assumed were bedrooms. The room was uncluttered, immaculate, and scary in its fanatic purity.

The color scheme didn't seem to go with the warm-blooded Damaris Bauza. Nor did it impress me as anything

Haysoos might be interested in. I was wrong. Haysoos had indeed chosen the decor, a point made by the half dozen books in the room. All dealt with law enforcement, meaning Detective Bauza was in charge. Mrs. Bauza and FBI studies on sexual homicide didn't seem to go together.

Haysoos was a neatness freak. Who would have thought it? I sent Gavilan to find ice for his mother's swollen ankle. Then I escorted her to a plastic armchair beside the phone and suggested she have the ankle X-rayed for broken bones. She thanked me for bringing her home, then said she didn't like doctors. Her son would take care of everything.

She removed her shoes and placed them in her lap. Since Haysoos seemed to be in charge, she'd probably been warned about leaving personal items lying about his neat little kingdom.

I placed Mrs. Bauza's ankle on one of the wire chairs as gently as I could. Ordinarily, Puerto Rican women didn't interest me. Most don't have the sense to peel a banana before eating it. As for looks—Puerto Rican males have mustaches in order to look like their mothers.

Damaris Bauza, however, gave me a sad, sweet smile, and I felt like knocking myself out to please her. She wore too much lip gloss for my taste, and she looked like a turboslut, but I could be persuaded.

I saw her as good-hearted and stupid, loyal to people who didn't deserve it and inclined to involve herself with crazies who kept changing the rules. Her kind side would nurse you back to health when you were sick. In a pinch she'd even watch your clothes spin-dry for you. But she had her brainless side as well. This Damaris Bauza enjoyed being sad, always picked the wrong man—and didn't learn from her mistakes.

Gavilan returned with a glass of water, some ice cubes wrapped in a hand towel, and a small bottle of pills. Mrs. Bauza assured me the pills were Valium. Before I could say I didn't care what they were, she had popped four. Her bright eyes said she wanted to gulp down a few more. Gavilan handled the situation by gently taking the bottle from his mother, then applying ice to her damaged ankle. Technically, Mrs. Bauza was the parent, but I sensed she needed watching.

Without his jacket and cap, Gavilan appeared smaller and more vulnerable. He wore his hair in a buzz cut and had a swelling under one eye. The gash on his cheekbone had stopped bleeding. Remembering he'd been kicked by his stepfather, I asked if his stomach still hurt.

"I don't need your help," he said, refusing to look at me. "I don't like cops."

Mrs. Bauza said, "Gavilan, apologize to Detective Meagher. He did help us. Now go on. Apologize."

Gavilan eyed me over his shoulder. You'd have thought his lunch had fallen into the toilet and I'd ordered him to fish it out by hand. Holding my gaze, he silently challenged me to make him atone.

I removed my hat, remembering Gavilan didn't need me. But I did need him. It behooved me, therefore, to avoid a shouting match with this little fuck. As for Mrs. Bauza, her husband was playing around. What better payback was there than ratting him out.

But to get her, I had to turn Gavilan, and that wasn't going to be easy. I was a cop. In his eyes, as big a jerk-off as his stepfather.

"You did good standing up for your mother," I said to him.

"I don't need you to tell me that," he said. He looked at me like I was a canker sore. "Nobody disses my mother. He want to marry his girlfriend, that's cool. But he can't insult my mother to my face. He can't say she look old and she don't take care of herself no more."

I said, "So your stepfather hit you because you spoke up for your mother."

"Man, fuck that dude," Gavilan said.

"Gavilan, please," Damaris Bauza said. She'd had enough confrontation for one day. Her soft brown eyes pleaded not to be embarrassed. I also had the feeling she wanted her son to calm down, to back off from hating his stepfather for the time being. Family violence was not unheard of in the Bronx. It could be that one day soon Gavilan might decide it was time for Haysoos to take a dirt nap.

You had to wonder if this apartment was big enough for the three of them. Great hatred, little room, as Yeats said of Ireland.

I decided to change the subject. "You named after the fighter?" I said to Gavilan. "You know, Kid Gavilan."

Damaris Bauza's eyes widened. "You heard of Kid Gavilan?"

"He don't know shit," Gavilan said. "He just jiving you."

"Kid Gavilan's real name was Gerardo Gonzales," I said. "And he was Cuban. He was welterweight champ back in the fifties, until he lost to Johnny Saxton. He fought Bobo Olson for the middleweight championship and dropped a fifteen-round decision. He had a hundred and forty fights, won a hundred and five and lost twenty-eight. He had six draws and one no-decision."

"Wow," Damaris Bauza said. "You know all that?"

"Kid Gavilan was a hell of a fighter," I said. "He was never knocked out."

"My father knew him," she said. "He was a boxer, my father. Middleweight like Kid Gavilan. They were good friends. Sometimes my father worked as his sparring partner. Daddy had two daughters, no sons, so when I got pregnant, he offered me and my first husband, Angel, a thousand dollars if we name our son after Kid Gavilan. He never gave me the money, but I don't hold that against him."

"What name did your father fight under?" I said.

"His own name. Frankie Vidal." Her voice sounded slurred. The Valium was kicking in.

"I've heard of Frankie Vidal," I said.

"You never even met my grandfather," Gavilan said. "How come you lie like that?"

I shook a cigarette loose from the pack and looked around for an ashtray. When I failed to spot one, I began telling the Bauzas about the 1963 welterweight title fight between the champion, Emile Griffith, and a Cuban named Benny "Kid" Paret. They fought here in New York, I said. Each man had beaten the other once. Each was at the top of his game. People expected a war, I said. What they got was a tragedy. During the fight Paret set the tone by calling Griffith *maricon*, faggot, because Griffith enjoyed designing lady's hats. Griffith blew his stack and handed Paret some ferocious punishment, connecting with twenty-one punches in the twelfth round before the referee finally stopped the fight. By then it was too late for Paret, I said. He never regained consciousness and died ten days later.

I rolled the unlit cigarette between my fingers. "I have a film of that fight," I said. "I also have a fight poster. Frankie Vidal's name is on it. He fought on the undercard."

Gavilan looked down at the floor, then up at me. He scratched his head and drew his eyebrows together. Some of the gangsta-rap attitude had disappeared, but he had yet to fall victim to my boyish charm.

"After that night my father didn't fight no more," Damaris Bauza said. "He didn't want what happened to Benny Paret to happen to him."

"He went out a winner," I said. "He beat Joey Viscaino that night. TKO fourth round. What's your father doing now?"

"He's dead," Damaris Bauza said. "Got killed in a hit-and-run three years ago. The cops don't know whether it was an accident or murder. He owed money to some people and couldn't pay."

I said it sounded like her father was a gambler.

"He couldn't stop," she said. "Gambled away every dollar he ever made. When he died, he owed three thousand dollars to some Cubans. Cops thought these guys might have killed him, but they couldn't find any proof. That's how I met Jesus. He was one of the detectives investigating my father's death. I should have listened to Angel, my first husband. He was Gavilan's father. He said to stay away from gamblers. They was bad news, he said."

I asked about Angel, and Damaris Bauza turned misty-eyed, which probably had as much to do with the Valium as it did with nostalgia. She and Angel Logart had been together from the night they'd met in a Dominican dance hall. According to her, he was the greatest guitar player who ever lived. He'd have been a star, she said, if he'd only gotten the breaks.

I thought, *Au contraire.* Angel had been a born loser, because Mrs. Bauza was only happy with losers.

Angel had wanted it all, she said. His own studio, record company, town house, and chauffeured limousine. Big dreams, it turned out, for someone who couldn't read music or write a check. He played Latino dance halls and social clubs and did session work for salsa companies, Damaris said. None of this paid well, and to make ends meet he took up driving a cab. Eventually, he was stopped by a cop who busted him for using his cab to deliver drugs. Angel lucked out when the cop let him go, first relieving him of thirty-five hundred in cash and four ounces of cocaine, none of which reached the station house.

Three years ago Angel had hooked up with a salsa band, then taken off on a South American tour. On the return trip a customs dog in Miami had sniffed out thirty kilos of cocaine hidden inside Angel's guitar amplifiers. He was now doing twenty-five to life in Lewisburg.

With Angel away at college, Damaris had gone looking for someone else to smother with love. She just had to get mugged again. And that's where Jesus came in. The lady had a talent for finding people who brought her down.

"So how come you know so much about boxing?" Gavilan said to me.

I said it was my hobby. I was obsessed with the sport, which I found exciting and beautiful. I was drawn by the danger, the excitement, and, above all, the skill. I liked people who went all out. In the ring you committed yourself totally, or you went under. Physically, mentally, emotionally. A boxer gave it everything he had.

"I like computer games," Gavilan said. "Built my own computer to play them. Got over two hundred, mostly copies. I trade with other kids so we can save money."

"Isn't copying illegal?" I said.

"So what? Hey, you ever box?"

"No. I have some natural ability, and I'm big and I'm not afraid to get hit. Thing is I don't have the discipline to be a boxer. I don't exercise at all as a matter of fact. I don't see any point in getting exhausted just so I can live another five years without my teeth."

Damaris Bauza giggled and gave me a sleepy smile that

went right into my pants. Gavilan didn't laugh, chuckle, or guffaw. He was still checking me out.

"Why you here in the Bronx?" he said.

I said I was investigating the murder of some illegal immigrants.

Mrs. Bauza wasn't yet spaced out, but she was getting there. Both hands were in her lap, palms up, fingers curled. Her eyelids were drooping and her head leaned forward. But when I mentioned illegals, the lady came alive in a hurry. She sat up straight in her plastic armchair, opened her mouth to speak, then changed her mind. Instead, she stared through the picture window at a white crescent moon.

Gavilan tightened his grip on the ice pack.

"Lourdes was killed because she was a danger to somebody," I said.

"She was nice," Gavilan said. He kept his back to me. "Couple times her father brought her here for dinner. She told me she was having trouble with him. Like he was always after her. Following her into the bathroom. Feeling her up. Shit like that."

"Maybe that's why she ran away."

"Maybe." He shrugged. I waited for more. It never came. Finally, Gavilan said, "What did you mean 'she was a danger to somebody'?"

"I think she could have identified the killer of the illegals," I said.

Mrs. Bauza bit her lower lip, and Gavilan shifted the ice pack to her instep. They knew Jesus was tied to these murders. Neither looked at me.

I wanted to talk about Lourdes Balera, but forcing the conversation would be stupid. If I leaned on Gavilan, Mom would defend him to the death. Lean on her, and Gavilan would be all over me. Still, I had to do something. I decided to work Gavilan, but not to come on too strong. Follow the original plan. Get him, then Mom.

"Where did you live before moving here?" I said to him. He hadn't spent his life in a quiet suburb. Not this strand of barbed wire.

His grin was wolflike, shiny teeth and ravenous eyes. "Lived in the 'hood," he said. "South Bronx. Prospect Avenue near Crotona Park." He wore the address like a badge of honor.

Prospect Avenue. Piss-ugly and murderous. A place where kids like Gavilan killed you for meat.

"Moved to Riverdale two years ago," Gavilan said. "Man, the kids round here can't touch me. They too soft."

His hand came out of his pocket. I heard a click, then a knife blade shot from Gavilan's clenched fist. "Nobody *tried* me back in the 'hood," he said. "Nobody mess with me here either. 'Cause I got *juice*. I got me some respect."

Another click and the blade disappeared.

Gavilan gave me the beady eye and awaited my response. I was being tested. Would I make trouble over the knife or be cool. I decided to light up and not worry about ashes.

I blew a smoke ring at Gavilan and said nothing. As long as he gave me what I wanted, he could pull monkeys out of his ass with a pair of tweezers. I continued blowing smoke rings at him, three small ones in a row this time, each one perfect. Gavilan got the point. The knife went back into his pocket.

"Forgot to check the machine," he said to his mother.

He pressed the message button. A long beep was followed by a series of clicks; then a male voice identified himself as Mohammed. Mohammed wasn't calling from Baghdad or from a barge on the Nile but from Goldman's Pharmacy. Mrs. Bauza, he said, could pick up her thyroid pills anytime tomorrow. Caller number two was a Latina, a husky-voiced woman named America, and she just wanted to know how things had gone at the funeral home and did Damaris know what cemetery Lourdes was being buried in.

Caller number three was male. He was cheerful and breezy. Not at all grief-stricken as one might expect, given recent circumstances. The caller was Detective Robert Schiafino. Bobby Schemes himself.

"Attention, Kmart shoppers. Yo, J.B. This is Bobby. It's a madhouse out here. TV cameras, reporters, and dip-shit neighbors lined up in front of the house like I'm giving away money or something. Phone never stops ringing. Driving me nuts. The department, the press, Lynda's friends. Everybody wants to tell me how sorry they are. Like I care, right? Any-

*way, the Washington thing is on again. The client's meeting
our price. You fly down tomorrow night, do what the client
wants done, then hightail it back to the airport. It's last minute, but don't whine. You're getting fifty large for only four
hours of your time. Call me for details. Incidentally, I'll fill
you in on what I've got planned for Detective Meagher. I've
put Mikey on him. He's going to help me turn this bastard's
life inside out. As of now Meagher can put his head between
his knees and kiss his fat ass good-bye. Sex, drugs, and rock
and roll. I'm outta here."*

XIV
It's Not My Job

I sat with Gavilan in the dining alcove adjoining the Bauzas'
kitchen. Mrs. Bauza was sleeping off the Valium in a bedroom where the walls were coated in gray rubber and the
doorknobs in blue enamel. In the alcove a semicircular radiator sputtered and hissed, producing more noise than heat.
The picture window rattled under the March wind, some of
which had found its way into the living room and was now
freezing the back of my neck.

Gavilan was hunched over the dining table, toying with
two computer games still in their plastic cases. He shuffled
the cases, blinking slowly as though thinking something
through in great detail. One game was Mortal Kombat. The
other, NBA Jam. I took a final drag on my cigarette and
ground the butt into a teacup I was using for an ashtray.

"You wanted to talk," I said.

Gavilan smiled without making eye contact. "Schiafino
don't like you," he said.

"Is that right."

"You messed with his wife. My stepfather said so. Man,
you got to be crazy. Schiafino ain't gon' let you get away

with pumping his woman. Another thing. My stepfather ain't gonna forget you beat him up."

"I was hoping he'd find it in his heart to forgive me. I guess not."

I didn't believe in talking down to kids. I didn't pat them on the head or chuck them under the chin, and I didn't claim to understand them. Gavilan wasn't into talking shit, and neither was I.

"Homeboy kills Schiafino's wife," Gavilan said. "And Schiafino? Man, he on the phone like nothing happened. I mean that is *cold.*"

"Schiafino," I said, lighting another cigarette, "is a remarkable human being."

"I don't know about that," Gavilan said. "He been here a couple of times, and I do know the man is sharp. My stepfather is afraid of him. I know that much."

Gavilan opened Mortal Kombat, stared inside, then closed the box. But not before I'd seen the contents. The box should have held a compact disc. It didn't. Instead it held a folded newspaper clipping.

"This Mikey who's after you," Gavilan said. "You know him?"

I said I had no idea who Mikey was.

"Well, damn," Gavilan said. "You don't know him, how you gonna stop him?"

"That's probably how Schiafino sees it," I said. "Anyway, I've got other things to think about."

I tapped cigarette ashes into the teacup and thought about the message from Schiafino. Mikey wasn't going to kill me. Schiafino didn't work that way. Mikey had been brought in to rough me up, to make my life a waking nightmare until Schiafino decided to move in for the kill. Mikey was only the setup man. Schiafino wanted to bring down the curtain on me personally. The message also told me Jesus was a member of Schiafino's crew, the secret group of cops Lynda called scary. She'd tried to tell me about them, but like a fool I'd blown her off. Was it just me, or was everyone's life one long regret.

Meanwhile give Bauza credit for having found a way around the minimum wage. Fifty thousand dollars for only four hours' work. Something told me he wasn't earning that kind of money stuffing envelopes.

"Any idea why your stepfather's going to Washington?" I said to Gavilan.

I watched him open Mortal Kombat and unfold the clipping I'd spotted earlier. Slowly and with great care he flattened it on the tabletop. Finished, he covered the clipping with one hand.

"First off, my mother don't get involved," he said. "You and me. That's it."

He held my gaze, but his voice was shaky. I could understand. He was a kid banging heads with two cops while playing one against the other. His life and that of his mother were at stake. Gavilan was riding the razor blade. I didn't envy him.

I said, "I won't go near your mother if that's how you want it."

"That's how I want it," Gavilan said.

He pushed the clipping toward me. "I took this from my stepfather."

Gavilan never called Haysoos by name. There was no love lost between these two.

The clip, from a Washington newspaper, was five weeks old and dealt with a local murder. The body of twenty-eight-year-old LaShon Dallas, an unlicensed cab driver and sometime bartender, had been discovered by police in Rock Creek Park. He had been shot twice in the head. Three years ago Dallas had been convicted in the kidnap-murder of Anthony Sattino, fourteen-year-old son of an Arlington, Virginia, real estate developer. Dallas, then a security guard at an Arlington mall, had abducted Sattino from the mall and buried him alive in a Maryland woods, intending to release the boy once a ransom had been negotiated.

Sattino had been placed two feet below the ground, in a box equipped with a battery, food and water, and vent pipes to let in air. Dallas informed the parents of the burial, then demanded a million dollars in ransom. When it was dropped off, Dallas gave the family directions to the boy's burial site. The FBI found young Sattino twenty minutes later. He was dead. He'd suffocated when the crude air system in his prison box malfunctioned. Using a tire-track impression, the

FBI quickly located Dallas, who was tried and sentenced to life imprisonment without possibility of parole. A year later he was freed when an appeals court overturned his conviction, ruling that police had subjected him to physical and psychological abuse, thereby forcing his confession.

I finished reading and looked up to see Gavilan opening the NBA Jam game. He had another clip for me. It was from the same paper, a month-old account of the murder of Duwayne Jamil Shakur, a twenty-six-year-old ex-con with a record for homicide, drug dealing, and carjacking. Shakur's corpse had turned up in the trunk of a Ford parked at Dulles Airport. He had been shot twice in the head. Police were treating his murder as drug-related.

Shakur had been a chief suspect in the killing of Mrs. Ria Greenberg, sixty-five-year-old wife of the founder of the Blue Cow supermarket chain. Two years ago Mrs. Greenberg had been shot to death in a Maryland carjacking. The killer had stolen her Lexus, jewelry, and purse. She'd been murdered even though she'd offered no resistance.

Police were led to Shakur when one of Mrs. Greenberg's rings was found in the possession of a seventeen-year-old girl pregnant with Shakur's child. To avoid being charged as an accessory, the girl testified against Shakur at his trial. She said he'd bragged about killing Mrs. Greenberg, calling the dead woman a Jew bitch who had been robbing black people for years. Shakur's lawyer countered with his own investigator, who testified the prints found on the gun used to kill Mrs. Greenberg were too smudged to be identified as Shakur's. Not beyond a reasonable doubt. Shakur was acquitted.

I looked at both clips. Cops call them trophies. Keepsakes from crimes. Perps collect them, and so do cops. Dion had some. Bullets removed from his body on three occasions, a fedora belonging to Lucky Luciano, a handgun used in the Malcolm X assassination. My collection included news clips of two shoot-outs I'd survived, a hundred-dollar chip from an Atlantic City casino where I'd worked undercover on Chinese money launderers, a Beretta belonging to a Cuban hit man sent after me for blocking a Fidel Castro drug deal.

Jesus was a perp with a perp's outlook on trophies. He wanted to control his vics again, the way he had while committing the crime. That's why serial killers and rapists always took something from their victims—panties, eyeglasses, credit cards, even a body part—to be drooled over later as they recalled those happy times. Bauza saved newspaper clippings to remind him of that moment when he'd been god. When he'd enjoyed the power of life and death over some poor mook.

"Your stepfather kill these two guys?" I said to Gavilan.

"Why you think he's being paid all that money?" Gavilan said. "You heard Schiafino's message."

"You're saying Detective Bauza is a contract killer."

"Yo, I overheard him and Schiafino talking about doing some guy for money."

"You witnessed this?"

"Ain't that what I just said? I saw them talking right here in this room."

He went quiet, eyeing me while he picked his nose, a gesture which probably indicated a reflective turn of mind among Puerto Ricans. After removing nose oysters from both nostrils, he wiped his fingers on his jeans and continued staring at me. I had the feeling the ball was in my court.

"So ax?" he said.

"*Ax?*"

"Ax me why I didn't go to the cops and tell them what I saw."

"The word is *ask*, not *ax*. So why didn't you go to the police?"

"You think I'm stupid or what? You can't trust cops. They always protecting each other, and they lie. I tell them what I saw, next thing they be after me."

He broke off eye contact and nervously drummed his fingers on the glass tabletop.

"Know what I think?" he said. "I think talking to you ain't gon' do shit."

"Oh? Why's that?"

"Schiafino's posse be too much for you."

"Is that a fact."

"They kill people," Gavilan said. "And they get away with it 'cause they protected."

"Protected? By who?"

"I don't want to get involved, understand what I'm saying?"

"Want to know what I think?" I said. "I think you're losing your nerve."

"Ain't my job to catch Schiafino." He shrugged. "That's why you getting paid. It's your job. Cops running around shooting people in the head. Hey, you deal with it. Tell me something. Why should I go for your show? Like I'm suppose to trust *you* to protect me against *your* people? Man, fuck that shit."

He closed his eyes. "I don't feel like dying on account of good eyesight, know what I'm saying? I don't wanna die 'cause I seen too much. I said all I'm gonna say. These are your people. You take 'em on. You don't need my help to get killed."

He rose from the table and gave me a look of disgust, as though he'd finally gotten tired of watching me chew with my mouth open. He said, "See ya. Wouldn't wanna be ya."

XV
Student Discipline

A frightened Gavilan stood in the kitchen, his back pressed against a wall covered in green studded rubber. His eyes bulged, and I watched him rub the back of his neck as though in pain. I wasn't looking at a South Bronx bad-ass anymore. I was looking at a very scared schoolboy who was breaking down under the strain of having to fight his battles alone. Some days the effort had to be too much for him. This was one of those days. I watched him face the rubber wall, slam it with his forehead, then pound the surface with both fists. He whimpered softly. His body began to shake. He tried to hold back the tears and failed.

I left the glass table, walked to the kitchen sink, and found the towel used on Mrs. Bauza's ankle. I soaked it in cold water, wrung it out, and handed the towel to Gavilan. He used it to hide his face.

91

Feeling thirsty, I opened the fridge. Like everything else in the house, it was unsullied and unspoiled. It couldn't have been more perfecto if they'd sent it out to the dry cleaners. The inside gleamed, and there wasn't a stain to be seen. Bottles were capped, food securely wrapped in tinfoil, and each shelf featured an open box of baking soda to reduce odors. Haysoos was so tidy he probably ironed the spaghetti.

There was a choice of club soda, Tab, low-fat milk, orange juice, and beer. The beer was Heineken, a tad pricey for me but easily affordable by anyone moonlighting at fifty thousand dollars a day. I removed a bottle, opened it, and stepped out of the kitchen.

Back at the table, I sucked on the Heineken and watched Gavilan. He stood with his back to the kitchen wall, staring at a gray tile floor. He'd needed to cry, preferably without anyone seeing him.

The most important part of being a cop is knowing how to deal with people. Computers have their place in police work. So does the ability to gather physical evidence, develop informants, and locate suspects. But all of this is wasted unless you can talk that talk.

"Cops cry," I said to Gavilan. "No reason you can't."

Gavilan raised his head. "What they got to cry about?"

I swallowed more Heineken, then said, "They cry when another cop gets killed."

"You mean like Schiafino's wife?"

"Her name was Lynda. Yes, like her."

"You cry when she got killed?"

"I cried, yes."

Gavilan pushed himself away from the wall and wiped his face. Then he sat down at the table and nervously wound the towel around his wrist.

"I keep it all inside," he said. "I can't tell people half the shit that's going on in my head. My own mother don't know. She's nice, but sometimes she can't handle things, and she 'pose to be grown-up."

"Being strong has nothing to do with age," I said. "I know fifty-year-olds who are nothing more than grown-up children. You owe your mother. Take care of her."

"I got no problem with that," Gavilan said. "But it's hard to know what to do sometimes."

"Like whether or not you should talk to me."

"That's right."

"Your stepfather kills people," I said. "That's a fact. It's also a fact he and his friends took out Lourdes. The minute Bauza or his buddy Schiafino decide you and your mother are a problem, you're gone. I don't think you realize what a snake Schiafino is. They don't call him Bobby Schemes for nothing."

"You don't have to tell me about Schiafino," Gavilan said. "I know all about that dude. I seen him hurt my stepfather one night. I ain't ever gonna forget that. He ain't right in the head, Schiafino. Thing is you go after him and my stepfather, you ain't just fighting two cops. You fighting a whole bunch of cops."

"You mean Schiafino's crew?"

"They killing people in New York and Washington," Gavilan said. "That's how they got their name."

"What name?"

Gavilan said he'd been here in the apartment three weeks ago and heard his stepfather on the phone with Schiafino, the two of them arguing because Schiafino wanted Bauza to do a special job in Washington that weekend and Bauza didn't feel like going. Gavilan had overheard enough of these conversations to know what *special job* meant. In any case Bauza wasn't interested. He was taking his girlfriend, Gina, to Puerto Rico for a week. She was a topless dancer with blond hair down to her ass, Gavilan said, and his stepfather was talking about marrying her. The way Bauza had put it to Schiafino, he was spending a fortune on Gina, and he wanted to enjoy what he was paying for. Let Schiafino give the Washington job to somebody else.

Gavilan said Schiafino kept pressing, refusing to take no for an answer. He would have done the job himself, he told Bauza, but he couldn't leave town because he was working on something very important. Bauza had to help him out and do the Washington thing. Bauza was good. He was reliable. Take the job. No way, Bauza said. He was going to Puerto

Rico with Gina, and that was that. Eventually Bauza's temper got the best of him and he slammed down the phone.

Later that same night Gavilan was awakened by noises coming from the living room. Someone was crashing into the furniture. Gavilan didn't know what to think. His family was in bed. So what was the racket about? A break-in, maybe. Some crackhead with a crowbar had John Wayned the front door and was tossing the place, looking for stuff to sell. That's what Gavilan thought until he heard his stepfather's voice. Heard him whining like a bitch: *"Bobby, please. Please, man, I'm begging. Don't do it."* Bobby, Gavilan knew, meant Schiafino. He cracked his bedroom door, praying his mother had taken enough Valium to knock her out.

What he saw shocked the living shit out of him, Gavilan said. His stepfather lay on the living-room floor. Schiafino was on his chest, Schiafino's knees pinning Bauza's arms so he couldn't fight back. As Gavilan watched, Schiafino sealed Bauza's mouth with duct tape. Then, taking a small can from the floor, he squirted liquid into Haysoos's right palm and lit it with a cigarette lighter. The liquid, Gavilan would later learn, was lighter fluid. Bauza went crazy, throwing both legs in the air and groaning, doing his best to throw Schiafino off. Waste of time, Gavilan said. Schiafino was bigger. He just sat on Bauza. Rode his ass like he was a horse in the rodeo, Gavilan said.

Bauza lay shaking, scared out of his mind, with Schiafino talking to him, saying the two of them had to get on the same page right now. No hanging up on me again, Schiafino said. Not if you want to keep on living. I let you diss me, Schiafino said, and before you know it, everybody's dissing me. He also wanted Bauza to stop spending so much money on his girlfriend, because it was bound to attract attention.

Schiafino was cool, Gavilan said. Never raised his voice. Never got excited. He told Bauza the Washington job was top priority because it was for the rabbi. The rabbi was their first line of defense. He was their protection. Without him the group couldn't function. Bauza was going to take the Washington job. No niggers this time, Schiafino said. The rabbi wanted Bauza to pop a white man.

Two days later Bauza went to Washington, Gavilan said.

He came back with a lot of cash, which always happened anytime he went to Washington. He also saved a newspaper clipping on the hit. Gavilan had seen it. Sure enough, the victim was a white guy, some kind of broker who'd cheated people out of fifty million dollars and never did a day in prison. A judge had given him probation, community service, and a five-million-dollar fine. The broker had been shot twice in the head, Gavilan said. That was a specialty with Schiafino's crew, the cops he called the Exchange Students.

XVI
Identifying Mr. Clean

The next morning I had breakfast with Dion in our garage.

We shared a two-story, white clapboard house in Woodside, Queens, a working-class Irish neighborhood until the seventies, when the affluent Irish moved out and the old Irish retired to Ireland and in came the ethnics with their turbans, electronics stores, fried bananas, and slitty eyes.

Woodside was now crawling with Asians and Hispanics. Fortunately, some things hadn't changed. A good number of bars and pubs remained Irish, with Dublin street signs on the walls, snooker tables, blood pudding, and blue-eyed barmaids from Kildare, Kerry, and Cork. Dion and I ate at an Irish tavern around the corner from our house. We avoided Mondays, though, when the Irish papers arrived from Dublin and the bars were packed with Micks.

We owned two cars, a 1990 Ford and a compact called the Henry J. The Henry J was a relic, forty years old but still getting twenty-five miles to the gallon. It was Dion's pride and joy. I'd never seen another one, no surprise since the Henry J had been a flop. When small cars were introduced during the fifties, Americans picked the Volkswagen over the Henry J. By 1954, the manufacturer of the Henry

J had gotten the message and stopped making it. Dion treated his better than some men treat their wives, keeping the car in the garage to avoid damage and minimize the chances of its being stolen.

He preferred working on the car in the morning, when the neighborhood was quiet and he was less apt to be disturbed. Today he was messing around with the spark plugs. As usual, the radio was tuned to a jazz station. I recognized Artie Shaw's "Begin the Beguine," but only because Dion had pointed it out to me years ago as a jazz classic.

I didn't like jazz. The music was too cold for my taste. I preferred country and western. Not Dion. He hated country with a passion, calling it music to fuck your sister by.

My taste ran to Travis Tritt, Garth Brooks, and Reba McEntire. My favorite was Jerry Lee Lewis, the Killer, the man who could shake your nerves and rattle your brain. I liked him because he had talent and because he was a wild man. At twelve he'd shoved his three-year-old sister, Frankie Jean, over a cliff for being a pain in the ass. He'd married his thirteen-year-old cousin while still married to wife number two, and he'd put two bullets in his bass player while taking potshots at a Coke bottle. All this plus a God-given gift for entertaining. You had to love the Killer.

He was playing the Village next month, three days, two shows a night, every show sold out. I'd had no luck getting tickets for Lynda and me, not that it mattered anymore.

For breakfast this morning I'd carried two cups of black coffee from the kitchen. I handed one to Dion.

"Black as hell and strong as death," he said. "The only way to drink this stuff." He offered his usual toast, *Pogue mahone*, Gaelic for "Kiss my ass."

I felt the coffee warm my hand as I enjoyed the morning stillness. The temperature was forty degrees, downright tropical compared to the past few days. I wore a sport jacket, corduroy shirt, and black tie, warm enough provided I didn't stay outside too long.

The garage smelled of gasoline and more than a few Chinese take-out meals, Dion's favorite nosh. I watched a lone robin peck at bread crumbs I'd sprinkled on the sundeck. The barbecue grill, coated in winter ice, glowed red under an early sun. Ordinary things. Run-of-the-mill and common-place. At the moment I found them restful and relaxing, a lifetime removed from Lynda's murder and cops who were executing citizens and a loony detective who was messing with my head with a view toward taking my life. I didn't feel happy. But then I rarely did. The best I could do was not feel unhappy for a while. It never got any better for me.

I stood beneath the upraised garage door and watched a neighboring couple leave for work. They were the Mukerjees, an Indian husband and wife who'd moved next door a year ago. Both were round-faced, dark-eyed, and as polite as can be. Today Mrs. Mukerjee wore a lambskin coat over a yellow sari and what appeared to be white gym socks with sandals. Topping it off was a red dot in the middle of her forehead, the significance of which escaped me. Mr. Mukerjee had shiny dimples, an enthusiasm for bow ties, and carried a laptop. He waved to me. As usual I ignored him. The way I saw it, bad manners were better than no manners at all.

"What happened in the Bronx yesterday?" Dion said. He looked red-eyed, sounded tired, and needed a shave.

He'd spent last night with his girlfriend, the bank officer, a five-time divorcée who paraded around naked in high heels and who more often than not left teeth marks on his ass. Right now he couldn't stop yawning. He appeared more dead than alive, his usual condition after a date with the much-married Maggie O'Keeffe. I was glad Dion had the day off. He looked like he could use it.

We hadn't spoken in twenty-four hours, so I brought him up to date. I told him about the Exchange Students, Bauza's family problems, and Bauza's run-in with Schiafino. I also told him about Bauza's girlfriend. I said I wouldn't be con-tacting Gavilan. The kid was to call me if he had anything.

I didn't tell him about my scheduled meeting with Lisa Watts. Yesterday I'd phoned her from Bauza's apartment. She had refused to come to the phone. Another cop had blown me off with the excuse she was working on an over-due report. Still playing games, our Lisa.

I'd left a message: she either called me back in ten min-utes, or I'd be dropping in to see her bright and early tomorrow morning. She called back at once. She would talk to me. But not over the phone. And not in her office.

We were meeting at nine-thirty this morning at a restaurant in Queens.

I planned to ask her about Lynda's alleged trip to Kennedy Airport the night of the murder. I also wanted to know if Lynda had ever mentioned the Exchange Students to her. Dion wanted me to stay away from Lynda's murder, which meant stay away from Lisa Watts. Which is when I decided to keep my own secrets.

Dion eyed me over his coffee cup. "This Gavilan kid righteous?"

I said, "I think so. He's right about Schiafino torching people. Remember that incident in Brooklyn a couple of years ago with Schiafino and some Puerto Rican? The Rican claimed Schiafino had pressured him to sell stolen dope. When he refused, Schiafino burned his hand."

"I remember," Dion said. "The spic disappeared, so the charges were dropped."

"Word is, Schiafino scared him off. Gonzales or Gonzaga or whatever his name was is supposed to be in Puerto Rico somewhere. Schiafino being Schiafino, he's probably still setting citizens on fire. It's starting to add up. The cops Lynda tried to tell me about. Her fear the last time we saw each other. The Washington newspaper stories. The message I heard on Bauza's phone. Lynda was right about Schiafino running a crew of rogue cops."

"His rabbi worries me," Dion said. "Sounds like a major player, the kind you don't fuck with."

Rabbi was the name cops gave to a department higher-up, someone distinguished, exalted, and on your side. You needed one if you wanted to rise in the NYPD. He was no less than the Supreme Being, the hidden hand and the maker of all things. He moved you through red tape and roadblocks. He arranged for a promotion.

He said the word and got you transferred out of a black neighborhood and into a white one, where you were apt to live longer. When you retired, he speeded up the paperwork and arranged for the unobstructed flow of pension checks. Schiafino's rabbi could do all of this and more. At the moment he was blocking my investigation into eight murders and getting away with it. Schiafino's rabbi was almighty and all-powerful, if not downright omnipotent.

"Taking this to the department," Dion said, "is like bringing the king bad news." He drew his finger across his throat.

I told him I was steering clear of the department for now. I wouldn't be talking to anybody until I had solid proof the Exchange Students existed. I had zilch at the moment. No witnesses, no audio- or videotapes. Absolutely nothing to prove that police in two cities were executing criminals turned loose by the courts. Even Schiafino's phone message to Bauza was useless. I had listened to it three times, and Schiafino never mentioned killing anybody.

"What about Bauza's burned hand?" Dion said. "Won't that prove he and Schiafino had a beef?"

I said it wouldn't prove anything because Bauza would never cop to being hurt by Schiafino. He was too frightened. To make Bauza rat out Schiafino, I had to put the fear of prison into him.

"The clippings," Dion said. "What about them?"

"No crime there. Anybody can cut stories out of newspapers."

I said I believed Gavilan had overheard Bauza and Schiafino talk about whacking a Washington stockbroker. But it came down to Gavilan's word against Bauza's, and as a cop Bauza would have more credibility. Even finding hard evidence at Bauza's apartment wouldn't have helped me. I had entered the premises without a search warrant. Therefore, nothing I uncovered could be admitted as evidence.

I said, "Bobby Schemes, spellbinding wizard that he is, appears to be ahead on points. Maybe they're right about him. Maybe the guy really can walk between the raindrops without getting wet."

"Covering up evidence in multiple murders ain't easy," Dion said. "Takes big daddy to pull that off. I'm talking chief of detectives, deputy commissioner, the DA. Maybe even the police commissioner. I suggest you switch to plan B."

"Whatever happened to plan A?"

"Ain't good enough," Dion said. "Not for Schiafino's rabbi."

He had a point. People that powerful usually gave you two choices. You could suck up to them and hate yourself for it. Or you could stand up to them and risk getting hurt. No wonder Dion was looking like he'd just been served a fish with the head still on.

"Schiafino's crew reminds me of those Brazilian death squads," Dion said, kicking a tire lying at his feet.

I said that's probably where Schiafino got the idea. He was certainly aware of these squads. Every cop in the world knew about them. I couldn't attend a police seminar, conference, or convention without the subject being brought up.

Death squads were composed of cops and soldiers who took the law into their own hands and murdered anyone they thought deserved it. Lynda had said Schiafino favored death squads. He saw courts and judges as useless, whereas with death squads a cop made his point the first time around. Rio de Janeiro had some of the most famous death squads in the world. But then it also had one of the world's worst crime problems. By comparison, life in the South Bronx was the equivalent of sipping champagne in front of a crackling fire.

Rio's crime problem was caused by street kids. They swooped down from the city's hillside slums, sometimes in gangs of a hundred or more, armed to the teeth and attacking tourists wherever they found them. Beaches, hotels, museums, restaurants. The little shits were everywhere. Tourists were avoiding Brazil in droves, costing hotels, airlines, and shops millions of dollars. That's where the death squads came in. Businessmen had hired them to kill these kids, and kill they did, at the rate of a thousand or more a year.

While I had no sympathy for perps, murdering children struck me as the wrong way to go. On the other hand I wasn't a businessman being besieged by herds of gluesniffing little pricks with switchblades. And there was the side of me that admired anyone willing to fight back and fight dirty.

"Look at Miami," Dion said. "Some spook jacker kills a tourist. What happens? Tourists stop coming, and the state's out a half billion dollars."

I said it was the same in California, where jackers were going after Jap tourists. Every time one got killed in southern California, a thousand Nips in Tokyo canceled plans for an L.A. vacation.

"Speaking of shooters," I said, "I think I know Mr. Clean's identity."

"And the winner is . . ."

"Not winner," I said, *"winners.* Gavilan says it works this way. Washington Exchange Students only do contract killings here. New York members, like Bauza and Schiafino, only kill in D.C. It's smart. Think about it. You have strangers killing strangers, leaving investigating officers without a motive. That's why I couldn't get a handle on the Ecuadoran killings. I couldn't find a motive."

I finished my coffee, then said, "A Washington Exchange Student flies to New York, takes out his vic, then returns to D.C. No hanging around to catch a Broadway show. He kills, then he disappears. A New York Student goes to D.C. and does the same thing. In and out. The quicker, the better."

I turned my empty cup upside down, letting the last few drops fall to the garage floor. "The cops don't know their vic," I said. "And the vic doesn't know the cop who does him. There's no connection between the two. Advantage number one. Advantage number two. We're talking cops, people who know how to mess up a crime scene big time."

I said this crew cleans up after itself. They collect shell casings, cigarette butts, fibers, whatever. If someone should accidentally leave evidence behind, *no problema.* The Exchange Students and the rabbi protect their own. Which is as good as it gets in this world of bad deeds and foul play.

I lit a cigarette. "Mr. Clean is a group effort," I said. "He's a combination of rogue cops from two cities. And he comes with serious backup. His intelligence is handed to him by other cops. They also furnish him with an untraceable weapon and destroy evidence that might connect him to the crime. They slow down any investigation. Think about it. You're a killer cop and you need protection. Well, what better protection is there than other cops. No wonder Lynda was terrified. Who wants to take on cops who kill and get away with it?"

"So how do you fight something this big?" Dion said.

"For starters, get your girlfriend to run a credit check on Bauza. Also run one on his main squeeze. Her name's Gina Branch."

"No problem."

"Check on their spending habits. And while you're at it, check on Schiafino's as well."

"Schiafino's slicker than spit on a doorknob," Dion said. "I can't see him throwing his money around. Bauza's a different story. Latinos and spooks are into broadcasting. Pissing their money away on gold chains, Rolex watches, and a new Jeep every month. They're too dumb to know any better. That's not Schiafino."

"Check on him anyway," I said. "We just might get lucky. Far as Bauza is concerned, I need a reason to lean on him. I think I know who hired Schiafino to take out the Ecuadorans. But I want Bauza to confirm it for me."

"I'll save you the trouble," Dion said. "Jonathan Munro."

I looked up from my empty coffee cup. "Son of a bitch," I said. "How'd you figure it out?"

"I taught you everything you know," he said. "But I didn't teach you everything I know."

Dion tapped his temple with an oily forefinger. "Observe the old master at work," he said. "Bauza's tied to the murders of the Ecuadorans and the runaway girl, right?"

"Right."

"Schiafino and Bauza work together, and they don't work cheap."

I said, "Do I spy the old master tiptoeing down the money trail?"

Dion grinned from ear to ear. "What department-store owner has been getting hit by greasers and is rich enough to have them killed?"

"Doing the nasty with Maggie O'Keeffe hasn't affected your brain."

"Might have helped it some," he said. "You and me, we were overlooking the obvious."

"We got conned by Munro," I said. "He whined about the hijackings costing him money. He bad-mouthed cops for not doing their job. He cried about his drivers getting hurt.

Everybody believes his sad story. They see him as a victim, not an instigator. The rabbi's pulling his strings. Bet on it."

I said it was the money, fifty grand for four hours' work, that set me thinking. Call it justice, payback, or a game at which two could play. In a fucked-up world the Exchange Students promised parity. For a price.

I said, "I asked myself who'd want the Ecuadorans dead and could afford it. Came up with one possible. Our boy Munro."

"He's tight with the mayor, Munro. He can make trouble."

"Bringing him down won't be easy," I said. "Not with his lawyers and his money. Let's start with you getting in touch with Mrs. O'Keeffe forthwith."

"I'll telephone her at the bank this morning."

"No phone calls," I said.

Dion rolled his eyes. "Christ, I was so busy patting myself on the back I forgot," he said.

It was something else Dion had taught me. You never used the phone when you were investigating a cop. When you wanted information, you talked to people face-to-face. A phone call could be overheard or recorded. And it warned your suspect before you could get to him or to those individuals who might give him up.

I looked at my watch. Almost 9:00 A.M. Time to meet Detective Watts. I headed for the house. Dion followed. He had to pee, or in his words, shake the dew from his lily.

My topcoat was folded across the back of a kitchen chair, Maurice Robichaux's rap sheet still in the pocket. I'd been too tired to read it last night. Seeing the report reminded me of something I'd asked Dion to do. He was in the downstairs toilet, located in the kitchen. To my knowledge, Dion and I were the only ones in the neighborhood with a crapper in the kitchen. I mean dead center.

I knocked on the bathroom door.

"Finished in a minute," Dion said.

"Don't rush. I just want to know if you've spoken with your guy at JFK."

Dion knew an ex-cop who worked security at the airport. I wanted to know about the lights at the parking lot where Lynda's body had been found.

"Yeah, we talked," Dion said. He sounded resentful, which wasn't like him. Usually, he was glad to help out. Anything for a chance to do police work.

He opened the bathroom door but remained inside, washing his hands. "According to Robby, all the bulbs are less than a month old."

"New bulbs. So why weren't they working two nights ago, when Lynda was killed?"

"Vandals. Robby says it happens all the time. Some schmuck shoots out the lights with an air gun, a twenty-two, a slingshot. It happens."

"Why *now?*"

"Give it a rest," Dion said. "Lynda's murder is a closed case. Listen to me: stay away from this thing before we both end up with our butts in a sling. You got other things to worry about. Like Lynda's letter. Shouldn't you be trying to find it before Schiafino or the department beats you to it?"

I said, "The department, the DA, the mayor's office— they're all blowing smoke. Lynda wasn't killed at the airport. She was killed somewhere else, then brought there. The parking lot isn't a crime scene. It's a lot of things, but it's not a crime scene. And I never said Robichaux didn't kill Lynda. What I am saying is he moved the body, and I want to know why."

Dion stared into the mirror. I'd seen that look before. And it wasn't pretty. It was a look of anger and pain and a lot of hatred. He was thinking about the three bullets he kept upstairs in a dresser drawer. His trophies. Bullets taken from his body on three separate occasions. Bullets fired by blacks.

He spoke to his reflection. "A cop killer didn't get away. Case closed. OK?"

Not for me. Not until I knew why Robichaux had played games with Lynda's corpse. That's why I was on my way to meet Lisa Watts. I wanted to know what business, if any, Lynda had at the airport the night she was murdered.

As though reading my mind, Dion said, "You're likely."

Meaning if I continued poking around Lynda's murder, I was likely to go down hard. And being human, he was hoping I wouldn't take him with me.

XVII
False Witness

I met Lisa Watts in a small Greek restaurant in Astoria, the Little Athens of Queens. Astoria was old-world Greece, with Mediterranean faces, worry beads, taped bouzouki music, and meat shops with sheeps' heads in the windows. It was men with mustaches and dark eyes arguing in *kaffenions,* Greek coffeehouses. Walk the main streets—Broadway, Ditmars Boulevard, Thirty-first Street, and you hear more Greek than English.

Many Astoria restaurants stayed open twenty-four hours a day and catered exclusively to Greeks. I'd eaten around here before. I'd met informants in these places and set up phony drug deals here as well. In that time I'd learned Greek restaurants operated under an unwritten law. Red-and-white checked tablecloths must be used at all times, and the walls had to be decorated with murals of goofy-looking shepherds standing guard over flocks grazing in the Greek countryside.

The restaurant chosen by Lisa Watts had the required tablecloths and mural. It also had black vinyl banquettes, hanging plastic plants, and counter stools with padded backs. Except for a lone mailman eating breakfast at a back table, the place was empty. There were no English menus. You ordered by walking to a steam table up front and pointing to what you wanted.

When I arrived, Lisa Watts was alone at the counter, chain-smoking, reading a folded newspaper, and drinking coffee with her pinky in the air. She was a birdlike woman of thirty-five with sunken eyes, a short chin, and wide nostrils. To me she looked like a pit bull in a green pantsuit.

She was self-centered, impatient, and power-driven. In her world, things were black or white, with no room for gray.

We'd met for the first time a couple of months ago, right after Lynda and I started seeing each other. I'd been in a Woodside bar, waiting to meet Lynda for drinks, when a hard-faced little redhead tapped me on the shoulder and introduced herself as Lisa Watts, Lynda's partner. She'd seen me with Lynda a few times, she said, and was here to hand over a forensic report Lynda wanted. I said I'd see that Lynda got the report, thereby freeing Lisa Watts to be on her way. She immediately got testy. The report, she said, had to be handed to Lynda personally.

I knew she was lying. There was no report. Being a snoop and knowing that Lynda was fooling around, she'd dropped by to check me out.

This world is full of people who think they're being frank when they're just being surly. Lisa Watts was one of those people. Straight up she told me I wasn't good enough for Lynda, that one unstable cop in her life was enough. I decided to be just as forthright, so I called her a bug-eyed little bitch and said being with her didn't exactly leave me with a sense of wonder and well-being. I suggested she buy herself one of those ratlike little dogs to play with and cut down on the caffeine. Above all she should keep her nose out of my business. Watching her charge from the bar was the first hint that our friendship wasn't going to be a full-time occupation.

She was lighting a cigarette when I climbed onto the stool beside her. A freshly opened pack of menthols lay beside her coffee cup.

"And a good, good morning to you," I said.

"Is it a gift, or do you work at being a prick?"

"I want to talk about Lynda."

"Lynda's dead. Put a tick next to that dream, and get on with your life."

"Tell me why she went to the airport," I said.

A fat-lipped counterman appeared at my elbow with a pot of steaming coffee. I nodded, and he pulled a cup from under the counter. He filled both cups, mine and Lisa's.

When I told him I just wanted coffee, he walked away looking disappointed.

"This case is closed," Lisa said. "You got a problem with that?"

"I have a problem with people who use that expression. Let's talk about Lynda. She was your partner."

"What's that supposed to mean?"

"If I have to spell it out, you shouldn't be a cop."

Lisa Watts took a drag on her cigarette and refused to look at me. There were tears in her eyes.

"I loved Lynda," she said. "Loved her as much as you did, if not more."

"Suppose I tell you she wasn't killed at the airport."

Lisa Watts swung around to face me. "A white cop gets murdered by a homeless black man whose rap sheet reads longer than *The Winds of War*. They've got this spook cold. No ifs, ands, or buts. Now you come along with some half-assed theory that nobody, especially the commissioner's office, wants to know from."

"I see word's gotten around."

"What in God's name makes you think the mayor, the department, not to mention the DA's office, will stand by and watch you throw shit in the game. Did I mention this is an election year?"

"Is Schiafino leaning on you?"

Lisa Watts swallowed more coffee, then took another drag on the menthol. There was a tic near her left eye.

"I'm not scared of Schiafino," she said.

"I didn't say you were."

She shrugged. "OK, so he did call. He said you're bad-mouthing Lynda when she's not here to defend herself. What he said was 'Fear Meagher has no bladder control. He keeps pissing on my wife.' Schiafino never came out and told me to stay away from you. The man's too slick for that. He just said he'd remember anyone who helped protect his wife's good name."

"What happens if he thinks you're not helping?"

Lisa Watts stubbed out her cigarette. "He carves his name on your spine with a piece of broken glass."

She lit another cigarette. "He's telling the world you're a sick puppy. Care to hear why?"

"Make my day."

"Well, Clint, it's like this. Schiafino says you hit on Lynda and she turned you down. So you decided to get even. You're doing it now, when she's in her grave. You're saying she was a slut who slept with every cop she worked with. You're telling people she wasn't qualified to be a cop, that being inept—"

"Got her killed. Tell me something I don't know."

"How about this," she said. "He says you showed up at the cemetery drunk out of your mind, tried to pick a fight with him, and had to be restrained. You told everybody Lynda was in love with you, that she planned to divorce Schiafino. He, on the other hand, says he and Lynda had no plans to divorce. According to him, they were devoted to each other."

"Makes me sound confused and misled. You believe any of this shit?"

"I'm not a fool," she said. "I know you and Lynda were seeing each other. She liked you a lot. Don't ask me why. About Schiafino, she once told me she'd fallen in love with his cock, then made the mistake of marrying the whole man."

"How'd you find out about us?"

"You made her happy," Lisa said. "And it showed. When I asked the reason for this euphoria, she told me. Look, Schiafino's not stupid. I'd say he knows about you and Lynda. That's why he's messing with your head. Blackening that part of your reputation you haven't already blackened yourself. Eventually, he'll get serious. At this point I suggest you hire a food taster. The man is spooky."

She poured a packet of NutraSweet into her coffee, then stared at me for a long time. "What makes you think Lynda wasn't killed at the airport?"

I decided to be truthful for a change. My trip to JFK was no secret. By now the whole world knew the commissioner's office had warned me to stay away from this case. I had nothing to hide. I mentioned the lack of blood at the crime scene, a dead giveaway that something was wrong. I also said the investigation of the murder scene couldn't have been more sloppy if it had been planned that way.

"None of this gets Robichaux off the hook," I said. "It just leaves me with my own opinion, which is that Robichaux didn't kill Lynda at the airport."

Lisa Watts stubbed out her half-smoked cigarette and immediately lit another. She blew smoke at the ceiling, then gave me her well-known barracuda smile.

"No one gives a fuck about your opinion," she said. "You don't figure into the equation, bunky. Not on this case."

I said, "You told investigators that Lynda might have been meeting an informant at the airport."

"That's right."

"And you claim not to know the informant's identity."

Lisa Watts stubbed out the new cigarette. "Right again."

"You sure about that?"

She continued screwing the cigarette into the ashtray. Finished, she stared at the pulverized weed. "I'm sure."

My gut said she was lying.

I watched her place both elbows on the counter, bringing the coffee cup to her mouth. But she didn't drink. Instead she looked straight ahead, eyes glazed and unblinking. "The day Lynda was murdered, she told me you'd walked out on her. You haven't forgotten that by any chance, have you?"

I said, "I've spent the past forty-eight hours wishing I could tear that day from my brain. No, I haven't forgotten."

We sat and drank coffee for a while.

"I know what you think of me," Lisa Watts said. "No good at running my own life. Quick to run everyone else's. Separated from my husband and a stranger to a ten-year-old daughter who's with day care more than she's with me. Nothing to be proud of, right? But I am proud of being a cop and proud that when Lynda needed me, I was there."

I shook a cigarette loose from the pack. "Not much I can say to that, is there?"

Lisa Watts placed a hand on my forearm. "That was a cheap shot. I'm sorry."

"I wasn't there when she needed me. End of story."

"I think I speak for all of America when I say you're an asshole. But Lynda adored you, which says a lot. You're probably wearing home-of-the-Whopper underwear and have a name for your dick."

"Humphrey," I said.

"What?"

"Humphrey. The name of my dick."

Lisa Watts closed her eyes. "Jesus, I had to ask."

She opened her eyes. "That last day when Lynda returned to the office, she was upset. Couldn't stop crying. She said you two had argued. She'd written a letter that could make trouble for you."

The counterman returned with a fresh pot of coffee and topped off Lisa's cup. I waited until he'd gone, then said, "She say what was in the letter?"

Lisa shook her head. "No. And I didn't ask."

"Am I hearing correctly?"

"Some things I'd rather not know about," Lisa said. "I'm up for promotion. I've a shot at making detective second grade, and I'm not about to rock the boat. Look, remember when I said I didn't know the name of the informant Lynda was meeting at the airport?"

"I remember."

"I wasn't telling the truth," she said.

I waited.

"He forced me to lie about Lynda's murder," Lisa said.

"Who forced you to lie?"

"Schiafino," she said. "He's got me involved in a cover-up."

XVIII
Family Protector

"He said we owed it to Lynda," Lisa said. "Jullee had to be protected. What could I say? Lynda had just been murdered, and I wanted to do something. *Anything*. So I went along with him. I lied to protect Jullee. The informant story I told investigators? That was Schiafino's idea, not mine.

The truth is Lynda did go to the airport that night. But she went because of Jullee."

Lisa was nervously cracking her knuckles, starting with the pinky and working her way up to the thumb. A slice of baklava in front of her remained untouched. She breathed deeply, like a drowning man coming out of deep water. She sat slumped on her padded stool, looking straight ahead at a restaurant mural showing women in skimpy white tunics dancing around the columns of an ancient Greek temple. Her place mat was gone. She'd shredded it, then placed the pieces in her empty coffee cup. As I watched, she cracked first one thumb, then the other, setting my teeth on edge.

I told her to relax, go slow, and tell me everything. After a few tears I got the full story.

Jullee had telephoned Lynda two days ago at the precinct, with Lisa present. Jullee was in trouble. Again. She'd sold her car to a guy who turned out to be a deadbeat. He'd paid with a bad check and was refusing to make good on it. A furious Jullee wanted to kill him. He was a cargo handler working at Kennedy Airport and tonight she was going there to confront him with a baseball bat. Either she got her money, or Deadbeat would end up with busted knee-caps. Lynda had failed to calm Jullee down, Lisa said. Baby sister had to get this guy tonight because he was leaving tomorrow for a Colorado ski trip.

Lynda had been worried, and with good cause. Using a baseball bat as a weapon was felony assault, and that meant serious prison time. It ended with a compromise. The sisters would go to Kennedy together, where Lynda would flash her badge, talk tough, and scare the cargo handler into paying up.

Jullee had a talent for trouble, Lisa said. Drugs, shoplifting, truancy, vandalism. You name it and little sister had done it. Lynda had protected her by pulling strings and calling in favors. If she hadn't, Jullee would have been behind bars long ago, hammering out license plates when she wasn't slow dancing with bull dykes.

The sisters' different lifestyles, Lisa said, might be attributed to different mothers. Unfortunately, both mothers were dead, and Oz Lesnevitch, Jullee's father, was nothing more than a driveling old geezer with one foot in the grave. He couldn't tie his shoes let alone discipline an unruly and outrageous Jullee. Lynda couldn't do it either. Not while working a full shift plus overtime. Little sister was a major complication in anybody's life.

"A couple of hours after Lynda's murder," Lisa said, "I get a call at home. It's Schiafino. At first I thought he was calling because he was broken up and needed a shoulder to cry on. Not him. He was calm, and believe me, far from tearful. He's calling to say we have to protect Jullee."

"Protect her from what?" I said.

"Protect her from what he called a possible misunderstanding. We had to keep quiet about her phone call to Lynda, he says. We had to dummy up about the deadbeat who'd ripped Jullee off for her car. According to Schiafino, Jullee didn't go to the airport that night. She came down with a case of food poisoning and ended up staying home. Lynda went to Kennedy alone and ran into Robichaux, and that prick killed her."

Lisa picked pieces of her place mat from her coffee cup and rolled them between her fingers. Her hands shook as she arranged the bits of paper into a crude garland around the base of the cup.

"Schiafino reminded me that Carmine Lacovara can be rough when it comes to a cop killing." Lisa shivered. "They don't call him His Holiness for nothing. We're talking the wrath of God here."

She looked at me. "If Lacovara learns Jullee was to have accompanied Lynda to the airport, he'll be all over that kid. He'll tear her to pieces. She'll be a basket case when he finishes with her. Schiafino thinks she'll fall apart, and I agree. Hell, she's just eighteen. He wants to protect her. We both want to protect her. For Lynda's sake if nothing else."

I said, "Hang on. Give me a second, and let me think. This *is* Schiafino we're talking about. The man whose idea of bringing love to the world is to spend his day fucking people?"

"At the time I thought he was right," Lisa said. "Jullee had nothing to do with Lynda's murder. So why involve her in something this heavy. Especially when it involves her sister. So I went along with Schiafino's bullshit about Lynda going to Kennedy by herself to meet an informant. Now I feel sick to my stomach because by keeping Jullee out of it, I withheld evidence in my partner's murder. Goddamn Schiafino. The man rots everything he touches."

I said she'd made a mistake, and she agreed. We also agreed she couldn't change her story and continue being a cop.

"I've given a sworn statement," she said. "Change it now, and I'm fucked. My promotion goes south and my career along with it. Anyway, what's the harm? Jullee's innocent. I simply stopped her from having her chops busted by the God-fearing Carmine. Lynda went to the airport alone, ran into Robichaux, and got unlucky. End of story."

I said the whole world was revolving around Jullee, which is how Jullee thought it ought to be.

Not long ago Jullee had gotten arrested for speeding. Being Jullee, she'd given the cop a lot of attitude, forcing him to place her under arrest. At the station house a search of her purse turned up four joints. Charges of drug possession were added to speeding and resisting arrest. Suddenly, little sister was scared.

Lynda was less than sympathetic. It was time, she said, for the wild child to grow up.

She refused to bail Jullee out, not while there were lessons to be learned. Check out your cell mates, Lynda said. See what happens when you don't get your act together. So Jullee spent three days locked up with whores, junkies, muggers, shoplifters, and various psychos. Seventy-two hours of pure hell, she'd say later. She hated every minute of it. Most of all she hated Lynda for leaving her there.

"So Schiafino asked you to lie about Lynda's murder," I said to Lisa.

"Let's say he was motivated. And not just by a desire to keep Jullee away from Lacovara."

"What are you talking about?"

"The heart has its reasons of which reason knows nothing," Lisa said.

"We know this in countless ways," I said. "It's Pascal, and what's he got to do with Schiafino and Jullee?"

"I'm impressed," Lisa said. "Lynda did say you read a lot."

She looked at the dancing temple maidens. And she was smiling through her tears. Lisa Watts knew something and was dying to tell me about it.

"Cut to the chase," I said.

She said, "Schiafino's interest in his sister-in-law has become up close and personal."

"You mean he's pumping her?" I said.

"No more phone calls, please. We have a winner."

Lisa shoved her cigarettes into her purse. "Lynda hit the roof when she found out. I mean she absolutely, totally freaked. Her husband fucking her sister."

"She never mentioned it to me," I said.

"You never gave her a chance, did you?"

Lisa slid off her stool. "Duty calls. Do me a favor. Stay away from me, OK? We met, we talked. *Finito.* Meanwhile, get with the program. Lynda's killer has been arrested. That's all that counts."

"You sound like my father," I said. "One more question."

"One. And make it snappy."

"Did Lynda mention anything to you about a crew called the Exchange Students?"

Lisa Watts backed away from me in a hurry.

"I don't know anything about rogue cops," she said. "And don't ask me."

"I never mentioned rogue cops."

"Good-bye, Meagher," Lisa said. "And please don't look to me for further positive reinforcement because after today there ain't going to be any. And watch your back. You're asking the wrong questions, and you're asking them about the wrong people. I'll leave you with the secret of happiness: good health and a bad memory. Want to stay healthy? Forget we had this conversation."

I said, "Other than that, Mrs. Lincoln, how did you enjoy the play?"

Lisa Watts gave me a smile of the nervous rather than happy persuasion, then took off like a bat out of hell.

XIX
Wild Child

I left the restaurant ten minutes after Lisa Watts made herself scarce, bought a newspaper, then walked to my car and drove east on Grand Central Parkway toward Flushing Meadows Park in Queens. I wanted to talk to Jullee Vulnavia or whatever Lynda's kid sister was calling herself this week. I had a question about her car problem.

If Schiafino was shtupping Jullee, this would explain protecting her from Carmine Lacovara and interrogation hell. But why stop there? A true guardian angel would have finished the job. He'd have gone after the guy who'd scammed Jullee out of her car.

Schiafino was as mean as a striped snake. A few charred fingers and the cargo handler would have come to understand that the payment of debt was necessary for social order. So why had Schiafino passed up the chance to impress his favorite teenybopper? He'd ignored her car problem, allowing Lynda to handle it. *Why?*

I also wanted the name of the cargo handler. I needed a serious answer to a serious question. Had he seen Lynda at the airport the night she was murdered?

Queens is the largest borough of New York, six times the size of Manhattan and mostly residential, with thousands of one- and two-family houses and as many parks as the other four boroughs combined. I've lived here all my life and know every inch of it, from the deserted chewing-gum factories near the Queensboro Bridge to the swamp village of old shacks floating on wobbly piers in Jamaica Bay. The strangest place out here, if not in all of New York, has to

115

be Flushing Meadows–Corona Park, which is near where Jullee lived.

It's located at Northern Boulevard and Grand Central Parkway, thirteen hundred acres running south along what used to be the Flushing River. It has soccer fields, a skating rink, the New York Hall of Science, and signs announcing that it hosts the U.S. Open tennis championship every summer. What makes the park strange are its ruins—pavilions, fountains, and metal sculptures left over from the 1939 and 1964 world's fairs—most of them now nothing more than moldering junk standing in the middle of weeds and vines and looking like the remains of a space-age civilization hit by a nuclear blast.

Jullee and her father, Oz Lesnevitch, lived near these ruins, which might explain why Jullee was so demento. I'd dropped Lynda at the house a few times. To avoid problems, I'd come at night and never gone inside. I'd sat in the car and stared at the ruins, expecting condemned souls, Beelzebub, and assorted devils to appear any minute.

I arrived at Flushing Meadows Park at ten in the morning, when the ruins appear less hellacious. The Lesnevitches lived in a one-family redbrick home on a quiet block with blue-and-white street signs. The house had a tiny lawn, a flagstone walk, and an empty garage. The garage's contents—spare tires, broken headlights, power tools, and old golf clubs—were scattered in front of the house. In the driveway, workmen were mixing cement. Apparently, the garage was getting a new floor.

I'd found a parking space near the driveway, behind a blue Dodge minivan with vanity plates, JUL S GR8. Jullee was a lot of things, but great wasn't one of them. She owned the van, that much was true. But she also had an aversion to manual labor. So how had she managed to pay for this nice new set of wheels? The van was too expensive for a do-nothing kid whose father was snowed under by medical expenses.

According to Lynda, Oz Lesnevitch had owned a Long Island City factory that manufactured women's handbags. He'd retired with a nice nest egg, expecting to enjoy his golden years in the company of Jullee's mother, his second and much younger wife. But rather than spend her days pulling pages off the calendar, the wife had taken up with a Brazilian soccer player, divorced Oz, and won a large settlement. The money had gone into a mediocre singing career, which ended when she and the Brazilian were beheaded in a Las Vegas car crash. At the moment Oz had a roof over his head but not much more. So where did he get the money to treat Jullee to a new van?

I wrote down the license number, hoping Schiafino had made his first mistake.

I wasn't being paid to check on Jullee's finances. I had plenty of work to do. Enough to keep me in overtime for months. And I'd been warned to leave Lynda's murder alone or risk having my balls squeezed. But I needed to know the truth about her death. Maybe I hoped to ring the bell and have Lynda answer the door. Maybe someone inside would help me justify the way I'd treated her. I stood in front of the Lesnevitch home, knowing the Irish were right. *There was hope from the sea and none from the grave.*

My ring was answered by a rose-scented male, thirtyish and gay, with a long neck, flat nose, and green eyes that turned downward at the corners, giving him a cranky-looking squint. He wore a blue blazer, penny loafers, black skullcap, and a gray tie stamped with clefs and sharps, which I assume put him in the music business. He looked natty and well groomed and was probably the type of fag whose sense of perfection irritated the shit out of everyone who knew him.

I figured he was here for *shivah,* the vigil Jews kept for the dead. He introduced himself as Gordon Eisen, Lynda's cousin, then gave me the kind of power stare you're supposed to use in business negotiations if you want to get that contract signed.

I identified myself and asked to speak to Jullee.

Gordon flared his nostrils. "What is this, a detectives' convention?"

"What do you mean?" I said.

"Jullee's upstairs with two detectives right now. If I didn't know better, I'd swear she's trying to corner the market."

I was caught off guard. I'd been told Schiafino had arranged for Jullee to be kept out of the investigation. So why were detectives interrogating her?

"I'll tell your friends you're here," Gordon said.

I said they weren't my friends and not to bother them. I was here unofficially and just wanted to see Jullee. I didn't say I wanted to talk to her alone and without witnesses, especially witnesses who might charge me with obstructing a homicide investigation.

I said, "Is Detective Schiafino one of the officers with Jullee?"

Gordon looked at me as though I'd just blown my nose on his tie.

"I know Bobby Schiafino," he said. "So I can say without fear of contradiction that he's home in Brooklyn, with journalists gathered on his doorstep in hopes he'll show his face and allow them to profit by his misery. Wherever he goes for the next few weeks or so, the media will follow. Since the media isn't camped outside, we'll assume Bobby's not here."

"When you stop assuming," I said, "I'd like to talk to Oz Lesnevitch."

"And why would you want to do that?"

"We'll assume it's none of your business," I said. Lesnevitch might know who bought Jullee's car, something I wasn't ready to discuss with Gordon.

I watched him tighten his jaw and consider a snappy comeback. In the end he passed on insulting me. "Oz is upstairs with Alma, his nurse," he said. "I'll take you there."

We walked from a black-tiled vestibule into a living room with a maroon leather sofa, corduroy-covered armchairs, black standing lamps, and a baby grand piano covered with family snapshots. Near the piano were baskets of fruit from relatives and friends. The parquet floor was covered with a soft green carpet. Two curtained windows overlooked the front yard, and a sweet-smelling fire crackled in a marble fireplace. A collection of white ceramic pigs and jugs sat on a gray marble coffee table. On the left side of the room, a staircase led to the bedroom floor. Under the staircase were bookshelves with pieces of jade tucked among the books. The room held a dozen or so mourners, men and women who stopped talking and gave me the look civilians usually have when encountering cops, the one that says something nasty is about to happen.

I followed Gordon upstairs to a shadowy hallway covered in brown carpeting and lined with flowered wallpaper. We passed a bathroom with white plaster walls and a raised tub sitting on a platform. Adjoining the bathroom was a room whose door was decorated with stills from Vincent Price movies. In each shot the face of the female costar was covered over by a snapshot of Jullee. Also on the door was a license plate reading DTFKWME.

For a split second I considered eavesdropping outside the room, then decided against it. Gordon might question my actions, thereby drawing the attention of the detectives. I kept walking, wondering why the DA had decided to come after Jullee.

At the end of the hallway, Gordon knocked cautiously, very cautiously, on a mahogany door. "Alma? Gordon," he said. "Someone here wants to speak to Oz."

Long seconds passed before the door opened, and when it did, I found myself looking at the chubby, sad-eyed black woman I'd seen with Oz Lesnevitch at the cemetery two days ago. Up close she was fortyish, with a protruding lower lip, wide nostrils, and a mole between her eyebrows. She wore a blue cardigan over nurse's whites, and a gleaming black wig, and she fingered a pair of bifocals on a gold chain around her neck. She looked as solid as a rock and set in her ways, not to mention certain in her mind. She probably saw Gordon and me as two dumb-ass white boys, neither of us any more threatening than a bowl of soggy cereal. "He's a detective," Gordon said, jerking his head in my direction.

I flashed my shield.

Alma was neither dazzled nor electrified. She dismissed me with a snort and turned to Gordon. Folding her arms across a sizable bosom, she stared at him until he looked down at his shiny loafers.

"Mr. Lesnevitch is my patient," she said. "Nobody comes in here 'less I say so."

"I just want to ask him one question," I said.

"I know you," she said to me.

"I was at the cemetery," I said.

"That's not what I'm talking about," she said.

Gordon looked at me from the corner of his eye. Suddenly, he snapped his fingers. "Meagher," he said. "I knew I'd heard that name somewhere. You're the cop who made trouble for Bobby at Lynda's funeral. You've got your nerve showing up here, you know that?"

Score one for Schiafino. Thanks to him I was now walking around with a KICK ME sign on my butt. Whether she meant to or not, Alma stopped me from trashing this little queen. She removed a tray of dirty dishes from a chest of drawers and shoved it at Gordon, forcing him to grab the tray in self-defense.

"Take this downstairs," she said. "And try not to get nothing on that nice new jacket."

She motioned me into the room, then shut the door in Gordon's face.

"Nurse Tyson," she said, offering her hand. Her grip was firm, unshakable. I had the feeling Oz Lesnevitch was being well taken care of.

"Where do you know me from?" I said.

"From in front of this house," she said, pointing to a window overlooking the street. "You helped Mrs. Schiafino bring a rocking chair to the house. But you didn't come inside."

Two weeks ago Lynda and I had gone shopping for a rocking chair, a present for her father, who'd wanted one for years. It had been Lynda's idea, a spur-of-the-moment thing. He's dying, she said. If the chair makes him happy for a day, it's worth it.

We found one in a shop on Queens Boulevard, a beauty carved from Vermont oak and stained black, with tiny red roses hand-painted on the back. It was also big, chunky, and weighed a ton. Somehow we managed to fit it into the trunk of my car, but at her father's house the chair proved too heavy for Lynda. So I'd carried the chair to the front door, my first and only time out of the car. Alma had been watching, proving Oscar Wilde had been right when he'd said that no good deed goes unpunished.

I looked around Lesnevitch's bedroom. It was small and beige-colored, with brown ceiling stains caused by water leaks. Despite a radiator and heater, the room was chilly. Most of the space was taken by twin beds. One held Alma's purse and scarf along with two books on Judaism, which suggested Oz Lesnevitch was in the process of making his peace with the ruler of heaven and earth. An oxygen tank was propped against an old sea chest that served as an end table. On top of the chest were a telephone, prescription drugs, and a small TV set tuned to the Home Shopping Network. A wooden ceiling fan was still.

Lesnevitch was in the other bed. He'd always been a small man, and now he was even smaller, scaled down by disease and old age, his bald head blotchy with liver spots, his teeth just brown stumps in a mouth without lips. His tiny hands were nothing but swollen joints and blue veins. His wrinkled flesh seemed too big for his arms and neck, and he smelled like a wet dog who'd just taken a shit. He was propped up, facing the window overlooking his driveway. A glassy-eyed stare made him look brain-dead.

"I see you met Gordon," Alma said. "Mouth almighty and tongue everlasting, that boy. Right now he downstairs gossiping his fool head off. When he finish, you and Mrs. Schiafino be the biggest thing since Whitney Houston and Bobby Brown."

"What's he know about me and Mrs. Schiafino?"

Alma's expression said I'd failed to bedazzle her with my brilliance and should refrain from baffling her with my bullshit.

"Detective Meagher, there is no denying the fact of death in this house. Daughter dead. Father just 'bout hanging on. After death ain't nothing left but the truth. It's your business, you and Mrs. Schiafino. But she phoned you from here. I heard her. And so did someone else."

Six to five someone else was Jullee. Which explained how Schiafino came to know about Lynda and me.

"I liked Mrs. Schiafino," Alma said. "She was decent. Woman had a good heart. Can't say that about everybody."

"What's your opinion of Mr. Schiafino?"

Alma took a tissue from her breast pocket and began polishing her bifocals. Finished, she refolded the tissue and returned it to her pocket.

"Can't say nothing good," she said, "don't say nothing at all."

I was beginning to like Alma.

I asked if Lesnevitch could answer one question. Alma said he might, he might not. I'd have to take my chances.

I asked Lesnevitch if he knew who'd bought Jullee's old car. He turned his glazed eyes to me, opened his mouth, and drooled. Not a pretty sight. That's when I knew that asking him to function normally was asking him to make a promise he couldn't keep.

Alma said don't press him, not when he's like this. Besides, he probably didn't know anything about Jullee's car. The two didn't talk much. In Alma's opinion Jullee was under *nobody's* control. When Mrs. Schiafino was alive, even she couldn't rein in that girl. The two never got along, Alma said, and it wasn't because Mrs. Schiafino didn't try.

While listening to Alma, I reminded myself that Maurice Robichaux had no motive for killing Lynda. He was guilty, no doubt about it. But someone else had a better motive, and that someone was Jullee. She hated Lynda. She'd also arranged for the two of them to go to Kennedy Airport the night of the murder. Motive and opportunity. Jullee had both.

Homicide investigators hadn't been given this information. Nor had they been told that Jullee had an uncontrollable temper. Had Jullee hated Lynda enough to have had her killed? Robichaux claimed a white man had lured him to the murder site. But suppose he'd gotten it wrong. Suppose it hadn't been a white man but a white woman.

Robichaux wasn't in his right mind. Thanks to booze and drugs he was one fucked-up spade. The man probably couldn't pick his nose at this point without poking himself in the eye. But was he so confused that he couldn't tell the difference between men and women? Was it possible he and Jullee were acting out a scenario known only to them? I'd been a cop long enough to know anything was possible. That's why I was going back to the airport. Maybe not today, but I was going back. Back to find the cargo handler who'd bought Jullee's car. And to see if a connection existed between Jullee and the douche bag who'd murdered her sister.

"Somebody steal Jullee's car?" Alma said. "That why you here?"

I lied. I said plates registered to Jullee had been seen on a car involved in a hit-and-run. I knew she'd sold her car, and I wanted the name of the new owner. Right now Jullee was in her room being interrogated by homicide detectives in connection with her sister's murder. I planned to talk to her when the detectives were through. Meanwhile I wondered if Mr. Lesnevitch would know who'd bought his daughter's car.

"He don't know her car is gone," Alma said. "Anyway, she driving around in a new van."

"I saw it. Expensive. Where'd she get the money?"

"It's a present from Detective Schiafino," Alma said.

"How do you know?"

Alma said young girls will talk, especially when they got a married man willing to play the fool, and that's all she was going to say about that.

I said, "Do you know if Jullee went to the airport with Lynda the night of the murder?"

Alma said the two could have gone anywhere. All she knew for sure is she'd seen them leave the house together. But Jullee must have come back because she was in her room the next morning when police came. The way Alma saw it, the good Lord had spared Jullee. Praise the sweet Savior.

"Looks like the Savior spared her from food poisoning, too," I said. "Evidently she didn't get sick that night."

"Jullee? No reason for her to be sick. Girl's strong as a horse."

"Didn't she come down with food poisoning the night Lynda was killed?"

"Who told you that?"

I didn't mention Lisa Watts. Instead I lied again.

"A reporter," I said. "He said Jullee never left the house that night because she was sick with food poisoning."

"She and Mrs. Schiafino left the house together. I saw them with my own two eyes. And she didn't have no food poisoning or any other kind of poisoning. She get sick, I'm a nurse and I'm right here. That child didn't call for me. Reporters. I tell you some people ain't got the sense they born with."

"Tell me about it," I said. "By the way, have the police talked to you about Mrs. Schiafino's murder?"

Alma shook her head, then patted her wig to make sure it hadn't moved.

"Nobody talk to me 'cept you," she said. "Look here, they got the man who killed Mrs. Schiafino. He's black so everybody know he did it. You black, you guilty. Justice is for other men, not brother men. Police don't need to talk to me. Don't need to talk to nobody now."

Robichaux had been found on the set, lying beside Lynda's corpse, weapon in hand. Guilty? Absofuckinglutely. But this was a racial homicide, and I didn't look for much sound reasoning from Alma. Blacks wouldn't make a decision about Lynda's murder based on the evidence. They saw Robichaux's arrest as just another example of the white man's justice, whose sole purpose was to fill American prisons with innocent blacks. I had news for Alma. The brothers were getting arrested because they were committing crimes and because they were dumb enough to get caught.

I watched Alma check Oz Lesnevitch's pulse. As she fingered one bony wrist, he raised the other hand, pointed to the window, and said, Lynda's in the garage. Would Alma make sure she visited him before leaving?

"Shame," Alma said. "He been going on like that since she died. Thinks she's still alive. Guess he don't want to let go of her."

I thought, neither do I.

Suddenly, the door burst open, and there was Jullee.

Her eyes found me. "I hear you want to talk," she said.

"Gordon tell you I was here?"

Alma gave Jullee a look that would have stopped a charging rhino. Being more stubborn than the rhino, Jullee saw nothing.

"Girl," Alma said, "don't you believe in knocking?"

Jullee addressed herself to me. "You want to talk or not. I don't have all day." She didn't sound broken up about Lynda's death.

I looked over Jullee's shoulder. The door to her room was open.

"What about the detectives?" I said.

"What about them?" Jullee said. "If you must know, they're gone."

Her voice was whiny and nasal, the sound of a self-centered wiseass. She was long-legged, looked older than eighteen, and had dyed red hair with black roots purposely left visible. She wore a nose ring, dark glasses, and black nail polish embedded with fake gems. Both ears were pierced, with a half dozen gold earrings in each. A heavy bust and full mouth gave her a sexy appearance. Her clothes were black and expensive—studded leather jacket, leather mini, black tights, and Doc Martens with white laces. What stopped her from being beautiful was a receding chin and short neck, both of which made her look like a turtle with its face out of the shell.

"Lead the way," I said to her.

I thanked Alma, who nodded, then gave Jullee a few parting words, the gist of which was knock next time, or there'd be trouble in paradise. Jullee responded with Yeah, right.

I closed Oz Lesnevitch's door and followed Jullee. From the hall her room appeared even smaller than her father's. Drawing closer, I saw dark-green walls, a four-poster bed made of bleached wood, and a windowsill holding a boom box and piles of CDs. I followed her into the room, where she quickly spun around to face me. Her smile raised the hairs on the back of my neck. *Too late.* The door slammed shut behind me, and I was hit above the right ear by something rock hard. My hat went flying. I dropped to my hands and knees, a blinding pain in my head. Whoever hit me had wanted the blow to hurt. It did.

"Stop beating on the man," a male voice said. "Leave off that shit till we get to the boat. If he can't walk, we got to carry him, and that don't look right. Let him march out under his own power."

I opened my eyes and saw a thin fortyish black male standing over me. His clothes said money. He wore an expensive overcoat around his shoulders, the way mob guys did. His suit was gray, double-breasted, and tailored to fit. His shirt was blue silk, with matching tie, and his Gucci loafers gleamed. Both wrists glittered and jingled, one with a thin gold watch, the other with several silver bracelets. Another cop living beyond his means.

One hand toyed with the change in his pants pocket. The other, at his side, casually gripped a .38 Smith & Wesson. He came with a born cool, a man who didn't have to work at it.

"Sorry about your head," he said. "My partner's got a beef with you."

Behind me a gravel voice said, "Be up to me, you'd be dead. Busting your head was just a start. Right now I want you on your knees, hands behind your neck. Get cute, and I'm gonna rock your world. You follow?"

I did as I was told. From the corner of my eye, I could see Gravel Voice from the waist down. If his partner was into styling, this guy had no style at all. He wore dirty jeans, a black raincoat, and scuffed brown shoes with broken laces. His hands were large, with broken knuckles indicating he'd punched a few people in his lifetime. My guess was he'd enjoyed himself.

One hand held a blackjack. He pocketed it before patting me down. When he found my Glock, he grunted with approval. It was new and had cost me nine hundred dollars before customizing. He shoved it in his belt, next to a hefty beer belly. He said, where you're going you ain't going to be needing it no more. My ankle gun went to the spook in the upscale clothes.

He was Detective Larry Aarons, and we'd worked together last year on a drug task force. He was called Lethal Larry for his habit of killing unarmed perps, then dropping a knife on the corpse to make the shooting look righteous. Gravel Voice was Detective Aldo Sinatra, a red-eyed ginzo in his thirties with double chins and a slow-motion walk that made him look older. He was a cousin of Danny Baldazano, the ex-partner I'd helped send to federal prison. When Aldo had gotten in my face for testifying against Danny, I'd punched him out. He'd promised to get even.

Larry Aarons took a cellular phone from his pocket. It was small, shiny, and real cute. He dialed a number, whispered into the phone, then handed it to me.

"Friend of yours," he said.

I put the phone to my ear and waited.

"Attention, Kmart shoppers," said a male voice. "Guess who's about to be hung by his eyebrows from skyhooks over a hard pavement."

The voice belonged to Schiafino.

XX
A Win-Win Situation

I knelt on the carpet in Jullee's room, cellular phone to my ear, and waited for Schiafino to play his mind games. With nothing better to do, I stared at a movie poster hanging on a closet door. It featured Vincent Price and a pretty blonde chained in a cellar, both looking uneasy, which was understandable. Peter Lorre was walling them up alive.

My future didn't look much brighter. Not with Schiafino's cops standing over me with guns. Blood flowed down the right side of my face. I felt shaky.

"Leave it to you to find new and better ways to fuck up your life," Schiafino said to me. "Don't you know you're not supposed to leave the scene of a crime?"

"What crime?"

"You tried to rape me," Jullee said.

"No shit," I said.

"No shit, indeed," Schiafino said.

Jullee slipped into a U.S. Army overcoat and rolled up the sleeves. A small suitcase was on the bed beside her purse. The case was made of black metal, edged in brass, and had a double combination lock. I'd seen it before but couldn't remember where.

"She's got you cold," Schiafino said. "And with witnesses, too."

I looked at Larry Aarons, one of the witnesses. He

grinned back. He seemed to view me as a source of genuine amusement, not to mention a real fun guy. Behind him Jullee sat at a black lacquer dresser, putting on purple lipstick and eyeing me in the mirror.

"Just when did I commit this rape?" I said to Schiafino.

"Tomorrow. Jullee's leaving town right now. She'll return tomorrow and file her complaint. The crime is attempted rape, by the way. The aforementioned witnesses—"

"Heckle and Jeckle," I said, "aka Detectives Aarons and Sinatra."

"Correcto. Fortunately, they were at the house paying their respects to my late wife. That's when they saw you enter Jullee's room and attack her. They came to her rescue and placed you under arrest."

"I see promotion here," I said. "Maybe even a photograph with the mayor."

"Never thought of that. Anyway, you came to the house claiming Lynda owed you money, and if her father didn't pay up, you were going to make trouble."

"How much money?"

"Two thou," Schiafino said. "I wanted to make Lynda generous but not stupid."

At the dresser Jullee was tucking her hair under a black Stetson. We were still staring at each other in the mirror. I saw her as the weak link.

"Detectives screwing teenage girls," I said. "Who'd have thought."

I wasn't talking to Schiafino. I was talking to Jullee, and she knew it. She shook her head in disgust. Then slowly, and at her own leisurely pace, she gave me the finger.

Schiafino sighed into the phone. "Forcing yourself on a grieving teenager. Have you no shame?"

I said if Jullee was grieving, Elvis was downstairs selling peanut-butter-and-bacon sandwiches on the front lawn. And forget about forcing myself on Jullee. If she'd fuck Schiafino, she'd fuck anybody.

A cold-cream jar flew past my head, hitting the movie poster. The top of the jar came off on impact, slopping white goo on Peter Lorre. Hit or miss, Jullee was just getting started. She snatched a nail file from the dresser and hurled herself in my direction and might have reached me if Aldo hadn't caught her from the rear, an arm around her waist and a hand over her mouth. He said, Shut up, or I'll sit on your face. He followed this with a smutty grin aimed at Larry Aarons but received no response because Lethal Larry hadn't taken his eyes off me. I was still on my knees, cellular phone in hand, holding Aarons's gaze because we both knew that when the time came, I'd go for it. Lethal Larry's job was to stop me. And he only knew one way.

Aldo removed his hand from Jullee's mouth. She took a deep breath, then let me know it wasn't over. "I'm going to get you for that remark," she said to me. "You better watch your ass, because I'm going to get you."

"You'll have to stand in line," I said to her. "Your boyfriend's got first dibs."

I said to Schiafino, "Someone mentioned something about a boat."

"Oh boy," he said. "Now you've done it. You may have to change your name and relocate 'cause the girl's gonna bring it to you good. She scares me sometimes. Now, about the boat. Some friends of mine are going to run you through a little Q and A. That means you get to join the harbor patrol."

Schiafino intended to stash me on a police boat—a cruiser or a tugboat used by the Harbor Unit to police the city's rivers and ports and pull dead bodies out of the water. This way he could keep me on the move, cut off from the world. Keep me sailing hundreds of miles of rivers and waterways in New York. He could move me to New Jersey and Connecticut if he wanted to. I'd be cut off from friends, telephones, and lawyers. I'd be cut off from Dion. And Schiafino's goons could work me over at their leisure.

"Exactly what is it you want to know?" I said.

"I want to know why you're sniffing around Jullee," Schiafino said. "I also want to know what you and Lisa Watts talked about. The two of you had a sit-down this morning in Astoria."

"Why don't you ask Lisa?"

"Can't. She's in the wind. Seems she heard I wanted to

talk to her, so she upped and disappeared. Not to worry. I'll find her."

Schiafino's people had followed me or Lisa this morning. I knew for a fact he had someone on me. Mikey. That was the name on Bauza's answering machine. Mikey was good. In two days I'd yet to spot him.

"Maybe I can help you out with Lisa," I said. "We talked about Lynda. What else do you want to know?"

"You're shitting me, right?" Schiafino said. "I mean, you actually believe you can outthink me. Go ahead, be my guest. But if I were any further ahead of you, I'd be on the fucking moon. You and Lisa didn't spend the morning exchanging recipes. And you didn't drive out to my father-in-law's house to see if Jullee did her homework. Forgive me, but I can't quite picture you as warm and fuzzy."

"How are you going to explain my absence? You know, when I'm on the boat with your friends."

"Thought you'd never ask," Schiafino said. "You're going on leave for a week. Every cop's prerogative. Personal leave time."

"What about my leave papers?"

"Being taken care of. Someone's filling in the forms even as we speak, including your signature. The papers should be approved by noon today. I'll have seven days to pick your brain, and nobody's going to miss you. I mean, is that good or what?"

"That's good," I said. "My compliments to the rabbi."

"What did you say?"

"I said my compliments to the rabbi."

Larry Aarons stopped grinning while Aldo lifted his chin and stared down his big nose at me. Jullee had been touching up her lipstick, which had been ruined by Aldo's hammy hand. When she heard the word *rabbi*, her jaw dropped.

"The rabbi," Schiafino said.

He exhaled into the phone for a long time.

Finally, he said, "The prevailing mode of function on that point is, if you know about him, you know too much."

"Coming down to the dock to see me off?"

"Afraid not. I'm in mourning, remember? Black armband, wreath on the front door. Sad music. The whole nine yards."

"You sound dazed with grief."

"Well, I try to look on the bright side," Schiafino said. "The nuns used to say, One may weep at night, but joy cometh in the morning. With me, I guess it's morning already."

"You and Jullee," I said. "And speaking of your main squeeze, why are you protecting her?"

"I'll be in touch," Schiafino said. "I'm thinking of having my guys videotape your Q and A. I want to see your eyes when they break you."

I looked at Jullee, who was still at her dresser, where she was stuffing cosmetics into her purse. She knew what Schiafino had planned for me, and she didn't care. This was one tough kid. Maybe tough enough to have killed her sister.

I said to Schiafino, "A boat trip and a rape charge. A full schedule by anybody's standards."

"A win-win situation for me," he said. "If it works, you go down. If it doesn't, you still lose. Your reputation will be destroyed, you'll go broke fighting the attempted rape charge, and in all probability, Sherlock, you'll be off the force. You don't fuck my wife and get away with it."

I said, "So you jerk me around for a while. Then when the time is right, you drop the hammer."

"You mean kill you? Don't rush me, I'm enjoying myself. I want to see you suffer, that's what I want. My boys give you a tune-up followed by the good part, which is you, an ex-cop, doing ten years in the joint. Of course you can always come out and do a Nixon bounce. You know, rehabilitate yourself in the public eye. Or try to. I'd like to see you become another Robichaux, a dumb-ass boozer hitting up people for spare change. Kill you? Something to think about. Right now, though, I'm in no hurry. That could change, however."

Larry Aarons snatched the phone from me and put it to his ear. He was anxious to get going.

"Say, homes," he said to Schiafino, "later for this mental bullshit. I got to be in court this afternoon. I want to settle up here. We brought the case to Jullee, so how about letting her hit the road so we can take Meagher to the boat and get that thing started."

Aarons listened, then said, "Right."

He closed the phone, put it in his coat pocket, then snapped his fingers at Jullee. If she was a tough girl with other people, she knew her place with Aarons. She nodded nervously at him, grabbed her purse and the metal suitcase, then left the room.

Aldo closed the door, then resumed his position at my back. In front of me, Aarons stared at his buffed fingernails.

"You know about our group, about what we do," he said to me.

I said I knew.

"Then you can't leave the boat," he said. He sounded sorry, as though he regretted being forced to kill me. I almost believed him.

"I was a dead man when I entered this room," I said. "I was dead because I'm making Schiafino nervous. He's jerking me around, but the bottom line is he wants to kill me. Today, tomorrow, doesn't matter. We've got a beef, and it can only end one way. He also gets nervous whenever a cop gets too close to Jullee."

"I tell you who's nervous, you fuckhead," gravel-voiced Aldo said to me. "My cousin Danny. He's nervous every day he's in Atlanta because of you. He's dying down there. Has to wear magazines inside his shirt so he don't get stabbed. Every month he pays three niggers a hundred apiece to keep from getting raped. He don't pay, he's meat. Danny owes you big time, and I'm here to deliver the message."

Aldo and Danny weren't just cousins. They were more like brothers. They'd grown up together, gone through the academy together, been best man at each other's wedding, and bought adjoining homes on Staten Island. Danny had taken a bullet for Aldo in a Jackson Heights drug raid, binding them even closer. Even without any of this, it was a fact that Italians raised in the same neighborhood ranked their loyalty to each other over any obligation to God, country, and/or the NYPD. At the moment, however, I wasn't thinking about homeboys and their sense of duty. I was thinking of the metal suitcase. I remembered where I'd seen it.

I'd once busted some Nigerians working as Manhattan

bank guards and janitors so they could steal banking and credit-card information. Like your average perp, the Nigerians were creatures of habit. When committing a crime, they stuck with what worked for them. They'd become partial to this particular metal suitcase, which they used to send money and fake credit cards back to Africa. They knew the case inside and out. Knew its capacity, how much punishment it could take, and how to break it down to create secret compartments. When I busted them, I found two dozen similar cases stacked in a Brooklyn room, just waiting to travel.

Apparently, Schiafino was also partial to this case. And partial to Jullee as a courier.

"We're going downstairs," Larry Aarons said to me. "No cuffs because that might raise questions. But guns do go off accidentally, you dig? I won't kill you. Not here. But if I have to, I'll blow out your knee."

He gave me my hat, then ordered me to stand. When I was on my feet, he handed me one of Jullee's teddy bears and said, Wipe the blood from your face. I did it while he and Aldo snickered.

Time to hit the road. Aarons nodded and Aldo reached for the door. His hand was on the knob when someone on the other side knocked in a way that said he or she was on a mission.

"Detective Meagher, it's Nurse Tyson. You in there?"

"Yes," I said.

"You got to come quick. It's your car. Jullee banged into it."

"Say you're busy," Aarons whispered to me. "You'll see her later. Remember your knee."

I said to Aarons, "Jullee told the nurse you'd left. You shoot me, and she'll know you're here. She'll also know Jullee lied."

I said they'd sent Jullee to invite me to her room, which could make a rape charge hard to prove, Jullee being eighteen and me having the nurse as a witness. I said if the nurse sees us leave together and I turn up dead, guess who homicide detectives will want to talk to.

I had Aarons frowning, thinking, and before he could make a decision, I said loudly, "Come in, Nurse Tyson."

She pushed against the door, and Aldo pushed back, and the door cracked, allowing them to eyeball each other. A few seconds of this, then Aldo slammed the door in her face.

"The hell's wrong with you?" Alma shouted from the hall.

A tense Aldo looked at Aarons, who deliberated, then finally said, Open the goddamn door.

He did, and there stood Alma, scowling and holding a bedpan, definitely not pleased with the door incident. Aldo, meanwhile, didn't like being so close to the bedpan. It wasn't empty. He could smell it, so he backed into the room, stepping on my feet. That was my chance. I quickly caught him in a bear hug, pinning his elbows to his sides. He cursed as I lifted him from the floor and swung around to face Aarons. I ordered Alma from the room, telling her not to ask questions, just leave the room and shut the door. She did.

I threw Aldo into Larry Aarons, sending both to the floor, arms and legs entangled. I had a clear shot at Aldo, so I kicked him in the face, sending blood gushing from his nose and mouth. He dropped onto his back, arms spread wide. Aarons drew himself into a sitting position, back against the four-poster and a hand in his overcoat pocket. Whipping off my hat, I backhanded it at his face, and as he batted it away with his empty hand, I stomped on his left knee, driving my heel into the kneecap. I heard him scream. The .38 was in his right hand, pointing at the floor. I stepped on the gun, pinning it to the rug, then crouched and punched him in the throat. Aarons's eyes bulged, and he was gagging when I picked up the gun and swung around to cover Aldo. I must have kicked him hard, because he sat dazed in the middle of the room, staring glassy-eyed at his bloodied raincoat. Suddenly, he noticed me and went for the Glock in his belt. He moved slowly. Too slow to do him any good. One step brought me close enough. I pressed the .38 into his left eyebrow, digging into his flesh and letting him see my face, knowing I wouldn't have to say anything. He sucked air through his open mouth and showed me his empty blood-stained hands.

I took back my Glock and my ankle gun. I also took Aldo's .38. Then I walked to the door and cracked it just enough to see Alma. She looked confused. And a bit curious. But when a cop tells a civilian to back off, that's usually what they do. What I told Alma was there'd been an argument, strictly cop stuff, and nothing for her to worry about. I'd take care of everything.

She said she'd come to tell me Jullee had deliberately rammed my car. Rammed it twice before driving away. Alma and the garage workers were witnesses.

Jullee's temper had saved my life, but I couldn't tell Alma that. I simply closed the door and turned my attention to the cops who'd planned to take me on a one-way cruise.

Aldo sat in the center of the room, head down, a handkerchief held to his nose. Aarons was where I'd left him, sitting on the floor with his back against the bed and massaging his damaged throat. He was having trouble breathing.

"I won't waste time filing a complaint," I said. "You've got Schiafino and you've got the rabbi, and I know when I'm wasting my time. One or two questions, then I'm out of here.

"Where's Jullee heading?" I said to Aarons.

He let his head fall back against the bed. Then he closed his eyes, ignoring me.

Stepping to the windowsill, I picked up Jullee's boom box, then turned and dropped it on Aarons's bad knee. He opened his eyes in a hurry.

"D.C.," he said. "Chick's driving to D.C."

"What's in the case?"

"Money."

"How much?"

"Fifty K."

"The going rate for you guys. Nice work if you can get it."

I asked Aarons if he knew the rabbi's identity, and he said no, that only Schiafino dealt with the guy, and he wasn't about to share that information because it meant sharing power, something Schiafino didn't do. Aldo chimed in, anxious to protect his partner, saying Aarons was telling the truth and that if I broke every kneecap they had between them, they couldn't tell me what they didn't know.

I looked at the bloodied teddy bear and remembered Aarons snickering at me. I told him to get Schiafino on the cellular phone. As he dialed, I said I was keeping his gun and Aldo's. They could explain the loss of their weapons to their superiors, and if they were lucky, all they'd get is a fine, maybe a week's suspension. Taking their badges was a possibility, but it would have been a waste of time. Most cops have copies made of their badges, keeping the original in a safe or bank. Lethal Larry and Aldo might have to explain having been beaten up. But with the rabbi in their corner, they might not have to explain anything.

Aarons was about to speak to Schiafino when I tapped him on the shoulder.

"Sing 'Ol' Man River' to Bobby Schemes," I said.

"Say what?" His voice was husky, as though he had a very bad cold.

I gently touched his damaged knee with my foot.

" 'Ol' Man River,' " I said.

Aarons sang. Or rather he croaked, pained eyes on me all the time. *"Ol' man river, dat ol' man river, he mus' know somethin', he—"*

He stopped and shook his head. He was hurting, and he'd taken a pounding, but there was still pride in him. Pride as a man. As a cop. He wasn't going to sing any more. I'd have to kill him first. I took the phone from him and listened.

Schiafino was in stitches. Laughing his ass off.

Thinking he was talking to Aarons, he said, "Fucking hysterical. What's with this nigger shit all of a sudden?"

I said, "I'm canceling my cruise. Can I have my deposit back?"

Schiafino went quiet in a hurry. In his silence I could hear his rage, his deep and total hatred of me.

He finally said, "What did you do to Larry and Aldo?"

"Aldo's going to need a nose job, and Larry may never dance again. Before I forget, you'd better call the rabbi and have those leave papers withdrawn."

"You're still standing in quicksand, dickhead."

"Why are you so anxious to protect Jullee? She didn't kill Lynda, by any chance?"

"Rhythm and blues," Schiafino said. "I got the rhythm, and you got the blues."

"Doesn't look that way to me," I said, feeling good for the first time in days.

"Look again, asshole," Schiafino said. "Win-win situation, remember? Before you called just now, I was sitting here thinking about you and Lynda. And I came to the conclusion that when you run out of luck, it don't matter how long your dick is. You know that letter Lynda wrote? The one that can send you to prison? I think I know where she hid it."

XXI
A Second Suspect

I spent the next forty minutes driving around Queens, looking into my rearview mirror for Mikey, the guy Schiafino had on me. Mikey was good. I didn't spot him or anything that looked like a tail. Then again Mikey might be off saving the earth or watching cartoons. Or he could be inviting me to sit back and put my feet up while he moved in for the kill.

Mikey's timing wasn't the only problem I had with him. To start with, I didn't know what he looked like. I also didn't know if he was working alone or how far he was prepared to go. Was he only doing surveillance on me, or was he planning to shove a screwdriver through my eye at some point? With Mikey on the job, Schiafino could cause me to lose a lot of sleep.

I wasn't used to being followed. It was starting to get under my skin. If I wanted peace and quiet, not to mention a trouble-free mind, I had to remove Mikey from the equation.

It was almost noon. I hadn't eaten all morning, so I stopped on Northern Boulevard for some scrambled eggs, then telephoned Dion at home. I told him about my run-in with Schiafino's crew and about Schiafino's relationship with

Jullee. I also told him about the altercation with Jullee, which had left my Ford with broken headlights, a dented front bumper, and a damaged grille. If I continued driving around in something this wrecked, I'd wind up in traffic court. The car was going into the shop right after I talked to Dion.

Then I told him about Schiafino and Lynda's letter.

"He doesn't have it," I said to Dion. "Not yet. He knows the letter's out there somewhere, but as of now he doesn't have it. The man lives to do a number on my head. If he had the letter, he'd have read me the gory details. He wouldn't have missed a chance to prey on my nerves. Anything to make my teeth chatter."

"Goddamn Mikey," Dion said. "He's in the picture one day, this guy, and suddenly the whole world knows about Lynda's letter. One way or another Schiafino's people find a way to kill you."

"Maybe Lisa's run off because of Mikey," I said. "Could be he's got her scared."

"What you do is you find Lisa, and you make her give up Mikey. Maybe she knows what he looks like. Find her before Schiafino does. She gives you Mikey. You and him talk, and you convince him to stop being so fucking inquisitive."

"Something else is bugging me," I said. "Besides Mikey."

"What?"

"Jullee. And not just because she trashed my car. You know that fifty grand she's carrying to Washington?"

"What about it?"

"Scumbag that he is, Larry Aarons didn't tell me the whole story. He held back. I know it. There's more to this courier thing. A lot more."

"You want more?" Dion said. "Here's more. Schiafino and Jullee are playing hide the wienie. There's your more. Hey, the kid's chump change. She's a mule, period. The advantage she has is she don't look like she's sitting on fifty K. Makes her the perfect courier."

"So why isn't the perfect courier flying to D.C.?" I said. "Beats the shit out of driving."

"So she hates to fly," Dion said.

I said Jullee did what Schiafino told her to do. If he said fly, Jullee would be on a plane to Washington even if it meant dressing up as a Hasidic Jew and letting passengers think she was Michael Jackson. She was driving to D.C. because that's how Bobby Schemes wanted it. To him a woman was a clipped coupon, to be cashed in. If Jullee had gotten a van out of their relationship, Schiafino was getting more. A hell of a lot more.

I lit a cigarette. I was standing in a pocket-size coffee shop, looking through the glass front at the corner where some stubby Mexicans were working in the cold, unloading large plastic bags of raw octopus from a truck and carrying them into a nearby Jap restaurant. One stopped to blow on his chilled hands. Immediately, a squat Nip overseeing the unloading began angrily waving his arms. He wanted the frozen Mex to resume working. The Mex probably had a two-digit IQ, which is all the job required. But with that came a bloodcurdling aura inherited from his Aztec forefathers, because he stared at the Nip as though wanting to carve his heart out with a stone knife. The Nip felt it, too. He stopped flapping his arms and took one step back.

"Jullee isn't traveling light," I said. "She's taking money to Washington. Then she's bringing something back. The van's primarily for the return trip."

I said yesterday's phone message from Schiafino to Bauza had him flying to Washington tonight to fulfill a contract for the Exchange Students. Since Haysoos had business in D.C., why not give him the courier job? Why give it to Jullee?

And then there was Schiafino's well-known stinginess. As the Irish would put it, he'd skin a flea for its hide. Cheap John, Lynda used to call him. This was the man who limited his gift giving to Christmas and then to stuff bought from a fence for next to nothing. Over Lynda's objections he'd once installed a cheesy alarm system in their home, a useless collection of wires and buzzers she'd been forced to replace at her own expense. Schiafino was moving to California, she said, so he could get paid three hours earlier. A guy that chintzy wouldn't pop for a twenty-thousand-dollar van when a round-trip plane ticket to Washington only cost a few hundred dollars.

"Maybe Schiafino's dealing," Dion said. "Big bucks in pharmaceuticals. Just ask any Colombian in a silk shirt and gold chain."

"A waste of the rabbi's talents," I said. "This guys thinks. He cogitates. He knows you sell drugs, you do drugs. You do drugs, you're an addict, and addicts are sick fucks who'd sell you out in a minute. Do business with dope fiends, you're stepping on your dick. That's not how the rabbi operates."

I said the rabbi had hooked up with two police departments and some very affluent people and this kind of talent didn't get together just to peddle nickel bags. Neither Schiafino nor the rabbi was a mental defective. Both knew drug dealing had its downside. Such as twenty-four-hour police surveillance. Or competitors who believed the best way to increase their market share was to kill you and every member of your family.

Forget about the rabbi being in drugs. Not when the people who hired the Exchange Students were paying to have drug pushers' eyes shot out.

"So if Schiafino's friend isn't dealing, what's his hustle?" Dion said.

"Haven't a clue," I said. "But whatever Jullee's bringing back from D.C., the rabbi's reaping the benefits."

"What makes you so sure?"

"Because Schiafino hasn't gone out of his way for anyone except this guy."

I mentioned Gavilan's story about Bauza's refusal to do a hit for the rabbi and how Schiafino had convinced Jesus to rearrange his priorities, with Jesus responding by going to Washington and promptly icing a stockbroker. He'd done it for the rabbi, for the man Schiafino called their protection . . . their first line of defense. That's why Jullee was going to Washington in a twenty-thousand-dollar van. And that's why I was still out on the street.

"Right now I should be getting booked on a bogus rape charge."

"Even as we speak," Dion said.

"Fingerprinted, photographed, and paraded in front of TV cameras with a raincoat hiding my handcuffs. But for some reason Schiafino had to postpone that pleasure. He had to let Jullee make the Washington trip. Then, and only then, could she come back and hit me with attempted rape."

"Strange when you think about it," Dion said. "Schiafino wants your ass. Yet with a chance to nail you, he backs off."

"He had no choice," I said. "Without the rabbi he's fucked. Like it or not, he couldn't put the hurt on me at Jullee's place."

"Bobby Schemes protecting his guardian angel," Dion said. "Ain't that a kick in the head. He doesn't want Jullee blabbing about the rabbi, so he keeps her away from the DA. Keeps her away from you as well. And you get booked on a sea cruise just to see what you know about this guy. Could be you're right. Like maybe there's more going on here than just some cops moonlighting as expensive shooters."

We were interrupted by a recorded voice from the phone company saying time was up and demanding more money. Dion asked for my number and said he'd call back. I hung up and pulled the newspaper from my overcoat pocket. I'd been too busy thinking about the rabbi and making notes on Jullee and Schiafino to do more than glance at the front page.

The headline said Maurice Robichaux's attorney was charging police with brutality in the matter of his client's arrest. I had no problem with Mr. Maurice getting his lumps. Seeing him suffer made me believe life was worth living.

The paper also had an article by Carlyle Taylor on the Schiafino homicide. I elected to pass, figuring it was the usual liberal crap about Lynda having been a member of a white occupying army who had been murdered by a black freedom fighter or some such shit. Instead I read an interview with First Deputy Mayor Ray Nathan Footman. Ordinarily, I'd have had no interest in this dick-brain reformer, but he was talking about cops, and I wanted to check out his latest theory on exactly how the department could benefit from his wisdom.

Seems Mr. Footman wasn't just satisfied with bringing ci-

vilians into the NYPD to replace experienced police officers.
Not him. He now wanted a monthly meeting between police
brass and a select committee of new civilian employees.
These meetings, he said, would make the department more
culturally sensitive and intellectually diverse. Footman was
a reminder that the asshole business was a growth industry
with more than its share of idiots.

The phone rang. I picked up on the first ring.

Dion said, "Want to hear about the spending habits of
your friend Detective Bauza?"

"Can't wait."

With his girlfriend's help Dion had learned Haysoos was
spending wildly on Gina Branch, the twenty-two-year-old
dancer who worked at the topless club owned by Haysoos,
Schiafino, and Eugene Elder. This was the babe Haysoos
planned to marry.

Schiafino had ordered Bauza not to throw his money
around. But as Dion was fond of saying, when your dick
gets hard, your brain gets soft, and at this point in time it
would appear Haysoos's brain was decidedly mushy.

So far this year he and his Gina had traveled to Puerto
Rico three times, eating in the best restaurants, renting expensive cars, and bouncing from one San Juan club to another. On their last visit Bauza had treated his lady to a
Rolex watch, seven pairs of shoes, and a Versace suit. Other
recent charges included a new Jaguar for Bauza and liposuc-
tion to rectify imperfections on Miss Gina's bod.

I knew how much a detective made, and cops like Jesus
were asking for trouble when they started playing high
roller. His credit charges for the past three months exceeded
his yearly salary as a cop. Talk about having a leak in your
think tank.

I wasn't exactly dumbfounded at hearing this news. Dirty
cops have no wish to be wise. I'd never known one to make
a pile, then have the good sense to lie low. The Bhagavad
Gita says that the immediacy of the pleasure is the undoing of man. It's definitely the undoing of dirty cops. They
spend money as fast as it comes in, letting the world know
just how stupid they can be. As for the department's posi-

tion on all of this, it didn't know because it didn't want to know.

Something was missing. I asked Dion to read the charges again.

"You're paying attention," he said. "What's missing are hotel charges."

"Bingo," I said. "Haysoos own property there or what?"

"He do indeed. But it's undeveloped land just outside San Juan. Nothing on it at the moment. Probably an investment of some kind. The reason there're no hotel charges is because when Bauza goes to the island, he and his lady stay at a friend's home."

"This friend have a name?"

"Try Jonathan Munro."

"The same Jonathan Munro who's no longer hung up about greaseball hijackers?"

"The very same," Dion said. "Maggie tells me he owns one of the island's most beautiful homes. A real showplace. She's always reading magazines about luxury homes. Says it's the closest she'll ever come to owning one. She tells me Munro's house is constantly getting written up. Says it's got everything from a private movie theater to a Jacuzzi for his horses. He owns two San Juan department stores plus a shitload of other businesses, ranging from a cab company to software stores. Married and divorced twice. Last wife was a Miss Puerto Rico from the sixties. Loves Latin women, this guy. Some of this shit came out when he had that tax problem, remember?"

I remembered. Last December the pope visited Puerto Rico around the time Roger L. Tucker, our beloved spade mayor, declared himself a candidate for reelection. Tucker wasn't the sharpest knife in the drawer, but he recognized a photo opportunity when he saw one. He'd hopped down to Puerto Rico, figuring New York's Latino voters would be pleased and delighted to witness him sucking up to God's vicar on earth.

In San Juan he stayed at the lavish home of Jonathan Munro, his close friend and chief fund-raiser. Munro knew the island's movers and shakers, so Tucker had no trouble getting his papal audience. New York newspapers and TV stations gave the audience major coverage. Our beloved mayor had gone to the island with a Bible in one hand and a tin cup in the other, and made good use of both.

But if Tucker thought this trip would turn the ground around him into a sacred cathedral, he was mistaken. The day after his return to New York, a couple of papers reported he'd secretly given Jonathan Munro a thirty-million-dollar tax break. Tucker, the papers said, was trading tax breaks for campaign contributions. Suddenly, the mayor's trip to Puerto Rico looked like a political payoff. It probably was, but the trick was not to get caught playing that game.

Two more New York VIPs were hit with charges of mooching a free papal trip from Jonathan Munro. One was the ever devout and divine Carmine Lacovara, the prosecutor who talked to God. The other was Con McGuigan, deputy police commissioner and the NYPD's number two man. Both had allowed Jonathan Munro to spring for airfare and hotel rooms for them and their wives. The joke was McGuigan had made the trip to arrest the pope for passing himself off as Lacovara.

Lacovara wasn't laughing when the press reported he'd gone to Puerto Rico to discuss a planned run for governor two years hence, with Roger Tucker as his running mate for lieutenant governor and Jonathan Munro as their chief fundraiser. An ambitious game plan to be sure, but it had nothing to do with worshiping at the feet of the foundation stone of the church and probing the deeper mysteries of religion.

As for McGuigan, he'd also used this trip to go in search of his golden dream. He'd paid the pope a quick visit, then hopped a plane back to the U.S. But instead of returning to New York, he'd stopped off in Washington to do a little job hunting. For three days he was the guest of the largest private-investigative firm in the country, which had been trying to recruit him for a long time. As he'd done in the past, he ended up deciding to stay put in New York. Unfortunately for him, Carlyle Taylor got wind of his side trip and crucified McGuigan in her paper, claiming he was trying to get out of working with a black mayor and a black police chief.

McGuigan was street-smart, hardworking, and familiar

with everything about the NYPD, from its history to the ins and outs of its seventy-five precincts. He'd put himself through law school at night while working as a full-time cop. His life revolved around his ambition to be police commissioner, and he wasn't very good at seeing other people's points of view.

He was qualified to be commissioner, but he hadn't a chance in hell of getting the job. McGuigan was white, a political liability in a city where a majority of the population was nonwhite. These very same citizens had seen fit to elect a black mayor who'd campaigned on the promise of bringing in a black police commissioner.

To keep that promise, Tucker had reached out for Carl Dowd, a plump, fifty-year-old black who'd been D.C.'s police chief and whose main qualification for any job appeared to be the ability to turn himself into a high-priced stooge. These days you needed a crowbar to pry Dowd's nose out of Tucker's ass.

Dowd had a ferocious pride, drank too much, and was just about impossible to please. Had he been good at his job, none of this would have mattered. But he was incompetent, easily bored, and unwilling to be bothered with the day-to-day running of the department. He wanted everyone to like him and couldn't understand why people insisted on remembering the shitty way he treated them.

In today's politically correct world the Dowds were immune from criticism. You approached these losers with loving-kindness and goodwill, or you kept your distance and watched them go wrong.

Cops described Tucker, McGuigan, and Lacovara's papal trip as Curly, Larry, and Moe say the rosary, and we all got a chuckle out of the press going after these moochers. But the story didn't hold the city's attention for long. In this town you had widespread apathy and people long resigned to the worst in their public servants, and this combined with stonewalling and fancy footwork on the part of the public servants in question pretty much killed the story in a week or so. Tucker, McGuigan, and Lacovara insisted they'd done nothing wrong and had broken no laws and were being made scapegoats by a press that had lost all sense of responsibility. Nevertheless, each of these freeloaders expressed a desire to set the record straight, whatever that meant, and would therefore pay for the Puerto Rico trip out of his own pocket.

Besides dumping on McGuigan, Carlyle Taylor had something else to say about this outing to view the holy father. She took it on herself to defend the mayor, and that meant playing the race card, something she did more often than I spilled food on my shirt. The attack on Tucker, she wrote, was one more white attempt to bring down a black leader and destroy black unity. I thought she was wide of the mark as usual. But that was her mission in life, to stand on the rooftops and tell the world that if you're black and get caught, just find someone else to blame. Preferably someone white.

"Anything on Schiafino?" I said to Dion.

"Nothing. No credit cards. Mortgage paid off. No car loans, no gambling debts, no collection agencies on his tail. The man's a closed book."

"The man's smart. Check on Jullee under her real name, Judith Lesnevitch. See if she has a credit card and, if so, what kind of money she's spending. You can get back to me later on this one."

I dropped my cigarette butt on the floor, stepped on it, and then yawned into the phone. I touched the sore spot on my head where Aldo had smacked me, feeling the clotted blood and wishing I'd gone upside his head just a bit harder. I let a long minute go by without saying anything. Dion listened to my silence, knowing I was trying to work out something and that the best thing he could do at the moment was keep the peace.

Finally, I said, "I'm thinking about the rabbi."

"I thought maybe you were thinking about Lynda."

"Her, too. But right now the rabbi. Let's start with Munro. He's got the Exchange Students working for him."

"Looks that way," Dion said.

"Eight to five he's got Schiafino's crew killing for some of his rich friends."

"No bet. Way I see it, Schiafino would be a fool not to bring up the idea, and he's no fool."

"So here's what we have. Munro's down with the Exchange Students. And he's down with McGuigan and Lacovara, two very sharp characters."

"Except when it comes to free travel," Dion said.

I said free travel aside, McGuigan and Lacovara were nobody's half-wits. Far from it. Without McGuigan the NYPD would fall apart. When it came to law enforcement, he was an Einstein. Tucker may have put Dowd in the commissioner's chair, but it was McGuigan who was keeping him there. Without him Dowd would die standing up.

As for Lacovara, even if he did see himself as a window through which God's mercy shone on the world, that didn't make him a moron. He had the highest conviction rate of any DA in the city, and no one could remember the last time he'd had a case reversed on appeal. Washington loved him. He had a standing offer to work for the Justice Department any time local politics got too boring. One Wall Street law firm had offered him a million a year for five years plus bonuses and perks, the whole package guaranteed.

"As a prosecutor he's A-1," I said. "You're talking law enforcement, you have to rate him and McGuigan as one, two. But here's what interests me more than anything else. They're tight with Munro. That's what the Puerto Rico trip was all about."

"Munro's tight with a lot of people. The man's got connections up the wazoo."

"That I know. Now here's where it gets interesting. Munro's using the Exchange Students, and he's tight with McGuigan and Lacovara. What's that tell you?"

Dion grunted. He was starting to catch on.

"You saying what I think you're saying?" he said.

"I'm saying McGuigan or Lacovara could be the rabbi."

"That's what I was afraid of."

Neither of us spoke for a while.

Finally, Dion said, "The NYPD's number two man and the city's top prosecutor. Either one could be involved with contract killers. The fucking end of the world, that's what it is."

I said whoever the rabbi was he was doing a hell of a lot of damage. As long as the city's courts were dispensing half-assed justice, Schiafino's crew would have more than its share of clients. The more clients, the more killings. Lourdes Balera and the eight Ecuadorans were just the tip of the iceberg. The rabbi was stonewalling more than one murder investigation, and to do that you had to be able to pull a lot of wires.

"The Exchange Students are rough," Dion said. "What you got here is a bunch of eight-hundred-pound gorillas. Almighty, full-blooded, double-edged gorillas. You can't cover for this crew unless you're a king-size heavyweight yourself. I'm thinking, and you're not going to like this, I'm thinking maybe the rabbi's two men. Suppose McGuigan and Lacovara together are the rabbi."

It was the last thing I needed to hear because it clearly put me between a rock and a hard place. McGuigan and Lacovara were primo. Alone they were brilliant. Together they were unstoppable. Throw in Schiafino, and you had the kind of crime dream team the average perp could only fantasize about.

I hung up and flipped through the newspaper, wondering if things could get any worse for me. Dion was saying if McGuigan and Lacovara actually were a team, it was the romance of the century. I only half-heard him. I hated to think of myself as panicking, but I had to admit I was starting to feel troubled and uneasy. If Dion was right, I was in over my head. I couldn't see anyone believing me, let alone helping me take on both Lacovara and McGuigan.

And just like that, I forgot all about the rabbi. It happened when I glanced at Carlyle Taylor's story on Lynda's murder. Fact is I didn't just glance at it. I read the whole thing. I had no choice.

She was still pounding out the message that an innocent Maurice Robichaux was being framed by racist cops. Surprise, surprise. This time, however, she didn't stick to the usual script. She went off on a new trail, one that left me feeling terminally ill, if not on the critical list.

According to her, there was another suspect, one police were protecting because he was one of them. This suspect was a detective who'd once worked with the murdered Lynda Schiafino. During their partnership he'd committed a crime, then terrorized Mrs. Schiafino into keeping quiet about it. Worried about her safety, she decided that should this detective ever kill her, he wasn't going to get away with it. She'd put the details of his crime in a letter, which she'd then hidden. Carlyle Taylor wanted to know why police weren't going after this detective, since the missing letter gave him a strong motive for killing Detective Lynda Schiafino.

XXII
Mac Attack

When I arrived at my office around two that afternoon, Jack Hayden was on the phone within seconds. He was whispering. And he sounded panicky.

"You're giving me a fucking heart attack is what you're doing," he said. "The man's in my office, and he's not leaving till he talks to you. Any idea what it means when a double-barreled honcho from the department makes a surprise visit to talk to one of *my* detectives?"

I said it probably means the detective's in deep shit.

I'd seen the first sign of trouble downstairs, a black Mercedes idling in front of the building and the driver, a young Latino detective, relaxing with the sports pages, knowing he wasn't going to be ticketed for illegal parking because the beat cop would sooner pick up needles with his butt cheeks than tag a car belonging to the first deputy commissioner.

Another indication I just might be standing on a slippery slope happened minutes before when I stepped off the elevator and cops looked at me, then quickly turned away, treating me as though I were sick unto death and the sands of my life were running out.

"McGuigan's next door in my office," Hayden said, his voice still low. "He's been waiting twenty minutes to talk to you. This wouldn't have anything to do with the Carlyle Taylor story, would it?"

"What story's that?"

"Don't shit me, cowboy. You know the story I'm talking about."

I said I hadn't read it and asked if he wanted to hear about yesterday's trip to the Bronx before or after I spoke to McGuigan. I said the Ecuadoran murders were planned executions and that I had a line on the killer. Hayden acted as though he hadn't heard me, demanding that I get my ass in his office now. Now, as in ten seconds ago. Then the line went dead.

I hung up my coat, remembering it was no secret I'd been accused of stealing drug money. Baby Cabrera, the coke-dealing fruit I'd busted with Lynda, had testified under oath that I'd skimmed twenty-five grand from his safe. Until now I'd dealt with this allegation fairly directly, which is to say I'd lied and hoped the whole thing would go away.

But life wasn't so simple these days. Not with Carlyle Taylor out to stick it to me.

She'd decided Robichaux was innocent, meaning someone else had to be guilty. Today's story said she was zeroing in on me as a chief suspect in Lynda's murder.

She hadn't mentioned me by name, which didn't mean anything. She obviously had me figured as the cop who'd terrorized Lynda, the cop whose name appeared in a letter qualifying him as a prime suspect in her murder. Hayden had certainly read the Taylor story, which is why he was more paranoid than usual. The arrest of a rogue cop meant the end of his career and his commander's as well. When I went down, I'd be taking Hayden with me.

That's why I wasn't surprised to hear him sounding so wired. Very much on the ragged edge and ready to fall on his sword, having decided McGuigan knew about my misdeeds and had come to take away my badge. I imagined Jack the Ripper being more twitchy than usual, pacing his office and waiting for me to show my face and at the same time thinking of ways he could slowly recede into the distance, leaving me friendless on the fifteenth floor.

I was more than a little uneasy myself. I liked being a

cop. Without my badge I had no identity. It was my power, my manhood, my place in the world. Losing it meant losing everything. Just the fear of losing it was enough to drive some cops over the edge.

Every year a dozen officers kill themselves, their suicides usually coming after being suspended or arrested. I'd known two cops who'd swallowed their guns, one a close friend who'd been kicked off the force after taking up with a female informant. He'd left his wife for this hot tamale, only to have her clean out his bank account and run off to Santo Domingo with a teenage coke dealer.

I'd always told myself I'd never stick a gun in my mouth. No hara-kiri for this kid. But you have the bottle and you have the gun, and you never know. You just never know.

I lit a cigarette, did a little thinking, and suddenly found a reason to smile. I blew a smoke ring at the ceiling. I wasn't going to be arrested. Not today.

There was a time when you couldn't beat a public hanging for family fun. Why was the community at large permitted to witness some schmuck take the long drop? Because it was believed his fate would discourage rascally behavior on the part of criminal wannabes.

But word soon got around that watching some poor bastard get strung up was amusing, if not enjoyable and gratifying. Pretty soon Mom and Pop started bringing the kids, then telling their friends, and before you knew it, thousands were enjoying themselves at what folks in the Old West liked to call a necktie sociable.

Still and all, nothing lasts forever, and along came humanitarians, social workers, and other kind persons, and together they rang down the curtain on this cherished form of recreation so beloved by American families from sea to shining sea.

For an up-to-date necktie sociable, check out the arrest of a police officer. Without knowing jack shit about the case or whether or not the officer is guilty, a bloodthirsty crowd usually gathers to watch him being handcuffed and taken into custody. Attending this modern lynching are police brass, prosecutors, civilians, fellow officers, and members of the media, everyone and his cousin as happy as a kid in a sandbox because they just know the cop had it coming.

When I'd entered the building, this lynch mob had been nowhere in sight. McGuigan was doing a solo. I wasn't going to be arrested.

This didn't mean I was out of the woods. Not by a long shot. McGuigan wasn't planning to take my badge. But he had a reason for coming here, and I wasn't going to like it. He wasn't known for being compassionate, nor was he the type to pay a social call during working hours. McGuigan could hurt me, and I wasn't talking about minor injuries.

I'd been caught off guard by his surprise visit. There was no time to react or find a way around this guy. All I could do was remind myself to say as little as possible, look respectful, and don't shoot myself in the foot. The more I thought about it, the more I felt this was very much the rabbi's style, a preemptive strike guaranteed to catch me napping and push me into making a mistake.

When I entered Hayden's office, McGuigan, bifocals perched on the tip of his red nose, sat behind Hayden's desk, filing his nails.

"If you don't know you're in danger of losing your badge," he said, "you're the only one in America who doesn't."

He was a beefy fiftyish Mick with a bull neck, soft voice, and heavy lids drooping over his eyes. With his large size and graying crew cut, he looked like a refrigerator. His sleepy, deadpan stare hid a steel-trap mind, and he had a reputation for dumping anyone to whom he felt obligated. There were two dime-size scars under his left eye, mementos from the night when, as a patrolman, he'd been shot twice in the face, the shoot-out occurring when he'd interrupted a SoHo restaurant robbery in progress, then gone on to kill the two perps who'd wounded him, shooting one and strangling the other to death with his bare hands. The twin facial scars had earned him the nickname Ditto Head. He expected to be obeyed and respected. God help you if you didn't.

He wore a double-breasted gray suit, matching shirt, and a black tie that he'd tied in a perfect Windsor knot. I'd never seen him in other clothes, leading me to believe the rumor he was color-blind and had nothing in his closet but a half dozen gray suits, a dozen gray shirts, and four black ties. He wore garters to hold up his socks, and there was a monogrammed pink handkerchief in his breast pocket, supposedly sewn in place by his wife so that it wouldn't be lost and replaced by one in the wrong color. He'd lost the tip of his right thumb to a pit bull in a Harlem drug raid, and there was a *fáinne*, a small gold circle in his lapel, indicating he spoke Irish.

And then there was Hayden. He'd decided to stand, probably thinking it made him look tough. Arms folded across his chest, he'd positioned himself beside McGuigan, feet apart and slightly crouched, a combat shooting stance without the gun. To calm his nerves, he furiously chewed gum and massaged his elbows. He was a man waiting for a bomb to go off.

An empty chair, one of those fake antique jobs left behind by the nutcase who'd owned the apartment before the OCCB moved in, had been spotted slightly to the right of Hayden's desk. The chair was deliberately positioned to catch the full light of the sun coming through one of the windows. The chair positively glowed.

Someone wanted me to feel uncomfortable.

I moved the chair out of the sun and sat down.

I felt a slight tingling in my arms and legs, and there was a dryness in my mouth. Nerves.

I'd been hard hit by Lynda's murder and by learning Schiafino and Carlyle Taylor knew about her letter. Now I had to deal with McGuigan. As deputy commissioner he could turn me into a nobody in a nanosecond. All he had to do was lift a finger, and I had my tit in the wringer.

As a kid I'd had to account to people who'd held my life in their hands, and I'd hated it. I'd had no power, and they'd had it all, and they'd busted my balls, the whole time telling me it was for my own good and that I'd thank them one day. The day I'd thank them would be the day dykes stopped using vibrators.

Old, unhappy, far-off things, Wordsworth called the past.

Wrong, Willie. Old and unhappy, yes. But far off? I don't think so.

I watched McGuigan put down the nail file, remove his bifocals, and massage his eyes with a thumb and forefinger. He spoke with a huge hand covering most of his face.

"Short and sweet," he said. "Back off, or I'll personally see to it you're suspended without pay, pending a complete investigation of your behavior in the Lynda Schiafino case. Is that understood?"

I said it was.

McGuigan placed his bifocals beside Hayden's phone, put his elbows on the desk, and continued massaging his eyes.

"I take it I am getting through to you."

I said he was.

"Then we've nothing more to talk about."

Hayden smirked like he'd never smirked before.

"Before you leave," McGuigan said, "I want you to take something with you, that something being a quick lesson in racial politics. The mayor has the black vote in his hip pocket. In that same pocket is the Hispanic vote, along with Asian votes, the gay vote, and what's left of the guilty white liberal vote, a commodity best described as fast shrinking and soon to become extinct. You might see all of this as impressive numbers. You'd be wrong. If Mayor Tucker wants to keep his buns in place for another four years, he needs a crossover vote. White votes, in other words. More than he has at the moment. You being a police officer, I'm sure you know the conservative white vote and black crime are not entirely unrelated. Black crime is very much on the mind of your average Caucasian. It could well be his worst nightmare. Unfortunately for Mayor Tucker, it happens to be his worst nightmare as well."

McGuigan said Tucker's success hinged on how he approached black crime. Criticize it, and he'd lose black support. On the other hand, keep quiet about it, and there'd be no white votes, and without the white votes Tucker was history. A solution to the problem seemed out of the question. That is, until Tucker got lucky. This luck could best be described in two words: Maurice Robichaux.

McGuigan said out of this luck had come what City Hall

insiders were calling TAP, as in tapping into the white vote, or more realistically, Tucker's African Plan. The brains behind TAP was none other than First Deputy Mayor Ray Footman, who according to McGuigan didn't let being a big-time liberal and sensitive, caring soul get in the way of wanting power. Footman, in fact, was a power freak. Couldn't get enough. He'd hitched his wagon to Tucker's star in order to get power and didn't want to lose it now. He was no friend to cops, but he was certainly a friend to Tucker, who couldn't get through a day without talking to him a dozen times. As far as the election was concerned, it was simple. Without Footman, Tucker didn't have a prayer of getting reelected.

TAP, according to Footman, went like this: go for the Jews. Twenty percent of the Jewish vote, and Tucker just might have his second term.

All he had to do was come down hard on Maurice Robichaux. Smart move, McGuigan said. Tucker had to condemn black crime if he wanted to make his bones with the Jews. At the same time he couldn't afford to lose the black vote. To pull this off, Tucker needed a soft black target. Enter Maurice Robichaux, cop killer, wacko, drug addict, possessor of a criminal record longer than a drum solo, and best of all, he was black. McGuigan said Tucker wouldn't win over all the Jews and didn't expect to. But he'd win over enough to increase his chances of being reelected.

The outcome of the election hung on TAP. That's why the Schiafino murder case had to stay closed and the killer had to stay black.

It's politics, McGuigan said, and politics wasn't about right or wrong. It was about being able to count votes. The mayor didn't want murder charges dropped against Maurice Robichaux. Totally unacceptable, McGuigan said. Totally unfuckingacceptable.

"You're a bubble who thinks he can take on the ocean," McGuigan said. "Stay away from the Lynda Schiafino case, or you're finished as a cop. That's all, detective."

I left without saying nighty-night. My hands were clammy, and I was slightly out of breath.

I thought about my choices. I could back off as ordered

or act like my answering machine was broken and I'd never gotten the message. Whatever decision I made would cost me. And in the past few minutes the price of everything had gone up.

In my office I sat on the windowsill, smoking and staring at low white clouds being pushed by strong winds across a leaden sky. I'd made Tucker's shit list. If this didn't put my career on hold, nothing would. The next time our beloved mayor went to church, let him light a candle in my memory. *Thank you, Lord, for sending a black politician like myself the kind of enemy he needs in an election year, specifically a big-assed white cop who doesn't want me to win a second term, who's been brought up on brutality charges against colored folks, and who stole money from a drug dealer. Thank you, Lord. Thank you, thank you.*

Offhand I'd say it was time to get out of Dodge. Leave Lynda's murder alone if I wanted to keep my badge.

I put a cigarette in my mouth and rolled it between my teeth without firing up and asked myself again why had McGuigan come here. True, he wanted my head on a pole. But why come here when he could just as easily have cut off my head at police headquarters.

There was a knock on my office door.

I continued staring out the window, figuring it was that prick Hayden come to kick me when I was down. He wasn't content just to gloat over the phone. Not him. He'd dropped by to celebrate his victory in person. The thought of him standing outside smacking his lips was enough to make me want to put a couple of rounds through the door. Then again the caller could be McGuigan come to twist the knife.

I walked to the door.

Well, well. My visitor was the Latino detective who drove for McGuigan. He was slim, twentyish, with small ears, no neck, and a scarred eyebrow that looked like a souvenir of a knife fight. There was a coldness in his handsome face that said he didn't need anybody and absolutely couldn't be trusted. The ideal driver for McGuigan.

"Detective Meagher?" he said. "I'm Detective Luis Bonilla. I was wondering if you could direct me to the men's room."

I thought, What kind of shit is this? Bonilla had just walked past dozens of cops, secretaries, and clerks. Any one of them could have pointed him toward the crapper. So why come to me? Weird.

I thought about slamming the door in his face but decided I didn't need more trouble with McGuigan. So I told Bonilla to make a right and keep going. The john was at the end of the hall.

He thanked me, then offered his hand. I thought, Aren't we being neighborly. As we shook, he pressed a small piece of paper into my hand. Ice Man Bonilla had passed me a note. He watched to see my reaction, eyeing me the way a wolf looks at a sheep.

I put the note in my pants pocket, and Bonilla took off for the john. I watched him for a few seconds, then closed the door. The phone rang. I ignored it and read the note.

Leave the office now. Go downstairs, head east on 57th Street. Keep walking. We'll make contact if you don't have a tail. Ten minutes and no contact means you're being followed. Meeting canceled. Robichaux didn't kill Detective Schiafino.

There was no signature. No name. Not even an initial. No identification was necessary. Considering what the note said, I'd have thought twice about signing it myself. You couldn't put your name on something like that and look forward to an assured future.

Not if you had any sense of survival and one day hoped to become police commissioner.

XXIII
My New Best Friend

I sat with McGuigan in the backseat of his black Mercedes. We were stuck in traffic on East Fifty-seventh Street, in front of a new bronze-and-glass high-rise. The building had a lobby with a pink marble floor and a miniature waterfall. You had to go through the lobby to reach a small bar run by Jerry Costello, a little Mick with big ears and an overbite, and a fat parrot he kept near the cash register. If Costello was in a good mood, you could say to him, "I want a Stoli with a twist," and he'd squint, show his buck teeth, pretend he was Japanese, and say, "OK. Once upon a time . . ." If Costello was in a bad mood, he'd say nothing.

Later he'd feel guilty and buy you a drink. The last time I'd told the joke, he'd said nothing. He owed me a drink, and I wanted it now.

"Did you know Robichaux's gay?" McGuigan said.

"Fags are innocent, right? Tell you what. I'll just get out at the next corner."

McGuigan avoided looking at me and instead stared through a tinted-glass window at a construction crew hard at work digging up a nearby crosswalk. When he spoke, his soft voice was almost hypnotic, like one of those New Age tapes that tell you to love and create and brighten the corner where you are.

He said, "If Robichaux's gay, then he couldn't have raped Lynda Schiafino, as reported in the press."

"Lynda's murder doesn't concern me anymore, remember?"

"You're not soft in the head, Meagher, so don't act like it. I didn't have to come uptown to do damage. One phone call, and your ass would've been hung out to dry. Even as we speak, your dick's dangling over the fence, and somebody else is holding the knife."

He was arrogant but with a twist. He did it casually, making him appear to be setting a standard of behavior we should all look up to.

"You're right," I said. "I'm not a retard. That's why I know you want something from me. Otherwise I wouldn't be here. You're a man with objectives, and I'm sure we'll get around to discussing them sooner or later."

He finally decided to look at me. He pulled his top lip back from his teeth in what was meant to be a smile. Instead he came across like a junkyard dog greeting a midnight caller.

"Smoke and mirrors," he said. "I think Hayden bought it. By the look on your face back there, so did you. Hayden will spread the word you've been chastised. That should leave you free to maneuver a bit."

Hell, I saw it coming. McGuigan was a smart bomb homing in on its target, which happened to be me. He was one of those people who found out what you wanted most in this world, then used it against you. He knew about me and Lynda, and as sure as Halloween brings candy apples, he had a strategy to exploit that knowledge to his advantage.

We stared at each other without speaking. The traffic started to move, and the car crept up to the corner, where it hung a right on Second Avenue, then headed downtown. McGuigan's eyes grew hooded, which I assumed meant he'd seen as much of my face as he could stand. So he eyed his nails, which were bright and flawless and maybe a bit too long for a deputy commissioner, not that anyone was going to tell him.

"You're back on the Schiafino case," he said. "Strictly unofficial. On your own time and with no help from the department. And you'll report directly to me."

Stunned wasn't the word. I was stupefied. I couldn't have been more surprised if McGuigan had told me his most secret dream had been to attend a Barbie-doll wedding. He was telling me to break the rules, to put my career on the line for him, and to expect no assistance or backup. The man had balls. Either that or he was one Hail Mary short of a rosary.

I thought about working for McGuigan, and the first words that came to mind in this connection were *sick* and *wrong*. His ambition was out of control, and he couldn't be trusted. Loyalty wasn't one of his strong points. This was a man who when told an aide was trying to get his wife into a drug-treatment program promptly dropped him from his staff.

"Not interested," I said. "This one's a stacked deck from the get-go, and it's all in your favor. I can't see myself coming out alive, let alone coming out ahead. Thanks, but no thanks. I'm going to heed your warning and stick to what's already on my plate."

McGuigan pressed a button in the armrest to his left, and a plastic shield slid from behind the driver's seat, cutting us off from Bonilla.

"How's ten years in prison sound?" McGuigan said.

"If I didn't know better, I'd swear you were threatening me."

"Let's talk about Lynda Schiafino's letter," McGuigan said. "The one Carlyle Taylor wrote about today."

My hands went clammy again. I felt light-headed, as though I'd been lying down and gotten up too quickly.

"A lot of people would like to get their hands on that letter," McGuigan said. "Schiafino, Carlyle Taylor—but that you already know. What you don't know is there's another player."

"You?"

"Try Ray Footman."

I wasn't surprised. Not after what McGuigan had told me back in Hayden's office. I read it this way: Footman and Tucker didn't want me to clear Robichaux. Not when it would cost Tucker the election. Footman had to take me out of the equation. The best way to do that was with Lynda's letter.

According to McGuigan, Footman wanted the letter badly enough to bring in a private investigator to find it. He'd also reached out to certain people in the NYPD, offering big bucks to anyone who turned the letter over to him. The liberal and very ambitious Mr. Footman viewed me as the cop from hell, if not the turd in the punch bowl.

He was telling anyone who would listen that given my record of civil rights abuses, I was long overdue for a prison term. McGuigan saw me doing a nickel to a dime. Five to ten surrounded by cons with razor blades wrapped in tissue paper and coated with Vaseline, the blade jammed up their asses so the guards couldn't find it, but the cons could find it fast enough to slit the throat of any cop dumb enough to go to prison.

"I would think you'd want to avoid that," McGuigan said. "Which is why you should consider accepting my help."

"What kind of help?"

"Say the letter does turn up. Since the department will have to discipline you, I'll be one of the first to see it."

"This is supposed to leave me happy and content?"

"The letter could disappear or be misplaced. Maybe even rewritten so as to make you appear if not less guilty, then less blamable. Hop on board, Meagher. There's something in it for you."

"It's called getting butt-fucked."

Puckering his thin lips, McGuigan frowned at the car ceiling and tugged at an earlobe. He was trying to control himself, which wasn't easy. I'd just gotten in his face, something cops didn't do.

I didn't care. The way I saw it, he was trying to dick me in his own quiet way. Which is why I didn't feel the need to be ingratiating.

"A word to the wise," McGuigan said. "Ignorance is curable, but stupidity is a lifelong affliction. Don't be stupid."

"According to you, Robichaux didn't kill Lynda. Want to tell me who did?"

"And have you go ballistic? Pass. Your report card is mixed. You're a good cop, you get things accomplished. You deliver the goods, and you make the people you work for look good. That, and not your winning personality, is what's kept you on the force. But let's face it. You can be autonomous on occasion. So no names. Not until I'm sure you're a team player."

"In other words, I get nothing until you're sure you can control me."

"We're talking conspiracy, one reaching all the way to City Hall. Lynda Schiafino's murder is part of it."

I said I knew Lynda, and she wasn't involved in any conspiracy.

"Her husband is," McGuigan said. "So's his sleazy lawyer. She died because she happened to be in the wrong place at the wrong time."

"You mean being at the airport got her killed. Well, let's just say I have my own theory about that. Meanwhile I know about Schiafino and Elder and the Exchange Students. I assume that's what you mean by conspiracy. Lynda tried to tell me about this crew, but I wouldn't listen. Speaking frankly, how do I know you're not a player? The thought has crossed my mind."

"If I were," McGuigan said, "we wouldn't be having this conversation."

"We would if you were trying to set me up. Suppose, just suppose, you don't really want to know about Lynda's murder. Suppose you're jerking me around."

"Why would I do that?"

"To find out what I know about the Exchange Students. To set me up to get killed."

"You could die," he said. "But it won't be me who pulls the trigger."

Reaching inside his overcoat, McGuigan brought out a white envelope and placed it in my lap.

"Preliminary medical report on the Schiafino killing," he said. "It's one of two copies, so treat it like gold. The public won't get to see it. The Exchange Students will make sure of that. The public's getting a second report, one that's been doctored."

McGuigan said the report aimed at the public was twisted shit from the beginning. A king-size con job from the Exchange Students, who had enough clout to get to the medical examiner's office as well as the DA's office. They were pulling out all the stops, McGuigan said, because Robichaux absolutely, positively had to go down for Lynda's murder.

I watched him massage his mutilated thumb and stare out

the car window at a bicycle messenger, a young male black in goggles and oversize earphones peddling furiously to keep up with the Mercedes. Bonilla also saw the spook. He floored the Merc and the messenger was left behind. I caught Bonilla's eyes in the rearview mirror. He was smiling.

McGuigan said, "Back in December, I went to Puerto Rico with Lacovara. Went there to meet the pope."

I said I knew about their trip. The part I liked best was when he and the others had to give Munro back his money.

McGuigan eyed me from a corner of his eye and snorted. When the car stopped for a red light, he looked forward.

"Seems the dynamics of our relationship have changed," he said.

"I get that way when I feel I have nothing to lose."

"I'll try to remember that. Anyway, down in Puerto Rico, I saw Munro with Detective Robert Schiafino. I wasn't meant to see them together. When I asked Munro about Schiafino, he swore Schiafino wasn't in Puerto Rico. He was lying, but I didn't push him."

McGuigan said it was just as well he hadn't pushed. Otherwise he'd never have learned about the Exchange Students. The day McGuigan saw Schiafino was the day one of Munro's rich Puerto Rican friends, a man named Santos Colón, came to see him. Colón owned most of the parking lots in Puerto Rico and was terrified. A local gang was trying to extort money from him. Fifty grand a month or they would start blowing up the cars in his lots. If Colón didn't get the message after the third car, the gang was going to blow up a fourth car, one with Colón's five-year-old daughter in the trunk.

Suspecting a San Juan police captain of leading the extortion crew, Colón stayed away from local cops. Instead he reached out for his amigo Jonathan Munro, who suggested that Schiafino be hired to kill the gang, starting with the police captain. Colón turned him down, then turned to McGuigan, who listened to Colón's story and told him to speak to nobody. Let McGuigan handle everything.

"What happened after that?" I said.

"Two days later Colón died."

"Schiafino."

"Don't think so. He died of natural causes. Doctors feel it was a brain hemorrhage, but no one's sure. Why did you say Schiafino?"

"He's the cautious type. He didn't like the idea of Colón knowing he was a hired gun, so he popped him. And he got away with it. Regardless of what you think, Colón was murdered."

"I know everything there is to know about Schiafino," McGuigan said. "He uses fire as a recreational toy, and the nurse who was his first wife ended up with a plastic hip after he deliberately ran her over with a motorcycle. He used to be a state trooper, reads books on psychology, and collects prints of houses designed by Frank Lloyd Wright. He was a junior-college wrestling champion, plays bass guitar, and plans to live on a houseboat in California in the not too distant future. I also know he had nothing to do with Santos Colón's death."

I said, "Here's what I know. If you think you can control Schiafino, you're wrong. He'll outsmart you every time. How the hell do you think he got his reputation?"

"How do you think I got mine?"

"He's still got the edge. He's unpredictable. Bound to do the unexpected. The only thing you can count on is getting the short end of the stick when you do business with him. Meanwhile there's this so-called conspiracy of yours. The one you say reaches to City Hall. Why haven't you told the commissioner? That's your job, isn't it?"

"My job is to survive," McGuigan said. "We have a black mayor, a black police commissioner. Trust me when I tell you neither one's a rocket scientist. Liberals, however, would have you believe these two are somehow superior to us greedy, conniving whites."

He threw up both hands. "I know Tucker and Dowd, and nobody's better at covering their asses than these two. Neither knows the meaning of the word *morality*. Matter of fact, they don't know the meaning of a lot of words. Mention conspiracy to them, and they'll look the other way. Or do whatever it takes to cover things up."

McGuigan was right. I should have known better. Tucker and Dowd had enough power to make every white man in the city afraid of them. I couldn't see them giving that up just to be on the side of the angels, which didn't pay nearly as much.

"This thing is about power," McGuigan said. "And it's bigger than the Exchange Students. Schiafino's cops are only a means to an end, nothing more."

I asked if he knew the rabbi's identity. If so, what was the man's game. McGuigan said, All in good time. I'd get an answer when he felt he could trust me. As of now we hadn't reached that point.

"Then let's talk about something else," I said. "You want Dowd's job. But these days it's not politically correct to yank the rug from under a black man. So you have to find someone to take him down for you."

"You, for instance."

"Fear Meagher, fall guy and all-around chump. Has a ring to it. I turn up evidence showing the department botched the Lynda Schiafino investigation. I give said evidence to you. Next thing I know, Dowd's out and you're in. Naturally, if anything goes wrong, you've never heard of me."

McGuigan smiled. He was about to enter a new period of happiness, and all because of me.

"Me using you," he said. "Now there's a concept."

He did his best not to laugh in my face.

"You loved Lynda Schiafino," he said. "And being human, you can't stand the guilt that comes with her death. So I'll go on record as saying you'll work for me. You do have some sense of right and wrong, Meagher. I don't think you can stand the idea of hanging by your fingernails over the private snake pit that's your conscience. Therefore, we're going to be business partners after a fashion. Regarding my objectives, don't worry about them. All you need to know is I'm one of two people who can help you do the right thing."

I said, Who's the second.

"First things first," McGuigan said.

He tapped the white envelope in my lap.

"Read this," he said. "Then tell me if you think Robichaux's the killer."

"They found him beside Lynda's corpse," I said. "He had

the murder weapon in his hand, and he's black. What's the problem?"

"Let's talk about blood," McGuigan said.

Something must have shown on my face because McGuigan eyed me for a few seconds, then pointed to the envelope again.

"Postmortem lividity," he said. "It's in that report but won't appear anywhere else. When the victim's lying prone, blood settles in the body within two to four hours."

"Cut to the chase."

McGuigan said, "When Lynda's body was discovered, she was lying face down. The remaining blood in her body should have been in her face and chest. It wasn't. Postmortem lividity revealed her blood to have settled on her back. She was killed somewhere else, then her body was brought to the airport."

"Well, at least we agree on one thing," I said.

"Even if you wanted to walk away, Lynda Schiafino's husband won't let you. I heard about that scene between you two at the cemetery."

"I'm having problems with him."

"I might be able to help you there," McGuigan said.

"Meanwhile nothing you said gets Robichaux off the hook. He could have killed Lynda, then moved the corpse."

"If this was *Jeopardy!* you'd never make a dime. For starters, Robichaux's not big enough to have carried Lynda Schiafino anywhere. He'd need help. An accomplice, a vehicle, something. We've found no signs of any assistance. The man's a loner."

McGuigan used his perfect nails to gently rub his facial scars.

"Question," he said. "What's your overall opinion of the investigation so far?"

"It sucks," I said. "In fact it looks like somebody's throwing shit in the game."

"They are," McGuigan said. "Evidence is being mishandled, the crime scene's been fucked over, and there's a shit storm of paperwork flying around designed to hide the truth. That's why you have to work alone. Run your investigation your way. You turn up anything, you hand it over to me and to me only."

"A minute ago I mentioned the rabbi," I said. "You didn't seem surprised or upset."

"You think I'm the rabbi?"

"I know a mob guy out on Staten Island," I said. "Tall, skinny ginzo who's older than water. Very smart. Operates like you do."

"And exactly how is that?"

"Keeps his enemies close so he can watch their every move. Makes them capos, underbosses, drivers. Lets them run certain clubs, whorehouses, even parts of his Atlantic City operation. They think he doesn't know what they're thinking. They couldn't be more wrong. He knows everything because they're not out of his sight."

McGuigan gave me his junkyard-dog smile. "And that's what I'm doing?"

"Let's just say you're capable of it."

"Let's talk about the other person who can help you investigate Lynda Schiafino's murder."

"What's his name?"

"Carlyle Taylor." He giggled.

"You can hold a gun to my head," I said, "but I'm never working with that woman."

"Never say never."

"She's gone from accusing me of police brutality to tagging me as a suspect in Lynda's murder. Know what I'd like to do? I'd like to introduce her to Ike Turner. That ought to keep her busy."

"She says Robichaux's innocent. I think she knows something. Find out what it is."

"Who cares what Carlyle Taylor thinks? Besides, nobody with a single brain cell believes Robichaux is innocent."

"She can help you clear the Ecuadoran murders."

McGuigan was playing me like a violin. Just when I was ready to write him off, he'd found a way to get my attention. Mr. Slick.

"What's her connection with Tonino's crew?" I said.

"She's seeing Elder again," McGuigan said.

I must have looked surprised, because McGuigan nodded.

"Figure on some pillow talk between Elder and Miss Taylor," he said. "All you have to do is get her to repeat the conversation to you."

"Nothing to it," I said. "I'll tell her I'm Dr. Ruth, and she'll spill her guts."

"Carlyle Taylor got her information on Lynda Schiafino's letter from Elder. He got it from Schiafino. You need any more reason to suck up to the lady?"

I didn't. And we both knew it.

"Anything else?" I said.

"Robichaux's family," McGuigan said. "They're not talking to cops. They're not talking to whitey, period. I wouldn't care except they're saying they have evidence proving Robichaux's innocence. I'd like to know what it is. They've probably told Carlyle Taylor. Get her to tell you."

I said I was in. But the minute I caught McGuigan fucking me over, I was bailing. Gone.

"Feel free," McGuigan said. "You know this shit with City Hall and the Exchange Students? Reminds me of the thirties. Back when whites ran the old Cotton Club in Harlem. Goes to show you things never change."

"Want to explain that?" I said.

"Check it out for yourself. I can't do all your thinking for you."

I was trying to bring down the rabbi, and for all I knew, here he was giving me advice on becoming an independent thinker. Weird.

So far McGuigan had been the one handing out all the surprises. Now it was my turn.

"Lisa Watts," I said. "Where've you got her stashed?"

McGuigan's jaw tightened. A vein popped out just under his jaw. His two facial scars turned bright red.

I said, "When I mentioned the Exchange Students and the rabbi, you didn't bat an eye. Didn't ask who they were or where I'd gotten my information. You even knew Schiafino and Elder were down with this crew. I got my information from Lynda, as did Lisa Watts. You either got yours from Lisa, or you're the rabbi. Which is it?"

"Lisa Watts doesn't concern you," McGuigan said. "Think Carlyle Taylor. And Detective Robert Schiafino. If that letter comes in before you bring me anything, you're gone. I won't be able to help you."

The plastic shield slid down.

"Luis," McGuigan said. "Next corner. Detective Meagher is leaving."

Minutes later I sat at the counter of a grubby little pizza joint on Second Avenue and Thirty-third Street, eating pork braciola with a calzone on the side and thinking McGuigan was either the rabbi or a supremely ambitious cop out to climb the greasy pole of success. In any case he'd been fun to watch. You don't often get the chance to see a prime mover and world-class puppet master up close while he's working his show.

XXIV
A Hatred Intense and Everlasting

When I returned to the office that afternoon, a message said Hayden wanted to see me. I found him with both feet on his desk, hands behind his head, and a half smile on his boyish face.

Ordinarily, he was a cagey little bastard, tight-lipped and self-contained and not one to let you know what he was thinking. But at the moment he made no attempt to hide his joy at having watched McGuigan climb up my ass. As far as he was concerned, I'd had it coming, and he was well satisfied.

"Where were you just now?" he said. "Tried you a couple of times. Got no answer."

He was congenial, a gracious winner talking to a loser.

"A late lunch," I said.

Hayden said, "Next time keep a bottle in the desk drawer. Saves having to eat out."

He shook his small head in disgust, having assumed

McGuigan had sent me racing from the building in search of something to dull the pain. Hayden's twisted smile suggested that I should have gone out and hung myself, thereby making the world a better place.

The truth was I hadn't touched a drop all day. Not that anything I could've said would have convinced Hayden. He was a cynical little putz, cynicism being his shield against changing times and real or imagined competitors. He was, as H. L. Mencken might have said, the kind of man who'd smell flowers, then look around for a coffin.

I'd stayed away from alcohol because of McGuigan. I wanted to know where we stood, so I decided to think about our little chat, to kick it around in my head, and for that I wanted to be sober. At lunch I'd stuck to decaf and thought about what McGuigan and I'd talked about, at the same time wondering what I stood to gain by getting involved with him and, more important, what I stood to lose.

When it came to playing low down and dirty, McGuigan was an absolute genius if not an out-and-out virtuoso. Underestimate him, and I'd be making a mistake, and since mistakes tend to multiply, I'd soon have a heavy load to haul. Had he meant what he said? Had he said what he meant? Who the hell knew.

He had his eyes on the prize, that much I knew, and he wasn't about to allow questions of moral behavior to slow him down. His plan to dump the police commissioner was something even Machiavelli wouldn't have dreamed of, let alone tried to pull off. But here was McGuigan, steady-pushing his scheme to bring down Commissioner Dowd for obstructing a murder investigation, a cop's murder no less. Once the throne was empty, McGuigan intended to plunk himself down and live happily ever after.

As schemes go, this one should have carried a surgeon general's warning. It was health threatening, not to mention risky, dicey, and subject to chance. Worst of all, I was in it up to my hairline, the obedient Igor to McGuigan's mad scientist. By my third decaf I'd decided that my best chance to survive was to spend as little time as possible doing McGuigan's dirty work. I told myself two days, no more.

Two days of looking into Lynda's murder and after that, catch you later, Ditto Head.

But that was before I'd read the medical examiner's report he'd given me.

"These Ecuadoran hits," Hayden said. "You mentioned something about having a line on the shooter."

Hayden was smirking, still under the impression that my run-in with McGuigan had pushed me into some serious soul-searching. The way he saw it, I'd been redeemed. I was no longer flying high but walking orderly. I'd seen the light, and Jack the Ripper couldn't be happier.

Fear Meagher. An awakened soul.

Not exactly.

I thought, Jack, baby, hell on earth has arrived, and then I told him he wasn't going to like what I had to say. I began by describing yesterday's trip to the Bronx and my meeting with the family and friends of Lourdes Balera. In my story Gavilan and his mother became anonymous callers. The Exchange Students could be all over the department. Until I knew who and where they were or until I'd nailed the rabbi, I didn't want Hayden mentioning names.

I also felt sorry for Gavilan. He was as cut off from his own childhood as I'd been from mine. He had no protection from cops who were hit men or from king-shit know-it-all prosecutors who cared nothing about justice and only wanted to see their names in the paper.

Gavilan and I weren't close, and we probably never would be. What little I knew about this kid indicated he was no sweetener of human life by any means. I could knock myself out for him, and he still wouldn't be grateful. In his world you didn't look for favors or rely on them. If he'd ever had the slightest inclination to be thankful, experience had knocked it out of him. Still, I wanted to do what I could, to give him the help I'd never had until Dion.

They say the road to hell is paved with good intentions and that all men mean well. I meant well by Gavilan and his mother, but in the long run my help wasn't going to amount to much. Withholding their names from Hayden was nothing more than temporary protection, a short-term fix at best. Sooner or later I'd have to turn in a written report, one with the names of everyone involved in my investigation. The report would be introduced as trial evidence, and from then on Damaris Bauza and Gavilan would be in the crosshairs.

I said to Hayden, "My chief suspect in the Lourdes Balera–Tonino Cuevas murders is a cop."

His feet slid from his desk, and he sat up in his chair, suddenly whiter than Casper the Friendly Ghost. He'd just been punched between the eyes and now had the air of a man caught in a bad joke, one that threatened to leave him tied naked to a traffic light in Times Square. There was a storm brewing, and we both knew it.

"This cop didn't pull the trigger," I said. "But he's still dirty. He used Lourdes to locate Tonino, then arranged for them both to be hit. Would you believe he's Lourdes's godfather?"

"He's what?"

"That's why she had to go. She lives, she ties our boy to Tonino's murder. That's the same as tying him to eight murders, because he and his cop friends are smoking the Ecuadorans."

Hayden looked queasy. He picked at a bump on his nose and couldn't stop blinking.

He said, "You're telling me there's more than one cop involved?"

"Jonathan Munro's paying them. He wants to send a message."

"What kind of message?"

"Stay away from my trucks. The hijackings have stopped, so I'd say the message is getting across. Munro's complaints about police inefficiency are bullshit. It's all an act."

Hayden pressed a clenched fist against his temple. He took a deep breath and exhaled for a long time. Finally, he slammed both palms down on his desktop and stared at me with bug-eyed disgust.

"The hell have you come up with *this* time?" he said.

"Cops moonlighting as contract killers," I said. "They work out of New York and Washington and call themselves the Exchange Students."

"The what?"

I talked and Hayden listened with eyes closed, and what I saw was a man whose worst fears had finally come to him. Jack the Ripper wasn't scared; he was terrified. I was telling him he'd have to investigate cops, the last thing he wanted to hear.

A cop who investigates other cops is on the lowest rung of the food chain, on a par with lawyers and child molesters. He's a cheese-eater, a rat of the lowest order and a threat to the freedom, career, and peace of mind of his fellow officers. No cop on the force is more of an outcast. He can expect to have his locker smeared with dog shit, his tires slashed, and threatening phone calls made to his family, proving there is nothing uglier than a frightened cop.

I finished telling Hayden about the Exchange Students, then watched him pinch his nose and frown at the chandelier, a man in an intense state of indecision. I'd put the fear of God in him, for sure. In effect, he'd been asked to step in front of a speeding car. Needless to say, he was in no hurry to comply.

I'd given him two choices: He could kill my investigation and protect the department, or he could allow me to proceed, thereby throwing the department into a panic. The second choice meant going out on a limb, something one didn't associate with Jack Hayden.

I could understand his reluctance to commit himself. The NYPD had over twenty-six thousand cops, any one of whom could be an Exchange Student. These guys could be anybody, including people you worked with or even members of your own family. They had power, they had the legal right to carry a gun, and they had the rabbi. They also had a few borderline psychotics on their roster.

"Did I hear right?" Hayden said. "You did say cops here and in Washington are killing people?"

"And getting away with it."

"Fucking unreal. You have any idea what happens when the press gets wind of this? Someone like Carlyle Taylor, for instance."

There it was. My window of opportunity. My chance to bring Hayden over to the side of the angels.

"This thing crosses state lines," I said. "So sooner or later the Justice Department and the FBI will cut themselves in. That's the feds for you. Biggest glory seekers alive. They smell a case like this, with killer cops and rich people, and right away it becomes theirs. They get written up in *Time* magazine, and we get cornholed. Unless we're so far ahead they can't do it without us."

Hayden's little face beamed. I had just answered the unspoken but ever-present question, to wit, what's in it for me.

I watched him remove a purple crayon from a coffee mug, reach for a memo pad, and begin sketching a flower with very pointed petals. His eyes widened, and as usual whenever he had a crayon in his hand, he spoke without looking at me.

"This cop who had his goddaughter killed. What's his name?"

"He's an old friend of yours," I said. "Detective Jesus Bauza."

Hayden stopped doodling and squeezed the crayon, breaking it. Then he tore the doodle from the memo pad and crumpled it in his hand.

Hayden was a sneaky fighter, a guy who never came at you from the front and whose preferred method of attack was backstabbing. He checked the odds and always left himself an escape route. He picked his enemies carefully, making sure he knew who could hurt and who could help. But when it came to Bauza, all rules went out the window. Hayden hated Bauza, a hatred best described as intense and everlasting.

Lord Byron called hatred the longest pleasure and a delightful passion, something to make us all happy for the rest of our days. If so, Hayden stood to be happy far into the future, and he owed it all to Jesus.

XXV
What's in It for Me?

Five years ago Hayden and Bauza had been with the Brooklyn Organized Crime Bureau, assigned to work an informant named Ida Dilascio, a twenty-four-year-old redheaded clerk in the Brooklyn DA's office. She'd been charged with stealing intelligence files, then passing them on to Alfonse "Allie Boy" Carneglia, the hulking, twenty-six-year-old car thief who was her main squeeze.

Allie Boy had given the files to Little Augie LaTempa, a fifty-year-old pint-size dago who was a capo in the Drucci crime family. Little Augie was also a sociopath, a headcase with a fondness for Puccini and for stuffing his enemies into a car trunk, then running the car through a crusher, reducing it to a metal chunk before melting it down in a blast furnace.

Ida Dilascio had agreed to wear a wire and testify against Little Augie. In return the DA would drop all charges and relocate her.

What happened next was unanticipated and in its own way as unexpected as old age. It began with Hayden's pregnant wife suddenly going into labor and him rushing her to a Queens hospital, leaving Bauza and Ida in Ida's apartment. It ended with Hayden's wife giving birth to their third daughter and Ida being found alone in her locked bedroom, dead of a heroin overdose, the hypodermic syringe still in her arm.

Having discovered no signs of foul play, the coroner ruled her death to be self-inflicted. Her bedroom had been locked from the inside. The lock hadn't been tampered with, and she was a known drug abuser. Case closed.

The DA disagreed. He tried to pin Ida's death on Hayden and Bauza, claiming they hadn't protected his chief witness, thereby depriving him of sending Little Augie away, something the DA had wanted to do for years. Hayden and Bauza were hit with manslaughter charges, which went nowhere. Next came charges of witness tampering and dereliction of duty. Again nothing happened.

Enter the NYPD, promising punishment just short of the pains of hell. What it handed out was far less agonizing. Hayden and Bauza received transfers and thirty days' suspension without pay. A letter of reprimand was added to each man's file. As punishments go, this one fell somewhere between a mild case of the runs and being forced to refold a road map.

The exact cause of Ida's death turned out to be a hot shot, a combination of pure China White and enough strychnine to wipe out a college marching band. It would appear that Ida had been just one more doper who'd gotten what she wanted out of life and died from it. But word on the street had Bauza giving her the bad dope on behalf of Little Augie, who detested informants. Bauza made out like a champ, supposedly getting $250,000 for silencing Ida.

Little Augie blamed Allie Boy for the Ida situation and its high-priced solution. Rumor had him coming down hard on Allie Boy, who at the end of their last meeting was stuffed into the trunk of a Chevy Nova and driven screaming to a junkyard in Red Hook. Minutes later Little Augie pissed on the metal chunk that had once been the Chevy, then ordered it taken to New Jersey for a meltdown.

"When Bauza capped Ida," Hayden said, "he put my career on hold. Not a day goes by I don't want to pull his spinal cord through his pink asshole."

"Do it soon, because Bauza's going down," I said. "He's broadcasting. Spending two, three times what he makes as a cop. The man's dirty."

Hayden sat back in his chair and rolled the crayon between his palms.

"The usual shit," he said.

I nodded. "Girlfriend, gambling, travel. He also owns Puerto Rico real estate and a new Jag. I've run him through a computer, and the man's got access to some serious money. More than he earns as a detective second grade, believe me."

I said Bauza's spending was bound to attract attention; he'd go to prison or get whacked. We had to squeeze him while we could.

Hayden agreed.

I said we should also lean on Jonathan Munro. Let him know that prison was no place for a nice Jewish boy. And there was Bauza's girlfriend. Plus the brother and cousin of the late Tonino Cuevas. Maybe they'd seen Bauza and Tonino together. That's why we had to reach the illegals before the Exchange Students did.

I said I had a statement from the manager of the Hotel Langham that he'd seen Bauza with Tonino and Lourdes. While the statement didn't tie Bauza to the murders, it proved he was lying when he said he hadn't found the kid.

Hayden said, "Show Bauza's photograph around Times Square. Let's find more people who'll put him in the area."

I agreed it was a good idea.

"This anonymous female caller," Hayden said. "The one who told you she'd been in a social club and heard Bauza and some cop talking about the Exchange Students and whacking a Washington stockbroker. Think she could be Bauza's wife?"

Talk about a trick question. If I said no, Hayden would be suspicious. If I said yes, I'd be bringing Gavilan and his mother into the picture. I decided to let Hayden play what-if to his heart's content.

"Anything's possible," I said. "Bauza's spending a fortune on his girlfriend, so he's definitely thinking with his dick. I can see his old lady wanting to get even."

Hayden said, "Your caller says she's in Bauza's apartment and spies a pile of cash on the bed. Near the cash are newspaper clippings about a couple of Washington murders. Sounds like the wife to me. I mean, who's got better access to the husband's bedroom than she does."

I nodded. What a time for Hayden to get smart.

"I'm not actually saying it was the wife," Hayden said. "Could be Bauza had been porking some bimbo. He drops her, she wants to get even. So she gives you a call. I say the wife could have done the same thing for the same reason."

The NYPD had its total fools. But Hayden wasn't among them.

"Something else," he said. "Watch out for Schiafino."

He grinned. He'd caught me napping. It must have been all over my face.

I willed myself to appear unruffled and unshaken. It wasn't easy.

"What's Schiafino got to do with this?" I said.

"Contrary to popular opinion, I don't spend all my time brown-nosing the brass. Schiafino and Bauza have been living in each other's pockets for years. Everyone knows these guys are tight. They were together two nights ago, when Schiafino's wife was murdered. Along with three or four cops. They had box seats at a Garden hockey game. Guess who the box belongs to?"

"Who?"

"Jonathan Munro. He was at the game with them."

Something else I hadn't known. So Munro figured in Schiafino's alibi. Now, that bothered me. Because as alibis go, this one was obvious. Too obvious. A big-time businessman and Bobby Schemes plus a handful of cops, and they're all on view in front of a sellout crowd at the Garden. Flawless. Absolutely flawless.

"If Bauza's down with the Exchange Students," Hayden said, "so's Schiafino, seeing as how he's got a hook in Bauza's nose. I hear they own points in a topless club on the East Side. Name's Shares. You might want to check that out."

I wasn't surprised that Hayden knew what Bauza was up to. When you hated someone the way Hayden hated Bauza, you entered into his mind. Just like Schiafino was doing with me.

In mentioning the Exchange Students, I'd deliberately left out Schiafino. I'd had no choice. Not if I wanted to protect Gavilan.

I also lacked any evidence against Bobby Schemes, the guy being a hell of a lot smarter than Haysoos. There was no paper trail, no one to put him at the murder scene. No one to see him drooling over newspaper clippings about the people he'd killed. Gavilan could testify he'd witnessed Schiafino and Bauza arguing over a contract killing. But you didn't need to be Einstein to know both cops would deny the incident ever took place. It would be their word against that of a kid who hated cops and looked like a sawed-off felon in drop-crotch jeans.

Hearing Schiafino's name also reminded me of the medical report on Lynda's murder, given to me by McGuigan. After reading it, I decided that evidence in this case was being withheld or tampered with. In addition, the crime scene had been contaminated, and the investigation was being deliberately bungled. Innocent or guilty, Robichaux was getting fucked.

I wasn't all that concerned about his rights or about him having access to due process. If he wasn't getting a fair shake, too bad. As far as I was concerned, he'd killed Lynda, and I wasn't about to lift a finger to get him off. But what did bother me was McGuigan's claim that Lynda's death led all the way to City Hall. I had to know how a roach like Robichaux and the Exchange Students could end up in the same conspiracy. In the meantime I decided to obey the signals that told me never to trust McGuigan.

District Attorney Lacovara had released a statement claiming Lynda had been overpowered by her killer. McGuigan's report told a different story. It noted defensive cuts on Lynda's hands and arms along with bits of human tissue under her fingernails. She'd fought back, taking on her killer the way she'd taken on an abusive husband and the department when it had contested her right to be one of us. I thought about the courage she'd needed to go through all of this shit and still have the ability to love, and the guilt I felt made it impossible for me to think straight.

Would the release of McGuigan's medical report change anything? Probably not. We may have been living in the nineties, but certain attitudes remained carved in stone, and one said that any black man accused of killing a white policewoman had better pray for a miracle because nothing else was going to save him.

Lynda's killer, the report said, had grabbed her by the

ankles, then yanked hard, dropping her headfirst on cement.
His grip had been strong enough to leave bruises on her
ankles. Like everyone else who'd made Robichaux for Lynda's murder, I hadn't looked too closely at specifics. Black
perp, white vic. Case closed.

But certain facts just wouldn't go away.

Such as Robichaux's being five feet four and 120 pounds,
a fag wasted on crack and cheap hooch. Lynda had been
bigger, stronger, a jogger who kept herself in good shape
and weighed in at five feet ten, 145 pounds. Either Robichaux was stronger than he looked, or he'd gotten lucky and
caught Lynda off guard.

The killer, McGuigan's report said, was right-handed. The
DA had him as left-handed. Just like Robichaux. Everyone
agreed the killer hadn't worn gloves. That's why there'd
been no problem with prints. They'd been found on the
murder weapon, an eight-dollar linoleum knife you could
buy in any hardware store. The prints belonged to Robichaux. But according to McGuigan's report, no prints had
been found on Lynda's boots.

Other facts mentioned only in McGuigan's report were
lividity and the lack of blood at the crime scene, which I'd
noticed when visiting the crime scene. And where were the
plans to run DNA tests on the tissue found under Lynda's
nails, tests that could send Robichaux away or cut him loose.

Guilty or innocent, one thing was sure: The department
had closed this case too fast.

Hayden said, "You ID any more cops in the Exchange
Students?"

"Two. Aldo Sinatra and Larry Aarons."

"Lethal Larry. The old back-shooter himself. I hear you
have a beef going with Aldo. Something to do with his
cousin Danny Baldazano."

I said Danny Baldazano and I had been partners until he
hired two spics to give me a Colombian necktie, which is to
say he wanted them to slice my throat, then pull my tongue
through the opening and down onto my chest. I'd killed one
hit man, wounded the other, and testified against Danny at
his trial on corruption charges. He was now doing a bit in

Atlanta, where he was having a hard time, a setback in his life which Aldo blamed on me.

Hayden said, "How'd you manage to connect Aldo and Lethal Larry to the Exchange Students?"

This time I told the truth with only slight alterations.

"Lynda's family is sitting *shivah* at her father's house," I said. "This morning I went there to pay my respects and ran into Aldo and Aarons. They told me to lay off Bauza and stop asking questions about the Exchange Students. Words were exchanged, after which we went our separate ways."

"Hurt your head?" Hayden said. "You keep feeling it, like you got hit or something."

I touched the back of my skull. Damn right it hurt. Fucking Aldo.

"Must have been some exchange of words you guys had," Hayden said. "In any case I'd like you to zero in on Cuevas's missing relatives."

"His younger brother and cousin."

"Doesn't matter if they didn't see Bauza with Tonino and Lourdes. We'll lie and say they did. Now get out of here while I do some thinking."

I left Hayden leaning back in his chair, eyes closed. He wasn't dozing. Not after this conversation. I figured he was back to shitting bricks, desperate to pull through this mess while doing the right thing. Like it or not, he was about to begin the journey of life in earnest. I left him alone to ponder whether or not he had a mission on this earth and, if so, what were his chances of surviving it.

When I returned to my office, I put in a call to Gavilan at home. He told me Bauza had spent the past couple of nights at his girlfriend's apartment and that his mother didn't want Bauza back. She'd thrown his shit into the hallway—clothes, shoes, books—then found herself a lawyer. It was his idea that she change the locks, which a locksmith was doing while Gavilan talked to me.

I asked if Bauza had received any calls, and Gavilan said Jonathan Munro had called twice. He'd been pissed off because he couldn't reach Schiafino, whose line was busy, probably with people calling about his dead wife. Munro wanted to hear from Schiafino or Bauza immediately. The problem was Harvey, Munro said. He was getting nervous, and someone had better straighten him out real fast. I asked if Gavilan knew Harvey, and he said no. But he knew Harvey worked at a bank. Bauza had telephoned him there a couple of times.

Another caller had wanted to speak to Bauza right away. A woman, Gavilan said. A reporter named Carlyle Taylor. She'd left numbers where she could be reached.

I told myself she wanted to ask questions about Lynda. Like Munro, she'd probably tried Schiafino, gotten a busy signal, and decided to reach out for some of his friends.

One of my other lines rang, and I told Gavilan I had another call. I said to be careful around Bauza and to give me a ring if there was any trouble.

The new caller was Lou Sobkavich, a blue-eyed fifty-year-old Polack who was the oldest homicide detective at Manhattan South. He rarely slept more than five hours a night, looked fifteen years younger than his age, and was nicknamed the Polish Prince. We'd met three years ago while investigating Yugoslav gunrunners operating out of Manhattan's West Side, a bunch of psychos who'd punished two gang-members-turned-informants by forcing one to castrate the other with his teeth.

Sobkavich had jurisdiction over the Cuevas-Balera homicides but had agreed to cooperate because of my interest in the hijackers. He had a slow intelligence, which I found irritating at times, and he tended to follow the same approach in every investigation. He also had a habit of saying nothing for long periods, making people around him nervous. Still, he managed to clear a good number of his cases, and that was the bottom line.

He spoke six languages, and since one was Spanish, Sobkavich had an abundance of Latino informants. A snitch of his had just spotted Tonino's brother and cousin on the Lower East Side, buying guns and letting it be known that *la policia* had them scared shitless. In other words, the Ecuadorans knew who was hunting them down:

It also meant they could connect Bauza to the Times Square killings. I didn't let on to Sobkavich that I was

pleased to hear from him. I wasn't opening myself up to
him or to any cop at the moment. Call it paranoia or forward
planning, but since I didn't know who to trust, I kept quiet
about the Exchange Students.

Sobkavich's bust was set to go in thirty minutes. He said
he'd allow me to show up with the understanding that I
watch and not participate. He was to have first crack at
interrogating the Ecuadorans. After that I'd get my shot.

I asked him for the address and said I was on my way.

XXVI
Go for the Gold

The Lower East Side was one of Manhattan's ugliest downtown neighborhoods. Over the years it had probably
changed less than any other part of the city. A hundred
years ago it was a slum for Jewish immigrants. Today it was
a slum for Puerto Ricans in decaying walk-ups, old Jews too
poor to move out, and black vagrants living in cardboard
boxes.

Marcos Cuevas and Paco Nieves were hiding out in Alphabet City, the area between Avenues A and D where
drug dealers operated openly and around the clock, stopping
only when they ran out of goodies to sell. Most buildings
were bombed-out shells, a good number being permanently
abandoned. On vacant lots vagrants lived in rickety shacks
and cardboard boxes and huddled around oil-drum fires to
keep warm, and you knew that for them and anyone else
down here, it was always winter and night.

I arrived on the set just before sundown, with the weather
still cold enough to leave me tight-assed. The Ecuadorans
were holed up in a six-story building, a dump standing alone
on an empty lot. There was no front door, lights, or glass
in the windows. A blackened fire escape hung precariously

from the rear, and one side was covered by a mural representing the black version of Mount Rushmore, the faces of dead white presidents having been replaced by those of Nelson Mandela, Malcolm X, Marcus Garvey, and Bob Marley. At the moment the street in front of the tenement was dealer free, police having cordoned off the area, preventing anyone from entering or leaving the block.

I checked in with Sobkavich. He was as icy as the weather and in no mood for small talk. He directed me to watch the action from a bodega opposite the tenement, and I didn't argue. Then he turned his attention to a broad-shouldered detective in a belted leather jacket who'd just returned from scouting the building. I forgave Sobkavich his frosty welcome, knowing that in his place I'd have done the same. He had to bring in two armed fugitives and keep his men alive. If anything went wrong, it was his ass, not mine.

The small, grimy bodega smelled of dried fish and coconut. I was alone with German Montalvo, a gap-toothed Rican who owned the place and didn't waste money on heat. He wore a sweater, gloves, and a red hunting cap with a missing ear flap. He was a jumpy little dude whose half-hearted smile tagged him as a man with something to hide. I suspected him of dealing, a suspicion he confirmed by flicking his eyes between me and the display of breakfast cereals and laundry detergent in his store window. Down here window displays were sometimes a code indicating the type of drugs sold on the premises.

I told Montalvo to chill, that we had no interest in him. If we did, he'd have seen the warrant by now. I said to look across the street because that's where it was happening. We wanted two guys in connection with a double murder. When we had them, we were out of here.

Montalvo smiled some more, grabbed a fistful of tissues from a box on the counter, and wiped perspiration from his forehead and hands. He offered me a beer. I told him to make it coffee, and that's when I heard *pop-pop*. Gunshots. From the tenement. I turned in time to see a man dive through a top-floor window and fall toward the ground, arms and legs churning, a full-throated scream marking his plunge. He landed facedown on the roof of an unmarked police car, the impact driving one of his legs through the windshield. His skull hit the revolving police light with enough force to shatter it. Blood covered the windshield and car roof. The car alarm went off.

Cops froze. Then came pandemonium.

Cops raced from the tenement and doorways, from behind empty storefronts and parked cars, uniforms in riot helmets and detectives in bulletproof vests, clutching shotguns and tear-gas guns, kicking empty beer cans as they ran to the leather-squeak sound of police utility belts heavy with handcuffs, bullet pouch, Mace canister, and nightstick. A uniform appeared at the jumper's window, looked out, and shook his head before turning to speak to someone behind him.

Cold wind teared my eyes and tore at my hat as I stepped outside the bodega to walk across the sidewalk and stare at the death scene. I wasn't going any farther. Now wasn't the time to talk to Sobkavich. I'd check him out later, when he had a handle on things.

Some cops hung back from the corpse. For them it was probably the first time they'd ever seen a pizza, a jumper smashed beyond recognition. Reality was more than putting in your twenty and walking away with a pension and permission to continue carrying a gun. Cop reality came out of ugly deaths. Like this one.

A few things made it difficult for me to see the death scene clearly. The sun was disappearing, and I was across the street from the jumper, who was now surrounded by Sobkavich's people. Still, I knew the jumper hadn't been a cop. I'd gotten a good look at his clothes before he'd started to draw a crowd. Strictly bargain-basement. Cheap stonewashed jeans, white socks, and plain-as-can-be running shoes.

He was wearing one thing that interested me: a green-and-white warm-up jacket with a photograph of the Brazilian soccer team on the back. I'd seen it before today, when I'd gone through Tonino Cuevas's effects and found a photograph of his younger brother Marcos. Smiling over his shoulder, Marcos had been pointing to the Brazilian team picture on a jacket like the one across the street. I remembered something else about the photograph, and that was

Marcos's face, childlike and eager and ready to do anything in the name of youth.

I was pretty sure he hadn't killed himself. I thought of the gunshots I'd just heard and decided whoever airmailed Marcos through the window had also put two bullets into Paco Nieves's brainpan. I saw a phony murder-suicide scenario emerging, courtesy of the Exchange Students.

The bodega telephone rang. Turning his back to me, German Montalvo snatched the receiver from a phone near the cash register. He cupped his hand around the mouthpiece and started whispering. I thought, a drug deal *now?* The man had to be crazy.

The call was for me.

I took the receiver from Montalvo, thinking it was Sobkavich calling to put me in the picture. A slight miscalculation on my part.

I said, "Detective Meagher."

At the other end of the line, a man laughed like a loon.

"Yo, Sparky," he said. "How's life at Asshole Central?"

Schiafino. The bodega became colder. I felt a sharp pain where Aldo had cracked my skull. My breathing roared in my ears.

He'd called to show off, to swagger and prance and make sure I'd gotten the message. His people had just killed Nieves and baby brother with me looking on. And they were going to get away with it.

Schiafino wasn't satisfied just to be Mr. Clever in the privacy of his own home. He had to let me know how good he was. He had to personally tell me he was the master and a shock to my system, the unexpected coming at me out of the darkness.

Every time I turned the corner, there he was. One step ahead of me. And it was beginning to weigh me down.

"I'd tell you to have a nice day," Schiafino said, "but that puts all the pressure on you, and the way I see it, you're under enough pressure already. I mean you just got pimped. Screwed, blued, and tattooed. And in front of a zillion cops. Offhand I'd say fate is laying waste to your ass."

"What do you want?"

"Just calling to act on all the positive energy flowing out of that neighborhood at the moment."

"Fuck you."

"Now, now. Is that any way to talk to someone who's a lot smarter than you'll ever be?"

"And modest, too."

"With a surgeon's touch," Schiafino said. "You're talking to a man who can tap dance on a charlotte russe and never dent the cherry."

"So could Hitler. And look how he wound up."

"Hey, don't knock the guy," Schiafino said. "Wasn't for him, wouldn't be any Israel. Wouldn't be any high five either. The man did some good."

"You smoked Cuevas and Nieves to protect Bauza. Your cops are out there in the street right now. How many you got watching me?"

"A wise man once said animals can smell fear and chicks know when you don't have money. I can smell your fear all the way out here in Brooklyn."

"You saying I'm afraid of you? Tell you what. Why don't we get together and talk about it?"

"Man, if Lynda could see you now. Hands sweating, looking over your shoulder. Looking for me. Come on, admit it. You're sleeping with one eye open these days, and the reason is Bobby Schemes."

I hit him where I knew it would hurt.

"I was sleeping with your wife," I said. "And you're right, I did work up a sweat. Want to hear the details?"

He went quiet. For a while I thought the line had gone dead. Then I heard him take a deep breath and let it out.

When he spoke his voice was dead, an icy monotone.

"Nice try," he said. "But you want to play with me, you need to rise to another level, and frankly I don't think you have it in you. I'm out in front, and all you can do is stare at my ass. You're messing with my future, and that's enough to make me come for you. But you also messed with my wife, and for that I want your blood. Your fucking blood. And nothing, I mean nothing, can save your ass. Understand what I'm saying?"

"You're there, I'm here. I understand that. What say we meet private? Just you and me."

"Oh, that day will come," Schiafino said. "Never fear. And when it does, you're going to wish you'd never laid eyes on me. Meanwhile let's talk about how you blew it. Really dropped the ball."

"I should have killed you at the cemetery," I said. "That what you're saying? You could be right."

Schiafino gave me his sicko laugh again. He was playful, jovial. In a festive mood. Definitely not in mourning.

"Pay attention," he said. "You ripped off Baby Cabrera, right? And you got, what, twenty-five K? Chump change. I mean, considering what was in the safe, you should have gone for the gold. You get just as much time for stealing twenty-five thousand as you do fifty. Am I right, or what."

I nearly dropped the receiver.

Schiafino had Lynda's letter.

XXVII
Street Eyes

I had dinner with Dion that evening at Kennedy Airport. We ate in the International Arrivals Building, where Maurice Robichaux had hustled tourists. Much as I hated to admit it, Schiafino had pushed me into coming here. I wanted to know whether he'd given Lynda's letter to Internal Affairs, and the person who could tell me that was McGuigan.

I didn't see approaching McGuigan empty-handed. With him I felt it best to proceed on the pay-as-you-go plan.

So I intended to check out the murder site again, to see if forensics and homicide had overlooked anything. I also planned to talk with security guards, porters, and baggage handlers and, if possible, to those panhandlers who hadn't been scared away by the increased police presence. Somewhere in all this I was hoping to find one or two individuals who could pinpoint Robichaux's movements the night of the murder.

I wasn't about to waste time looking for the mysterious cargo handler who'd allegedly cheated Jullee out of her car. Jullee had lied. The guy didn't exist, and Lynda hadn't come to the airport to meet him. On the other hand Jullee, jive-ass little bitch that she was, might be connected to Robichaux in some way. I planned to look into that possibility while here.

Dion and I ate Chinese food in a glass-enclosed cafeteria on the terminal's second level and washed it down with Mexican beer. We sat near a bay window facing a mini-mall of shops and newsstands, scarfing noodles and checking out a steady stream of passengers headed for outbound flights. One floor below us was the lobby where Maurice Robichaux claimed to have met a white man who'd given him a hundred-dollar bill every day for a week. The more I thought about Maurice, the more he appeared to be a man whose sense of reality was seriously impaired. Were he Chinese, his name would have been Won Dum Fuk.

I told Dion about the latest Ecuadoran killings, Schiafino's phone call, and Bauza's marital problems. I also told him about my private meeting with McGuigan, who wanted me to hook up with Carlyle Taylor. Then I handed him the medical report and said McGuigan thought Robichaux was being framed.

"McGuigan says that, he's got an angle," Dion said. "This guy didn't get where he is by being softhearted. He's standing in a pool of blood. Better to distrust him than have him screw you is what I say. By the way, want to hear what I think about Schiafino's telephone call?"

"I'm listening."

"A con job," he said. "He took you for a ride. I don't think he has the letter."

"So how come he knows about the twenty-five grand?"

"The same way we all do," Dion said. "Carlyle Taylor mentioned it in her story. Or did you forget that little fact."

Suddenly, I didn't feel like eating. Dion was right. I'd been taken. Diddled by a master.

Dion tapped his temple with a forefinger. "He's smart, this guy. A regular whiz kid. He has two spics whacked with you looking on. Then he calls, knowing you're watching the crime scene and maybe you're agitated by what just happened. You're not thinking clearly. He catches you off guard."

"He had me going," I said. "He really had me going. Christ."

"Let me ask you something. How come he didn't read you the actual letter? Use Lynda's words to stab you in the heart. Because that's his way."

I'd been taken. With ease. Schiafino hadn't even worked up a sweat. He'd done it with one hand tied behind his back, using bullshit with just enough truth in it to get over. I hated to think what he could do with hard evidence and time to plan. Bobby Schemes. Black as hell and dark as night.

Dion spoke with his mouth full of brown rice. "Some things to consider. The department hasn't come for you, there's been no phone calls from McGuigan or Hayden, and the union hasn't offered to get you a lawyer. Also the press isn't here. So we know one thing for sure. The department doesn't have the letter."

He dug into his lemon chicken, eating with gusto. I'd ordered a spicy beef dish and barely touched it. Not to worry, Dion said. He'd eat anything I couldn't finish.

"In the outhouse of life," he said, "Schiafino's a splinter in your ass. The man didn't tell you anything you don't already know. And forget this crap about him sending you to prison. He wants to do you himself, and we both know why."

That we did. Schiafino's dago pride demanded he personally kill me for messing with his wife. For most guys in that situation, killing me would have been enough. Not for Bobby Schemes.

First the bastard had to poke me full of holes. Take the shine off me. Then and only then would he kill me.

Men go to war, someone wrote, because women are watching. That was Schiafino. He had an active imagination. In his mind's eye he saw Lynda watching him and me go at it. And what she saw was me getting cut down to size.

"The difference between a Sicilian and an elephant," Dion said, "is the elephant eventually forgets. Sicilians don't. Schiafino owes it to himself to do you. If he gets the letter, the department ain't gonna see it. Not in this life. But he'll still find a way to use it against you, never fear. Meanwhile it's you and him. Especially since you've just told him you did steal the money. Because that's what he got out of the phone call."

Good news and bad news. The good news: for the time being, I didn't have to worry about being indicted. The bad news: I'd let Schiafino trick me into not thinking. I was thinking now, and it was making me angry. For some reason this brought back my appetite.

I ate most of my spicy beef, then polished off a dish of fresh pineapple, washing everything down with beer. I wasn't as crazy about Chinese as Dion, but for the most part I could eat anything and drink what I wanted. Lately, though, my nose seemed to be getting redder, leading me to wonder if I'd end up like a lot of cops, with gin blossoms, a bad liver, and slurred speech, all marks of a thirsty soul. I decided I didn't care. I enjoyed drinking too much to worry about my nose changing color.

I ate and drank while Dion told me what he'd learned about Gina Branch, the twenty-two-year-old topless dancer who was Bauza's main squeeze. While her name appeared on the lease of a Manhattan apartment and on a recent doctor's bill for collagen injections to enlarge her chin, Jesus was picking up the tab. He was also treating his Gina to cable television. The pleasures of love didn't come cheap.

"About Jullee and Schiafino," Dion said. "There's nothing to connect them on paper."

"That's why he's Bobby Schemes."

"Yeah, well, I'm Dion Meagher, and I didn't come up empty."

I grinned. "That's my dad."

"Jullee doesn't have a job," Dion said. "Never worked a day in her life. At least there's no record of it. Yet she gets a bank loan without no co-signer, no collateral, and she gets it faster than shit going through a tin goose."

"How fast is that?" I said.

"How about the same day she applies for it?"

"I ask you, who among us doesn't love miracles? How much was the loan for?"

"Try twenty grand."

"Explains the van," I said.

"She got the money five weeks ago," Dion said. "Around the time she bought the van from a dealer out on Long Island. Two weeks later she repays the loan. All of it. In cash, with interest."

"Schiafino," I said. "He gives twenty grand to the banker, who then passes it to Jullee in the form of a phony loan. She buys the van, whereupon Schiafino gives her another twenty grand. She gives that to the banker, who takes a thousand for his trouble and returns the rest to Schiafino. A little paperwork and nobody's the wiser. You wouldn't happen to have the name of Jullee's friendly banker by any chance?"

"So happens I do."

Dion put on his reading glasses and looked at his notebook. "Works at Courtline Trust in Manhattan. He's not just a loan officer. He's a senior vice president, name of Rafaelson. Harvey Rafaelson."

I said *bingo* and asked if Dion was sure about the name. He was.

"Where do you know this guy from?" he said.

"Gavilan."

I reminded him about Munro's phone message which told of a nervous Harvey who needed to be straightened out by Bauza or Schiafino. This Harvey also worked at a bank. Just like Jullee's Harvey. With Schiafino involved, both Harveys had to be the same guy.

Dion flipped a page in his notebook.

"Jullee has two accounts with Harvey Rafaelson," he said. "Both in her own name. Five thousand and change in one. A little over six thousand in the other. She makes a deposit every week, sometimes every ten days. Eight hundred to a thousand dollars each time. Always cash."

He closed the notebook. "And she's still unemployed."

"She's Schiafino's courier," I said. "Among her other duties."

"That's the thing with whoring," Dion said. "You can sell it and still have it, then sell it again."

"That's not what I mean. Harvey knows what's going on. He's dirty. That's why he rang up that phony loan for Jullee. He's Schiafino's boy. Find out what Margaret's computer has to say about him."

Dion spoke through a mouthful of noodles and broccoli. "What are we looking for?"

"A trail that leads to City Hall."

"Hell, I can give you the answer right now. Rafaelson's tight with City Hall."

"You serious?"

"Serious as a heart attack," Dion said. "He's working with Munro to raise money for Tucker's reelection."

I lifted my glass. "Way to go, D."

"We got some liberals working at our place," he said. "Fucking dildos. They're supporting Tucker because he's black. Ask them for a better reason, and they look at you like you're crazy. They keep trying to talk me into backing him. Good luck. One of them gave me an invitation to a fund-raising party for Tucker this weekend at Rafaelson's townhouse in the Village. I said if I didn't show to start without me."

"McGuigan was right," I said.

"About what?"

"About everything leading to City Hall. Lynda's murder to the Exchange Students to Robichaux himself. And now you can include Harvey the friendly banker. Meanwhile I'm thinking we should start looking for the money trail. That's the heart of any investigation. There may be people who want to see Tucker win a second term, but Schiafino's not one of them. He's in it for the money."

"He's got it," Dion said. "Fifty grand a hit."

"Suppose he's looking for more," I said. "He just told me I was messing with his future. To me that sounds like he's playing for higher stakes. I think that's why he jumped in between Jullee and me and why he's being asked to straighten out Harvey."

"Harvey's been a naughty boy," Dion said.

"Suits like Munro and Harvey speak the same language. They should be able to work out their problems."

"Unless the situation calls for Harvey to get his ass kicked. In which case you bring in Bobby Schemes."

"True enough. But I keep thinking there's more going on here than just Schiafino's trips to Washington. I think Harvey and I should talk."

I looked over Dion's shoulder, not searching for anything special. Street eyes, we call it. Since anything can happen on the street, you learn to be alert at all times. You watch your back, expect the worst, and you trust nobody. After a while, it becomes natural to be on the lookout, even in your dreams.

That's how I spotted her. She was headed toward the cafeteria, on a course that would take her past me and Dion. She'd have seen us, and we'd have seen her, and I didn't want that to happen. As usual she was chic and sleek, this evening decked out in a red coat down to her ankles, a red cloth hat with a small black feather, and dark glasses. She walked fast, a lady in a hurry.

It was Carlyle Taylor, and she was on a mission.

I hid my face behind a menu. McGuigan or no McGuigan, I'd get together with Schwarzenigger in my own good time.

I certainly didn't want us to meet here. Not while she was trying to pin Lynda's murder on me. Did I have a persecution complex? Not from where I sat. Live long enough, and no matter who you are, your paranoia will be justified.

I warned Dion she was coming up behind him. Duck, I said. Stay down until I give the all clear. Shielding the side of his face with one hand, Dion all but dove into his food.

I peeked at Carlyle Taylor from behind the menu. She had no carry-on luggage, no ticket in her hand. Since she was in the general area of the crime scene, I figured she was looking for information that would prove Robichaux innocent and me guilty. She seemed absorbed in her own little world, making her deaf, dumb, and blind to everything around her. She never noticed she was in danger.

She passed the cafeteria without seeing us.

Looking up from his food, Dion saw my face. "What's wrong?"

I said the sooner we caught up to Carlyle Taylor, the better her chances of staying alive. I raced from the cafeteria with Dion at my heels.

XXVIII
Down Under

Dion and I spent the next few minutes in the terminal's shopping area, tailing Carlyle Taylor and the two men following her. Identifying the two males was easy. Both were NYPD detectives, the kind you wouldn't want to meet in your worst nightmare.

One was Aldo Sinatra, who now had a bandaged nose and swollen lip to go with his customary tacky raincoat and who sported his usual expression, one identifying him as a man whose mind tended to wander. His buddy was broad-shouldered and in his mid-thirties with a flat nose and red buzz cut that exaggerated his big ears. Red, as I called him, wore the same belted black leather jacket he'd had on in Alphabet City an hour ago, when I'd watched him and Lou Sobkavich go over their plan for taking down the late Paco Nieves and Marcos Cuevas.

Losing one parent, Oscar Wilde said, may be regarded as a misfortune, whereas losing both seems like carelessness. The last two Ecuadoran hijackers had gotten themselves capped a couple of hours ago, and Red had been there, in the flesh and big as life. So much for misfortune. Now he was in the company of a lowlife sleazebag like Aldo, an association which to my mind went beyond carelessness. Aldo was an Exchange Student, and since birds of a feather flock together, you could bet the house that Red was one as well. Carlyle Taylor had gotten herself into one hell of a jackpot.

Good luck to her. Robichaux was heading upstate, and God in his heaven couldn't keep that from happening. True, Robichaux wasn't getting a fair shake. Not the way this investigation was being handled. But that wasn't my problem. He'd killed Lynda, and since justice for cop killers wasn't a priority with me, I wasn't about to lose any sleep over his bad karma. At the moment I was more interested in knowing why Miss Taylor had attracted the attention of the Exchange Students.

It was almost 7:30 P.M. when Dion and I joined her, Aldo, and Red on a walk past gift shops, newsstands, and posters warning passengers not to take packages from strangers. Carlyle Taylor never looked back. Never saw fat Aldo, a folded newspaper under one arm, trailing her and trying to look like his mind was everywhere except on her. The newspaper was a surveillance tool. If Aldo suddenly found himself in her range of vision, he'd pretend to read it.

Not too far behind him was Red, smoking a long, thin cigar and playing the window-shopper. Dion and I kept a Brazilian flight crew between us and Red, who seemed to take a lot of pride in his leather jacket, brushing real or imagined cigar ashes from its sleeves while sneaking admiring glances at himself in store windows. Red had the swagger and strut that goes with belted leather jackets and long, thin cigars. He reminded me of someone who wears sunglasses at night because he thinks it's cool and isn't above snapping his fingers to get your attention.

Suddenly, Red picked up the pace. He closed in on Aldo, and the two began jogging, and I thought, Christ, we've been made. They've seen us. I was wrong. Red and Aldo were only trying to keep up with Carlyle Taylor, who'd suddenly lengthened her stride and was starting to leave them behind. I shouldered my way through the Brazilians, Dion behind me. If I lost sight of Aldo and Red, it was going to be a rainy day for Carlyle Taylor.

As things turned out, the lady had her own agenda. As I was wondering how best to keep her alive, she disappeared around a corner. Stopping at a newsstand, I caught Dion's arm, bringing him to a halt. We hung near the checkout counter, watching Aldo and Red stop at the corner taken by Carlyle Taylor. Aldo was calling the shots. He looked around the corner, and apparently the coast was clear, because he lifted a forefinger in a signal to Red, and then they were gone.

I waited a few seconds, then strolled to the corner, peeked around it, and saw what appeared to be a side wing of the shopping area. It was small and undergoing renovations. At the moment it was deserted, and as far as I could see, there hadn't been any work done there in a while. Vacant, half-constructed stores were lit by grimy bulbs hanging from ceiling wires. A layer of dust covered emptied cement bags, dried mortar troughs, and overturned wheelbarrows. Hanging on a sawhorse blocking the entrance was a sign describing the renovation as another quality job from CCCH Construction of Brooklyn, New York.

I'd run into the CCCH name before. Earlier today I'd seen one of its panel trucks outside the Lesnevitch home, where the family garage was being renovated.

Meanwhile, missing from the set were Carlyle Taylor, Aldo, and Red.

Dion whispered, "Where'd everybody go?"

I said, "That's what I'm about to find out. Stay here."

"I'm going with you. You got two shooters, remember?"

I said, "I need you covering my back. Mikey's out there somewhere. If he's watching us, that means we're caught between him and Aldo and Red. I need you here, D."

"I understand."

He did. And he didn't. He was a proud man, still capable of a full day's work. And he could get it up twice a night, no mean feat at his age. I'd told him more than once that he ought to have his johnson bronzed and put into a museum. In his mind he hadn't lost a step. He could still hang in there with the best of the young cops, but then cops pushing walkers and ten years into Social Security felt the same way.

I'd trust Dion with my life, but no matter what the poets and philosophers said, old age is old age. I was about to take on two killer cops in an area that looked as though it had been hit by a hand grenade. Maybe Dion could find his way around without twisting a knee, and maybe he couldn't. For sure I knew shots could be fired, and if possible, I didn't want anyone shooting at him. And I did need him watching my back. Neither of us had seen Mikey, but Dion was an experienced cop, a hunter who was able to recognize another hunter when he saw one.

I started with the first shop on my right. And promptly put my foot in it. I stepped on a loose plank, snapping it in two and making a noise loud enough to wake the dead. Quickly drawing my nine, I froze, eyes going in every direction while I waited for disaster to strike, and when nothing happened, I continued my search, wondering if going on a diet would have made a difference and deciding it was a case of shoulda woulda coulda since I'd never dieted in my life and wasn't about to start now.

The search. I looked under an overturned sales counter, in an empty supply room, and in a cramped bathroom where a cracked toilet bowl held rust-colored water whose surface was bright with a mysterious crud. I snagged my overcoat on a loose wire, got paint on my shoes, and inhaled dust by the carload. And I never stopped thinking about Aldo coming up behind me with a length of pipe and bad intentions.

The next shop brought results. By now I'd gotten around to using my lighter, and while the tiny flame wasn't much, it was better than nothing. With its help, I uncovered a recent footprint. It was on an old copy of *USA Today*, stamped in white plaster dust, and while the print meant nothing by itself, crushed in the heel lay the remains of a long, thin cigar. Print and cigar were in front of a closed door, and the cigar was still warm. Hello, Red.

The most dangerous part of police work is going through a door. Anyone can be waiting for you on the other side, and in these days of wackos and assorted schizzed-out looney tunes with AK-47s, anyone means someone planning to do you grievous bodily harm. I'd gone through a door last year and been jumped by a pit bull whose vocal cords had been deliberately severed to allow it to attack without making a sound. I'd put half a clip in the pit bull, then loosened the teeth of the drug dealer who'd sicced the dog on me.

I hadn't felt the terror most cops feel in that situation. I'd felt a rush. A boost, if not an unholy joy. Hair-raising as it might have been for others, for me there was no more exhilarating time than going through a door. The unknown excited the hell out of me. Without it I would shrivel up and die of boredom.

The door. Stepping left and out of the line of fire, I cracked it just wide enough to stick my gun hand inside. I saw a small, empty room, probably a supply room or an office. It was dusty, lit by a dim bulb, and had a hardwood floor covered by sheets of old newspapers. Three of the walls were plywood, temporary stuff until the real thing went up. Straight ahead a narrow brick wall had been knocked down to reveal a hidden shaft. I tiptoed across the floor to the shaft and looked inside. Actually, I looked down, because the shaft's wooden ceiling was just over my head. At my feet a rusty steel ladder descended into a pitch-blackness where the wind howled and sent cold air rushing up to smack me in the face. I could hear voices.

I took off my hat, put my keys and change inside, then placed the hat on the floor. The nine went into my belt. Then I slipped on my gloves, stepped on the ladder, and began my descent.

XXIX
Hiding Place

I climbed down carefully, one rung at a time, hoping the worn bolts wouldn't tear loose from the wooden wall and send me free-falling to China. The farther down I went, the colder it got. A little taste of hell for you, Meagher. Down into a darkness smelling of garbage, urine, and God knows what else, all of it making me sick to my stomach. The smell of fresh cigar smoke kept me going. It meant Red wasn't far away. All I had to do was reach him before I threw up.

The sound of male voices grew louder. I was nearing the bottom of the shaft. Look on the bright side, Meagher. If you're going to fall, you don't have far to go.

And then I heard Aldo say *party time* and laugh his dumb laugh. Red mumbled something in response. My foot touched bottom. I stepped off the ladder onto a wooden floor and turned to face the voices.

I was in a windy passageway, dark and smelly. Since I couldn't see anything, I felt around and discovered the rusty ladder marked one end of the tunnel. The voices came from the other end. There was light there, too. I made the distance between me and the light as ten feet.

Light and voices came from a small room on the right, where some kind of struggle was going on. I figured it was one-sided because Aldo and Red were laughing and I heard nothing from Carlyle Taylor.

My instinct was to get to her immediately. First things first. I reached overhead, brushing a wooden ceiling with my fingertips. Then I spread my arms to the sides. I ended up touching wood with both palms. I had my bearings. I could move around without bumping my head or bouncing off walls.

One final check. I needed to know what was on the floor. I flicked on my lighter. I had a three- or four-second peek at the ground before the wind blew out the flame. Up ahead in the room, someone broke a bottle.

I was in a rubbish-strewn wooden passageway, around ten feet in length and reeking of mildew, urine, and shit. The airport probably didn't know it was here. Most likely it didn't show up on any architectural plans, and over a period of time it had been forgotten. It might have been a storage area or a connection between old offices in a previous building. The CCCH crew had discovered one end but had stopped work before checking out the entire area. There was probably more than one way into this little hideaway. Judging by the trash and the smells, someone had found it.

The ground was littered with crack vials, empty wine bottles, newspapers, abandoned pizza cartons, and beer cans. It added up to an obstacle course between me and the room at the other end. If I wanted to get to Carlyle Taylor, I'd have to be careful. And very, very lucky.

The noise from the wind would help. That and Aldo and Red being preoccupied.

I drew my nine. Time to get down.

I inched forward, keeping close to the right wall. My foot brushed a wine bottle. Pushing it aside with my toe, I continued forward. Ahead, the struggle in the room was still going on. Aldo whooped and cackled, enjoying himself. I needed him and Red to stay preoccupied a few seconds longer.

I reached the end of the tunnel, squeezed the nine, and peeked inside the room. It was small and dark, a filthy cubbyhole with water-stained wooden walls. There was trash everywhere—old newspapers, empty cardboard boxes, grease-stained paper bags, and a stink the cold air couldn't hide. Red held the only light, a flashlight. His back was to me, which was good. What wasn't so good was Carlyle Taylor's predicament. She was lying stomach down in the debris, mouth and eyes covered with duct tape. Both hands were taped behind her back.

Red had his flashlight trained on her while Aldo sat straddling her bare thighs. He'd pulled her pants down to her knees and was using a penknife to cut away her panties. A frantic Carlyle Taylor tried to buck him off and couldn't do it. Aldo was getting turned on, and Red was enjoying the show.

I stepped into the room and slammed the nine into the back of Red's skull. He fell into a kneeling position. I clubbed him in the jaw with the gun, knocking him sideways, and he fell with the slackness of someone unconscious and about to stay that way for a while. The flashlight slipped from his hand. Picking it up, I aimed the beam at Aldo, blinding him. His arms came up to cover his face and he said, *The fuck's going on here, Red.* I wanted to put a bullet between his eyes, but that would present problems. So for the second time that day, I kicked him in the head, knocking him backwards into darkness.

I shone the flashlight on him again. He was on his hands and knees, shaking his head. I thought about what he'd just tried to do and remembered how as a kid I'd punched out a priest-rapist, then fled the orphanage and ended up getting shot in the heart, and it reminded me what sick fucks rapists are, and I thought about doing Aldo, I really did, but instead I jammed the heel of my foot down on the back of his right hand, putting my full weight on his bones, feeling them crack. Aldo shrieked and fell onto his back, cradling the hand to his chest. I pulled his .38 from his belt holster, then checked Red. No problem there. Big-eared Red was still out cold.

I shone the flashlight on Carlyle Taylor. She lay on her side facing me, breathing hard and listening. I pulled the tape from her eyes and mouth as gently as I could, then turned the flashlight on my face. I figured it might calm her. It didn't. She was terrified. Her eyes were all whites. She shook her head violently and backed into the wall. She didn't want a man near her. Not now.

I reached for her, doing it slow and speaking softly, telling her she was safe, that all I wanted to do was take the tape from her wrists. That's all. She wouldn't stop shaking, but she let me remove the tape. When I'd finished, I covered her with my overcoat. I told her no one was going to touch her, that I was taking her out of here. I couldn't think of anything else to say.

In her place I'd have felt fear and shame, and I'd have hated every man who'd ever been born, and I'm sure I'd have wanted to kill as many as possible. It was no good saying she hadn't been raped, that she'd been lucky, and that as bad as tonight had been there were rape victims who'd gone through worse. Aldo and Red had put her through hell, and that was enough for her. After tonight her life would never be the same. No amount of counseling would change what had happened here. I didn't have any quick answers. I never did in these situations. I only knew that if Carlyle Taylor had asked me for a gun so she could kill Aldo, I'd have handed over his .38 and left the room.

Ignoring Carlyle Taylor for the moment, I made a further check of the room. Something had brought her here. And it wasn't the decor. This pigsty had been home to someone. A cardboard box contained a pair of rancid-looking running shoes, greasy head rags, empty McDonald's containers, and old copies of *Jet* magazine. Six to five the previous tenant had been Maurice Robichaux.

It became clear when I checked out his stash that I hadn't been blowing smoke. Maurice had chipped a hole in the wall to hide his goodies. The hole, just inches deep, was just above Carlyle Taylor's left shoulder. When I reached for it, she flinched.

Maurice's stash. I found a Walkman, earphones, cassette tapes by Miles Davis and Wynton Marsalis, and an old newspaper photograph of a well-dressed, smiling Maurice Robichaux as a young man facing the camera and proudly balancing a trumpet on his thigh. Carlyle Taylor had written about him as having been a promising trumpet player until drugs, emotional problems, and what she called institutional racism had messed up his head.

There was something else in the hole, a small box the size of my hand. When I opened it, I found a trumpet mouthpiece in mint condition. Under the flashlight beam it glittered like a polished gold nugget. There wasn't a mark or a scratch on it.

Also in the box were three one-hundred-dollar bills, each bill brand-new and, as far as I could tell, absolutely genuine.

XXX
Phone Call

I spent most of the next hour on my living-room couch, whiskey in hand, as I pondered the attack on Carlyle Taylor. I usually did my thinking with a fight film for company. Tonight I ran the 1952 title fight between heavyweight champion Jersey Joe Walcott and challenger Rocky Marciano and tried to decide if the money in the tunnel had been put there by Robichaux or Carlyle Taylor.

If she'd hidden the money with the intention of helping Robichaux, she was skating on thin ice. She could go to prison for impeding a murder investigation and kiss her credibility as a reporter good-bye. Was she crazy enough to take that kind of chance? Who knows.

On the other hand, suppose she'd found the money in the tunnel. And the money really did belong to Maurice. My normal reaction would be to say he'd stolen it. But if he hadn't stolen the money, then we were left with the story about him and a bearded white man who gave away hundred-dollar bills.

I'd asked Carlyle Taylor if she'd planted the money in the tunnel, and she said she'd never do such a thing. She'd learned about the tunnel from Robichaux's mother. Apparently, Mom and Robichaux had gone shopping for a new telephone for her, the old one having been taken in a burglary of Mom's Harlem apartment, the third in the past six months. Robichaux had surprised Mom by paying for the phone with one of several hundreds he'd been carrying.

Asked where he'd gotten the money, he'd told Mom about the philanthropic white man he'd met at Kennedy Airport. Not everyone at Kennedy was so kind. Robichaux told Mom about his secret airport hideaway. That's where he went to escape his fellow vagrants, a nasty bunch of spooks who'd rob anybody to keep themselves in crack and cheap wine. Since he was the only one who knew about the hideaway, it was a good place to stash his cash. That's what he'd told Mom, who'd passed the information on to Carlyle. Mom wasn't about to talk to the police. Not after they'd framed her son for murder.

When I asked if Carlyle Taylor knew why Aldo and Red had attacked her, she said they were probably racists. She'd been receiving threatening phone calls and letters for years, usually from whites who didn't like her politics. It was just her bad luck that she'd run into a couple of these crackers at the airport. I didn't give her my opinion, namely, that she was now under surveillance by rogue cops and that she could be attacked again, and that the guy to worry about was Eugene Elder because he was reporting her every move to Bobby Schemes.

At the moment Carlyle Taylor was upstairs taking a shower. Afraid to be alone, she'd asked if she could stay with me for a while, and I'd said yes. She was free to stay for as long as she liked. We hadn't talked much, not that we'd had many long conversations in the past. Despite what happened at the airport, it was still a little too soon for us to fall into each other's arms and promise to be palsy-walsy forevermore.

After cleaning up, she planned to make a few phone calls. She'd get a friend to drive her into the city. She said she couldn't spend the night alone and would probably stay with somebody. My guess was the somebody she had in mind was none other than Eugene Elder. Old Daddy Duke himself.

At no time was there any talk about Carlyle filing charges against her attackers. I'd identified Aldo and Red as cops, going so far as to write down their badge numbers. But she'd shown no interest in wanting to get these guys.

I figured pride had a lot to do with it, pride being something Carlyle Taylor possessed in great abundance. With it came the image of a militant black woman ready to do battle with whitey at the drop of a hat. The last thing Carlyle needed was to be seen as weak and defenseless, a breakable human being who couldn't take care of herself. She had to come across as a ferocious soul sister. That's how she earned her money.

She planned to consult an attorney before deciding what to do about her attackers. At least that's what she said. I was betting the attorney would be Eugene Elder. What she didn't know is that Daddy Duke took his orders from Bobby Schemes. In other words, Carlyle Taylor would be told it wasn't in her best interest to file a complaint. The attack in the tunnel? What attack?

Dion was in the kitchen, putting together fresh fruit, tea, cheese and crackers for Carlyle when she came downstairs. Neither of us was used to having women around the house, let alone a black woman who didn't like white cops and was trying to convict me of murder.

But life is full of surprises, pleasant and unpleasant, and you have to ride with the tide and go with the flow. I'd had no choice but to help Carlyle Taylor. When I became a cop,

I'd taken an oath, one that meant doing my job in a way that allowed me to live with myself. We do what we must, Emerson said, and call it by the best names.

I wondered how Carlyle Taylor would take the news when I told her the stuff we'd found in the tunnel was useless, that if her goal had been to help Robichaux, she'd missed the boat.

To be entered as evidence, the money would first have to be photographed in the tunnel, with detectives witnessing the discovery. The same detectives would then have to voucher everything—bills, cassette tapes, newspaper photograph—making sure the paperwork was correct and duly witnessed. It was too late for that to happen now. The stuff was in my living room, in an envelope on a coffee table. I'd broken the chain of evidence. Genuine or not, the evidence was now contaminated.

The Walcott-Marciano fight was winding down. Old Joe was a crafty jig. At the time, he'd lied about his age, telling the world he was thirty-eight when he was forty-two, if not older. But for twelve rounds he'd handled the twenty-nine-year-old Marciano with ease, showing that at forty-two or fifty-two he still had some glide in his stride and some cut in his strut. He'd taken the younger, stronger Marciano apart and was ahead on every judge's card. He'd had the world believing that old age and cunning really did beat youth and strength every time.

But the thirteenth round was coming up, the one where Marciano would hit Joe with the hardest punch ever thrown in a heavyweight title fight, a punch that would knock Joe stone-cold and bring doctors into the ring, wondering whether or not he was still alive.

I felt a tap on my shoulder. I didn't want to be interrupted. I wanted to see the look of joy on Marciano's bloodied face, this small, chunky guinea who was the new champ and the most determined and best-conditioned fighter in his class and who would become the only heavyweight in boxing history to go through his career without being defeated.

When I looked around, I saw Dion, frowning as though his stomach was more gassy than usual. He put a finger to his lips and with the other hand pointed to the ceiling. I whispered, Carlyle? He nodded, then signaled for me to follow him.

He led me to the kitchen, then pointed to the telephone. The receiver was off the hook. Picking it up, Dion held the receiver so we both could hear, and what we heard was Eugene Elder telling Carlyle Taylor that I was behind the attack on her at Kennedy Airport.

XXXI
Consider the Possibilities

Elder said, "Baby, you got to get out of there. I can't have you hanging around that Paddy Meagher. I hear what you're saying about him coming to your rescue. But let me ask you something. Ever consider the possibility he may have set you up so he could step in and play the white knight? The fat white knight."

Elder's deep voice was soothing and ingratiating, a painkilling narcotic.

"It's a fact of living, baby," he said. "You do not put your faith in white bread."

"Gene, believe me," Carlyle Taylor said. "Meagher wasn't putting on an act. He really did go after those men. I mean he left them bleeding. Like you, I'm no Meagher fan. But if he hadn't come along when he did, I might be dead. I still can't stop shaking. He saved my life, and at the moment I don't feel like trashing him. If you're a woman and you're about to be raped, having Fear Meagher come to your rescue isn't such a bad idea. His being white didn't make a blind bit of difference. Tomorrow it might. Right now it doesn't."

Elder appeared irked. Almost jealous.

"Sounds to me like you're pleased and honored to be blessed with the opportunity to be in Mr. Charlie's company. If I didn't know better, I'd swear you're grooving on the man.

You got eyes for the cat, you can tell me. Daddy Duke's been around. He knows about these things."

"Gene, don't start that shit. Not now."

"What shit we talking about?"

"I'm in no mood to sit back and watch you play the professional nigger. Pick another time to do that, if you don't mind. You talk black, but you live white, and you think green, and don't bother denying anything because I'm in no mood to have you lie to me."

"The hell's gotten into you, girl?" Elder said. "I'm trying to stop Meagher from running a game on you, and this is how you thank me, dumping on me like that. He tell you why he just happened to be at the airport same time you showed?"

"I didn't ask, and he didn't say," Carlyle said. "Believe it or not, I had other things on my mind. Tell you this much. I don't think Meagher killed Mrs. Schiafino. I just don't."

"Girl, you are a wonder. You don't think Robichaux did it, and now you're telling me Meagher's as pure as the driven snow. Maybe he didn't kill the woman, but when it comes to Robichaux, hell, you're the only one who doesn't believe that nigger killed my client's wife."

"Gene, I don't feel like arguing right now. I'm upset, I'm on the verge of tears, and I know I'll have nightmares. Just tell me when you're coming to pick me up."

Elder said, "I'm on my way now. Oh, before I forget. That shit you found at the airport, the money and mouthpiece."

"Meagher's got it. He wants to check it out. Which reminds me. I have to call Maurice's mother and thank her. Everything was where she said Maurice hid it. Gene, he's telling the truth. Impossible as it sounds, a white man did give him that money. I mean it has to be. A brother like Maurice can't get his hand on a dollar bill, let alone a hundred-dollar bill. Thank God for Maurice's mother."

Elder said, "Never mind Maurice's momma. I want you to get that shit back from Meagher. Tell him you've changed your mind. You want to take it with you."

"After what he did for me? He can keep it for as long as he wants. I don't have to write about it immediately."

"Write? Girl, you living in a dream world. Didn't I just say you're the only one who wants to cut Maurice loose? The

brother did a cop, a white female cop at that. He's going down. Look, just do what I tell you. Get that money back from Meagher. I need it, you understand?"

There was a silence. Then Carlyle said, "What do you mean you need it?"

Elder didn't answer.

Carlyle said, "Gene, I asked you a question. What do you mean you need it?"

Elder said, "What I meant to say was I need it to give to Mrs. Robichaux. I thought it might be nice to give her the money since it does belong to her son."

Carlyle said, "You want the stuff so bad, you talk to Meagher. Me, I've had my fill of confrontation for the moment. I still don't know whether or not to file a complaint. I have to be honest with you. I don't want what happened to get out."

"You got that right," Elder said. "It's never smart to put your business in the street. Bad for your image, know what I'm saying? The men who attacked you could be pretending to be cops. Couple white boys unhappy with a sister standing up for her race. You think they're cops, you're bound to go looking in the wrong direction."

"They never identified themselves as cops," Carlyle said. "They just came up behind me. Look, I don't want to talk about it, OK? Meagher says they're real cops, and I believe him."

Elder said, "Meagher's a jive ass. Only thing he knows is how to bust black heads. Dig, he's white, and white is not the color we should be concerning ourselves with. The man got me kicked out of the prosecutor's office, remember? Ain't about to forget that. I can see where Mr. Charlie is messing with your mind. Sooner I get you away from him, the better. One more thing. You still going to write about Bauza and Robichaux?"

Carlyle Taylor said, "Can't we talk about that later?"

"We'll talk about it now. Robert Schiafino is my client. That story's going to hurt him."

"Gene, I'm a reporter. It's my job to write about this killing."

"You don't have to hurt me, and that's what you do when you embarrass my clients."

A weeping Carlyle Taylor was close to losing it.

"Gene, you are one self-centered nigger," she said. "Why the hell do I bother with you? After all I've been through tonight, all I get from you is me, me, me. You're saying I shouldn't write about something that's already a matter of public record."

"I'm saying don't do Gene wrong, baby. Treat your Daddy right, and Daddy will treat you right. You know I never stopped loving you. Like the man says, you got me chewing on my coffee and drinking my meat. You're steady on my mind. Sorry about upsetting you. Honest to God I am. I'm on the way out there now. You be ready. Meagher won't give you the stuff, don't worry about it. I'll deal with him. Everything's cool. Daddy's going to take care of you. Later."

He hung up. So did Carlyle. And so did I.

I hurried to the living room, Dion on my heels. The fight film was over. I hadn't seen Marciano knock out Jersey Joe, but I'd learned something from Carlyle's phone call. I'd learned Elder was worried, which meant Schiafino was worried. And what they were worried about was Carlyle's story on Bauza and Robichaux, a story that could lead to Schiafino.

I went to the foyer, opened the closet, and pulled the copy of Robichaux's arrest record from my overcoat pocket. I'd been too busy to read it, so I'd ended up carrying the thing around with me.

Returning to the living room, I plopped down on the couch and began examining the list of Maurice's misdeeds and transgressions. There were more than a few. When it came to right and wrong, Maurice appeared to have drawn a mental blank.

"I'm guessing," I said to Dion, "but it would seem to me that any connection between Bauza and Robichaux would be that of arresting officer and perp."

"I'll buy that."

"When I spoke to Gavilan today, he told me Carlyle Taylor had called wanting to speak to Bauza. We now know why. She's doing a story on Bauza and Robichaux and apparently it's making Elder, excuse me, Schiafino, very nervous. Why's that, I wonder?"

Dion said, "What do I win if I come up with the right answer?"

"All the macaroni salad you can take home in a suitcase," I said. "Ah, what have we here, boys and girls . . ."

There it was. Third page, fourth from the top.

I said, "Bauza was doing temporary duty at Kennedy with the Port Authority. That's when he arrested Robichaux for wienie waving. Three months later Bauza pops Robichaux again. Also at Kennedy. This time the charge was stealing luggage."

Dion said, "Two arrests. Same cop, same mutt. What's the problem?"

"Let's say you're Schiafino," I said. "You're always scheming, always conniving. You're a regular Wile E. Coyote, Mr. Intrigue himself. Now suppose you have something in mind which requires a fall guy, a loser. Not just any loser, mind you, but one immediately recognizable as such. This scheme of yours is set to go down at Kennedy Airport. You mention it to your good friend Detective Bauza, who says I have just the man you're looking for. The man Bauza has in mind is none other than Maurice Robichaux, with whom he is quite familiar."

Dion shook his head. "You're playing with dynamite. You're saying Schiafino knew his wife's killer. If you're right, it explains why Elder's so jumpy."

"Here's what we know for sure," I said. "We know Elder thinks Carlyle's story on Bauza and Robichaux is bad for Schiafino. We know Carlyle probably told Elder about the tunnel, and he told Schiafino. Schiafino then sent Aldo and Red after her. Aldo being Aldo, well, things were bound to get a little out of hand. I wonder if Elder knew he was setting his lady up to be raped. If he did, he's even more of a dirtbag than I think he is."

I said Schiafino never did anything without a reason. And if he wanted to eliminate all ties, real or imaginary, between himself and Robichaux, then there had to be a reason, such as Schiafino being the white man who'd given Maurice those hundreds.

XXXII
The Truth Will Out

When Carlyle Taylor came downstairs, I was in the living room rewinding the Walcott-Marciano film. Dion sat across from me in an armchair, watching *Jeopardy!* on television. He was the only one I knew who could explain the game or even cared how it was played.

Carlyle had asked to borrow a change of clothes. Since we didn't keep women's clothes on hand, the best I could do was some of Dion's stuff. With her thin face scrubbed clean of makeup and dressed in Dion's sweater and stone-washed jeans, she looked twenty years old. There was an attractive soapy smell about her, and for the first time I noticed that her eyes were green.

Her purse hung from one shoulder, and she carried a black plastic garbage bag, which she held out to me. I placed the bag on the couch. It held the clothes she'd worn earlier tonight.

"I never want to see them again."

"I understand." I pointed to the food.

Her smile was sad, pained. "No appetite," she said.

"Tea?"

"Tea would be fine."

She took a seat on the couch and started to shiver. The room was warm, but not warm enough for a woman as frightened as she was. I poured her a cup of tea, then went to the foyer closet. I returned with a green cardigan belonging to Dion and put it around Carlyle's shoulders.

She smiled her thanks, then touched her throat. "Thyroid problems," she said. "It's messed up my circulation. Just one of the things affecting me at the moment."

Dion said, "There's a heater in my room. I'll get it for you."

She shook her head. "Tea and the sweater will do me just fine. I'll be leaving soon. Someone's coming to pick me up. He should be here within the hour."

"That's nice," I said, looking at Dion, who smiled and said *friends* with all the sincerity of a lawyer promising never to lie for the rest of his life.

I said, "Speaking of friends, if you decide to go after the men who attacked you, I'll back you up."

She looked at me as though I'd just offered to dissect a frog and eat it in front of her.

"You'd help me go after cops?" she said.

"They're not cops. They're dirtbags who shouldn't be carrying a badge."

"Forgive me for saying so, but I never thought I'd hear that coming from you."

"It goes to show you never can tell. At least that's what Chuck Berry says."

She smiled. "My ex-husband can probably tell you everything about that song, including what Chuck was eating for breakfast the day he wrote it."

Dion said, "Your ex-husband, he a musician?"

"No," she said. "He's professor of journalism at Howard University, in Washington. That's how we met. I was one of his students. I was born and raised in Washington. Family still lives there. Billy, my ex-husband, he's a frustrated musician. Plays guitar. He's not bad. Come to think of it, he's not good either. He writes music articles for magazines and scholastic publications. Jazz, blues. Nothing past 1960."

Dion nodded his approval. "A man who knows. More power to him."

I said jazz wasn't my kind of music. Country and western did it for me. Dion knew all there was to know about jazz, I said, and had met everyone from Art Tatum to Charlie Parker. I said that few people, black or white, knew as much about black music as Dion.

Carlyle's eyes widened. "Excuse me, but you two take the cake. One's ready to do battle with white cops on behalf of a black woman. The other's an expert on black music. What next? You two planning to join the Nation of Islam?"

"Just as soon as I can get Jesse to cosign my application," Dion said.

A grinning Carlyle said, "Don't hold your breath. Anyway, I want to thank you both again. You didn't have to help me back there." She looked at me. "Not after what I've written about you."

I said, "With all due respect, Miss Taylor—"

"Carlyle. My father named me after the writer. Are you familiar with his work at all?"

"Your father's or Thomas Carlyle's?"

Carlyle bowed her head. "I stand corrected."

"No problem. What I started to say was you and I don't agree on a lot of things, and we probably never will. But what happened at the airport wasn't about race. It was about right and wrong. Dion and I didn't discuss whether or not we should become involved. There wasn't anything to discuss. You do or you don't. That's all there is to it."

Carlyle looked into her cup of tea. "Right and wrong. Doesn't sound all that complicated, but it is. Right and wrong. The story of my marriage, you could say. Billy thought it was OK for him to screw his adoring female students. I disagreed. With black men it's Daddy knows best, so you can imagine how the argument ended. They say you always marry one of your parents. I'm here to tell you that's a fact. Billy was fifteen years older than me. Which in his case meant I'd married a grown-up child."

She leaned back on the sofa and spoke to the ceiling. She herself was a grown-up child, she said. That happened when you were the only child in a well-to-do family. Being an only child with money also gave a girl a head start on becoming a boss bitch, a survival mechanism Carlyle couldn't do without. Daddy, bless him, had spoiled her rotten. Even today Carlyle couldn't go home for a visit without him offering her everything from a new car to a year's rent on her East Side apartment. Daddy was Washington's most successful black undertaker. Twice he'd turned down the chance to run for mayor rather than disclose his considerable financial worth. Carlyle's mother, a former model and actress, wasn't doing too badly either. She ran a travel agency which made most of the travel arrangements for Washington's black congressmen.

Carlyle had attended private schools, been treated to ballet and piano lessons, and traveled to Europe three times before she was twenty, and that was the problem, because her family's money had fooled her into thinking she was safe. Safe from racism and the dangers that came with it. At the age of fourteen, the real world caught up to her. After that nothing was ever the same.

XXXIII
Visitors

The night it happened, fourteen-year-old Carlyle was attending a slumber party at the Washington home of Vanessa Carter, a black girl who was her age and also her best friend. An hour into the party a carload of drunken white cops drove through the neighborhood, shooting so-called wild dogs, *nigger* dogs, and suddenly there were bullets breaking the bedroom window, and Carlyle screamed as Vanessa fell to the floor, the front of her flowered nightgown darkened by a red stain. She died with her eyes open and unseeing, her blood on Carlyle's bare feet.

The cops were never brought to justice, Carlyle said. A white judge ruled Vanessa had died at the hands of party or parties unknown. Case closed, to be forever forgotten. Except by Carlyle, who'd devoted her life to making cops remember Vanessa. She'd written for newspapers in Washington, Virginia, and Maryland and done a year of television before deciding she hated it, and in that time, on Vanessa's behalf, she'd become a cop's worst nightmare.

I said, "In your place I'd have done the same. While we're

clearing the air, I've like to say something about the trouble between me and Eugene Elder."

Carlyle sat up straight. "How'd he get into the conversation?"

"It's no secret you two are seeing each other again," I said. "I figure you'll tell him about the airport. He'll then say I'm the lowest form of life on the planet. You think I framed Elder to get him out of the prosecutor's office. That's not the way it happened."

"As a matter of fact, Gene is coming here to pick me up," she said.

"When he shows," I said, "don't be surprised if a spontaneous aversion breaks out between us."

She narrowed her eyes. "I won't."

"Hear me out," I said. "Elder wasn't framed. He did the crime but not the time. He stole money and drugs from the DA's office and never did a day in prison. He pulled off one hell of a scam. And you went for it."

"Gene told me you framed him. Now you're asking me to believe you didn't."

"In your eyes Elder was the real deal. You were in love, and I was the wrong color. Did he say why I framed him?"

Carlyle raised both eyebrows. "Are you sure you want to maintain this level of candor? I don't mind if you don't mind."

"Fire away," I said.

"Gene said you belonged in the Klan with a sheet covering your fat white ass. He said the day they took away your badge, black people should declare a national holiday."

"He doesn't like you," Dion said.

I said it sure looks that way.

Dion said, "Fear also enjoys killing the spotted owl. Put that in your story next time you write about him."

"Don't mind Dion," I said. "Every time they start *Jeopardy!* something comes over him. I take it you agreed with Elder that I'm morally challenged?"

Carlyle nodded. "To be frank, yes. But that was then. Right now, I don't know what to think about you."

"And the rest of the story?" I said.

"You already know it. You got to Gene before he got to

you. You framed him. Instead of you being out of a job, Gene had his career ruined."

"If Elder got a raw deal, as he claims," I said, "how come he didn't sue me or the city? And where were the press conferences proclaiming his innocence? What better time to tell the world you're a victim and should be paid for it."

Carlyle turned to face me. There was something appealing about her honesty, especially when she wasn't being ballistic. She really cared about Elder, which was a shame. Because the man didn't deserve her.

She said, "Gene didn't sue for the same reason he asked me not to write about his resignation. He didn't want bad publicity. He wanted to go into private practice without notoriety. As he told me, crybabies don't get the big clients. He was black and proud, and he walked away from a job he loved without whining. He showed the world he could take anything white people dished out and not break. Look, I'm sorry. I don't mean to be disrespectful, but you did ask me."

I said, "No problem. Your friend Gene sounds like he can do everything except make his own spaghetti. Did you know that he, Schiafino, and Bauza own an East Side topless club called Shares?"

She looked shocked. "You're wrong. He's the club lawyer. He told me so himself. The club's owned by a Japanese company."

"Check the liquor license," I said. "His name won't be on it, but if you keep plugging, the trail will eventually lead to him. Also, talk to the people supplying his liquor, food, linens, and vending machines. Talk to the girls who work there. Elder, Schiafino, and Bauza also own a Shares in Washington."

"He spends time in Washington. That I know. But he never mentioned any topless club down there. Look, what's this got to do with you getting him fired?"

I said it showed she didn't know Elder as well as she thought she did.

Carlyle said, "You're forgetting something. He didn't go to prison. We both know that black men accused of crimes usually end up behind bars. Guilty or innocent, it doesn't matter."

I said *innocent* wasn't a word that came to mind whenever I thought of Elder. A more appropriate term was *slippery*.

"He conned you," I said, "and I'm betting it wasn't the first time. That's Daddy Duke. He didn't do time because he made a sweetheart of a deal for himself. Care to hear the details?"

"Enlighten me," Carlyle said.

I said Elder knew the DA's office couldn't afford to try him. The minute he was indicted, all of his cases could be overturned. Putting him on trial meant freeing as many as ten thousand criminals, each convicted and sent away by Elder. At the very least you could count on the bad guys appealing their sentences. The state was looking at a nightmare, and Elder knew it. So he proposed a deal. He was to go free. No prison time, no fines, no disbarment. In return he'd keep quiet, and the courts wouldn't be tied up for the next twenty years with appeals of his cases. The state had no choice. It took the deal.

Carlyle Taylor shook her head. "I don't believe you."

"You don't want to believe me. How about believing the case file? Read it and draw your own conclusions. I'm betting Elder talked you into taking his word and not looking too closely at the facts. Continuing the spirit of candor we've got going here, I'd say you didn't do your job as a reporter. He played the race card, and you let him get away with it. You never really investigated this case, did you?"

Carlyle looked away.

"There were additional police investigators on that case," I said. "Other witnesses as well. Check with them, then tell me who's lying. Oh, here's one more source you might want to look up. Someone who wanted to see Elder convicted in the worst way. His ex-wife. The one you had words with when you two ran into each other Christmas shopping. Who threw the first punch?"

Carlyle laughed. It had been some time since I'd heard a woman's laughter in the house. The sound was warm. Pure pleasure.

"She hit me first," Carlyle said. "Esther damn near took my head off. Gene had told me he was getting a divorce. Apparently, he forgot to tell her."

"Some things just slip the mind," I said. "Could happen to anybody."

"Let's change the subject, shall we? I owe you and your father for what you did tonight. I can't help the way I feel about cops, but I do know you didn't kill Lynda Schiafino. I was told you loved her, that you did everything possible to help her career. I think that's called being someone's rabbi."

I said, "I don't know about being Lynda's rabbi. But as far as my feelings for her are concerned, let's just say I think she was a good cop. One of the best I ever worked with."

"I understand. In other words you loved her but don't want to talk about it."

"What else did Lisa Watts tell you?" I said.

Carlyle nodded to show she was impressed. "Very good. Lisa said you were no dummy. Smart-mouthed, but no dummy."

"Next time you speak to her, give her my regards. Tell me something. Ever hear of a crew called the Exchange Students?"

"No. Who are they, and what do they do?"

I said I might have a story for her, maybe the biggest of her career. But to get, she'd have to give. She could start by doing me a favor.

"Robichaux and his family aren't talking to white people," I said.

"Can you blame them?"

"Be that as it may, I'd like you to set up a meeting. I think you'll want to be there. You might find it interesting."

Carlyle leaned toward me. "You saying Maurice is innocent?"

"Let's just say I'm not as anxious to see him go away as I was a couple of days ago. I think he met someone at the airport the night Lynda was murdered. Just like he said. But that someone refuses to come forward, and I don't think he intends to. It's all tied up with the Exchange Students and city politics. Like I said, it's a big story, and you might want to follow up on it."

Carlyle leaned her head to one side and studied my face. "I'd like to know about these Exchange Students."

"I'm sure you would. Just as I'm sure there're things you're not telling me at the moment. Maybe we'll sit down one day and open our hearts to each other. Until then trust me when I tell you I have to see Robichaux."

"I definitely want to be there."

"Any chance we can keep this between ourselves?"

"You mean don't tell Gene."

The doorbell rang.

"Guess who?" Dion said.

A tense Carlyle Taylor looked toward the front door. When the bell rang a second time, she flinched. What a soap opera this was. A black woman caught between the black man she couldn't forget and the white man who'd saved her life. A white man who was also holding out the promise of a big story, meaning the more ambitious she was, the harder it would be to ignore me.

I left her in the living room freshening her lipstick and walked toward the front door. At the foyer closet, I took my nine from the shelf and tucked it in the small of my back, under my shirt. Having overheard the Carlyle-Elder conversation, Dion would also be packing. Daddy Duke was on a mission for Schiafino. He wouldn't be traveling alone.

I opened the door to see the tall and elegant Eugene Elder standing in the cold darkness, dressed in an ankle-length mink coat, white silk scarf, white leather cap, and Gucci loafers. He appeared prosperous. Even the steam floating from his nostrils looked high-priced. There was a silver Rolls parked at the curb, which had to be his because it wasn't mine. He smelled of Paco Rabanne, and judging by the way he curled his top lip, his loathing for me was as intense as ever.

He'd brought some friends with him, three young wide-bodies, two of them white, the other black, each one a ste-roid freak with a swollen neck, gargantuan chest, and matching thighs. I figured them for bouncers who worked for Shares and were being paid extra for leaning on me. They were about to learn it never paid to expend too much energy in hope and expectation.

I stood in the doorway dressed in a shirt, pants, and slippers, no socks, the cold air smacking me in the chest as I watched Carlyle throw herself into Elder's arms. He held her, but his eyes were on me.

"You have something that belongs to me," he said. "I want it."

"How's it going, Gene?" I said. "Club must be doing well. You look like you're rolling in it. Must be a fortune in silicone these days."

"Don't jerk me around, Meagher. Carlyle's told you I want what you found at the airport. Give it up so I can get out of here."

"Gene, Gene. We don't see each other for years and you show up with three mutants and a bad attitude. You call that being sociable?"

Elder gently passed Carlyle on to one of his goons, a big white guy with snot on his mustache. Snotty smoothly guided Carlyle behind him, then said to me, "Listen up, fuckhead. I don't like being called a mutant."

He started toward the house.

Elder held out a hand and restrained him. I didn't feel at risk. But I did feel cold, tired, and irritable. I'd had a long day, and I wanted to lie down in a quiet, dark room. Instead I was in my doorway, freezing my nuts off and talking to people I didn't like.

I said to Snotty, "You ever kill anybody?"

"Is that supposed to make me wet my pants?" he said. He gave me a look meant to indicate he'd seen it all. Being half my age, he hadn't seen much at all.

I shook my head. "No. But it's the wrong answer."

I said to Elder, "He doesn't think I'll kill him. What do you think, Gene? Think I'll smoke this dipshit if he tries forcing his way into my house?"

I flashed my tin and told Snotty and his friends that my father and I were cops and that we could kill him legally just for ringing the bell too many times and that if he or anybody else put one foot in the house, they were history.

Judging by the look on Snotty's face, Daddy Duke had been less than forthcoming. Snotty looked perplexed. And intimidated. Snotty looked at Elder, and so did Snotty's muscle-bound friends. Snotty said to Elder, "You never told me these guys were cops. You just said they were deadbeats who refused to repay a loan."

Elder glared at me but spoke to Snotty. "Dig, Richie. You're not supposed to wet your pants, remember?"

Snotty nodded. "Right." Holding up both hands, he looked at me and said, *Everything's cool.* He and his friends backed away.

That left me and Elder, with a shivering Carlyle looking on.

Elder said, "I'd like to come inside and talk."

I said, "I don't think so. Besides, we've nothing to talk about."

Looking up at the darkened sky, Elder blew steam toward the stars. "I can't tell you how fascinating it is to stand here in the cold and watch a man self-destruct. Last chance. Give me what you found in the tunnel. Otherwise—"

"Otherwise what?"

He took a step back. "If that's how you want it. You've broken the chain of evidence, so what you're holding can't help Robichaux. And if you think you can put Bobby at the airport the night Robichaux killed Lynda, think again. You just cranked it up for all of us. From now on, we play hardball."

He walked toward his car, a hand on Carlyle's arm, pulling her with him. She didn't like that. She pulled away, rubbed her arm where he'd held her, then said she'd been walking on her own for years. He said something I couldn't hear, and she shouted that he could go to hell. I was starting to warm up to Carlyle, even if her taste in men wasn't the best.

After the Rolls pulled away, I returned to the living room, where Dion, .38 tucked in his belt, held something out to me. It was Carlyle's card. Her home number was on the back. Score one for the fat-assed white guy.

Seating myself on the couch, I fingered the card and thought about something Elder had said. His threats didn't concern me. We'd always been enemies, and that wasn't going to change. What bothered me was this: Elder had gotten on me for even daring to think that Schiafino might have been at Kennedy when Lynda was killed, something I'd discussed with Dion just minutes ago.

XXXIV
Mikey

The next morning Jack Hayden called me at home while I was having coffee and going over Robichaux's arrest record again.

"It's official," he said. "Chalk up two more for the Exchange Students. The department's calling yesterday's action in the East Village a murder-suicide. Nieves killed Cuevas, then skied out the window."

Hayden sounded wired, a man sweating bullets. Was he rethinking his decision to go after the Exchange Students? I hoped not, because without him my investigation was up the creek. At the same time I couldn't fault the guy. He'd just seen the Exchange Students smoke two vics and go scot free, which was enough to make anyone fudge his undies.

Hayden had one thing going for him, namely, a deep and fervent wish to get Bauza. The downside was his desire to make captain, a factor which could easily induce him to betray anybody. The time for me to worry was when he started being pleasant. Hayden was always agreeable when he was stabbing you in the back.

"This should make Munro happy," I said. "No more lost merchandise. No more increases in his insurance premiums. Even the mob will think twice before hijacking his trucks.

Speaking of which, you know a CCCH Construction Company?"

"As a matter of fact, I do. Why the sudden interest?"

A cop's taught to pay attention to anything that catches his eye. Especially when it catches his eye more than once. I'd run across the CCCH name twice in one day, at the Lesnevitch home and at the airport. Instinct said check it out.

On the other hand, common sense told me not to mention the airport. Not unless I wanted to listen to Hayden blow his stack. Going to the airport meant I'd been looking into Lynda's murder, and that's all he'd need to hear. It could be the excuse he was looking for to close down the Exchange Students investigation. I also didn't think he'd be too happy to hear about my new and strange relationship with Carlyle Taylor.

I said, "Yesterday when I went to see Lynda's father, CCCH was repairing the family garage. I've seen the name around and wanted to know something about the company."

I didn't need Hayden to tell me CCCH was mob-owned. Wiseguys controlled New York construction down to the last hammer and nail. Construction companies, labor unions, carting companies, and security guards. The mob owned them all. It also set the price on every foot of concrete poured in this town, including projects commissioned by the city. New York rents were the highest in the country, and a big reason was the mob's stranglehold on construction.

"CCCH is a front for the Drucci crime family," Hayden said. "The company has Little Augie LaTempa on the books as a salesman. Plumbing equipment. You believe that shit?"

I said, "You don't suppose Schiafino got his father-in-law a deal on the garage job through Bauza. Haysoos talks to Little Augie, and Oz Lesnevitch gets a new garage at half price."

"Yeah, right. The hell's this got to do with your case?"

Cops work on instinct. On what some might call unverified supposition. I heard Hayden's question, but my mind was on the past two days, and then instinct took over, and the answer hit me between the eyes, and I wondered why I hadn't seen it before now. I became so hyped I nearly dropped my coffee cup. Across the room the kitchen window glowed with the morning sun. I stared at the crimson glass until it began to shimmer, until its red warmth surrounded me and I was standing in the middle of the sun, whose light revealed all secrets to me. The front doorbell rang, and I heard Dion say *I've got it*. I also heard another voice, this one belonging to Oz Lesnevitch. *Lynda's in the garage. She's in the garage.*

To give myself time to calm down, I asked Hayden for the names of CCCH clients.

"The city's a big client," he said. "School repairs, public housing, office renovations. Last month they installed new windows at City Hall. The Drucci family and Little Augie are in our files. In case you've forgotten, we do investigate organized crime."

I said, "Sounds like Little Augie's connected down at City Hall. Somebody important is giving that little greaseball a lot of business. Any idea who that somebody is?"

"Try Ray Footman," Hayden said.

I lit another cigarette. So Deputy Mayor Footman, the mayor's campaign manager and the city's chief bleeding heart, was pouring money into the coffers of organized crime. Marvy. Absolutely fucking marvy.

I said, "Does Footman know who these guys really are?"

"He knows," Hayden said. "But lying fuck that he is, he'll swear CCCH is legit. True, the guys who run it don't have prison records. They go to church every Sunday, build tree houses for their kids, and vote Republican. It's the people behind them you got to worry about. First Footman brings civilians into the department. Then he puts wiseguys on the city payroll. The thought of this Jew bastard dumping on the department for another four years turns my stomach. But if the mayor gets in, Footman gets in with him."

"Footman's good at raising money," I said. "Him and Jonathan Munro. That's how elections are won."

Hayden yawned into the phone. "Back to the Exchange Students. They impressed me with that shit in the East Village yesterday. They're good. We're up to our hips in dead Ecuadorans, and nobody seems to notice. Know what this says? Says this crew has a rabbi. Someone covering for them."

I said he was probably right and let it go at that. The dumbest thing I could do at the moment was name names. Tag McGuigan or Lacovara as the rabbi, and Hayden would go bananas.

"One thing's for sure," Hayden said. "Footman's not the rabbi. The man's no friend to the department. And speaking of cops, you left out one name in connection with the Exchange Students."

I waited, knowing what he was going to say.

"Schiafino," Hayden said. "Bauza's his yes-man. If Bauza's down with the Exchange Students, Schiafino knows about it. He has to."

"I had my reasons for keeping him out of it."

"His wife," Hayden said.

"People will say I went after him because of her. How do you answer that?"

"You don't. You make the best case you can and pray it holds up."

Lynda's in the garage. I couldn't think of anything else. I wanted to slam down the phone and get to Dion, the only one I could trust with my theory about Lynda's murder. The department wouldn't buy it; to do so would mean turning Robichaux loose and going after one of its own. McGuigan might go for it, but moral conduct wasn't exactly a priority with him, not as long as he had his eye on the commissioner's job. Carlyle Taylor was a possibility. She believed Maurice Robichaux was innocent, and she'd led me to the hundred-dollar bills. But there was the little problem of her relationship with Eugene Elder, and since this thing was about race, there was always the possibility of her cutting my throat in the name of black solidarity.

Hayden said, "Schiafino's got the department and the whole city on his side. Take him on, and you take them on. The press is camped out in front of his house around the clock. A TV show's offering him two hundred fifty thousand dollars for an exclusive interview. For that kind of money, I'd floss with the string from one of my wife's old tampons."

"You'd have to murder her first," I said.

Schmuck, I thought. *Not yet.*

I got lucky. Hayden let my remark pass without comment.

"Killing wives is Robichaux's department," Hayden said. "How'd he get a name like Robichaux anyway? I thought spooks had names like Washington and Jefferson. Know something? George Washington and Thomas Jefferson were probably the last two white guys to have those names."

"I've got a name for you," I said. "Detective Third Grade Carl Keller. Big guy with red hair. Works with Lou Sobkavich out of Manhattan South. I make him as an Exchange Student. He was around yesterday when the last two Ecuadorans got smoked. And he hangs out with Aldo Sinatra."

"Keller," Hayden said. "I think I know the guy. The Keller I'm thinking of put eight shots into a perp's back and claimed self-defense. Got away with it. I'll check to see if it's the same Carl Keller."

After saying we'd talk later, Hayden hung up.

I stood with my hand on the receiver and thought about Lynda and how close I was to the truth. The longer I thought, the deeper I slipped into a flow of ideas, into a current of dark thoughts. When I heard the car horn, I nearly jumped out of my skin. It came from the front of the house. I walked to the living room and looked through the window in time to see Dion slide behind the wheel of my Ford. He'd just taken delivery from Juan Cedeño, the big-nosed fifty-year-old Puerto Rican who'd done my repairs for years. I didn't see Juan, so I assumed he was heading back to the garage with my check for five hundred bucks. Not only was I on Jullee Vulnavia's shit list, I also had to pay for the privilege.

I left the house dressed in a robe, slippers, and boxer shorts, not the best way to tackle thirty-degree temperature. A bright sun had the hard edge of winter to it, and there were patches of ice on the lawn. The calendar said spring, but you could have fooled me.

In the car I switched on the heater and said to Dion, How's she look?

"Good as new," he said. "Juan knows his stuff."

I rolled up the window. "I think I'm on to something," I said. "I think I know where Lynda was murdered. I'm missing a couple of pieces, but I'm closing in on the whole enchilada. McGuigan's the one who started me thinking."

"What's old Ditto Head up to now?"

"He said the Exchange Students are part of a conspiracy, one reaching into City Hall. Said it reminded him of the Cotton Club. You're the Harlem expert around here. What's he trying to say?"

Dion toyed with the gear shift. "Who knows. All I can tell you is the Cotton Club opened in Harlem during Prohibition. Hood named Owney Madden owned it. Cold-blooded as they come. Nickname was the Killer. Born in England, came here as a kid, and took to crime like a duck to water. You had the Cotton Club in the middle of Harlem, but blacks couldn't set foot in the place. It was whites only. Blacks worked the joint as entertainers, waiters, cooks. All the greats played there. Lena Horne, Duke, Cab Calloway."

I said, "So McGuigan's saying the black mayor's just a front. That whites really control City Hall."

Dion adjusted the rearview mirror. "Who's the one man to see if you want anything from City Hall?"

"The smartest Caucasian of them all," I said. "Ray Footman."

"Sounds like the Cotton Club to me."

I thought, *bingo*. One step closer. I was about to tell Dion my theory when someone said, "Detective Meagher, may I speak to you a moment, please?"

The voice belonged to my ever affable Indian neighbor, Mr. Mukerjee. He headed toward us, trailed by his butterball of a wife, who wore a green cloth coat over a pink-and-gold sari. As usual, Mr. Mukerjee carried his laptop, spoke in a high-pitched voice, and was as friendly as a puppy.

He said, "We have something for you and your father if you would like. It is a television set."

I rolled down the window. What the hell was this all about? When I looked at Dion, he shrugged. I turned back to the Mukerjees, who seemed to be waiting for me to say something. I kept quiet. I didn't like practical jokes, especially when they were played on me.

My unfriendly expression must have made Mr. Mukerjee

nervous. Edging away, he said, "If it pleases you, we can deliver it to your house. And you may keep it for as long as you like. Return it when yours is repaired."

I'd had enough. I said, "Mind telling me why you think there's something wrong with my TV set? I mean, how come you know something I don't."

Mukerjee's eyes widened. He appeared apologetic, ready to make amends for having wasted my time.

He spoke quickly, anxious to finish and be gone. "Please forgive me for having disturbed you and your father. Two times the men came to your house to make repairs, and I thought perhaps something had gone wrong, so I—"

He didn't finish. The look on my face got to him in a hurry. I wanted to kill somebody. But not the Mukerjees. Unfortunately, they didn't understand that. All they saw was a big, ugly cop who looked as if he wanted to drink their blood. They scurried away.

I looked at Dion. He was overwhelmed. We both knew.

I left the car in a hurry and called out to Mr. Mukerjee. He stopped dead, rigid with fear. His wife, close on his heels, ran into him. Watching them bump into each other was funny yet sad.

Immigrants are usually afraid of cops. With good reason. Illegals fear being jailed or deported. Those with green cards or American citizenship have memories of the old country, where the cops are often rapists, thieves, and murderers, and the only difference between them and the bad guys is that one group of scumbags has badges and the other doesn't.

I said, "Mr. Mukerjee, you'll have to excuse me. I've been working hard and I'm a bit on edge. These repairmen who fixed my TV set. Could you tell me when they came to the house?"

His eyes widened. The expression on his face asked if I was jerking him around. In the end he did the only thing he could do. He gave it up. Me being a cop and him being a civilian, what else could he do.

He said, "Yesterday. Two in the afternoon, I would say. I had come home early, you see. There was no heat at work. Most uncomfortable, most unpleasant. From my window I saw them. Two men. Their van was parked in front of your house. Could it be they came to repair your television and your father did not tell you?"

"Yes, sir," I said. "That could be. Sometimes he forgets things."

Dion would love hearing that.

I smiled at the Mukerjees, the first gesture of brotherhood on my part since they'd moved next door. I thanked them for their offer of the TV set. Then came the hard part. I held out my hand.

I did it knowing I'd treated the Mukerjees like shit. And I'd treated them that way because I'd wanted the neighborhood to be as it had always been, filled with people who looked like me. Going up against criminal immigrants had me leery of gate-crashers, trespassers, and others not of my world. Anyone waiting for me to roll out the Welcome Wagon to outsiders would wait a long time. I didn't care where they lived so long as it wasn't in my backyard.

To be honest, I had to admit the Mukerjees were different. They weren't criminals. They lived quietly, were friendly enough, and never caused trouble. Any trouble between us had been in my mind, something I couldn't bring myself to admit to them or anyone else. Maybe I should have apologized, but all I could do was offer my hand and hope I'd have the chance to make things right between us. Especially since I now owed the Mukerjees big time.

A smiling Mr. Mukerjee shook my hand. His wife smiled. I smiled. Peace in our time.

In the midst of this sudden serenity, my mind went to Daddy Duke, well-known lawyer and topless-bar businessperson. He'd said I'd never be able to put Schiafino at the airport. Jesus had bragged about Schiafino being ahead of me all the way. I thought of how surprised I'd been to learn that Schiafino knew about Lynda's letter. Bottom line: if the Mukerjees hadn't been nicer than their asshole cop neighbor, the asshole cop neighbor wouldn't have learned his home was bugged and that Mikey wasn't a person but a microphone.

XXXV
Look What I Found

I spent the next few minutes searching the house, looking for wires and transmitters hidden by Schiafino's people. I located two bugs easily enough. One was in the base of the kitchen phone. The other was behind the living-room couch.

Both were miniature transmitters, flat bits of metal no larger than a child's fingernail. Neither was what I'd call state-of-the-art. Both had a limited range, and in bad weather static would make them all but useless. But they were capable of getting the job done, and if you didn't know what to look for, they were all but invisible.

I left the bugs in place. Take them away, and the snoop listening in would turn tail and run. He was somewhere in the neighborhood, recording every call and every conversation between Dion and me. I didn't want him scared off. Not before we'd had a little chat.

Dion sat on a footstool near the fireplace, the two of us carrying on a conversation as though everything was hunky-dory. The fact is we were both angry as hell. To the Irish, *home* is a strong word, on a par with good health and a clean conscience. *Yet dearer still / that Irish hill / than all the world beside / it's home sweet home / where e'er I roam / through land and waters wide.*

I saw the house as an old friend, a place I could come to and feel human again. I'd failed to protect it from trespassers, leaving me more than a little down in the mouth. It was a defeat I hadn't counted on. I wasn't always at home in this city, but I was at home here. The house allowed me to dream in peace, something Schiafino had now taken away from me.

Knowing Schiafino, I figured his people had more than

231

two bugs planted around the place. He might even have bugged my car. I wouldn't know for sure until I'd brought in a pro and had him sweep the house and the Ford.

Meanwhile Dion and I talked about everything and nothing in particular. He said he and Maggie were thinking about a trip to Aruba next month, provided she didn't have to attend a bankers' conference in L.A. We discussed *Bonanza* reruns, computer dating, whether bigger was really better, and what fags did in bed. I told Dion I needed a new office air conditioner but that the paperwork involved was mind-boggling.

"Speaking of the office," I said, "I'd better get a move on. Hayden just called. Sounded nervous. I think that shooting in the East Village got to him. He knows it wasn't righteous, but he sees Schiafino's crew getting away with it."

"Schiafino. Fucking dago eats shit and barks at the moon."

"I'll drink to that. Right now I'm going to have a quick shower and shave, then head to the office."

Signaling Dion to follow me, I led him upstairs to the bathroom, closed the door behind us and flushed the toilet. After lighting a cigarette, I dropped the seat cover and sat down. Dion turned on the shower and sink taps, then jumped in the air, landing flat-footed on the tile floor. It was a quick way to neutralize wiretaps.

"Schiafino," Dion said. "Fucking guinea bastard comes into my home. Into *my home.*"

"D., listen up," I said. "We've got a few things to do, and there isn't much time. Schiafino knows Gavilan's been talking to me. The kid and his mother have to be warned. They can't stay in that apartment."

"How you gonna reach them? You can't use our phone."

"I'll have to find a clean phone in a hurry. I should warn McGuigan as well."

Dion said, "McGuigan? Didn't you say he might be the rabbi?"

"I've changed my mind."

The bathroom was becoming a sauna. Moisture dripped from the walls and shower curtains, and the basin mirror was covered by steam. The shower curtain glistened with condensation, and I was working up a pretty good sweat myself. Dion didn't mind the heat since it loosened up his bad shoulder. On the other hand, his red face probably owed as much to rising temperatures as it did to anger.

I said to Dion, "Bring in Ned Ray. Get him here as soon as possible."

Ned Ray was a retired cop and former partner of Dion's who'd had a lifelong gambling problem. These days he worked as a private investigator for a lawyer whose mob clients took most of Ned's salary in gambling losses. When he wasn't handing over his paycheck to the wiseguys, Ned was an electronics whiz. He owed Dion money, enough to get him to come here and sweep the house.

"Don't call Ned until you hear from me," I said. "Stay by the phone until I call. That'll be soon. And I'll be calling from around here."

"You're not going to work?"

I shook my head. "What I said downstairs was for the benefit of Mr. Big Ears, whoever he is."

Grabbing a towel, I dried my face, then rose from the toilet.

Dion said, "Where're you going?"

I said I was going to find Mr. Big Ears and convince him the world was a dangerous place.

XXXVI
We Meet Again

I parked the Ford on Queens Boulevard at ten-thirty that morning. Then I stared across the street at Roosevelt Avenue, where a gray panel truck was parked in front of an Irish import shop specializing in Donegal china and Cavan crystal. On the truck's sides, in red letters, was THREE CROWNS TV REPAIR. The front seat was empty.

The truck was just six blocks from my house, close enough for Schiafino's people to step in should anything go wrong with one of their bugs. Evidently, something had. Which is how the Mukerjees ended up catching "repairmen" making a house call.

I figured the rabbi had to have put in a call to Fred Estevez, the local precinct commander, telling him the panel truck was on surveillance and should be ignored. He'd offered no explanation, and Estevez would ask no questions, having his hands full with Lynda's death and work of his own.

I'd left the house, keeping my eyes open for a TV repair truck. There wasn't anything on my block or the next. I also came up empty on Forty-sixth Street, where I left the car, ducked into Sally O'Brien's pub, and made a quick call to Gavilan. No one was home. I left a message on the service, warning that Bauza and Schiafino knew he'd talked to me. I told him to take his mother and get the hell out of there. I put off contacting McGuigan, who wasn't big on talking on the phone. It would've taken too long to get through to him, and at the moment time was something I didn't have.

Back in my car, I continued driving along Forty-sixth Street. At Roosevelt Avenue, I made a right, and there it was. A television repair truck. One not from the neighborhood. I drove past it without slowing down, circled the block, then crossed Roosevelt Avenue. When I reached Queens Boulevard, I parked in front of a Korean nail salon.

After lighting a cigarette, I settled back to watch the truck. Figure Schiafino to have people on my house around the clock. If so, there'd have to be a changing of the guard at the truck. But after ten minutes, when no one approached the vehicle, I decided to pay a call on Mr. Big Ears.

I left the car carrying a baseball bat. An Italian .45, mob guys called it. But I didn't cross the street. Not yet. Instead I stood on the curb, looked across Queens Boulevard, and watched a thin black man approach the panel truck. He walked with a limp, favoring his left leg. He wore wraparound dark glasses and the same cashmere topcoat he'd had on yesterday. One hand gripped a brown bag, probably food. The other held a couple of folded newspapers. The spook was none other than Detective Larry Aarons.

I made no attempt to hide. A wide boulevard and heavy traffic kept me out of his immediate range of vision. In any case, he wasn't looking for me. As far as Aarons was concerned, I was heading to work. I waited for him to knock on the panel truck's rear doors. He didn't. Instead he unlocked the doors with a key and set his food on the van floor. Then, gripping a door handle with both hands, he cautiously pulled himself inside the vehicle and closed the doors. Interesting. Lethal Larry was working alone.

I managed to cross Queens Boulevard on foot, no small feat when you had to avoid potholes, wild-riding bicycle messengers, and Pakistani cab drivers who thought a red light meant speed up. Once on Roosevelt, I approached the panel truck from the rear, the bat hidden behind my thigh.

At the truck I stayed clear of the windows and pounded a rear door with my fist.

I said, "Hey, buddy. You, inside. You're being towed. You're in a no-parking zone. Unless you want to go along for the ride, you best get out here."

I swung the bat, connecting with the bumper. "I'm hooking up. Know what that means? Means your truck's gone. City regulations."

I smacked the bumper again, this time putting my back into the swing.

I heard Aarons stirring inside and yelling something I couldn't make out. He was on his way to greet me. I stepped away from the doors. A second later one door swung open, and Aarons leaned out. One hand held a hero sandwich while the other gripped a door handle. A white napkin protected his tailored blue blazer. Lethal Larry was mad as hell. Ready to snarl and bite. But the sight of me left him in shock. Instead of offering resistance, he ended up dribbling half-chewed food on his napkin.

I said, "Know something, Larry? I've just learned my phones are bugged, so I'm really stressed out. You know what stress is, don't you? It's that basic confusion created when one's mind overrides the body's basic desire to choke the living shit out of some asshole who desperately needs it."

I pointed to his left knee with the bat and asked if he'd mind backing up so I could come inside. He flinched. But he moved. Tomato sauce was dripping from the hero onto the napkin, making it look as though Lethal Larry had just taken a bullet to the chest.

Once in the van, I closed the doors behind me. Talk about a dump. Cramped, dark, and cold. Your typical surveillance van. Everything—electronics, equipment, newspapers, blankets, empty fast-food containers, and overflowing ashtrays—was piled on one long metal table. A small black-and-white TV had been dumped in the middle of this mess. On-screen, a has-been blond actress with teased hair and a bad face-lift was hosting a morning talk show. Aarons's holstered .38 was beside the set, along with a pair of oversize earphones used for eavesdropping. Under the table a space heater glowed a bright orange.

I could have shoved my Glock in Aarons's face, but that would have constituted overkill. I'd already fucked up his knee, leaving him less than frisky. I did have the bat. And I'd caught him off guard. At the moment Lethal Larry appeared too overwhelmed to do anything but stare at me. I directed him to one of two folding chairs. Then I drew up a chair next to him, sat down, and placed the bat in my lap. Where he could see it.

"You bugged my home," I said. "I'm really vexed about that."

We sat facing each other, my hands on the bat. Aarons put down his hero, removed the napkin, and looked down at his brown-and-white shoes. Anywhere but at the bat.

"I just do what I'm told," he said. "Somebody else is calling the shots."

"And I know who," I said. "But I can't take it out on Schiafino. So I'm thinking maybe I should take it out on you. What do you say?"

I placed the fat part of the bat on Aarons's left knee, the sore one. He tried to stay cool, to maintain a poker face. The best he could do was blink and try to hold my gaze.

"What do you want to know?" he said.

He massaged his damaged knee. "This shit's your fault," he said. "Told them I got hurt playing basketball. I'm on sick leave, but I can't hang around the house, right? I get this call saying get my ass over here."

"Schiafino," I said.

"Whatever. All I know is I'm here since six this morning, and I stay till I'm relieved."

"And when will that be?"

"Noon."

I looked at my watch. Five after eleven. Plenty of time.

"About Jullee," I said. "You didn't tell me everything. You said she's the paymaster for the Washington Exchange Students. You forgot to tell me what she's bringing back to New York."

Aarons closed his eyes.

I said, "Larry, you tried to waste me. I haven't forgotten that. I suggest you save yourself some grief. Jullee's bringing back something from D.C. One way or another you're going to tell me what it is."

"Money," he said.

"Excuse me?" I tapped the bat with my palm.

"Jullee's carrying both ways," Aarons said. "She's paying our people down there. But that money ain't shit compared to what she's bringing back."

"Give me a figure."

"Last trip? Eight hundred grand."

"Eight hundred thousand dollars? Might I ask who's being so generous with the little bitch?"

"The people we service in Washington," Aarons said.

"Let me get this straight. Fifty grand a hit isn't chump change. So where do you come off collecting twice?"

"Fuck's wrong with you?" Aarons said. "Haven't you figured it out yet?"

We locked eyes. Finally, he looked away in disgust.

I put the bat on the table, leaned back in my chair, and let my mind go its own way.

I said, "Son of a bitch. Schiafino's blackmailing his clients."

Aarons shrugged. "Business is business."

"You kill, they pay," I said. "Then you make them pay again. And they don't have a choice. Either they pay or get tagged as an accessory to murder."

"That ain't all they got to worry about."

"You mean they're afraid of being killed."

Aarons brushed a crumb from his blazer. "We don't have a problem collecting, if that's what you mean."

I said, "So that's why Schiafino doesn't want me bothering Jullee. It also explains the problem with Harvey. Sitting on all that money is making him antsy."

Aarons frowned and said, "Harvey? Don't know no Harvey."

"Strange. And you look so intelligent, too. Your boy Jonathan Munro knows Harvey. He's worried about him. He wants Schiafino to straighten Harvey out."

Aarons's eyes went dead. "Don't know no Harvey."

I took the bat from the table. Slowly.

"I was at Bauza's apartment when Munro called," I said. "He left a message on the service about Harvey. I was there to see Gavilan. You do know Gavilan. You've been tapping my phones long enough."

Aarons put up his hands in surrender. "OK, OK. So I know Harvey. Man's always bitching about something. All Jews do is complain."

"Back to Jullee. She returns from D.C. with big bucks, which she then turns over to Harvey for safekeeping. What's to stop him from copping the money?"

Aarons grinned and said, "Common sense."

"You mean Schiafino?"

Aarons shrugged. "Call it what you will. By the way, that money doesn't belong to Bobby. Belongs to the man down at City Hall."

I said, "You mean the rabbi?"

Aarons blew into his cupped hands to warm them and said, "Don't be asking me about him. Bobby, he deals with that dude."

"You're being unfactual, Larry," I said. "Possibly even devoid of the truth. You know who the rabbi is. We both know. Just as we know the money Harvey's sitting on is meant for the mayor's reelection campaign."

Aarons chewed a corner of his mouth, then looked down at his two-tones.

Lighting a cigarette, I thought about Harvey and the

blackmail money. It had to add up to millions. And Bobby Schemes was planning to walk off with the whole bundle.

I said to Aarons, "How many Exchange Students are there?"

"Enough," he said.

I tapped his bad knee with the bat. A gentle tap, but Aarons had dark memories of me and his knee, so he flinched and drew back, almost falling from his chair.

"Wrong answer," I said.

Aarons closed his eyes. "Eight in New York. Another seven in D.C."

"Schiafino being a control freak, I assume he does the recruiting himself."

Rubbing his knee, Aarons nodded. "Bobby's careful. And he gets around. Police seminars, weapons conventions, union meetings, funerals."

"Schiafino recruits at police funerals?"

"You want to meet cops, you go where cops are."

"Makes sense," I said. "I'm also assuming you don't re-sign from this crew. Once in, you stay in. Right?"

Aarons didn't answer. He didn't have to. We both knew the only way to control cops like the Exchange Students was through fear.

I said, "How do you find your clients?"

"That's Daddy Duke's department," Aarons said. "Like I said, I just take orders."

"Daddy Duke," I said. "Big-time lawyer with rich clients. And rich friends like Jonathan Munro. Thinking out loud now. What are the chances of Daddy and Munro knowing affluent folks who want someone killed? Good to excellent, I'd say. And let's not forget Daddy meets clients through his clubs here and in D.C. Hit men and blackmailers. Not what I would call sensitive New Age guys, Larry."

"Don't understand you," Aarons said. "You should be with us, not sitting there pointing the finger. Dig. We ask for extra money, know what some people say? They say it's worth it. You got a father whose daughter's been raped and murdered. Now along comes somebody who says the law's not going to do shit. Pay me, and I'll take care of your problem. You're going to feel a lot better after I do the guy who did your kid. That father will pay anything. Anything. Know what this means? Means we got it going on. Means we're doing the right thing."

I said the Exchange Students were executing people without due process. Didn't that bother him?

Aarons smiled and said, "*You* do it. Don't see you losing no sleep over a dead perp."

"I don't kill for money. And I only eliminate people who try to eliminate me."

"Yeah, right. Gonna let you in on a little secret. Something white folks don't know. There's blacks and there's niggers, and I don't like niggers any more than you do. Niggers make the race look bad, know what I'm saying? Now I got a chance to change that. I got a chance to deal with the brothers who walked into a church in South Jamaica two years ago and shot my mother in the back of the head while she was praying. Killed my mother in church, and for what? For three dollars, 'cause that's all she had on her."

Aarons leaned forward, warming to his subject. "Think I'm down with Bobby for money? Shit, I'd do it for nothing. We got guys, black and white, who feel the same way. They're doing what people want done. It ain't wrong, man. No way is it wrong."

I said, "It is when you murder a cop and blame an innocent man."

Aarons drew back as though struck in the face. "Fuck you talking about?"

I stared at him until he turned away to pick at his hero sandwich, flicking bits of bread at the TV set.

"Don't want to get into that," he said.

I said, "You're black, and so's Maurice Robichaux. He's being framed for a crime he didn't commit. Happens to black men a lot these days. Doesn't that bother you? Believe it or not, it bothers me."

"Since when did you start caring about black people?"

"I don't. But I care about innocent men going to prison. I care because it's wrong and because it means the real perp's getting away. Robichaux didn't kill Lynda, and you know it."

Aarons wiped his fingers with his napkin. "You can shoot

my eyes out. But there's no way you get me to talk about that."

Want to make a perp confess? Get inside his head. I tried it with Aarons.

"You're loyal to Schiafino," I said. "I appreciate that. What I'd like to know is why?"

"Wasn't for Bobby, I wouldn't be living in a new house in Westchester with a backyard and a two-car garage. Wouldn't be sending my thirteen-year-old daughter to private school. Bobby's paying for all that. Plus I get the chance to do the right thing."

I said, "Schiafino has his own agenda, and it doesn't include you. Who do you think's going to walk off with all that money Harvey's got? The money the rabbi thinks belongs to him?"

Aarons's smile said he could be one deceitful brother when necessary.

"Got mine, Jack," he said. "Bobby wants to Jap the rabbi, that's cool with me. Meanwhile we never had this conversation. And one more thing: I'm not ratting out Bobby. No way, no how. Wasn't for him, I'd still be living in Harlem, tiptoeing through dog shit and waiting for crackheads to come through the back window. Bobby wants Harvey's money, he's welcome to it."

I said Schiafino was going to get him killed. At best Aarons would end up in prison, sucking dick to stay alive.

He said I was the one who had to worry. Bobby had my ass going around in circles. So what if I'd found the bugs. My worries weren't over, not by far. As long as I messed with Bobby, I'd be looking over my shoulder and hearing footsteps.

I ordered him to climb behind the wheel. We'd discuss my mental state on the way.

He made a face. "Where we going?"

"To mess with Bobby," I said.

XXXVII
Eeny Meeny Miney Mo

Shares was on Manhattan's East Side, facing the UN on First Avenue and Forty-fourth Street. If Shares was tits and ass and all sorts of wicked goings-on, the UN was six blocks of bad architecture and dimwits who believed they could change the world through press releases. The UN wasn't a part of New York or the United States. It was international territory, meaning when the delegates weren't punching out call girls, they were running up unpaid parking tickets.

Shares, on the other hand, was Schiafino's territory. Unlike the UN, it didn't have its own stamps and post office. But it did have its own army. I figured some were local cops hired to work security and discourage city inspectors from finding violations. Others were probably Exchange Students out for a bit of leisure. I had no idea how many were on the premises this afternoon. But I knew my coming here was the equivalent of riding the tiger. Still, I couldn't let Schiafino's attack on my home go unanswered.

From the outside Shares wasn't much to look at. It had a gold canopy that sagged in the middle and needed cleaning. On the front door was a brass plate engraved with the club name and the inscription: FOUNDED APRIL 1, 1993 A.D. The windows were covered by thick gray curtains and decorated with color photos of busty ladies in pasties, G-strings, and lots of lip gloss. All of the women—white, black, Asian—had blond hair. Those who hadn't been born with it wore wigs or sported dye jobs. According to Lynda, the all-blond concept had been Schiafino's idea. It also explained his nickname for the club—the House of Lemon-Flavored Pussy.

I followed Aarons into the club lobby, where he waved to a huge young Hispanic guarding the door. I had one hand in my right overcoat pocket, gripping the Glock. Aarons had his .38 back, minus the bullets. I'd told him just lead me to Daddy Duke, then he was free to go home to the suburbs. Get cute, and commuting wouldn't be his only problem.

A sign near the coat check said Shares was open noon to 4:00 A.M., and featured a hundred topless dancers, a hug-'n'-squeeze room, bottomless shows, happy hour, panties give-away, and a continuous showing of all stock and commodity quotes in real time. Shares also offered free admission, discount parking, and private dancing in its Happy Valley Room. For a night they would never forget, bachelors were urged to ask about the club's private bachelor parties.

Aarons told the doorman I was with him. The Hispanic neither smiled nor bid me welcome. He had the rigid, controlled face of a man trying hard not to give anything away. I made him as a born liar. In turn he made me as a cop. Nervously scratching his face, he told Aarons we were just in time for the noon show. This wasn't my first time in a topless club. So I knew the guy to see if you wanted drugs was usually the doorman. Which might explain our Hispanic friend's edginess around cops.

Aarons led me into the main room, where mirrored walls reflected dozens of colored lights and a gold ceiling. The lighting was dim, but not too dim to prevent patrons from seeing everything. There was the usual bass-heavy disco music, but it was being turned down as we entered. The air was gray with cigarette smoke and sweet with cheap perfume. Lethal Larry and I had to push our way through a packed house of males who'd crowded the bar and taken nearly every table. Noon shows were the most popular. A noontime terrorist attack on Manhattan topless clubs would kill enough CEOs to cripple the nation's economy into the next decade.

The waitresses wore lingerie. The bouncers—Shares called them floor managers—wore tuxedos. In the center of the room was a small stage with a pole running to the ceiling and visible from all sides. The first wave of "talent," a dozen dancers in low-cut gowns, stood onstage while being introduced by an unseen disc jockey who read the girls' credits over a loudspeaker. Meryl Streep didn't have to worry. The credits, such as they were, consisted of appearances in porn magazines, triple-X skin flicks, music videos, and, in rare cases, bit roles in legit films and commercials.

Meanwhile the girl being introduced would slip out of her gown and let the paying customers see what she was selling. At this point she wore a G-string and, in compliance with the law as I knew it, latex on her nipples. She'd then grab the pole, sliding up and down as though the pole was the mother of all joysticks. Some girls had pierced nipples and tattoos. But when it came to breast enlargements, all had taken the plunge. There was enough silicone onstage to lubricate every motor vehicle in North America.

Lethal Larry slowed down to eye a black dancer with short blond hair who'd just finished a split and now lay back on the stage, huge tits pointing to the ceiling. Her boobs didn't droop, sag, or hang to the side. Big as they were, there should have been some motion while she was flat on her back. Never happened. You could have whacked her maracas with a two-by-four and they wouldn't have budged.

I prodded Aarons with the Glock. Wakey, wakey, I whispered. I had no idea who'd seen me enter the club or who might be closing in on me. The wise thing was to put distance between myself and this crowd of dance aficionados.

Aarons led me across the room and to a narrow passageway. At the end of it was a small door with PRIVATE on it in gold letters. Aarons knocked and said, "Gene, you in there? It's me, Larry. I got the tapes from Meagher's house."

Elder said come in.

Aarons opened the door and I followed him in, kicking the door shut behind me. We were in a small, low-ceilinged office, the kind designed to hold a desk, a couple of filing cabinets, maybe a wastebasket, but not much else. A ground-floor, barred window offered a rear view of nearby brownstones. The office walls were covered in autographed photographs of naked and half-naked women with names like Infinity, Brandy, Siren, and Tiffany. Some space was given over to autographed pictures of local sports figures who'd been Shares's customers.

Elder sat on the edge of a black metal desk, talking into

a cellular phone and puffing a twisted Cuban cigar, the kind that were illegal in this country and cost a fortune to get hold of. He wore a gray pinstriped suit tailored to his lanky frame, and since he wasn't wearing a hat, I got my first look at the ponytail he'd grown. It wasn't much. Just some kinky hair at the base of his neck, tied into a greasy, egg-size lump.

Given the kind of hair black guys had, one wondered why they bothered with ponytails. But things have a way of evening out. To make up for what he'd done to their hair, God had given black guys big dicks.

At the sight of me, Elder became all eyeballs. He stopped talking and inhaled loudly through his mouth. Then he started blinking. Eventually, when he stopped blinking and I still hadn't disappeared, he resumed talking. Showing me how cool he was.

"I'm here, I'm here," he said into the phone. "Look, stay away from Gina Branch. She's Bauza's lady, and neither one of them wants to meet with the press. Especially when it involves a cop killing."

He was talking to Carlyle Taylor.

If he was unhappy with her, he was even more displeased with Lethal Larry for bringing me here. He gave Aarons one hell of a dirty look, to which all Aarons could do in response was shrug and shake his head by way of saying *what choice did I have?*

Meanwhile, Carlyle Taylor seemed to have a lot on her mind, because Elder was doing a lot of listening. Finally, he exploded. Leaping from the desk, he threw his cigar at the window.

"Meagher sent you to talk with my ex-wife?" he said. "Since when do you take orders from that fat Paddy?"

I took out my Glock, held it up so Elder could see it, then pried the phone from his fingers. I motioned him and Aarons back against the door, then spoke into the phone.

"Carlyle, this is Fear."

"Fear Meagher?"

"One and the same."

"What are you doing at Gene's apartment?" she said.

I said, "We're not at Gene's apartment. We're at Shares, the topless club he owns with Schiafino and Bauza."

"He told me he was calling from home."

"Did he now. Well, if that's the case, he's got a dozen women dancing naked in his living room and a hundred and fifty of his closest friends watching the show. Anyway, I just dropped by to tell Gene to stop bugging my house and tapping my phone calls. I gather he's still pressuring you to leave Bauza alone."

"Whoa," she said. "Slow down. Gene's tapping your phones?"

"Cute little rascal that he is, yes. But we'll discuss that another time. So tell me about Bauza."

"For the life of me, I don't see why Gene's so uptight about this. There's a connection between Robert Schiafino and Maurice Robichaux, and that connection is Detective Bauza, Schiafino's ex-partner. It's just coincidence, that's all. But it's something I feel has to be said if the story's to be complete. And speaking of complete, I put in a call to the airport this morning. Guess what? CCCH Construction is back on the job. They're in the process of closing off Maurice's little hideaway."

I said, "Where are you now?"

"At my paper. Forty-first Street and Second."

I said, Be downstairs in exactly half an hour, then hung up.

I said to Elder, "Tell Schiafino to stay away from my home."

"You tell him," Elder said. "He'll be happy to hear from you."

I sat on the edge of the desk, placed the Glock on my thigh, and dialed home. "Gene, Gene," I said. "What do you think would happen if the cops were to receive an anonymous call saying a naked black man was running loose in a topless club, waving his johnson around and scaring the shit out of the dancers?"

Elder and Aarons exchanged looks, then focused on me.

When I got Dion on the line, I said *do it*. I didn't mention his name, and I didn't tell him what to do. We'd worked that out before I left the house. He was to call Shares's precinct with the naked-black-man story, then call Carlyle Taylor to make sure the press knew about it. I wanted to close the club down. A day, a week, a month. It didn't matter. I wanted to let Schiafino know I could hurt him.

I was about to hang up when Dion asked me if I'd heard about Damaris Bauza. The story had just been on the noon TV news.

"Hit-and-run on the Grand Concourse last night," he said. "Driver came at her and the kid. She pushed the kid out of the way and took the hit. Car tore her leg off. Kid's OK. She's in the hospital. They don't know if she's going to make it."

I thought, *the wiretaps.*

I'd promised to protect Gavilan and his mother, and I hadn't done it. In my life, regrets were starting to take the place of everything else. I was sad and angry. And I wanted to hurt somebody.

I told Dion to make the calls, and I hung up.

Then I said to Elder and Aarons, "One of you is going through that door naked, and I don't care who. In the interest of fair play, here's how we're going to choose the lucky guy."

Using the Glock as a pointer, I moved from Aarons to Elder. I chanted, *"Eeny meeny miney mo. Catch an African American by the toe."*

I paused. "See?" I said. "Even a fat Paddy can be politically correct if he tries. Now where were we? Right. *If he hollers, let him go. Eeny meeny miney mo. My. Mother. Told. Me. To. Pick. This. One."*

Elder.

I told him to start stripping.

He didn't move.

I said, "Gene, you may have noticed that Larry's limping. He's limping because he didn't do something I asked him to do. I won't kill you. But I will hurt you. I leave it to you to decide whether or not I'm capable of doing it. Last time. Take off your clothes."

He did, breathing hard with anger and never looking at me. Finally, he said, "Before the sun goes down, you're going to pay for this. I swear on my mother you're going to pay."

I said, "There's a woman in a Bronx hospital who might

247

not live out the day. And all because Schiafino bugged my house. I feel responsible. Blowing out your knee might make me feel better. If I were you, I'd go through that door before I decide to act on that thought. One more thing."

I touched the back of my neck with the Glock. "Lose the dork knob, Gene. You're about five years out of date with that."

I told Aarons to go with him.

When they'd left, I cracked the door and saw the chaos, the disbelieving looks on the faces of dancers and customers, and heard the laughter, and I saw the bouncers' confusion because they didn't know what to do, since Elder was their boss. But the uniformed cops coming into the room from the bar knew what to do. They pushed through the crowd and cuffed Elder.

I left the club and began walking downtown to meet Carlyle Taylor.

XXXVIII
A Heated Discord

When I entered the Tribune-News Building, Carlyle was in the lobby talking to a uniformed security guard, a young female Hispanic with a small, pretty face. The Latina didn't look strong enough to peel a grape, let alone defend life and property. Noticing me, Carlyle said good-bye to the guard and seconds later was shaking my hand.

At the entrance she stopped to adjust her scarf, and that's when I noticed that her dark glasses didn't quite hide the fresh bruise on her check.

"I want to thank you again for last night," she said. "Most cops wouldn't have done what you did. Not for me."

"Wrong. Most would've done exactly what I did. That's

248

why they become cops. You didn't happen to check out Sinatra and Keller, by any chance."

"I did, and you're right. They're cops."

"What did Elder say when you told him?"

She hesitated before saying, "We didn't get around to that. We had what you might call a heated discord."

I touched my left cheekbone. "So I see."

She paused, hands on either end of the scarf. "Once in a while the things that turn you on turn you around. Anyway, over the phone you sounded like a man in a hurry. So where we going?"

I said she'd wanted to talk to Detective Bauza, so we were going to surprise him at the love nest he shared with a topless dancer who worked at his club.

Carlyle's smile was attractively wicked. "You are bad," she said, sounding as though I'd just done something far-out and excellent between the sheets. Then she asked why I was being so obliging.

I said, "I want to see Bauza's reaction when you ask him about Robichaux and Robert Schiafino."

"If he's anything like Gene, he'll throw a fit," she said. "All this fuss over a coincidence."

I said, "Suppose I told you it's not just a coincidence."

Carlyle tightened her grip on the ends of the scarf. "Don't do this to me, Meagher. Say what you mean."

"Robichaux didn't kill Lynda. So who did. And why frame Maurice."

Outside on the curb I held up my hand for a cab.

"I have another reason for doing this," I said. "Last night a hit-and-run driver tried to kill Bauza's wife and stepson."

"I know. Mrs. Bauza's lost her right leg."

I said I felt responsible. Her son had warned me of a conspiracy involving Bauza, Robert Schiafino, and Elder. I'd promised the kid I'd protect him and his mother. So far I hadn't done a very good job.

Carlyle said, "Who are you supposed to protect the boy from?"

"You're not listening. I just gave you three names. All three want Gavilan and his mother dead."

A yellow cab stopped, and we got in. The driver was a

bearded Russian with a neck like a tree stump and a taste for balalaika music. I gave him Gina Branch's address on the Upper East Side, then took off my hat. Leaning back, I closed my eyes and saw Gavilan's accusing face.

Carlyle said, "Why would Gene want Mrs. Bauza and her son dead?"

Eyes still closed, I said, "Let's have it."

Carlyle said, "What?"

I held out my hand, and after some hesitation she gave me the tape recorder. Opening my eyes, I switched it off and dropped it into my overcoat pocket.

"Slow down that march to glory for a few minutes," I said. "Besides, if the department knew I was talking to you, it would have me for lunch."

I told Carlyle I was talking to her because she and I were the only ones who believed Robichaux was innocent. That's why she'd been attacked at the airport and why her friend Elder was so jumpy. He'd driven out to Queens to get in my face, and he'd lied to Carlyle about Sinatra and Keller being cops. I called that being worried to the bone.

Carlyle nervously slapped her thigh with her gloves. "Maybe it's me. I have this talent. I only fall in love with men who can't make up their minds about me. They're sure about everything else in their lives. Jobs, sports cars, winter vacations. They can deal with all of it. They just don't seem to know what to do about me, and I wish I could understand why."

"Look, going after Bauza is part of my job. You don't have to come with me. I can let you out here. Or you can stay, and I can tell you why your friend Elder is so antsy."

Carlyle said, "I'm staying."

I told her about the Exchange Students, about Schiafino, Bauza, and Elder's connection with the group. I was investigating this crew, and that's why they were tapping my phone. Lynda had learned about their operation somehow so they'd killed her, then framed Robichaux. When it looked as if Carlyle might find evidence clearing Robichaux, they'd gone after her as well.

"It's not just about money," I said. "It's about winning an election. That's why City Hall's involved."

Carlyle thought and said, "I've never heard anything so incredible."

"Why do you think those two cops attacked you?"

She looked worried. "City Hall and Maurice Robichaux? I mean we've got a black mayor and—"

"And someone wants to make sure he's reelected. That same someone has figured out that a cop killing with a black perp is worth a few thousand votes."

She nodded. "So if you're right, Gene, the police, and this City Hall person conspired to murder Lynda Schiafino plus a number of people here and in Washington."

"Power corrupts," I said. "Tell me you've never run into that before."

"Not on the scale you're talking about. Never."

"First time for everything. Speaking of which, did you talk to Elder's wife?"

Carlyle shook her head. "Esther won't speak to me. I did find someone in the DA's office who knew about Gene's resignation."

"And?"

Carlyle shook her head. "She confirmed what you said. Gene did make a deal with the DA's office to stay out of prison. She said he blackmailed the DA and got away with it."

"The man's a cat. Lands on his feet every time."

Carlyle said, "And you said Jonathan Munro's in on it as well."

"He paid to have the Ecuadorans killed. You just might come up with a hell of a story, provided your friend doesn't put you in a coma first."

Carlyle said, "Taking this a bit further, Robert Schiafino obviously knows who killed his wife. Who do you think did it?"

"The answer to that can get *you* killed. Especially you, with your choice of friends. Before I forget, where's Lisa Watts these days?"

"When she called, she didn't say. But it turns out she's in Washington."

"Smart," I said. "It's the last place they'd look for her. She's hiding out from the Exchange Students. Schiafino finds her, she's history. She was Lisa's partner, so he figures she knows too much."

"And Schiafino allowed them to murder his wife. Christ, what some people won't do for money."

I didn't want to get into that, so I said, "I think Lisa Watts is in Washington compiling a list of names."

"Names?"

"Probably down there combing local papers and reading trial transcripts to see if she can come up with a list of Exchange Student clients. That's what I'd do. She certainly isn't talking to D.C. cops about the Exchange Students. Not if she wants to live out the week."

Carlyle said, "So she's also investigating this case."

"She's doing some work for an NYPD deputy police commissioner who also knows about the Exchange Students. He's Lisa's protector. My guess is he's banging her as well. He's nobody you want to get mixed up with. Did you tell Elder about Lisa?"

Carlyle shook her head. "No. The subject never came up."

"Did you tell him you were going to Kennedy Airport last night?"

She looked at the cab roof, made her face blank, and said, "Yes."

I said, "How long have you and Elder been seeing each other? This time, I mean."

She leaned away from me and said, "What's that got to do with anything?"

"I figure a couple of weeks," I said. "Want to know what I think?"

"No, but you're going to tell me anyway."

"I think the man who framed Robichaux was looking ahead. He knew what you'd do when a black man was charged with killing a white cop. You'd say the black guy didn't do it, but if he did, it's not his fault. The man behind the frame, we'll call him Mr. Schemes, he could live with that. After all, it's the same old shit. I mean, what else could they expect from you."

But suppose Carlyle got lucky, I said. Suppose she found evidence that could get Robichaux off. Mr. Schemes couldn't live with that. So he put Elder on her. Told Daddy Duke to get that loving feeling going one more time. And should Carlyle come up with anything that might hurt the game plan, Daddy and Schemes could discourage her. As they tried to do at the airport.

Carlyle Taylor said, "Go fuck yourself."

"Lady, you're the one getting diddled here. And I think you know it. You're not stupid. You know things aren't what they seem to be, starting with your friend Elder."

Most people expect you to sympathize with them no matter how badly they're behaving. That's because they're spoiled children, and to get them to think, you have to stick them in the eye with a fork. I wanted to shake up Miss Taylor. I wanted her to see that being black didn't automatically make Eugene Elder upright and chaste.

I laid it out straight because her feeling for Daddy Duke was so strong she was practically hypnotized. It would seem she was sleeping while awake. Then again, maybe she didn't want to wake up. Well, she'd have to if we were going to work together. Her life depended on it. And so did mine.

Carlyle's reaction? After telling me to perform the anatomically impossible, she looked at me with as much hatred as I'd ever seen in a woman's eyes. Behind that look was hurt vanity. *Proud people breed sad sorrows for themselves.*

"You're saying the only reason Gene came back was to use me?"

"That is correct."

"You're also saying he knew about Lynda Schiafino's murder before it occurred?"

"Right again. He's an accessory. You think love brought him back? Gene loves Gene. He uses women because he doesn't know any other way."

An angry Carlyle said, "You're a fat-assed, shit-eating redneck. That's all you are and all you'll ever be."

"I also suffer from love handles and high cholesterol, but with God's help the light of goodness may soon prevail."

"Why the hell should I listen to you?" she said. "You're the occupying army. You march in from the white suburbs every morning and into the black community, bent on busting black heads and getting rich."

I said, "Take it from me, the white suburbs ain't so white anymore. Speaking of race, if you care so much about black people, when are you going to write about the failure of blacks to hold their own responsible for the high crime rate in their community?"

She folded her arms across her chest. "When white cops stop shooting black kids in the back and taking payoffs from drug dealers and forcing fifteen-year-old black whores to suck cock at the point of a gun."

I said, "Isn't it wonderful the way we're hitting it off? About Elder. You won't be able to quit him when you want. It's like dancing with a bear. You don't stop when you get tired. You stop when the bear gets tired."

Carlyle covered her face with her hands. Time for tears.

I said, "Watch Lisa. The guy backing her's a nasty piece of work. He'll jerk you around the way Elder's doing. When am I getting together with Robichaux?"

Carlyle looked at me with a tear-stained face. Her hate-whitey mode was still going strong.

"I couldn't talk his mother into it," she said. "You're white. And a cop. Your friends framed her son and nearly beat him to death. She doesn't want you near him. Frankly, I don't blame her."

I spoke as if I'd never heard her. "You're going back to Mrs. Robichaux. And you're going to get her to change her mind."

Reaching inside my coat pocket, I removed an envelope and tossed it in Carlyle's lap.

She said, "What's this?"

"How should I know? I'm only a redneck. You're the college graduate."

Carlyle opened the envelope, pulled out the typewritten pages, and read in silence. A few seconds into her read she went wide-eyed and said, *Oh my God*. Then she looked at me. "Where'd you get this?"

I pried the pages from her fingers. "It's a preliminary autopsy report on Lynda. It's the truth as opposed to the bullshit being handed out by the city. The day I see Robichaux, you get your copy."

Carlyle was stirred up. *Impassioned* might be a better word.

"Maurice didn't do it," she said. She repeated the phrase as though it was a mantra given her by a Tibetan monk.

She touched my forearm. I was her amigo once more.

"You'll see Maurice," she said. "I promise you."

Then she quickly removed her hand and gave me a look I recognized as one people give you prior to hitting you with bad news.

She said, "I'm sorry about blowing up at you."

"I wish there'd been another way," I said. "All I can do is lay it out for you. The decision is yours."

She looked at the Russian's thick neck. "This isn't easy."

She took a deep breath. "Gene's working with a banker named Harvey Rafaelson to raise money for the mayor's reelection. I know Harvey from parties at the mayor's mansion. I just learned he's been helping Gene with something special."

She touched the bruise on her face. "The argument Gene and I had this morning was about you. I told him I was having second thoughts about sending you to prison."

"And he hit you."

Carlyle said, "He told me I didn't have a choice. I had to follow the plan."

"What plan?"

"Harvey's found Lynda Schiafino's letter," Carlyle said. "It was in a Manhattan safe-deposit box under the name of Lynda's mother. He's given it to Gene, who showed it to me. Gene wants me to use the letter to send you to prison."

XXXIX
Explanations

Neither of us spoke for a long time. Carlyle stared into a compact mirror, patted her face dry with tissues, and worked hard at avoiding eye contact. I sensed she wanted to say something, but at the last second she changed her mind and continued staring into the tiny mirror, even when the cab hit a pothole, lifting us both from the backseat.

I put a cigarette in my mouth but didn't light up. I thought about going to prison and what that meant for a cop—and the effect it would have on Dion. He'd had a drinking problem but had beat it with a twelve-step program and me taking him to meetings. If I went away, a guilt-ridden Dion would climb into the bottle again. And this time he wouldn't come out.

Snapping her compact closed, Carlyle said, "I've made it my business to know everything there is to know about you. When it comes to race relations, you're not exactly tactful or Daniel come to judgment, as they say down south. And I can personally testify you're no diplomat. But I've never heard of you taking a dime. Except this once. And you took, what, twenty-five thousand dollars? Thirteen-year-old drug dealers make that in a week."

I rolled down the taxi window. Then I let the cold air hit my face and told Carlyle that talking was a waste of time, that her mind was already made up.

"Look at me," she said. "Damn your white ass, look at me. And roll up that freaking window. It's freezing in here."

Black women. Straight to the point, as usual. I rolled up the window, then looked at her.

She took off her dark glasses and pointed to the bruise on her face.

"Does this look as if my mind's made up?"

I nodded. "OK. So you took a punch for me."

I tried to make light of it. But what she'd done couldn't be overlooked so easily. A black woman taking a hit for a white cop. *Rare* didn't begin to describe it.

She said, "I'd like to hear your side of the story."

"You'd like to hear *what?*"

"You think you know me," Carlyle said. "Got the black woman down pat. She's a fool for love except when she's being some kind of liberal doofus. You probably think I can be cured by having an enlightened white conservative sprinkle the cold water of reality in my face. Or by having a white cop shatter my few remaining illusions about love. Believe me when I tell you that to survive in your white America, black people have to be a lot tougher than your average Caucasian."

She leaned toward me. "You saw what Lynda had to go through just for a chance at a job for which she was qualified. Without your help she'd never have gotten that chance. Well, detective, black women have it twice as tough because we have to do it without much in the way of support from black men. That stuff you read in Alice Walker and Terry McMillan novels is factual. Black men are not the rock upon which to build your kingdom, but that's another story. In other words, I'm not blind, Detective Meagher."

I said, "Take away the racial shit, and you sound just like Lynda. She didn't think too much of men, and from where she stood, she was right."

Carlyle said, "Off the record, tell me about you two. You were in love, I know that much. I also know she was having trouble with her husband."

I said, "I'm not the type to bare my soul. Let's just say Lynda asked nothing and she gave everything and she made me believe the impossible."

Carlyle stared at me a long time before saying, "Definitely not your ordinary redneck. Why did you take the money? I have to know."

"Off the record?"

"Can't promise that," she said. "But I want to know why you stole once and never stole again. It's important."

I figured I had nothing to lose at this point. She'd read the letter, and she had the transcripts of Baby Cabrera's trial. So I told her about Dion and the IRA's threat to kill him and how ripping off Baby was the only way to save him.

I wasn't sure what Carlyle's reaction would be, but when I finished, what I got was silence. Not a word until we reached Gina Branch's apartment building. And then nothing about the letter.

XL
Love Nest

Gina Branch had a high-rise apartment in Manhattan's Yorkville, a German-Hungarian neighborhood running from Seventy-seventh Street to Ninety-sixth Street between Lexington Avenue and the East River. Most of the old community had moved out, leaving behind German delicatessens, bakeries, and photography shops with faded pictures of smiling Aryans in the windows. Yuppies had taken over, moving into buildings cut up into postage-stamp-size apartments to cater to the demand for single housing.

An eye-rolling Arab in a gray cap and matching long coat with gold epaulets opened the lobby door for Carlyle and me and said he'd call upstairs and announce us. I flashed my shield and asked if Detective Bauza was upstairs. No sir, he wasn't. He'd gone to the hospital to see his wife. He was expected back this afternoon.

I told the Arab not to announce us. Nodding many times, he ran ahead to hold the elevator and push the twelfth-floor button for us. Carlyle and I rode up in silence. I sensed her mind was on Lynda's letter and how to handle it. From where I stood, it came down to her choosing between me or Elder. Between white and black. And my money wasn't on white. Not in today's world.

I hadn't mentioned the earlier scene with Daddy Duke since I assumed Carlyle would hear about it soon enough. When a former prosecutor gets popped for wienie waving in a topless joint, you can expect people to talk. Even if Elder managed to keep it out of the papers, word would get around. I didn't know if Shares would be shut down, but I did know that Daddy Duke's feelings toward me had just taken a quantum leap forward on the nasty scale.

Twelfth floor. Leaving the elevator, we walked down a hallway with threadbare green carpeting and wallpaper decorated in beige Eiffel Towers. It smelled of carpet cleaner. There was also the odor of a disgusting onion dish emanating from one apartment. At Gina Branch's apartment I rang the bell, then held my shield up to the peephole.

On the other side a childlike voice said, "Who's there?"

"Police. Detective Meagher. I'd like to talk to you."

"About what?"

She wasn't from New York. The voice was midwestern and too trusting. It also promised death by perky if you weren't careful.

I said, "Do you know a Detective Bauza?"

"Uh, yes."

"And you work at his club on East Forty-fourth Street?"

"Yes," she said. "Could you tell me what this is about?"

"I prefer to talk about it inside, Miss Branch."

"I'm sorry, but Detective Bauza told me never to let anyone in when he's not here."

I said, "Miss Branch, where are you from?"

"Wichita, Kansas. Why do you ask?"

"Does your family know you dance naked for a living and are being kept by a married man?"

A smiling Carlyle whispered "Bad" in a tone that chilled the back of my neck, then quietly said that if Bauza wasn't here, why did we want to talk to Bambi?

I whispered, "I want to shake Bauza up, to let him know we're bird-dogging him. You'll see why when we get inside."

"Sure she'll open the door?"

A lock snapped. Then another.

"I'm sure," I said.

Gina Branch opened the door at a snail's pace. I'd been

told she was twenty-two, but in person she looked seventeen, which was probably what Haysoos saw in her. She had long blond hair, the bluest eyes I'd ever seen, and a perfect little nose to go with a perfect little chin. Jesus had probably paid for the nose as well as the majestic pair of hooters faintly outlined under a pink sweatsuit. She'd been jogging on a treadmill set up in front of a TV set tuned to a CNN newscast.

"Come in," she said in a girlish squeak. "And please don't talk that way in front of my neighbors again." There was nothing demanding in her manner. Just the openness of a beautiful child who'd always been the center of attention and knew she'd get her way because she was too adorable to be refused.

Stepping aside, I let Carlyle enter, then followed her into a studio apartment overlooking the East River. The apartment was small and low-ceilinged with a tiny kitchen and a single alcove containing a makeup table. There was a sleeper couch, a white wicker desk and chair, and an end table topped by a vase of dried flowers and a cordless phone. The only other large piece in the apartment was a cabinet with a glass front, a setting for a collection of dolls, combs, and seashells. One door, probably leading to the bathroom, was covered in Jayhawks pennants, souvenirs of Kansas, where college basketball was a religion.

Gina Branch collapsed into the white wicker chair and started fanning her face with a small towel. When she saw me looking at the pennants, she jerked her head in that direction.

"I was a Kansas cheerleader," she said. "Majored in dance and drama. Got bored, and my average wasn't all that high, so I left without finishing my senior year. Came to New York to study dance."

I said, "Before I forget, may I introduce Carlyle Taylor."

Gina stopped fanning. "Aren't you the woman J. doesn't want to talk to?"

"Five minutes of his time," Carlyle said. "That's all I want. No more."

She and I took seats on the couch, where I casually returned the tape recorder to her shoulder bag.

I said, "J.? That wouldn't be Detective Bauza, would it?"

"I can't call him Jesus," Gina said. "I was raised in a Christian family and don't believe in using the Lord's name in vain. So I call him J. He doesn't mind."

I said, "Were you at the final-four championship game when Kansas took Duke by one in overtime?"

Little Gina squealed with delight. "My God, yes. Yes, yes. I was so excited I lost my voice. That was the happiest day of my life."

"How do you think they'll do this year?"

She turned serious, saying that Kansas's low post game was weak, that the center was prone to early foul trouble and the guards weren't bringing the ball up fast enough. Miss B. knew her hoops.

I said having two starters declare for an early draft hadn't helped, and to that Miss B. nodded shrewdly. Common ground had been established.

I said, "Miss Branch, being raised in a Christian family, you know how important it is to do the right thing. Miss Taylor wants Detective Bauza's help in freeing an innocent man charged with killing a cop."

"That's right," Carlyle said. "Like you, I come from a strong Baptist family. Believe me when I tell you God-fearing doesn't begin to describe my folks."

Gina rolled her eyes. "Tell me about it. After a while, I couldn't stand all that Bible thumping. Had to get away. How'd you know I was a Baptist?"

Carlyle leaned forward and spoke in that we're-all-sisters-together voice. "Honey, everybody outside New York is Baptist."

I looked at Carlyle, who gave me a sly smile. If she'd been a used-car dealer, her name would have been Honest John and she'd be under indictment. She'd lied about being a Baptist. But she'd brought us closer to Miss Branch.

Gina dropped the towel in her lap and leaned back in the wicker chair, somewhat more relaxed now that she was among friends.

"You probably want to talk about Maurice Robichaux," she said. "I don't know how innocent he is, but he's the only one J. talks about who's killed a cop. That I know of anyway."

"I understand," I said. "We know Detective Bauza arrested Robichaux twice. It's a matter of public record."

"You're right," Gina said. "But he feels the press will get the wrong idea. That's why he doesn't want to talk about it. His friend Bobby might end up getting hurt."

I said, "You mean because people might see a connection between Detective Robert Schiafino and Robichaux where there is none?"

Gina nodded. "Exactly. You said you wanted to talk to me. What about?"

My turn to sell used cars. I said, "I mentioned that Miss Taylor and I are interested in proving Maurice Robichaux's innocence. To do that, we start with the fact that Robert Schiafino's lying about his whereabouts the night of his wife's murder."

Gina Branch put her hands over her ears. "I told J. the truth would come out, that you couldn't lie all the time. He just wouldn't listen."

Bingo.

Carlyle took off her dark glasses and looked from me to Gina. One hand went into her shoulder bag.

"A few of Schiafino's friends are lying for him," I said. "We know that."

Little Gina squeaked, "You do?"

"His attorney," I said. "A couple of businessmen and some cops. Detective Bauza among them. We know Schiafino's called here to make sure Detective Bauza backs him up on that hockey game story."

Schiafino was a control freak. He was phoning Bauza in the Bronx, so why not phone him in Manhattan. Schiafino had a reason to be on the horn a lot. He needed a solid alibi for the night of Lynda's murder. Because if he didn't have one, he had a problem.

Gina nervously wrapped the towel around one wrist. When she spoke, she seemed relieved to be telling all. That's what an old-fashioned Baptist upbringing will do for you.

"J. told me he had to do it," she said. "Bobby needed

him, and he couldn't let Bobby down. I said lying was a sin, but J. got mad. Told me to butt out."

I said, "The night his wife was murdered, Schiafino wasn't at Madison Square Garden. He was in Queens, wasn't he."

Gina nodded.

I looked at Carlyle. "With Lynda's sister, Jullee."

Gina said, "That's right," and Carlyle whispered, *Oh my God,* and then a key turned in the door, followed by a key going into the second lock, and then the door opened, and there stood Haysoos holding a bag of groceries. At the sight of me, he looked pained, as though he'd just been jerked off by a tiger. But he'd been around long enough to be cautious, and that meant staying cool until he knew whether or not my visit was official.

Finally, he tore his glance from me and glared at Gina. "Goddamn it," he said. "I told you don't let nobody in while I'm gone."

Gina leaped from the chair. "J., he's the police, just like you."

Jesus put the groceries down on the floor, took a handkerchief from his overcoat pocket, and blew his nose. Then he looked into the handkerchief before returning it to his pocket. He still hadn't closed the door.

"That bastard Mohammed," he said. "He never told me anybody was here."

"I wanted it to be our little secret," I said. "Say hello to Carlyle Taylor. She's been dying to meet you."

Carlyle rose and said, "Detective, I'd like to ask you a few questions."

Bauza pointed to the open door. "Right. You and Meagher, out. You're trespassing. I could kill you for that."

I said, "Sure you could."

"I'm not talking," he said and pointed to Gina. "She's not talking either."

"She's done her talking," I said. "Miss Taylor wants to ask you some questions about Robichaux. You know, the homeless guy you arrested twice. Good thing you did, too, because when Schiafino needed a fall guy to take the rap for his wife's murder, you had the perfect candidate. A black man with a record as long as your arm. Someone who had to be guilty even if he wasn't."

Carlyle gripped my arm.

Bauza's eyes widened. He licked his lips and said, "You know what you're saying?"

I turned to look at the seashells. "I'm saying Schiafino killed his wife, framed Robichaux, and you helped him do it."

Carlyle yanked on my sleeve with both hands, and Gina from Kansas began to cry. Jesus stiffened like a man who'd just been awakened in the middle of the night by a cold-water enema.

I said, "How's your wife, Haysoos? Seeing as how she's still breathing, I'd say your people didn't do such a good job. Unless you were the guy who drove the car that hit her. In which case I can understand why things didn't work out."

Bauza shoved his hand inside his overcoat. "You're leaving. Not gonna tell you again."

I grinned. "Haysoos, if you're not careful, you'll shoot your dick off. OK, OK, you talked me into it. We're leaving."

I said to Carlyle, "Did I ever tell you about Ida Dilascio? I'll fill you in on the details later. She was a protected witness in an organized-crime case, and Haysoos was guarding her. That is, until she suddenly died of a heroin overdose."

This time Bauza didn't just point to the open door. He banged on it with his fist. "Out. You and the bitch, *out!* You got no warrant, and I don't have to talk."

I said, "A quick call to my father, then I'm gone."

With everyone's eyes on me, I used the cordless phone to dial home. Dion didn't pick up and neither did the service. I'd told him to stay put until he heard from me. I listened to the phone ring at the other end, thinking it wasn't like Dion to go off without checking with me first.

Something was wrong.

XLI
None So Blind

Carlyle Taylor and I flagged down a cab two blocks from Gina Branch's apartment and headed across town to the West Side. I was about to make my second surprise visit of the afternoon, this one to Harvey Rafaelson at Courtline Trust. I wanted to talk to him about the Exchange Students' slush fund. Most of all I wanted to know who controlled the fund.

I hadn't planned on taking Carlyle with me, but my concern for Dion changed that. She saw the worry on my face, and as I hailed the cab, she took a cellular phone from her bag and handed it to me. I took the phone and said nothing when she followed me into the cab.

The cabby, a bony young Chink in dark glasses, drove along East Eighty-sixth Street, made a left onto Fifth Avenue, and entered Central Park at Eighty-fifth Street. He headed west on the transverse, overtaking and passing an empty horse-drawn carriage driven by a bored-looking fat man wearing a top hat and drinking from a brown paper bag. The Chink was so far down in the seat I wondered how he could see over the wheel.

I called the house again. No answer. So I phoned Maggie O'Keeffe, who said Dion had neither shown up for work nor called in. Next I reached out for Ned Ray, who said he'd spoken to Dion this morning, making an appointment to sweep the house this afternoon. He hadn't talked to him since.

"Could he have gone to the store?" Carlyle said.

I handed the phone back to her. "No. Something's not right. I can feel it."

"So what are you going to do?"

"Harvey's just across the park. I'll have my talk with him, then contact my local precinct and have them run a car past the house. After that I'll take things as they come."

On an empty baseball diamond in the park, a young woman on a shiny black horse was completing a home-run trot around the infield. Reins in one hand, she expertly put the horse through its paces. They'd done it before; the horse took the corners sharply, smoothly, making everything look easy, as the good ones always do. Watching them reminded me that the baseball season was due to start in ten days. I thought of Dion, who was a big Mets fan and hadn't missed a home opener since the team was founded in 1962. He was in trouble. I knew it as surely as I knew Carlyle Taylor was dying to ask me about Elder's involvement in Lynda's murder.

The cab left the park at West Eighty-sixth Street and headed toward Courtline at Broadway and Eightieth Street, just minutes away. It was time to dump Carlyle.

Before I could speak she said, "We have to talk."

"About what?" I said. "About how many years I'll get when you tell the world I'm a thief? The best way to help myself is to put together the best case I can and hope it weighs in my favor. No offense, but at the moment talking to you is the last thing on my mind."

"I can save you time," she said. "The sooner you get to Harvey, the sooner you can turn your attention to your father."

"What are you saying?"

"Courtline's a big bank," she said. "You could probably find Harvey on your own, but by the time you located him, he'd know you were coming. You want to surprise him, right?"

"So?"

"So we go in together."

I said, "I'll cover your ass, if that's what you're worried about. I won't mention the letter. I won't rat you out to Harvey."

Carlyle snorted. "I don't give a shit what you tell Harvey. As for Gene, you leave him to me. I know how to keep him in line. Believe me when I say he won't lay a hand on me ever again."

"He won't?"

"He wants something from me," she said.

We both knew what that something was. My head on a platter.

Carlyle said, "There's something I have to know. You wanted to shake up Bauza."

"That's what I said."

"Then tell me. Did Schiafino really kill his wife, or were you just out to rattle Bauza's cage? *I have to know.*"

I lit a cigarette and took my time answering. "What you want to know is whether or not Elder's implicated in Lynda Schiafino's murder."

Carlyle chewed her lip and waited.

"He's in this up to his hairline," I said. "Schiafino killed Lynda, and Elder helped him cover it up. They want to discredit me before I hang Lynda's murder on them. That's where you and your story come in. If you don't write, Elder's going to kill you."

Carlyle shook her head. "You're wrong. Gene wouldn't kill me."

" 'Nothing in the world is more dangerous than sincere ignorance and conscientious stupidity.' Martin Luther King, Jr."

Carlyle raised both eyebrows. "Whoa. Slow down. *Martin Luther King?*"

"When's the last time you read anything he wrote?" I said.

"I'm ashamed to say I can't remember."

I said, "You were telling me why I should let you tag along when I see Harvey."

"I can get in to see him anytime. Especially now."

"The letter," I said.

She nodded. "He might be on guard against you but not against me. And let's say I owe you one for getting me in to see Bauza, such as it was. Besides, I know Harvey. You won't have any trouble with him. He's what you call pliable."

"Weak, you mean."

"Like they say, white men can't jump. They can't pump either."

"Want to explain that?" I said.

She smiled. "Some other time."

267

XLII
Invitation to a Party

Courtline Trust is one of the most striking buildings on Manhattan's Upper West Side. It is colossal, an overgrown black monster occupying an entire block on Broadway and Eightieth Street. I'd been in the neighborhood before, but until today I'd never set foot in the 150-year-old bank.

I'd paid the cabby when I noticed another vehicle parked in front of Courtline. It was a blue Dodge minivan with a vanity license plate, JUL S GR8. Since the chance of there being two such vans was small, I had to assume this one belonged to Jullee Vulnavia and that she was inside the bank, consorting with Harvey Rafaelson.

Leaving the cab, I approached the van from the rear. No one behind the wheel. I touched the hood. It was still warm.

I felt Carlyle come up behind me. "Thinking of buying one?" she said.

I shook my head and said, "Too rich for my blood. This is Jullee's ride."

"Lynda Schiafino's kid sister?"

"She's inside," I said. "Remember that slush fund I told you about? The one the rabbi's putting together for Tucker? Jullee brings that money from Washington and hands it over to Harvey, who cleans it up."

Carlyle said, "Does she have any idea what she's into? I mean murder and money laundering, not to mention adultery?"

"Jullee lives by her own rules. If she met Charles Manson, he wouldn't hesitate to offer her a job."

"Can't wait to meet her."

With that Carlyle led me into the Courtline, past an iron gate and metal doors and finally into an immense open area topped by a forty-foot ceiling covered in blue-and-gold enamel. Dozens of tellers' cages, each made of black wrought iron, formed a circle in the center of a beige marble floor. Security was provided by able-bodied guards in blue blazers cut to hide shoulder holsters. One corner of the bank featured a sunken Japanese garden with blue rocks and a miniature waterfall. Community bulletin boards carried notices of local events—martial-arts classes for Girl Scouts and an upcoming Easter dance for gay men. A near wall contained a small bank of elevators and a series of offices. More offices lined a circular marble walkway overlooking the main floor and reached by a broad marble staircase.

I'd forgotten that Carlyle was a celebrity. Customers and bank employees stopped us to say how much they enjoyed her writing. No surprise. The West Side was Manhattan's most liberal ground, a hotbed of political correctness in New York. A place where quadruple amputees were described as physically challenged and dogs were called Canine Americans.

Carlyle didn't introduce me to her admirers, which was just as well since I was in no mood for small talk. My mind was on Harvey. I had to reach him before Jullee spotted me and pressed the panic button.

I wasn't paying attention, so I was caught off guard when Carlyle whispered that Harvey wasn't in his first-floor office. He was on the second floor, taking care of a special client. Then she took my arm, and we were on our way, heading toward the marble staircase.

Carlyle said, "Seems whenever Harvey meets this special client, it's never in his office."

"He doesn't want witnesses," I said. "No secretaries, no receptionists. Just him and Jullee and lots of dirty money."

Without Carlyle, I'd have gone searching for Harvey and Jullee from one end of this rock pile to another. The longer I searched, the more likely someone would have warned them I was coming, giving Jullee and Harvey plenty of time to head south. I didn't like admitting it, but at the moment I needed Carlyle.

At the top of the staircase, she pointed right, and we headed in that direction. We walked along the marble promenade, over the heads of tellers and customers visible on the ground floor below, until we came to a frosted glass door with 207 stenciled on it in gold letters. Taking a deep breath, Carlyle knocked on the glass.

Inside a male voice said, "Yes?"

"Harvey, this is Carlyle Taylor. It's about that letter you gave Gene. We have to talk."

Harvey whispered to someone, then said, "Carlyle, I'm busy right now. Can't it wait?"

"Gene doesn't think so," Carlyle said. "That's why I'm here. Look, it won't take long."

"All right. Just a minute."

Harvey unlocked the door, and I shoved it in his face, sending him back into the room. Motioning Carlyle inside, I shut the door and held up my shield. Harvey continued backing up toward Jullee, who sat at an oval-shaped conference table, chewing on a cheeseburger and talking on a cell phone. At the sight of me, she put down the cheeseburger and, shielding her mouth, whispered into the phone. As for Harvey, he stopped backpedaling and eyed my shield as if it were a drooling Rottweiler.

We were in a small conference room with matching table and chairs, all polished to an eye-blinding glare. Lighting the room was a pair of elaborate chandeliers in a high, ivory-yellow ceiling. The American and New York State flags stood between two large glass-enclosed bookcases, and the thick gray carpeting looked clean enough to lick. In front of the near wall was a huge bronze bust of a fat-faced bald man with muttonchop whiskers and a floppy tie, quite possibly the bank's founder. He stood guard over six metal suitcases, all carbon copies of the one I'd seen in Jullee's room the day before.

I'd interrupted Harvey's work. There was a laptop computer on the conference table, along with a fax machine, two small notebooks, and a pocket calculator. Also on the table were the remains of a McDonald's lunch for two. Someone was squawking on Jullee's phone, trying to get Harvey's attention.

His back to the conference table, Harvey nervously fingered his rimless glasses and stared at my badge. He was several inches over six feet tall and in his mid-thirties, with a small face that made his glasses look like a windshield. He had a full mouth, hairy ears, and narrow shoulders, with the stooped stance of a man uncomfortable with his height. He might have looked younger if he hadn't been losing his hair, a fact he tried to hide with a bad comb-over. He was dressed in a baggy gray suit that needed pressing, a blue shirt, and a tie with the color scheme of a barber pole. There was a red AIDS ribbon in his jacket lapel, along with a FUR KILLS button. If nothing else, Harvey was politically correct.

He was also ready to piss his pants. In a shaky voice he said, "Am I under arrest?"

Jullee, a slut babe in black leather and purple lipstick, said, "Shut the fuck up, Harvey. Just shut the fuck up, OK?"

Keeping her eyes on me, she spoke into the phone. "Carlyle didn't come alone. Meagher's with her."

I said to Carlyle, "Ask Jullee about her and Schiafino. He's on the phone with her now."

Carlyle nodded and stepped closer to Jullee. "Miss Lesnevitch, I'd—"

Jullee never bothered to look at Carlyle. Instead she took a bite of her cheeseburger and said, "Get your facts straight. My name is not Lesnevitch. It's Jullee Vulnavia. You ought to know that from hanging around Gene."

Carlyle lifted one eyebrow. It wouldn't take much more to push her over the edge.

Taking out her tape recorder, she said, *"Miss* Jullee Vulnavia. Where were you and your brother-in-law the night your sister was murdered?"

Jullee stopped chewing. "What's that supposed to mean?"

Carlyle said, "Well, for one thing it means the two of you were together. I've learned that during the murder Detective Schiafino wasn't at Madison Square Garden as he claims. In other words you are now his only alibi. I'd like to know—"

Jullee threw her cheeseburger at Carlyle's face, smacking her in the forehead. A shocked Carlyle took one step back, touched her forehead, then looked at the beef particles and bits of lettuce on her fingertips. "Girl," she said. "You want to play, I'll *play.*"

She charged Jullee, pinning her in the chair while the two clawed and screamed at each other. I ordered Harvey to stop the fight, and when he didn't move fast enough, I pushed him toward the action. With everyone occupied, I could make my move. I reached Jullee's handbag, ignored a roll of hundred-dollar bills, and removed two items: her address book and a small notebook. Both went into my overcoat pocket.

Time to focus on Harvey the peacemaker. He'd pulled Carlyle off Jullee and was using his long arms to keep the two apart. Jullee may have met her match. Red-faced and breathing hard, she sat and silently eyed Carlyle, who pushed Harvey's hand aside and bent down to pick up her tape recorder.

Jullee, meanwhile, decided on another tactic.

Picking up the cell phone, she said, "Bobby, you won't believe what just happened. That bitch Carlyle attacked me. I'm not kidding, she *attacked* me."

An out-of-breath Carlyle said, "You don't watch your goddamn mouth, this bitch is going to kill you."

"Yeah, right." Jullee held out the phone to me. "Someone wants to speak to you."

I ordered her to stay put and stay cool because this time Schiafino wasn't here to protect her.

She smiled. "I wouldn't be so sure."

I brought the phone to my ear. "Lo and behold, it's the bereaved widower."

Schiafino said, "Just the man I wanted to see. Heard from your father lately?"

I closed my eyes. I'd been expecting the worst about Dion. And Bobby Schemes was just the man to deliver the bad news.

"You've been a busy boy," Schiafino said. "My club's closed down for a couple days. You embarrass Gene, you give Aarons a hard time, and you've got Bauza hearing footsteps. Time you took a break."

I asked if my father was alive.

"Definitely," Schiafino said. "Alive and kicking, but for how long? Depends entirely on you, my man. You have something I want. Some one-hundred-dollar bills and the medical report from McGuigan. You have them on you?"

"I do."

"That's what your father said. Bring them with you."

"Where am I going?"

"You're invited to a party. Yesterday at the airport you John Wayned two of my people, namely Aldo and Keller. Now they want to return the favor. Actually, four or five of our guys want to get together with you."

"They call that banana style," I said. "Yellow and in a bunch."

"Whatever. I know this much. You're in for the mother of all tune-ups. Most definitely. The guys are getting sick of being harassed by you, and to keep them happy, I'm going along with their express desire to go upside your head. While I told them not to go overboard, it is possible you could die. But, hey, that's life."

"And Dion?"

"Entirely up to you," Schiafino said. "You show, we turn him loose. You stay away, and I assure you it'll only get worse for him. Look, why don't I let Aldo put you in the picture. I'm at home, but he's somewhere in Queens with your father. I'm putting us on a conference call. Take it away, Aldo."

Aldo said, "Meagher. You hear me?"

I said yes.

"That's good," he said. "While you were out leaning on Aarons and Elder, Bobby comes up with the idea for me and Keller to go to your house and grab your old man. He thought it was a dynamite way to get your attention. Know something? He's right. From now on when we say jump, you jump. Now say hello to Daddy."

"Fear? It's me, Dion." He sounded in pain and his breathing was labored.

"They broke my arm," he said. "Couple ribs. Listen. Don't come. They'll kill you. Fuck these maggots—"

I heard Dion cry out, then Aldo was laughing in my ear.

"A stand-up guy, your old man," Aldo said. "Busted his arm, he don't say shit. Kicked in a couple ribs, he still don't say nothing. Only time he makes a peep is now. When I smacked him in his broken arm."

Two things going on here, Aldo said. First Bobby wanted his shit—the money and the medical report. Then Aldo wanted payback for the pounding he and Keller had taken at the airport. If I wanted to see Dion alive again, I had to do the right thing. Because if I didn't, the next time I saw Dion, he'd be in a body bag.

XLIII
Nothing to Lose

Shortly after I became a cop, Dion clued me in about my gun. It's yours, he said, but only as long as you can keep it. Remember that whenever you go to arrest a man facing life imprisonment. This is the guy who'll try for your gun, Dion said. He'll do it because he's desperate and has nothing to lose.

I thought about that while listening to Aldo's threats. I didn't react to anything he said, figuring it might set him off and make things worse for Dion. Lose control, and I'd go down with Dion. With the Exchange Students, when you went down, you stayed down. My only chance of surviving was to become a man with nothing to lose.

A smirking Jullee was leaning back in her chair, smoking a menthol. She knew I was in a jackpot, a man with weight on his mind, and she was enjoying every minute of it. Harvey had his own agenda. He stared at the door as though planning to make a break for it. He didn't have the stones for something like that, but thinking about it gave him hope. As for Carlyle, she couldn't take her eyes off me.

I sat on the edge of the table and lit a cigarette. Dion had taken a beating because of me. If it was the last thing I did, Schiafino and Aldo were going to pay for hurting him. But for the moment, no trash-talking. Don't get mad, get even.

Laying the cell phone on the table, I removed my hat and coat, dumping them in an empty chair.

Picking up the phone, I said to Aldo, "You still there?"

"Hey, ass face," he said, "when I'm talking, you stay put. I got your fucking father, remember?"

"I want to speak to Schiafino."

"Right here," Schiafino said. "So, don't let me keep you. The sooner you get started, the sooner you see your father. Or what's left of him. And please. Whatever you do, don't show up empty-handed."

I looked at the metal suitcases and said, "The Irish say there're three things you can never understand—a woman's mind, the work of bees, and the ebb and flow of the tides. Pay attention because the tide's about to change. I'm going to let Harvey tell you all about it."

I handed the phone to Harvey and said, "Talk to Schiafino."

He licked his lips. "What do I say?"

"Just describe what you see. Pretend you're doing a play-by-play for your favorite team."

I said to Carlyle, "Schiafino's people have Dion. He's taken a beating. If I don't get him out, he's dead."

She said, "Is there anything I can do?"

"Lock the door, and don't let anyone in."

I said to Harvey, "Just call it like you see it."

Jullee first. I cuffed her hands behind the chair. When she cried out, I gagged her with my scarf. She gnawed at the scarf, gave me the hard eye, and lashed out with her feet. But behind all that attitude was a growing alarm and a lot of uncertainty about her immediate future. And Harvey? He followed instructions, using a confused monotone to keep Schiafino abreast of the action.

I walked over to the bronze bust of the fat-faced man, grabbed two suitcases, and returned to the table. Opening the cases, I found myself looking at bundles of fifty- and hundred-dollar bills, all bearing Washington bank stickers. I dumped the cash onto the conference table, causing Harvey to stop talking and stare at me. Digging my fingers into his shoulder, I said, *Don't stop now, you're on a roll.* Clearing his throat, Harvey resumed his description of the action. As he talked, I emptied the cash from two additional suitcases onto the table.

Harvey said to Schiafino, "I don't *know* what he's planning to do. All I can tell you is the money's piled on the table. No, I'm not going to interfere with him. He's got a gun. Yes, I'll ask him."

Harvey looked at me. "He wants to know what you intend to do with the money."

I took out my lighter, thumbed it into flame, and said to Harvey, "How much you figure is in these cases? All of them."

Harvey used a long finger to scratch one of his bushy eyebrows. "All of them? Uh, in excess of a million, I believe."

"In excess of a million," I said. I picked up a bundle of hundreds, set it afire, then tossed the burning bundle into the money pile.

Harvey's jaw dropped.

I ordered him to keep talking.

Had Harvey ever seen anyone set fire to money before? *Deliberately?* I didn't think so. He took a while to find his voice, and when he spoke to Schiafino, it was as though he were describing a death in the family. The money burned slowly, green bills turning black at the edges and curling into ash. Poor Harvey. His world was money, and whatever you did to it, you never burned the stuff. There were tears in his eyes, and he whispered the word *sickening* over and over.

I figured I had Schiafino's attention. But since there was a lot at stake, I decided to make sure. I placed a few bundles of hundreds on Jullee's lap, and to say the least, she knew what was coming. She squirmed, screamed against the gag, and tried to knock the chair over. Stepping behind her, I leaned on the chair to keep it in place, and saying *Happy birthday,* I fired the money in her lap.

She went pop-eyed, thrashing around in the chair as though possessed by the devil. She wasn't on fire; the money was. But you'd never have known that by the way she carried on. She rocked from side to side while I hung on, keeping her chair as upright as I could. When she couldn't knock over the chair, she did a bump and grind and used her steel-tipped boots to kick the underside of the conference table. Finally, she stopped struggling and slumped in the chair, weeping hysterically, wrists bloodied from pulling at the handcuffs. Harvey said, *Oh my God,* then whispered to Schiafino that I was burning Jullee alive.

I took the phone from Harvey and watched a red-faced Jullee come alive again. She did some more side-to-side rocking. This time she succeeded in throwing herself to the carpet, scattering the burning money across the rug. Carlyle took a step toward Jullee, then stopped, uncertain about my reaction. Harvey also started toward Jullee. He didn't get far. Grabbing his collar, I yanked him back into his chair.

"Leave her alone," I said. "I want her to go to school on this. Today's lesson is: You play, you pay."

I spoke into the phone. "How was Harvey? Think he's ready for *Monday Night Football?*"

Schiafino's voice was tight. He'd been caught by surprise, the last thing a control freak wanted.

He said in a soft voice, "You've made your point. Mind putting out the fire?"

"What's the rush," I said. "It's only money."

"Put out the fucking fire. *Please?*"

I took a drag on my cigarette. "Tell me something. Did my father say that? Did he say, You've made your point, now stop beating the shit out of me?"

Schiafino and Aldo were silent.

I ordered Harvey to put out the fire, making sure Schiafino heard. I said, *Use your jacket,* and Harvey nodded vigorously, as though this were one of history's greatest ideas. Jullee was weeping and drenching my scarf, so I sat her chair upright and told her to stop crying because nobody gave a shit, especially me.

Then I said to Schiafino, "Forty minutes. That's how much time you have to bring my father here alive. He shows up dead or you decide to get cute, and a million bucks goes up in smoke. And don't bother telling me that's not enough time. You're cops. You can do anything, remember?"

I said I wouldn't stop with the money in this room. I had

plans for *all* of Schiafino's money. I was going to break Harvey's fingers until he gave me the numbers of Schiafino's slush-fund accounts, at which point Schiafino could kiss them good-bye because I intended to open up new accounts all over the world. Accounts known only to me because Harvey wouldn't be in a position to tell anybody anything. Kiss it all good-bye, I said. Every dime.

Schiafino said, "That won't be necessary. Your father's on his way to you now. Aldo will see to it."

A shaken Aldo said, "Bobby, don't let him bullshit you. He's bluffing."

Schiafino said, "He's burning the money, and he's burning Jullee. Excuse me, but does that sound like bluffing to you? I'll say this once, Aldo. Don't even think about touching his father. Fun's over. Back off and leave the old man be. He dies, and the guy who whacked him is history. Don't make me repeat myself."

"You're the boss, Bobby."

"Sometimes I wonder. I want to talk to Meagher privately. And Aldo?"

"Yeah?"

"If I were you, I'd have someone else drive Meagher's father into the city. I wouldn't do it myself."

Aldo said, "Meagher don't scare me."

Schiafino said, "Dagos. Whenever they want to take a day off, they call in dead. I mean, we talking dumb here or what. Aldo, hear me on this. The last two times you've run into Meagher, he's waxed your ass. Seems to me he has your number. I'd say he owns you and there's nothing you can do about it. Anyway, I'm cutting you off so Meagher and I can talk privately. Bring his father into the city now, and I do mean *now.*"

Then Schiafino said to me, "How's Jullee taking this?"

I said, *Judge for yourself.*

Pulling the scarf from her mouth, I held the phone to her face. She was out of control. Red-faced and shrieking, she begged Schiafino to stop me from burning her alive. There wasn't a mark on her, but Schiafino couldn't see that.

I put the scarf back over her mouth and said to Schiafino, "I think someone's just had a reality check."

"Have her in front of the bank when we return your father."

"She's yours when I get Dion back alive. Otherwise she goes into the system. She gets popped for money laundering, and that means the feds will want a piece of her. She gets convicted on a federal rap, there's no parole. She does the full bit. Jullee and the bull dykes. How's that for a rock group?"

"Your father will be returned to you alive," Schiafino said. "Know something? You sound like a man who wants a crack at the title. How about a little one on one. You and me. What do you say?"

"I say let's do it."

He wasn't talking about basketball, and he wasn't talking about him and me challenging each other to Game Boy. He was talking about us getting together with only one man walking away.

Schiafino said I wouldn't have to come to him, that he'd come to me real soon, and then he hung up.

XLIV
Hurt Feelings

When I stepped from Courtline Trust that afternoon, Jesus Bauza was parked out front in his new Jag with the motor running. A dejected-looking Jullee was with me. I gripped her elbow with one hand and kept the other on the Glock in my coat pocket. Dion was nowhere to be seen.

Jullee blew her nose into a pink tissue, then looked straight ahead. Anywhere but at me. Carlyle was watching us from the bank lobby. I'd ordered her to stay inside in case of a shoot-out.

Where was Dion?

"Bobby's gonna kill you," Jullee said, trying to pull loose

from my grip. "You're not going to get away with what you did to me."

"You'd better hope I do. Because if there's any shooting out here, you'll be the first to go."

I dug my fingers into her elbow, and when she flinched, I said that if my father wasn't in Bauza's car, she and I were going back inside and resume our leisure activities. Jullee said, *You're an asshole and your mother sucks cocks in hell.*

I dragged her toward the Jag, on the lookout for a double cross by Schiafino. Jullee believed Bobby Schemes was ready to go the whole nine yards for love. I knew better. His first and only love was himself. He'd killed and schemed to build that slush fund, and he wasn't about to let me or anyone else walk off with it. Jullee was his mule, and she knew how the fund worked. Getting her away from me was the first step in keeping her quiet.

Holding on to Jullee, I walked toward Bauza's Jag. At the same time I clocked every car, pedestrian, and dog walker anywhere near me. I'd dissed Schiafino in front of his crew, and he couldn't let me get away with it. Not if he wanted their respect. He'd have to come back at me. And like he said, he'd do it real soon.

A fidgety Bauza looked at me, then jerked his head toward the backseat. The tinted back window slid down, and I saw Dion sitting alone, glassy-eyed and cradling his left arm. One eye was swollen, and there was blood on his forehead. At the sight of me, he grinned and blew a kiss.

"You done good, kid," he said.

"I had a good teacher. The best, as a matter of fact."

He said, "You should have seen Aldo's friends when they heard they had to cut me loose. Goddamn maggots couldn't believe it."

Touching his ribs, he flinched. "Best part was Aldo telling them about you burning the money and setting fire to Jullee. Man, the air went out of that tribe in a hurry."

Dion chuckled. "Hurts when I laugh, but it's worth it just to remember their faces. They didn't know whether to shit or go blind. I have to say it was beautiful. Fucking beautiful."

I said, "One of these days Aldo and I are going to get together and discuss what just happened."

Eyes closed, Dion shook his head. "He talks big, but he don't want no part of you. Not now."

I opened the passenger door, shoved Jullee inside, and slammed the door behind her. Then I said to Dion, *Let's get you to a hospital.*

I was helping Dion out of the car when Bauza leaned over the backseat and said, "I had nothing to do with this. Your old man will back me up. Go ahead and ask him. I wasn't even there when they worked him over. They drove him into the city, then turned him over to me 'cause no one else wanted to face you. That's the truth."

I said, "You're Schiafino's boy. Get out of here before I put a bullet in your head."

I slammed the back door and, tires squealing, Bauza took off.

There was a noise behind me. Drawing the Glock, I shielded Dion with my body. When I turned, I saw Carlyle rushing toward us. I quickly put the gun away and told her Dion needed a doctor. She never hesitated. Arms waving wildly, she tackled the traffic. She wanted to help Dion. I could see that. But I also saw something else. I saw a woman hooked up with the people who'd hurt my father.

She flagged down a taxi and told the driver we had to go to the hospital. I put Dion in the backseat, then told Carlyle she wasn't coming with us. Something in my face frightened her, because she leaned away from me. I said she'd never worried about white cops before, so why start now. Then I climbed in beside Dion, slammed the door, and told the Haitian driver to take me to St. George's Hospital on Fifty-fourth Street and Ninth Avenue. I'd hurt Carlyle, something I'd always wanted to do. Getting to her like that should have left me feeling good. The problem was, it didn't.

XLV
Expressions of Regret

The next morning when I came downstairs, Dion was in the kitchen frying eggs and link sausages. His left arm was in a sling, one eye was blackened, and there were stitches near his hairline. Every now and then he'd touch his cracked ribs.

Injuries or no injuries, he was still the early riser. And his morning routine remained the same. He'd left the house to get the papers, then returned to make breakfast. Chances were good he'd go out to the garage and work on the Henry J. It would be his way of saying *Life goes on*. How he'd managed to dress with one arm, I'll never know. I've had to do it a couple of times, and there's nothing more frustrating. I wasn't surprised to see Dion up and around. I'd only met a few people who were sure of their courage and Dion was one of them. Which didn't mean he was a fool. He'd left the house carrying his .38 Smith & Wesson, which now lay on top of the newspapers.

"Any calls?" I said.

"Two," he said. "Your friend Miss Taylor wasn't one of them." Dion was no fool. He sensed I wanted to talk to Carlyle, to try and make things right. Knowing him, he was probably thinking, *Why bother.*

I poured myself a cup of coffee. "I came down hard on her yesterday. I was angry about what happened to you."

Dion broke the yolks in a pair of eggs sizzling in the frying pan. "So you told me. Last time I looked, the woman wanted to send you away. Fuck her, I say. Has she mentioned anything more about the letter?"

I blew on my coffee to cool it. "Zilch. Not a word. I get the feeling she's still trying to figure out her next move. Elder thinks he's got her in his back pocket. All he has to do is play the race card and she'll come running. Normally, that's all it takes with her. But things aren't normal for Miss Taylor these days. She knows Schiafino killed Lynda, that he's boffing her kid sister and laundering big bucks through Harvey Rafaelson. And unless she's a retard, she also knows Elder's in this up to his stupid ponytail."

Dion said, "Will all of that make her forget about putting you behind bars?"

"Truth is I don't know what she'll do," I said. "You never told me how many bugs Ned Ray found."

"Five," Dion said. "Two downstairs telephones, two upstairs phones, and the one you found behind the couch. Ned thinks we should have a sweep once a week until this thing's cleared up."

"I'll think about it. What about those two callers you mentioned?"

Dion scooped eggs from the frying pan, adding them to a platter of sausages. Then, using the spatula as a pointer, he directed my attention to a pair of notes pinned to the refrigerator with magnets.

The first was from Jack Hayden; the second was from Detective Luis Bonilla, McGuigan's driver. Yesterday at the hospital I'd made a few calls while doctors were treating Dion, who explained his injuries by claiming to have suffered a subway fall. I'd called Hayden and Bonilla to warn them about the wiretaps found in my home. I'd also given Hayden several names found in the notebook I'd taken from Jullee's purse. Each had a Washington address along with a dollar figure beside it.

I'd told Hayden my phones were now clean, but he was taking no chances. This morning's message was short and to the point. In his words, the names I'd given him had a high temperature. Meaning they were involved with crime victims, and the courts had freed the perp, who'd then met a violent death at the hands of person or persons unknown. As for Bonilla, his message said Uncle wanted to see me and suggested I attend a fund-raiser being held tonight in the Village for Mayor Tucker.

I'd also called the Bronx hospital where Damaris Bauza was in intensive care and spoken to Gavilan. I told him about the wiretaps and took responsibility for what happened to his mother. He listened, then quietly said *thanks for calling* and hung up, leaving me with what Oscar Wilde called the wild regrets, and the bloody sweats. I thought about getting Gavilan and his mother police protection, but that would involve their becoming witnesses against the Exchange Students. Now wasn't the time to ask them to consider doing that.

Dion said, "You going to Tucker's fund-raiser?"

"I'm not sure. McGuigan will want to play games. Jerk me around a bit and see what I know. I'm pretty sure he knows Schiafino killed Lynda. But he doesn't want to be the one to accuse a cop of murdering his own wife. He wants me to do the heavy lifting."

Dion bit into a sausage. "You dig up the evidence, maybe go after Schiafino yourself, and McGuigan lets the world know that the police commissioner orchestrated a cover-up. Next day the commissioner's out and McGuigan's taking his place."

The phone rang. While I wanted to speak to Carlyle, I hesitated because I didn't know what to say to her. Dion picked up the receiver, said hello, and listened. Then he handed the receiver to me.

"The girl of your dreams," he said.

I said, "Detective Meagher."

"Carlyle." She sounded distant. Cold.

I said *how are you*, and waited.

After a long silence she said, "I've set up a meeting with Maurice Robichaux and his mother. Noon at Rikers Island hospital. I realize you might feel more comfortable if I wasn't there—"

"Listen, about yesterday. I shouldn't have—"

"As I was saying, I realize you might not want me there. But his mother doesn't trust white cops, and she insists I show up. She thinks you might harm Maurice."

I shook my head. "Did you tell her I think he's innocent, that I know who killed Lynda?"

"I'll leave it to you to win her over. You're such a charmer when you put your mind to it."

"The gardener who makes souls blossom," I said.

"I wouldn't exactly go that far. I did say you had your doubts about Maurice's guilt, and that as a personal favor to me I'd like her to see you. It'll be the four of us. I didn't think you wanted his attorney there. Not just yet anyway. If he were to learn who's involved in this, he'd bring in the press, the governor, and God knows who else."

"Good thinking. The guy's a public defender, which means he can't get work at a decent law firm. He'd only start filing writs and court papers and scare Schiafino's crowd into doing something I'm not ready for. Listen, about yesterday."

She said, "What about yesterday?"

I turned my back to Dion. "I was out of line. I said something I shouldn't have said. I was angry over what happened to Dion."

"And you blamed me."

"I blamed your friends. The ones who want you to send me to prison."

"Meagher, let me ask you something."

"Go ahead."

"Did it ever occur to you that I didn't have to tell you about the letter? That I could have gone ahead and written my story? That I could have hit you hard and without warning?"

I said, "I never thought of that."

"Did it occur to you that by mentioning the letter, I might be saying I had doubts about certain things? When it comes to white cops, I'm carrying a lot of baggage. I may have mentioned that to you."

"I understand."

"Like hell you do. You think I'm obstinate and stubborn, while you, on the other hand, are reasonable and wise. What if I told you that you are one bigoted, set-in-your-ways white boy who thinks he's so wonderful he ought to be cloned. It's your world, and you just let us live in it. Is that how it works?"

I said, "There are times when I wouldn't buy a used car from myself."

"Life's full of tough choices," she said. "Except for you. You're the only one I know who finds making choices just so easy. There must be an explanation for you, for people who want to live in a world without surprises, but I haven't thought of it yet. I'll see you at Rikers. Twelve noon. If you're not there, I'll have a hard time holding back the tears."

She hung up.

XLVI
A Positive ID

Rikers Island is in New York's East River, connected to Queens by a single two-lane bridge. Its ten jails and seventeen thousand inmates make Rikers the world's largest penal colony. Blacks and Hispanics form 92 percent of the population, most of whom are awaiting trial or can't make bail.

Maurice Robichaux was being kept in the island hospital, in a third-floor room guarded around the clock by two armed corrections officers. His room wasn't designed for gracious living. The walls were bare, the smell of disinfectant everywhere, and there was just enough space for a bed, night table, and tiny toilet. Maurice lay propped up in bed, his bruised face yellowed by sunlight coming through a barred window. He was talking to his mother and Carlyle Taylor, the two sitting knee to knee on folding chairs. I had a shopping bag with me. With nowhere to put it, I ended up hanging the bag from Maurice's bed.

Carlyle gave me a vague nod. I tried reading it, to see if all was forgiven or if she was still pissed about yesterday. In the end I gave up, figuring she'd declare herself soon enough. Meanwhile she introduced me to Mrs. Ina Rae Robichaux, Maurice's mother, who acknowledged my presence by looking me up and down, then turning away. Something said I was in for a long afternoon.

Ina Rae Robichaux was a pint-size woman in her late

fifties with shiny brown skin, a flat nose with large nostrils, and straightened hair dyed jet black and worn in evenly cut bangs. She was dressed in a pink suit, matching pillbox hat, and white pearls, along with black pumps and white gloves. Her outfit seemed familiar, and at first I had trouble placing it. Then it hit me. She was dressed like Jackie Kennedy in the early sixties, when JFK was president. It was a goony outfit, to say the least. She held Maurice's hand and stared at him with the sad wisdom of someone who'd finally come to see that life was nothing more than a series of cruel disappointments.

A plane passed overhead, causing her to look up. Only a hundred feet of water separated Rikers Island from La Guardia Airport. A short swim to freedom is how some inmates saw it. But anyone dumb enough to go that route quickly learned that escape wasn't in the cosmic game plan. The water had treacherous tides and currents. Escapees who didn't drown usually ended up floundering in the river until they were rescued by a police boat.

As for Maurice Robichaux, up close he was hard on the eyes. Even without his injuries he was one ugly jig, and getting hammered hadn't improved his looks. His jaw was wired, his left wrist was in a cast, and both his eyes were nearly closed. The fingers of his right hand were attached to wooden splints and an IV unit was connected to his left arm. His left ankle was shackled to the bed, and a few front teeth were missing. He still had his dreadlocks, but the mustache and goatee from his rap-sheet photos were missing. He wore a green hospital gown, and cradled in his arms was a shiny black trumpet, minus the mouthpiece.

His mother was something else. On the surface she seemed courteous, a courtly and refined lady who at some point in her life had taken deportment lessons in order to achieve an air of respectability. In reality, she was an assertive, rock-hard woman who was used to telling people how to run their lives. This might explain why Maurice ended up on the street. Having her talk to you was like being rapped on the knuckles with a ruler.

La-di-da aside, Mrs. Robichaux wasn't stupid. According to the press, she'd written two books on black history and currently managed a black bookstore on Malcolm X Boulevard in Harlem. On the personal side, she was a widow who'd once been married to a trumpeter in the old Basie band. Maurice was her only child.

"I'm told I should listen to you," she said. "As you can see, I'm complying with Miss Taylor's wishes, but most reluctantly. My opinion of you and what you stand for remains the same. Since that opinion is negative in the extreme, I will attempt to maintain civility so long as you do the same."

"Yes, ma'am," I said, choosing my words carefully. "I appreciate your seeing me. I'm after the man who killed Detective Lynda Schiafino. It's not Maurice. He's being framed."

She closed her eyes for a long time. Then she opened them and said, "A natural assumption would be by your white police department."

I removed my hat. "I'm afraid that's true."

She released her son's hand and turned to face me. "Then what brings you here? You're a member of that selfsame police department. Am I to believe you've been transformed, like Saul on the road to Damascus? I'm aware of your feelings toward black people, so forgive me if I bring your sincerity into question."

She looked at Carlyle. "I also question the wisdom of meeting the police without Maurice's attorney being present."

I reached into the shopping bag, removed a small cardboard box, and handed it to Mrs. Robichaux. The box contained a new portable CD player and a set of earphones. I told her to connect the earphones to the player and hand it to Maurice. Then I told Maurice to press PLAY and he'd be in business.

"Maurice doesn't have an attorney," I said to Mrs. Robichaux. "Certainly not one who knows what he's doing. You're stuck with a public defender who's getting peanuts from the city, leaving him or her with a tendency to plead clients guilty. Judges love guilty pleas. Speeds things up. Public defenders love them, too. Same reason. When you're representing fifty nonpaying nonwhites, the sooner you start dumping them, the better."

I said if she thought it was going to be different with Maurice, think again. My guess was he'd been assigned the dumbest attorney on the city payroll. Because the truth was, nobody wanted Maurice to get off. I said it wouldn't surprise me if Maurice's attorney was in touch with the people who framed Maurice. That's why I didn't want the attorney here.

A quiet Mrs. Robichaux sat rigid in her chair, holding my gaze without blinking. She continued staring at me as Carlyle removed the CD player from her hand, placed the earphones in Maurice's ears and pressed PLAY.

Maurice listened. Suddenly, his eyes brightened. Then he smiled at me and whispered one word. *Miles*.

I nodded. "My father recommended the album. He's the jazz expert in the family. There's instructions in the box on how to work the CD player."

"Milestones," Maurice said, naming the album. "Cannonball Adderley on alto. Red Garland, piano. Paul Chambers, bass. Philly Joe Jones, drums. Trane on tenor. I got the cassette, but mine don't sound nothing like this."

"Tapes can't touch a CD for sound," I said.

Mrs. Robichaux reached out for Carlyle's arm. "Is this man telling the truth about Maurice being framed?"

Carlyle said, "Yes." She nodded in my direction. "And he's stepping on a few toes. They've tried to kill him, and yesterday they went after his father."

Mrs. Robichaux pointed to the CD player and said, "Tell me something, detective. Did that come out of your pocket?"

"What difference does it make?"

She clutched her white gloves. "Answering a question with a question. Putting that aside for the moment, if, as you say, police framed Maurice, I can't see them sending him a get-well present. Can you?"

"No, ma'am," I said.

"Which means you paid for it, and I'd like to know why. What's your purpose in being so philanthropic?"

"This case is important to me," I said. "I knew the victim. To be frank, it's personal. I need Maurice to make an identification. Call the CD player an icebreaker."

Carlyle said, "Detective Meagher was in love with the dead woman."

Something passed across Mrs. Robichaux's face. Sympathy. Curiosity. Maybe even shock. Whatever it was, the emotion didn't last long.

"Personal," she said.

"Yes, ma'am."

Mrs. Robichaux looked at her white gloves. "Just like Maurice is with me. I couldn't keep him from the streets. But I can keep him from being used by reporters and by community activists in their little African caps and by outdated white liberals who just won't let go of the sixties. The question is, what kind of user are you, detective? You have a certain reputation in the black community, and as we both know, it's not exactly unblemished."

I said, "No argument there. Still, I think you should hear me out."

"Give me one reason."

"New York now has the death penalty for cop killers. And Maurice is about to be convicted of killing Detective Lynda Schiafino."

She stared out the small window, her face looking sadder and older.

"I marched in Selma against people like you," she said. "They put their dogs on me, attacked me with water hoses, and even shot at me. But I never gave in to them. Never. Now I've got to work with you. There's a certain irony here, don't you think?"

"With all due respect, Mrs. Robichaux," I said, "we're here to help Maurice, not to hold hands and skip down memory lane. I'm not interested in those days when you were changing the world and couldn't wait to get up in the morning because people paid attention to everything you had to say. They don't anymore, and I think it's time you got used to it."

Head tilted back in the position of offended royalty, Mrs. Robichaux gave every indication that I was soon to be banished from her kingdom. Carlyle was much too mortified to even look at me. I was on my own. Having opened this can of peas, I continued talking. In for a penny, in for a pound.

"This isn't about you, Mrs. Robichaux," I said. "It's about Maurice. What he needs is evidence proving someone else killed Detective Schiafino. Now, if you have a better way to handle this thing, I'd like to hear it. I really would."

I reached for my hat, fully expecting to be told to get out of Dodge. What happened next surprised the hell out of me.

Mrs. Robichaux said, "If I've offended you, Detective Meagher, I apologize. Common sense says if Maurice is being framed by police, your coming here puts you at risk. Is Miss Taylor also at risk?"

I nodded. "Yes, ma'am."

"And will you protect her?"

I looked at Carlyle. "I'll do the best I can."

I reached in the shopping bag. "Something else for Maurice."

I handed Mrs. Robichaux the trumpet mouthpiece found at the airport. When Maurice spotted it, he became excited. Quickly removing the earphones, he held out his right hand. His mother gave him the mouthpiece. Maurice tried attaching it to the trumpet. But between the splints and the cast, he couldn't do it. Carlyle did the honors, and Maurice thanked her. When he looked at me, I gave him a thumbs up. Grinning, he began stroking the trumpet as if it were a cherished house pet.

"Miles's trumpet was black," he said. "That's why I got me one."

I said, "My father says a trumpet player never lets anyone use his mouthpiece."

"Better believe it," Maurice said. "No matter how bad things got, I always took care of my mouthpiece. Never let it get dirty. Never sold it. Never let nobody touch it."

"Want to ask you something," I said.

I took a folded newspaper page from the shopping bag. Then, using a ballpoint pen, I drew a beard, mustache, and sunglasses on a two-column photograph that had appeared with the story on Lynda's murder. When I finished, I leaned forward and handed the page to Maurice.

I knew his vision wasn't good and he was on medication,

so I said take your time, study it, then let me know if you recognize this guy.

Maurice shook his head. "Don't need no time." His voice was the strongest it had been since we met.

"This is the dude," he said. "The one who gave me that money. Gave me them hundred-dollar bills and told me to meet him in the parking lot the night that woman was killed. What you just did makes him look exactly like the guy. Exactly like him."

Carlyle looked at the doctored photograph, then at me. "That's a picture of Detective Robert Schiafino."

Maurice pointed to me. "Something else, too. He had on a ring just like the one you got."

I held up my right hand. "You mean this gold detective's ring."

Maurice nodded. "Just like yours. And he had a fancy watch."

"Silver-link bracelet," I said. "Jeweled face. Gives the time in major cities around the world."

Maurice was pumped. Someone besides his mother was buying into his story.

"That's right," he said. "I ax him the time in South Africa, and he give it to me. You got a watch like that?"

I said no. But I did happen to be with Schiafino's wife two months ago, when she'd purchased one like it for her husband's birthday.

XLVII
Save the Children

At four o'clock that afternoon I was in Central Park, standing face-to-face with Jesus Bauza in the middle of the Great Lawn, a favorite spot in warm weather for softball, touch football, and soccer. But today wasn't warm, and the Great Lawn was empty.

"I came alone," Bauza said. "Just like I promised."

My hand was on the Glock in my overcoat pocket. "If you're setting me up, I'll be vexed."

Haysoos blinked at the high-rises surrounding the park. He had the jumps.

"Ain't nothing gonna happen," he said. "I don't feature being a target."

I'd called the office from Rikers Island and been told Bauza wanted to see me right away. Something was going down in D.C. tomorrow night. According to Bauza, I knew the person involved. Translation: the Exchange Students had a Washington hit on for tomorrow night. And I knew the vic.

I called Jesus at his girlfriend's number. He picked up on the first ring, sounding more than a little nervous. He didn't want to talk over the phone. And we had to meet now. I said I'd pick the spot. Outdoors, with plenty of space and clear visibility in all directions.

In Central Park we stood with our backs to the Delacorte Theater, on the edge of Belvedere Lake. The theater was closed until summer, when it offers free Shakespeare. Bauza cupped his gloved hands over his ears to keep warm. He tried lighting a cigarette, but the wind blew out the lighter flame. Furious, he threw the lighter into the lake. Then he crossed his arms and began slapping his shoulders to keep the circulation going, and finally he brought up the question we both knew had to be asked.

"You wired?"

I wasn't and invited him to pat me down. He looked at my eyes and decided to believe me.

"Let's walk," he said. "I'm colder than a polar bear's asshole."

I pointed east, toward the roof of the Metropolitan Museum of Art, which could be seen just over the trees. We headed in that direction.

"Tell me about the hit," I said. "And this vic I'm supposed to know."

"It's Jullee. Bobby wants me to go to Washington and whack her."

I stopped walking and so did Bauza. Jullee was a bitch, but she was also a kid and in over her head. A part of me felt sorry for her. The rest of me wanted to see her tried for Lynda's murder. But for that to happen, she'd have to be alive.

Haysoos said, "Jullee's shook up, and Bobby blames you. He's afraid you'll go after his money now that you know about her and Harvey. He's got to protect Harvey and the rest of the cash coming out of Washington. Bobby thinks you could scare Jullee into talking. Considering how much she knows, that's bad news. That's why she's got to go."

I said, "Why are you telling me all this?"

"I want out."

"Schiafino won't let you out."

"Don't I know it," Bauza said. "But I could still get out, provided you convince Jullee to testify against Bobby. Me and Gina. Gone."

"You're not going anywhere if Jullee mentions your name."

"I got that covered," he said. "I don't go to Washington tomorrow. *You* do. You go there and get Jullee out, and you make sure she knows Bobby wanted her killed. While you're gone, Gina and me take off. We'll lay low till Bobby's arrested. Then we come back and maybe cut a deal. Or maybe we don't come back, I don't know. All I know is tomorrow we're gone."

"And if I don't go to Washington?"

"Two people killed Lynda Schiafino," Haysoos said. "Bobby's one, but he'll never talk. That leaves Jullee. I figure you want to nail Bobby real bad. Bad enough to go after the one person who can tie him to his wife's murder. Get her talking before Bobby shuts her up for good."

He was right. I wanted Schiafino for Lynda's murder so bad I could taste it.

I said, "One of your D.C. guys could cap Jullee. Why doesn't Schiafino do it that way?"

"You don't shit where you eat," Haysoos said. "That's what makes this thing work. Someone from New York has to go down there and do it. Besides, Bobby would have to pay them to do it. He's a cheap bastard. He's asking me to do it on the arm."

He took a deep breath. "Another reason I want out is this killing would create a lot of heat. You whack a spook or a child molester, nobody cares. But Jullee's different. Her sister just got murdered, and her sister's a white cop. That's too much weight. Also, I don't feel like leaving New York."

I said, "Think something will happen to Gina while you're gone?"

Haysoos shrugged. "Bobby says it makes him nervous, you asking Gina questions."

"You've killed before. What's wrong with you killing Gina?"

Haysoos got angry in a hurry. "Fuck you. Why you say a thing like that?"

"I get these moods. You know how it is. Anyway, work with me on this. Jullee helped Schiafino kill Lynda, right?"

Bauza still hadn't cooled down. He blew steam toward the Met and said, "You asking me or telling me?"

I said, "I figured it started when she tricked Lynda into coming to their father's house in Flushing. Lisa Watts overheard that phone call, which is why Bobby Schemes wants to meet her for a little chitchat. Meanwhile Jullee told Lynda some bullshit story about a guy who'd bought her car then stuck her with a bum check and how she needed Lynda's help."

The park ground, frozen by cold weather, was as hard as

295

oak. A hungry squirrel came close to us and stood on its hind legs, begging for food. The wind blew dry leaves around my ankles and ruffled the lake's surface.

"Jullee's got a memory like a Sicilian," I said. "Never forgave Lynda for leaving her in jail for three days. At the time, Lynda wanted to teach her a lesson. I'd say the lesson didn't take."

I put a hand on my hat to keep the wind from taking it. In the distance a lone jogger worked his way down an empty driveway. The trees were still bare and without a hint of spring buds.

I said, "In Flushing, Schiafino and Jullee lure Lynda into the garage, where they kill her. The body and knife are then taken to Kennedy, where their fall guy's waiting. That would be Maurice. Good old Maurice. Black, homeless, and fried on a series of easily obtainable pharmaceuticals. And he comes with a bonus, a rap sheet ten feet long. A chump sent from heaven. Isn't that what you told Schiafino?"

Bauza chewed his lip and stared down at the ground, a man lost in his secret thoughts.

I said, "Next time you see Schiafino, tell him close but no cigar."

Haysoos looked ready to jump out of his skin. "What do you mean by that?"

"I mean the frame was less than perfect. Schiafino, Jullee, and Lynda were seen entering the garage together. In other words, we got ourselves a witness. A surprise witness."

I thought, *A dying man who still thinks his daughter will walk out of the garage alive.*

Haysoos wiped his runny nose with the back of his hand. "Who's this witness?"

"If Schiafino's interested, he knows where to find me."

"You're not going to give me the name?"

I said, "Jesus, what do I look like, the poster boy for stupidity? Let's get back to Lynda's murder. Suppose somebody digs up that nice new garage floor Little Augie's laying down for Oz Lesnevitch. What do you think they'll find? How about blood and skull fragments belonging to Lynda."

"That's Bobby. Got nothing to do with me."

"Wrong. You're an accessory. You found Maurice for

Schiafino, and then you joined the cover-up. And let's not forget those little trips you're making to Washington. Accessory? Buddy boy, you're a player. Big time. You want to stay out of the slammer? I want more than Jullee and it had better be good. Real good."

Bauza went back to staring at the ground and chewing his lip.

We were near the southeast end of Belvedere Lake, coming up on a bronze statue of Jagiello, king of Poland and grand duke of Lithuania. How the king of Poland rated a statue in Central Park was beyond me.

Bauza said, "You're saying I'm an accessory to a cop killing?"

"Does a bear shit in the woods?"

"What do you want from me? I'm giving you Jullee. Ain't that enough?"

"You're sending me out of town so you can go south. From where I stand, I'm doing you a favor. What do I want from you? Here's a hint. Tell me how Bobby Schemes got connected at City Hall. Give me a reason for doing your dirty work."

I said Schiafino seemed to have a lock on the rabbi. I needed to know how that came about.

Bauza said, "You're right. Elder's connected, but Bobby and the rabbi have their own thing. It has to do with the mayor's daughter, the kid who died of a heroin overdose."

Jesus refused to mention the rabbi's name. Not that it mattered, since I already knew it. Still, the story was a grabber. Schiafino used to drive for the rabbi, Bauza said, and what brought them together was Janine. She was Mayor Tucker's sixteen-year-old daughter, a young beauty with a modeling contract and a promising future. She had a crush on the rabbi, and one thing led to another, and according to Haysoos, the two began doing the wild thing. On their last date a phone call went out to Schiafino. It came from a Yonkers motel, where the rabbi happened to be with Janine, who happened to be very dead. She'd OD'd on smack, a habit picked up from her friends in modeling, where living in the fast lane was the norm. Schiafino recruited Bauza, and together they came to the rabbi's rescue. Janine ended up in a Harlem doorway, and Schiafino ended up owning the rabbi, body and soul.

I pushed for more. "Schiafino killed Santos Colón. How'd he do it?"

McGuigan had already told me about Colón's trouble with Puerto Rican extortionists and how the Exchange Students offered to solve the problem. Haysoos filled in the rest. Not only did Colón turn down Schiafino's offer, but he made the mistake of telling people about it. Schiafino reacted by shoving an ice pick up Colón's nose and into his brain, making it appear he'd died of a cerebral hemorrhage. It was an old Mafia way of killing, leaving doctors and forensic experts no choice but to declare death by natural causes.

I told Bauza I could request that Puerto Rican authorities exhume Colón's body. But they'd probably drag their feet unless I gave them additional evidence against Schiafino.

Haysoos said, "Turn Jullee and there's your extra evidence. At that point having Colón's body exhumed will be a piece of cake. I know you had a thing with Lynda. You couldn't save her, but maybe you can save her sister. Your call."

I said my call was to send Jullee away for life. But Lynda was dead, and death and guilt went together, and I'd feel guilty if I didn't try to keep Jullee alive.

Bauza nodded in agreement.

He said, "Schiafino's told D.C. there's a hit on Jullee and to cooperate as usual. There'll be a piece waiting in a locker at Dulles Airport, plus whatever information's needed. Plus an emergency phone number. When the shooter's finished, he's supposed to return the weapon to the locker. Somebody breaks the piece down and drops the parts in a few sewers. It'll never be found."

"Your Washington people expecting you or just anybody?"

"They don't know who's coming," Jesus said. "All they know is we're sending somebody. We never give out the name of our guy, and they don't tell us who they're sending here. You don't know, you can't say. I've never met any of the Washington guys. No reason to. I show up, do my thing, and I'm gone. At most I'm there one hour."

"I'll go," I said. "Provided you put twenty-five thousand dollars in a bank account for your wife and Gavilan. Do it by noon tomorrow. Then have her or Gavilan call me and confirm the money's there. If it is, I'll go to Washington in your place. Take it or leave it."

Bauza said, "Take it or leave it?"

I waited, knowing he'd heard me and was only hoping I'd come down on the price. That wasn't going to happen, and after a few seconds of us staring at each other, Haysoos said we had a deal.

XLVIII
Yes, Yes, Yes

When I returned to my office at five o'clock that afternoon, Jack Hayden was standing at the window. Back to me, he kept his grim face pointed at the soft white clouds being blown across the sky by a hard, north wind.

"Check your desk," he said. "Lower right drawer. I dropped by to give you the information I came up with on those Washington names in Jullee's notebook. I'm leaving for a dental appointment and didn't want this stuff handled by too many people. Figured to keep it between us for a while. Then I saw the blood on your rug near your desk drawer. And what I thought was a long string hanging from your desk drawer. I opened the drawer."

He shivered.

I saw the blood, too. And the string. Except I knew it wasn't a string. Dumping my hat and coat on the desk, I opened the drawer and found myself staring at a dead rat, the biggest goddamn rat I'd ever seen. It was bright eyed, still bleeding, and absolutely fucking hideous. The tail—the *string*—had to be three feet long.

I closed the drawer, taking care not to slam it too hard

and cut off the rat's tail. I hadn't eaten all day. Right now, I didn't care if I ever ate again.

The rat was a message. Someone in my unit knew I was investigating cops. Which made me a traitor to the brotherhood. A rat. And unless I could prove otherwise, that's how every cop in the department would see me from now on.

Hayden sat on the windowsill. "Building superintendent's sending somebody up. Whoever did this is sick. How'd he learn we're bird-dogging cops? I haven't said anything, and I know you haven't. Yet somehow this prick knows."

"Schiafino has friends everywhere," I said. "He mixes in a little bit of the truth, namely, my relationship with his wife, with a lot of bullshit. Finally, he relies on the average cop's suspicious nature. Face it, we thrive on paranoia. Anything that feeds our persecution complex is welcome. Gives our lives meaning."

Hayden looked at the rat drawer and shuddered. "I've seen this happen once or twice over the years, when they thought someone was with Internal Affairs. But I never had it happen here. Give me something to work with. Some hard evidence so I can show the fuck who did this that Schiafino's dirty."

I thought about Jullee. Getting her to talk would be the hard evidence Hayden was looking for. But after this thing with the rat, I didn't know who to trust around here. I decided to keep quiet about Jullee. I had my own plans for her. As Samuel Johnson said, *Three may keep a secret, if two are dead.*

Hayden pointed to my desk. "Have them scrub the fucking hell out of that drawer. Speaking of cleanups, you were seen leaving Schiafino's topless club just before it was shut down yesterday due to public lewdness on the part of a co-owner."

"Is that a fact?"

"I mention this," Hayden said, "because I got a call from McGuigan, who says he got a call from City Hall, where Schiafino and the naked co-owner possess some small influence. The club's reopening tomorrow, liquor license and all."

"Somebody's got a lot of clout," I said.

"You're to stay away from Shares. Walk on the same side of the street and you're suspended. That's McGuigan talking, not me."

Ditto Head was playing the game. I doubt if he intended to suspend me. He needed me working for him. Still, he had to make it look good.

There was a knock on the door. I said, *come in,* and a pudgy young Puerto Rican male in the building uniform, heavy gloves, blue granny glasses, and an earring in each ear walked in carrying a bucket and rags.

"You got rats?" he said, as though he were interested in buying some for his private collection.

I said, "Bottom right drawer and don't bother removing the rat. Just take the drawer, clean it, and bring it back. And don't forget the rug."

"Cool," he said. He looked at the rat. "Whoa. A big sucker. People don't got dogs that big."

The Rican was taking the rat's presence calmly, like a man used to seeing humungous rodents on the job or at home. He did what he could with the rug, then promised to return today or tomorrow with the drawer.

After he'd left, I said to Hayden, "That caller from City Hall. The one who's so protective of Shares. That wouldn't be Ray Footman, by any chance?"

Hayden raised an eyebrow. "How did you know?"

I said, "Elder's a fund-raiser for Mayor Tucker, who lets Deputy Mayor Footman jerk him around. Footman actually runs this city and wants to keep on running it. But he can only do that if Tucker wins a second term. To win, you need money. Reopening Shares keeps Elder happy, and a happy Elder is more inclined to kick in to Tucker's war chest."

Hayden picked up a paperweight and tossed it from hand to hand. "You say that as though it's supposed to mean something."

"It could. It definitely could."

The paperweight went back on the desk. "You were at Rikers today to see Maurice Robichaux. Same time as Carlyle Taylor. Your visit wouldn't have anything to do with the Lynda Schiafino case, would it?"

Think fast. I decided against telling Hayden about my arrangement with McGuigan. Touchy soul that he was, Hayden would see that as my having gone over his head. So I offered an altered version of the truth.

"I needed Robichaux to make an ID," I said. "And Carlyle Taylor was at Rikers when I got there. She and Robichaux's mother."

"Who'd Robichaux ID?"

"Bauza. The cop who popped him twice."

Hayden said, "You told me about that."

Came the lie. A basic spur-of-the-moment fabrication designed to keep the peace and save my ass.

I said, "Robichaux was in Times Square scoring crack around the same time Bauza was trolling for Lourdes Balera. He can put the two of them together."

Hayden shrugged. "Waste of time. The DA's got a cop killer in Robichaux. He won't let us have him to make a case against Bauza for any reason. Besides, Robichaux's got a reason to lie about Bauza. Those two busts, remember? That's what the defense *and* the DA will say. Nice try, but you've got nothing."

He looked at his watch. "Time to let the dentist drill for oil. Check with you later. I trust you didn't say anything to exasperate Miss Taylor?"

"You know me," I said.

"That's why I asked."

When Hayden had gone, I lit a cigarette and thought about the kind of cop who'd find a rat, kill it, and then hold on to it until he could dump it on me. At first I thought anyone could have put it there. Then I narrowed it down to some hard cases, two or three guys in the unit I didn't get along with. I glanced at the wet spot on the rug, and that's when the phone rang. I had two numbers. One went through the switchboard; one didn't. The non-switchboard line was for informants whose identity I preferred to keep secret.

The caller was Carlyle Taylor.

"Can you talk?" she said.

"I can also whistle a merry tune from time to time. You sound like Joan Rivers. Yeah, I can talk. What's up?"

"You made quite an impression on Mrs. Robichaux. Despite your complexion, she thinks you have a certain integrity and, as she puts it, a modicum of uprightness."

"Modicum?"

"Men," she said. "Always hung up on size. Anyway, she's fired Maurice's lawyer and asked for a new one."

"Good move," I said. "Tell her to keep an eye on him as well."

"I will. She said whenever you want to talk to Maurice, you can."

For some reason having Mrs. Robichaux's approval made me feel good.

I said, "Give her my thanks. And make sure she and Maurice keep quiet about our meeting today."

"She knows that."

"She's also to keep everyone away from Maurice. Except for you and the new attorney, no one's to talk to him. Let's hope the Exchange Students don't turn Maurice into a suicide while he's in police custody. If that happens, case closed."

"And Schiafino gets away with killing his wife. I have another reason for calling. I'm not going to write that story on you. The one Gene wants me to do."

I took my feet off the desk, the rat temporarily forgotten.

"This is going to frost Gene's socks," she said. "But that's too bad. Some things have nothing to do with black or white, and this is one of them. I owe you for the airport and for keeping quiet about it. Keeping quiet about you only seems fair. Sending you to prison means Schiafino goes free and Maurice is convicted, and I won't be a part of that. In any case, I do have an exclusive on the Exchange Students story, correct?"

"Correct," I said.

"Then provided you don't get yourself killed, I just may come out ahead in this thing."

Talk about Saul turning into Saint Paul. A week ago I wouldn't have given Carlyle Taylor the time of day. Now I was helping her expose dirty cops. Cops who'd just as soon kill me as write a parking ticket. I had her word there'd be nothing in print until I said so. Would she keep that promise? Who the hell knew?

I thanked Carlyle for not writing the story but warned her that Elder wouldn't take no for an answer. Not with Schiafino leaning on him.

She laughed. "I'm meeting that challenge head-on. I'm ducking Gene. I'm skipping tonight's fund-raiser for Mayor Tucker. It's a biggie. Features some heavy Hollywood hitters, the usual West Coast liberals who'd run naked through the snow for a photo opportunity with a black politician. I'd like to cover it, but that just doesn't seem feasible. Gene will be there, and I'm not ready for that kind of confrontation. As we say in our neck of the woods, it be's that way sometimes."

"What about a bodyguard?" I said.

"Bodyguard? I don't know. I mean how would I go about hiring one?"

"How about me?" I said.

She laughed. *"You?* Body-guarding *me?* That's hysterical."

"The deputy police commissioner will be there. He wants to see me, and that's an invitation I can't refuse. I'm also going out of town tomorrow in connection with this case. Nothing I can talk about right now. Before I leave, I want to rattle somebody's cage. He'll be at the fund-raiser. He's with the Exchange Students and no, I'm not talking about Daddy Duke."

"Are we in a position to name names?"

I said, "How about the rabbi."

"Mr. City Hall? The real mover and shaker in this thing?"

"I intend to get in his face. How'd you like to be there when that happens?"

Carlyle whispered, "Oh my God."

I said, Then it's a date, and she said, Yes, yes, yesyesyes.

XLIX
Your Name's on It

When I entered the limousine parked on Bleecker Street that evening, McGuigan was sitting in the backseat, a cell phone to his ear. The conversation must have been serious because he was scowling. At the sight of me, he said he'd call back in ten minutes and immediately broke off the conversation. Evidently, our meeting wasn't going to last long.

We were just four blocks from Mayor Tucker's fundraiser. McGuigan, however, had no intention of showing up. He'd had a last-minute change of heart. The reason? Me.

My situation within the department had worsened. McGuigan didn't want to be seen talking to me. In fact he didn't want to be in the same room with me. He couldn't afford to. In his words I was the Bermuda Triangle of law enforcement, and anybody dumb enough to come near me was lost.

So he'd set up a meeting on Bleecker, which is Main Street, Greenwich Village, with the largest concentration of restaurants, shops, bars, and wackos to be found down there. Carlyle and Detective Bonilla were down the street, having cappuccino at the Figaro Café. Which left me and Ditto Head to go *mano a mano*.

"Here's the bad news," McGuigan said. "The commissioner wants your ass. He's having an arrest warrant drawn up with your name on it. Corruption charges stemming from your relationship with Detective Lynda Schiafino."

"And the good news?"

"You have forty-eight hours until he serves the warrant."

"Great," I said.

"Dowd's heard about you and Baby Cabrera's drug money. I'm assuming this is the basis of the corruption charges. He also wants IA to launch an inquiry into your interference with a major murder investigation. I assume he means the Lynda Schiafino investigation."

"The murder which I'm now looking into at your request."

"The very same."

I said, "Something tells me I just got sandbagged by Bobby Schemes and the rabbi. And if I might be so bold, maybe even by you."

"That still leaves you with forty-eight hours to save your ass."

"I'm being set up. And Dowd's being used. Except he's too dumb to see that."

"Law enforcement is about many things," McGuigan said, "perception being one of them. This being an election year, Dowd is taking special pains to look good. He needs a quick and easy solution to Lynda Schiafino's murder, and anyone depriving him of that stands to get de-balled. He'd also like some more TV time, the kind that shows him coming down hard on corrupt cops. If you have any tricks up your sleeve, you've got forty-eight hours to make them work."

I looked out the window at a young white male, skinny as a rail and wearing a wedding gown, pointy aluminum bra, and white tiara. His gold sequined wand threw off sparks in the night, and despite the traffic, he was Rollerblading backward down Bleecker Street.

"I've got one trick," I said. "Whether or not it works, I'll know tomorrow."

"Don't tell me about it," McGuigan said. "If it works, I'll know soon enough. If it doesn't, I'd rather not be around for the fallout."

"Forty-eight hours," I said.

"If that."

L

How's It Hanging, Rabbi?

I stood sipping black coffee with Carlyle Taylor in the cozy library of a Washington Square townhouse located in the Row. Washington Square is considered the spiritual center of the Village, a claim you can't take too seriously when you see the public toilets in the middle of the park. A hundred years ago the square had been surrounded by fashionable homes. Today only a single block of these fancy redbrick houses remains. That block is called the Row.

The most elegant house belongs to a fifty-five-year-old record-company president with big hips, coarse, curly hair, and a taste for teenage girls young enough to be his granddaughter. He was the sunny host of tonight's fund-raiser for Mayor Tucker. Carlyle knew a little about Mr. Record Man. According to her, he was backing the recording career of the country's top female singer, a seventeen-year-old he'd been screwing since she was twelve.

He wasn't just investing in little girls. The library featured an original Renoir and a Rembrandt sketch of Rem himself, both wired to the wall and watched over by a security guard. Mr. Record Man was glued to Mayor Tucker, who held court in the center of the bustling library. Every time the mayor said something remotely funny, Mr. Record Man guffawed until he was red in the face.

"You know any of these people?" I said.

"Well," Carlyle said, "there's last year's Oscar winner for Best Actress, half the city council, and the pastors of Harlem's two biggest churches, neither of whom can stand the other. There's the chief justice of the state supreme court, three professional basketball players, the police commissioner, whom I'm sure you recognize, and a fashion designer who gets weekly collagen injections in his face to keep looking young. That good enough for you?"

It wasn't, but I kept my opinion to myself. The commissioner was deliberately avoiding me, and as for the others, I was trying to avoid them. I had no use for black activists with extended rap sheets, indictable politicians, models whose runny noses had nothing to do with cold weather, three drag queens pretending to be the Ronettes, and balding businessmen looking to get laid. I made several guests as freeloaders who considered party-crashing their life's work. They stopped white-jacketed domestics carrying silver trays of canapés and ate like famine was imminent.

Carlyle exchanged hugs with a cross-eyed black preacher while I warmed my butt in front of a wood-burning fireplace and watched the people around me look past one another for someone more important. All eyes were on Mayor Tucker and his entourage, which included Commissioner Dowd, Ray Footman, Jonathan Munro, and Eugene Elder. Harvey Rafaelson was there, too, doing his best to pretend I didn't exist. I called this crew the UDs. Unsatisfied demons. *The love of power is the demon of men, for men can have everything and still be unhappy, for the demon waits and waits and will be satisfied.*

Carlyle and I drew stares, and not just because she was wearing a pair of jeweled chopsticks in her hair. Two white cops eyed me with disgust but kept moving. A well-known black rabble-rouser, who I knew to be a secret police informant, maintained his street credibility by greeting Carlyle while deliberately ignoring me. Elder looked in her direction a couple of times and let it go at that. My attention was on the rabbi. I watched him whisper something to Jonathan Munro, a tall, fiftyish man with silver hair and a square jaw. A beaming Munro had his arm around a blond model who didn't look a day over nineteen and seemed bored out of her mind.

Suddenly, the rabbi broke away from the mayor's circle and started to work the room, and I realized that if I waited until he stopped schmoozing, I'd be here all night. This was a fund-raiser after all, and the rabbi's responsibility was to bring in the bucks.

Placing my coffee cup on the mantel, I said to Carlyle, *here we go*. I took her hand and began pushing through the crowd. Someone stepped on my foot. Nobody apologized, and I didn't bother stopping. I sensed Carlyle getting charged. One hand gripped my arm; the other squeezed my hand as tightly as she could. I was getting a little pumped myself. Face-to-face with the rabbi. Mind-blowing.

And then I was close enough to touch him. Deputy Mayor Ray Footman turned around, and his eyes immediately went to Carlyle, and because they were old friends she didn't suspect a thing. It was hugs and air kisses and glad-to-see-you and can-I-get-you-a-drink? and you're-looking-great and how's-everything-going? I watched in silence, and finally the thick-bodied, forty-five-year-old Footman looked at me, put a smile on his wide gap-toothed face, and extended his hand. His game plan called for him to act as if nothing was wrong. But his eyes gave it away. He blinked a lot, then forced his eyes open as though trying to stay awake, and in the end, his smile faded as well.

Ignoring his hand, I said, "They say once you've tasted power, you never want to give it up. How's it hanging, rabbi?"

Footman brought back his smile and said, "Public service and power seeking are two entirely different things. What did you just call me?"

"Rabbi," I said. "It's what Schiafino's cops call you. You know the cops I'm talking about. The Exchange Students. Now, there's a bunch of fun-seekers for you. Cutting down on the rate of recidivism while making a few bucks for you at the same time. Is that great or what. Back to the subject of power. Did you know that if you have enough of it, you can lie and make your lies come true?"

The tension between Footman and me literally rocked Carlyle back on her heels. Her jaw dropped, and she covered her mouth with one hand.

Footman stopped smiling. "Cryptic conversations are rarely worth the effort, detective. Now if you'll excuse me. Carlyle."

He kissed her hand and was about to leave when I said, "Been to Yonkers lately? I understand you used to spend a lot of time there. In fact, I hear that's how you and Bobby Schiafino came to be of one mind, so to speak. That cryptic enough for you?"

Footman was shaken. His jaw tightened, and he clasped his hands together, squeezing them until the backs were white. But he didn't get where he was by caving in easily. He leaned toward me and said, "I'd be very careful if I were you. I hear things, too. And I hear you're going to be up on corruption charges very shortly."

I said, "Let's talk about the way you protect the Exchange Students. It's a good system. Bring civilians into the police department, and make sure each one's beholden to you. And you, of course, are beholden to Bobby Schemes. How many murders have you and your *civilians* covered up so far? In round figures."

Footman said to Carlyle, "You in on this?"

Shocked, all she could do was shake her head.

Footman nodded and looked at me. "There's an old saying, *Never insult an alligator until after you've crossed the river.* I'm the alligator, and as yet you haven't crossed the river. You want to take me on? Fine. You've got your war, detective."

Then he said to Carlyle, "You should be more careful about the company you keep. I'd also advise you to take anything this man says with a grain of salt. Now, if you'll excuse me, I have to raise two million dollars tonight."

I said, "Ever hear of Davis Hookstadter and Barry Petras?"

Footman froze.

"They're from Washington," I said. "Hookstadter owns half the city's movie theaters and Petras used to be lieutenant governor of Maryland. His family's in gas and oil. Both had relatives who were murdered. Turns out the murderers are now dead. You and Schiafino wouldn't be collecting money from Hookstadter and Petras, by any chance?"

Footman shook his head as though he'd given up trying to convince me professional wrestling was phony. I had one more surprise. I handed him the newspaper photo of Schiafino, the one to which I'd added a beard and dark glasses. At the sight of it, Footman looked as if he'd just eaten some very bad clams. People tried to get his attention, but he ignored them and continued to stare at the photograph. Then he closed his eyes and fought for control, and in the end he crushed the photo in his hand, dropped it on the carpet, and walked away, to be followed by parasites, fawners, and flunkies.

Carlyle was on the verge of tears. "Not him," she said. "Anyone but him."

"You've just met the rabbi," I said. "Up close and personal."

"If it weren't for him, we wouldn't have a black mayor."

I thought, *On a scale of one to ten, the mayor sucks.* Footman had a lot to answer for.

Carlyle said, "If it weren't for Ray, we wouldn't have minorities and women in the police department. He's made this city better."

"He's made it better for cops who want to kill their wives," I said. "He's made it better for people who can afford to buy justice, and above all he's made it better for Ray Footman. He framed Maurice—him, Schiafino, and your boy Elder. And they're hiding behind a black mayor."

"I've had dinner with Ray and his wife," Carlyle said. "I know his two daughters. One's on her way to Harvard Medical School. He can't be the rabbi. He just can't."

"Can and is. That money you saw at the bank yesterday, the money brought from Washington by Jullee, it's meant to win the mayor a second term and keep Footman in power. Harvey knows he's the rabbi. So does Jullee and Schiafino. Jullee's a better witness because she also knows about Lynda's murder."

I said Footman's thing was power, and he had it in spades, no pun intended. To get more power, he was putting minorities and women into the police department. At present the beneficiary of this particular bit of Footman power was the Exchange Students.

And then Eugene Elder emerged from the crush of people to stand between Carlyle and me.

"Girl, you're looking peaked," he said. He glanced at me over his shoulder. "Must be the company you're keeping." A sweeping gesture of his arm took in the entire room.

"Feast your eyes," he said. "All these fine-looking black people around you. My people. *Your* people. Ebony, mahogany, high yellow, tan, bronze, and leather colored. Brothers and sisters coming in so many hues, and all members of the same tribe, the Mo'nig tribe. Mo' nigger than anything else. And beautiful to the bone."

He smiled at me, a multitude of teeth against purple gums. "How you like that, *Fear,* man?"

Carlyle said, "I need fresh air. Take me out of here. Now."

Elder's smile grew wider. He was a winner, and I was a loser, and I didn't like it. I watched him slip an arm around Carlyle's waist and say, "Baby, we are gone. Just let me tell a few people I'm leaving and then—"

She pushed his arm away and said, "Don't touch me. Not now, not ever. Gene, for God's sake, look at yourself. You want the world to think you're so black you cast a shadow on coal. Yet you're sucking up to any white man here you think can do you some good. And you're not exactly ignoring white women either."

There were tears in her eyes as she said, "It should be you in the center of the room, not Tucker. You, not him. That was my dream for you. I thought it was *our* dream, but I was wrong, wasn't I. God, you've broken my heart, you've just broken my heart. You're a racial pimp. It's taken me this long to see it, but that's what you are. I don't like what your friends have done to you, and I don't like what you're doing to me. Stay away, Gene. Just stay away."

I saw him draw himself up, prepared to tough it out. But he and I knew she'd drawn blood. There is a pain a man feels when he betrays a woman he loves, a pain unlike any other. I'd felt it every day since Lynda died, and tonight I saw it in Elder's face, a regret for things that might have been. In the middle of what should have been a great night for him, he suddenly had nothing. *Footfalls echo in the memory / Down the passages which we did not take / Towards the door we never opened.* . . .

But you can only rewrite your life in your imagination, and for Elder it was too late to even do that. He soon made his face iron hard, looked at Carlyle, and shook his head as though humoring someone who'd just been let out of an institution.

She moved closer to me.

I took her arm and said to Elder, "Guess this make me an honorary Mo'nig. What's the first year's dues?"

LI
Travel Plans

I arrived at the office the next morning to find my mail opened, cut up, and scattered across my desk. Say hello to police paranoia. As for my missing desk drawer—Mr. Rat's final resting place—it had yet to be returned.

When I searched the scraps of shredded mail for telephone messages, I found two, one from Bauza and the other from Gavilan. I called Gavilan first. He was still at the hospital with his mother and sounded exhausted. He'd just heard from Bauza, who'd called to say a new bank account had been opened in Damaris's name. Gavilan understandably thought Bauza was lying until my name cropped up. Checking with the bank, Gavilan had received confirmation of the account, but the bank refused to say how much was on deposit. After getting the name of the bank officer he'd spoken to, I told Gavilan I'd check it out.

"Thanks, man," Gavilan said. "Yo, maybe we can get together sometime. My stepfather wouldn't do shit for me unless you made him do it. Maybe you and me, we can hang out. Like, just for a while, you know?"

"No problem," I said. "I'm going out of town today on business. I'm back tomorrow. Give you a call then. We'll set something up."

"Cool." He sounded a bit more lively. "Talk to you tomorrow. And thanks again for what you did."

Jesus was next. I told him I'd spoken to Gavilan and would be contacting the bank. If the twenty-five K wasn't there, Bauza's ass would belong to me.

"Hey, I'm not about to play games with you," he said. "Not after what you did to Jullee. I mean you actually set fire to the bitch. Now, that was cold."

"She's alive," I said. "And let's keep her that way. Since it looks like I'm going to Washington, where can I reach her?"

"Hotel Duquesne, First Street and Maryland Avenue, not far from the Botanic Gardens. Hotel faces a little park that's part of the gardens. Jullee's in room three-seventeen."

I lit a cigarette and stuck my foot into the space formerly occupied by the rat drawer.

"And she's there now?" I said.

"Right now she's in and out. Doing the collection thing. Since the run-in with you, Bobby's changed things around. No more staying in Washington overnight and returning to New York in the morning. From now on she's traveling at night. This way she's back here when the city's quiet and nobody's out on the street. That's Bobby's thinking. Before she leaves, she'll phone him so he'll know when to expect her."

"What time's she calling him?"

"Seven. She leaves for New York right after that."

I bit into the jelly doughnut that was my breakfast, then looked down at my tie. It was sprinkled with sugar. I brushed the sugar away, remembering too late that sugar on the floor could attract rats.

"So if I'm there at seven," I said, "Jullee should be in her room."

"If she knows what's good for her, she will be. Bobby's expecting her call, and you don't fuck with him. Especially when it comes to money."

"Speaking of money," I said, "Jullee should be sitting on a pile. So what do we do with it?"

Haysoos chuckled. "Help yourself. Won't be the first time, right?"

I let that pass and said, *What about the locker at Dulles Airport?* Schiafino's Washington cops would be expecting someone to show up for the gun and information on Jullee's hotel. If I didn't clean out the locker, the Exchange Students might get suspicious and decide to visit Jullee's hotel.

Jesus breathed into the phone, thinking. Finally, he said, "I don't get it. I mean, what are you trying to say?"

"I'm saying it might be a good idea for me to pick up the gun. Play the game. Act like everything's normal, then go to Jullee's hotel."

"Right. Now I understand. Play like you're serious. Sure, you gotta do that."

Haysoos did some more breathing, then said, "How you getting her back?"

"If I tell you, we'll both know."

"Yo, I'm just curious. You got a safe house, or you stashing her at your place?"

I reached for my coffee. "Know how you keep an asshole in suspense?"

"No."

"I'll tell you later."

Bauza then became somewhat testy. "Man, you got an attitude problem, you know that?"

"I'm going to Washington," I said. "That's all you need to know. Jullee registered under her own name?"

"Mrs. Matthew Hopkins."

"Who? What?"

Haysoos said, "She digs Vincent Price. Bobby says she picked Hopkins because that's the name Price used in a movie where he went around burning witches."

"Speaking of burning people," I said, "you might want to leave town before your friend Schiafino decides to set fire to you and Miss Kansas."

"Don't worry. I was only waiting to get the word from you. Gina and me, we're outta here."

"I'd better get cracking. I've got a few things to do before I leave."

Haysoos said, "Washington shuttle out of La Guardia puts you in there in forty-five minutes. Once Jullee's gone, Schiafino's coming after her. You got to know that."

"Leave Jullee to me," I said. "You worry about finding a hiding place for you and Miss Kansas."

My next call was to Carlyle, who thanked me for escorting

her to the fund-raiser, then seeing her home. She did most of the talking, nearly all of it about how Elder bad let her down. I wasn't all that interested in Daddy Duke's evil ways, but she needed to talk so I listened. When her phone rang last night, Carlyle had refused to answer, knowing it was Elder. Later she checked her answering machine, and sure enough, there was Daddy Duke, weeping and sloshed, babbling on about her being the only woman he'd ever loved and blaming me for coming between them. Carlyle herself had ended up crying. Elder had finished by saying he wasn't as bad as Fear Meagher made him out to be. Fortunately, my days of making trouble for him were about to come to an end.

"I don't like the sound of that," Carlyle said. "I think you should be very careful the next few days."

I said I'd certainly try.

She said, "Your story about Ray Footman and Tucker's daughter also kept me awake last night. Ordinarily, I'd dismiss it as so much trash. But coming from you, I have to take it seriously. Mayor Tucker adored that girl. He'd kill Ray if he ever found out the truth. Believe me, he would."

"You going to give the mayor a call?"

"Not in this life," Carlyle said. "That's definitely not the kind of news you want to bring Roger Tucker about his daughter. Frankly, I don't think he'll ever get over her death."

"Desperate remorse swallows the present in a quenchless rage."

"What's that, more Yeats?"

I said, "No, it's Blake."

"Yeats, Blake, and Jerry Lee Lewis. Anyone ever tell you you're strange?"

"All the time."

Carlyle said, "This Washington trip you're not talking about. Is it dangerous?"

"Dion's coming with me," I said. "He's the only cop I can trust."

"Good luck to the both of you. And there's nothing you can tell me now?"

I said I'd talk to her tomorrow and hung up.

One problem I wouldn't have is explaining my trip to Hayden. He wasn't coming into the office today. Yesterday at the dentist he'd had a bad reaction to a Novocain shot. Which was a break for me. Had I told him what I had in mind, he'd have had no choice. He would have had me arrested.

My next call was to Dion. After giving him the name of the Bronx bank and the officer Gavilan had spoken with, I asked him to have Maggie O'Keeffe use her connections and see if Haysoos was telling the truth. I said if the new account checked out, the Washington trip was on. Get back to me as soon as possible.

No problem.

While waiting for Dion to call, I occupied myself by reconstructing my shredded mail. I didn't do too well. I was still struggling twenty minutes later when Dion phoned. There was indeed a new bank account under Damaris's name. Amount on deposit: twenty-five thousand dollars.

We were on our way to Washington.

I said I'd like to arrive in Washington in plenty of time to check out Jullee's hotel before moving in on her. If possible, I wanted to avoid being surprised. Dion agreed. I said I'd get back to him regarding the tickets and hung up.

I spent the next few hours alone in the conference room, examining maps of Washington, making arrangements for my flight, and booking a car for our return to New York. I also telephoned the Hotel Duquesne. One Mrs. Matthew Hopkins had checked in last night and was still registered. Meanwhile the building superintendent phoned to say he couldn't get all the rat blood out of my drawer. At three o'clock I left the office and headed for La Guardia Airport.

317

LII
Full Circle

I was alone in the motel garage. From the entrance I could see La Guardia Airport fifty feet away, where a night shuttle prepared to touch down on a darkened runway edged in gleaming white lights. I'd driven here six hours ago. In that time I hadn't left the airport.

I pulled a tuna-fish sandwich from my topcoat, unwrapped it, and shoved the cellophane into my pocket. Then I dug into the sandwich. It was my dinner, and it tasted like luke-warm goo.

While eating, I thought of Jesus Bauza. Yesterday I'd told him just what he wanted to hear, namely, that I'd go to Washington and grab Jullee before Schiafino could waste her. I'd lied. But then so had Jesus. The trip had been a setup.

I finished eating, then looked around to see if I'd dropped anything. The garage lighting was pretty dim, so I used a penlight to check the immediate area. Now wasn't the time to be careless. One mistake, just one, and I could end up on death row. As it turned out, I hadn't dropped a crumb.

The garage was located beneath a two-story motel, one of three built on flat land west of the airport. I'd been hiding here for over an hour. My first move had been to avoid security. No problem there. Security was an ex-cop named Cephas Purify, a bull-necked fifty-five-year-old black man with a major capacity for cheap booze. I knew Cephas. We'd met a year ago, when OCCB had used one of the motels as a safe house for a witness in an Israeli drug case. In his last year as a cop, Cephas had broken a kneecap chasing a suspect. These days he didn't get around much, preferring to remain indoors with his bad leg propped up on a cushion while sucking on a bottle of muscatel and watching *Days of Our Lives*. Eventually, I'd let him know I was here. But only after I'd taken care of business.

The garage was small and dark, with concrete walls, low ceiling, and barely enough lighting to keep you from bumping into stone pillars. There was room for just four cars. Tonight it held three, one a beat-up Mercury belonging to Cephas. Alongside the Merc was a beauty of a bike, a Harley in mint condition, its spoke wheels and leather saddle polished to a glossy finish. A brass U-shaped lock was clamped to the back wheel. I was waiting around for the owner. La Guardia had indoor and outdoor parking. What it didn't have was night security. At the airport the bike would have been stripped clean in minutes.

I checked my watch. Nine o'clock. Any minute now.

I hid in back of a pillar within sight of the Harley. Behind me a broken window failed to keep out the cold air. I blew into my gloved hands, then drew my Glock. No need to take off the safety. The Glock didn't have one.

How do you kill six hours at an airport? I'd ridden buses from one end of La Guardia to the other, reading Yeats's "The Secret Rose" and thinking of Lynda, my Rose. When I needed a men's room, I ducked into a snack bar. Once in a while I'd look toward Rikers Island and think about Maurice Robichaux lying chained to a hospital bed and about his mother, who wore pink Jackie Kennedy suits, and about Carlyle Taylor, who cried when she listened to her answering machine. Three blacks waiting for a white cop to deliver justice. Was that faith or what? Mencken called faith an illogical belief in the occurrence of the improbable. So where did I get off helping Maurice when I had problems of my own? Thou shalt not trust the advice of a man who's in deep shit.

I wore a black leather jacket, hooded sweatshirt, running shoes, and a black knit cap. To my knowledge I wasn't being followed, but a change of clothes did seem prudent. At the moment I looked like the wiseguys who hung around the airport freight terminals, stealing anything that wasn't nailed down when they weren't dealing drugs to pilots and flight attendants.

But where the mob has its crews, I was working alone. And at a time when I should have had a ton of backup. A team with radios, beepers, shotguns, and cars blocking off escape routes. But that would have meant playing by the rules, a luxury I couldn't afford. Instead I was alone in the garage, hoping to get lucky. Hoping I knew enough about the bike owner to have predicted his next move.

I wore gloves and wool socks, neither of which did much to keep my hands and feet warm. To get my circulation going, I laid the Glock on the windowsill and jogged in place. When I was loose, I began throwing punches. To make it interesting, I imagined myself in the ring with Sugar Ray Robinson, slipping his left, then hooking a right to the body and following up with more body shots, driving him into the ropes, forcing him to hang on and look to the referee. In my dreams.

Suddenly, headlights pulled into the motel, lighting up the garage and sending me reaching for the Glock.

False alarm. The vehicle turned out to be a cab dropping off a young couple, who entered the motel in lockstep, her head on his shoulder, his hand on her ass. I still had the garage to myself. But not for long. In time Cephas or another car owner would show up. I tried not to think about it. Instead I looked through a broken window at planes taking off and thought about the bike owner. *Tonight or never*, I told myself. After tonight, I'd never get within a mile of him. It had to be tonight. When he wasn't expecting me.

My legs began to ache. I'd been on my feet too long, and I needed sleep. I leaned against the cold garage wall, but the chill quickly worked its way into my spine, making me feel even more uncomfortable. I yawned, and the frozen air attacked my fillings. I wanted a cigarette and I wanted a drink, and I wanted this night to be over. Above all I wanted Lynda to forgive me for what I'd done and for what I was about to do. *Red Rose, proud Rose, sad Rose of all my days! / Come near me, while I sing the ancient ways.*

And then I saw him.

Walking toward me. Soundless. Menacing.

A shadow who'd floated out of the night. Life and death, past and future, and just feet away from the garage. He'd gotten close without making the slightest noise, and it was just dumb-ass luck I'd spotted him before he spotted me. At first I rejected the idea it might be who I was expecting. I told myself this was just another citizen come to reclaim his car. A businessman who'd finished pumping his secretary and was now going home to the wife. But my gut said, *he's here. Deal with it.*

I made myself invisible, easing behind the pillar while keeping the new arrival in sight. I watched him stop at the garage entrance and look around. A cautious man. Not one to stick his neck out. He wore the uniform of a motorcycle cop: black leather jacket, boots, and black pants, with his face hidden by a visored helmet. A gym bag hung from one shoulder. He was barrel-chested, with broad shoulders and muscular thighs, exactly what a coach wanted in a running back or in a wrestler. For long seconds he eyed the bike without moving. He kept one hand on his holster the whole time.

I thought, *he's seen me.* I held my breath, watching as he stood rigid for a long time. Were we playing a game? *First one to move loses.* He enjoyed a war of nerves. It was his specialty, and he'd take on anybody. Except with him the war was always undeclared and fought to the death, with no holds barred. He had me twitchy. More shaky than I'd ever admit. *He's made me,* I thought, *fucking made me.* Then his hand came off the gun, and he walked toward the bike. I relaxed. Just a little. You could never completely relax around this guy.

At the bike he hung the gym bag from the handlebars, took off his helmet, and tucked it under one arm. He rotated his head and rubbed the back of his neck. The man needed a little relief. He'd had an exhausting day.

I stepped from behind the pillar, the Glock aimed at his chest.

"Don't you look cute," I said.

The cop was Schiafino. And was he ever surprised.

I'd never known him to be speechless. Not Bobby Schemes, the old sharpie himself. But he'd just been hit with the mother of all surprises. By the look on his face, you'd have thought he'd caught his hand in a car door. I watched him open his mouth to speak. Nothing came out.

I said, "Turn around. Back to me. You so much as blink, and I'll cut your spinal cord in half."

He gave me his back. That's when his voice returned. "Man, you're like a fag without AIDS. One lucky cocksucker. Looking all over Washington for you, and you're here. Easy with the gun. I'm cool. I ain't no Steven Seagal."

I jammed the Glock against his spine, pulled his .45 from its holster, and stepped back. Then, placing his gun on the cement floor, I ordered Schiafino to turn around and back away from the piece. I kept the Glock aimed at his chest.

"You go away on a trip," I said. "You don't write, you don't phone, and after all we've been to each other. I feel used."

Schiafino tucked his helmet under one arm. "How'd you catch on?"

"We're cops, remember?" I said. "We get paid to think evil. Your first mistake was Bauza. Face it, the man's just not presidential material."

"Tell me about it. Cross a Latino with a gorilla, and you get a dumb gorilla. What did he do wrong?"

"Everything."

"I love it."

I said, "You told me you'd be coming for me real soon. Next day Jesus invites me to tour our nation's capital. How's that for timing?"

"Go on."

"Yesterday in the park we're discussing your sinful ways. I expected to be patted down for a wire. But no. Jesus takes my word I'm clean. Something wrong there. He should have covered his ass, seeing as how our little talk incriminated him in everything from money laundering to murder. As for him giving you up, I don't think so. You put the fear of God in Jesus a long time ago."

Schiafino nodded. "Still doesn't tell me how you ended up here."

"Well, it goes something like this. The minute Haysoos reached out for me, I smelled a trap. Had to be your idea, you calling the shots and all. I also knew you'd personally want to put a bullet in my head."

"Lynda was my wife. You seem to forget that."

"You're wrong," I said. "I remember all too well. That's why I called this meeting. Anyway, to kill me, you had to get to Washington. Before that you had to make your way past cops, reporters, and assorted perverts camped in front of your house. You could only do that by becoming invisible."

"That's me. The disappearing dago."

"This morning I put someone on your house. You had a visitor. Just one. A cop on a bike. Weren't you a state trooper at one time?"

Schiafino gave me a broad smile. "Made trooper of the month twice."

"Lynda says that's where you became interested in bikes. Anyway, this cop comes to see you, and he stays fifty-two minutes exactly. Put it another way. Fifty-two minutes after he arrived, you left the house wearing his uniform and helmet. Then you hop on the bike, and off you go. So who's the guy lounging around your house in his drawers, just counting the minutes until you return."

"Aldo," Schiafino said. "We're about the same size, except he has a bigger butt. Mind telling me who you had pulling surveillance?"

"My father," I said. "Couldn't keep him out of this thing. Not after what your guys did to him. He ran the bike plates. The bike's yours. Lynda said you treated your bikes better than you treated her."

"The bikes didn't give me any lip. Never saw your old man. Means he's a good cop. Tell him I said so. You still haven't told me how you knew I'd come here."

I said that was the easy part. "Last year's task force. The one we were on together, remember?"

Schiafino raised a forefinger. "Gasoline scam. Russians and wiseguys. Used to meet here. Schmucks thought leaving the city meant they wouldn't run into any more wiretaps. So that's how you came to be in this fine establishment tonight."

"Lynda helped me nail you. Funny, isn't it. She told me

about the bikes and how you're one cheap bastard. Said you'd rather shoot off a toe than spend money. Most cops expect a free ride, but you take the cake. On the way here I thought, he's flying out of La Guardia. Now where's he going for free parking?"

Schiafino nodded. "So Lynda told you about the bikes. My old man always said anything with tits or tires is gonna cost you. How right he was."

I said, "Cops stick together, something you counted on. My guess is that before coming to see you this morning, fat-assed Aldo came here. He shows up in a trooper's uniform, riding the bike, and he gives Cephas some bogus story about working undercover on an airport drug case. He asks if he can park in the garage, and Cephas says no problem. Come and go as you please."

Schiafino looked at his watch and said, "Close enough. Back to Bauza."

"You going somewhere? You keep checking the time."

"Well, I would like to get home before Aldo cleans out the fridge. The man lives to eat. How do you think he got that big butt?"

I said, "Let's cool it on any travel plans for the moment. Back to Bauza. I told him you'd left a witness behind when you killed Lynda. Guess what. He freaked. Know what I think? I think he saw himself going down with you. Meaning he was lying when he said he'd dumped you."

"Witness. Let's see. Someone who saw me and Jullee enter the garage with Lynda. Has to be Oz Lesnevitch or Alma. Nobody else was in the house."

I took a step to my right. Anything to keep Schiafino off balance.

I said, "Then there's Daddy Duke."

"Lawyers. Every time they sit down to make out a bill, the burglar alarm goes off."

"Last night I saw Elder, and he didn't mention the money or anything else I found in the tunnel. Mind you, this is the same guy who got in my face when I wouldn't turn this stuff over to him. But last night he was Mr. Mellow, as laid-back as can be. And this morning he leaves a message on Carlyle's service, in effect saying that my days are numbered. Kind of sets a man to thinking."

Schiafino fingered the zipper on his leather jacket. "Elder was ticked over what Aldo and Keller did to Carlyle at the airport. Wanted to go after them with a baseball bat. He wasn't down for raping her. She might want to know that."

Schiafino giggled. "Understand you and Footman had words. Something to do with his taste for brown sugar."

"I mentioned Yonkers, and he nearly barfed on my shoes."

Schiafino said, "He called last night, Footman. Talk about being highly agitated. Wanted to know how you'd managed to learn about him and little Miss Tucker. I said I had no idea."

"Right. Except we know Bauza won't say dick without your approval. You lied to Footman. But then you lie to everybody."

"Whatever it takes to close the deal, my man."

"A little of this, a little of that, right? The stuff about Footman and the mayor's daughter was true. The rest was bullshit. You probably figured I wouldn't notice the difference."

"Now that you mention it, that idea did cross my mind. But you know how it goes. Win some, lose some. Some days you eat the bear. Other days the bear eats you."

Schiafino scratched his eyebrow with a thumbnail, then looked at the garage floor and widened his eyes. He was keyed up. In a sweat and on the ragged edge. Not a healthy state of mind for a man with a short fuse.

He had to get back to Brooklyn before something went wrong. Before Aldo found a way to screw things up.

I said, "Why did you kill Lynda?"

"I ran out of gift ideas. Fuck you want me to say."

My outstretched arm was tired. Stepping back into the shadows, I let my gun hand fall to my side.

"Feel free to speak your mind," I said. "I'm not wired. And I'm alone."

Schiafino snorted. "Do I look like I give a shit? I own the department, I own the mayor. I snap my fingers, it happens. *Ba-da-bing, ba-da-boom.* You can't touch me, and neither could Lynda. Goddamn Lynda. She wants a divorce, right? So she starts collecting evidence. Got more than she bargained for. Overhears a phone call, me talking to Elder about a trip I'd made to Washington. About what I'd done there."

"So you killed her."

"If you're waiting for me to say I'm sorry, we'll be here a long time. Catch the wave, *Feargal.* Juries don't convict cops. Not even when we're wrong. Am I telling you something you don't already know? The public wants the bad guys eliminated, and at this point in time they don't much care how. The way I see it, one dead woman is a small price to pay for protecting the Exchange Students. You have another opinion, I say you lost your natural mind and you best go looking for it."

I watched his face. There was no remorse. No regrets. He could have been talking about painting his house. But he wasn't. He was talking about Lynda and playing her cheap, as he always did. *Red Rose . . . Sad Rose.*

Schiafino looked inside his helmet. "My people followed you to the airport. They saw you and your father board the Washington shuttle. What happened? You parachute out over Jersey or what."

I said I'd shown up at the airport, but there'd been a last-minute switch. The two men boarding the plane had been my father and a mechanic named Juan Cedeño, who was around my size, give or take a few pounds. Juan had worn my hat and coat, and kept my scarf over his face. Together he and Dion flew down to Dulles, then back to New York on the first available flight. Right now they were home watching *Jeopardy!*

I said, "I figured you couldn't stay in D.C. long. Not when you had to get back to Brooklyn. How's Jullee? She still alert and lively?"

Schiafino grinned. "She nearly became excess baggage, which would have been the case had you turned up in Washington. But you're here, so she's still breathing."

"Let me guess. You'd planned to kill her and blame me. Your guys in D.C. would then conjure up some bogus charge and claim I got shot resisting arrest. Speaking of Jullee, what's my motive for killing that little scamp?"

Schiafino held up his hand. "A question for you. Do people with dyslexia wipe their ass, *then* shit? How about you stop trying to swing dicks with me and just take me in."

"You seem to be having a good time," I said.

Schiafino looked into his helmet again. "Enjoy yourself, I always say. If you can't enjoy yourself, enjoy someone else. Anyway, let's get this farce over with. Make your call. Go waste a quarter."

I stepped from the shadows and said, "Kind of hard to do justice to the dead."

"The hell's that supposed to mean?"

"Means I wish Lynda were here to see this."

"Tell you what. Blow a hole in your dumb head. That way you meet up with my wife, and the two of you can have a nice long talk about me."

"She was too precious to be destroyed," I said.

Schiafino raised his voice. This was as close as he'd come to losing it. "Lynda was a liability," he said. "Understand that, OK? Doing her showed I was serious."

"So you did kill her."

"Let's just say I found her death meaningful. Now I *know* my people aren't going to give me any trouble. Not after this. Lynda learned something, too."

"Which is?"

"You married to me, you don't go spreading your legs for nobody. No-fucking-body. Now let's talk about you. The sun sometimes shines on a dog's ass. That means you got lucky tonight. Don't count on it happening a second time."

"There isn't going to be a second time," I said.

Schiafino scratched his head and pretended to look confused. "I'm not getting a crystal-clear picture here. Aren't you supposed to be reading me my rights, then calling for a car?"

"Any cop who shows up isn't going to arrest you. The minute I phone in, the word gets out. Next thing, your cops are on the set. They whack me, shove a kilo of blow in my jacket, and call it a righteous shooting. Meanwhile you leave and go on to a brighter future."

"I can live with that," Schiafino said.

"That's the problem."

I said as long as he was alive, the Exchange Students would be killing people. And he'd go on blackmailing anyone who hired him. As long as he was alive, none of his people would talk, because in prison or on the street he'd find a way to kill anyone who gave him up. I said I knew this as sure as I knew he'd never forgive me for being with his wife.

I said, "Full circle. First Lynda and now you."

"Now me?"

"You both died in a garage."

Schiafino leaned his head back. Working his jaw, he thought about what he'd just heard. He looked down at his gun, then closed his eyes. The gun was too far away, and we both knew it. I saw something else, too. He was starting to feel defeated. And he didn't like it. Not at all.

But he was Bobby Schemes. And he had one more card to play. One more chance to talk himself out of the shitter.

"Kill me, and you'll never find Lynda's letter," he said.

I said I'd thought about that and shot him twice in the chest, seeing him leave his feet and hit the bike, landing on the concrete floor, on his side, with one hand clutching the kickstand. A second later he released his grip on the kickstand and died.

I shoved the Glock in my belt, stepped to the bike, and opened the gym bag. I saw a priest's collar, black dickey, and dark glasses and a beard. Schiafino's disguise on the Washington shuttle. I poked around the bag some more but didn't find what I was looking for.

Someone was bound to have heard the shots. I'd be having company soon. I told myself to stay cool. I heard a woman shout, *The shots came from the first motel.* The one I happened to be in. My eyes went to Schiafino's helmet. He'd stared at it a number of times.

I picked up the helmet, looked inside, and saw a folded sheet of paper. Removing it from the helmet, I unfolded the single page and switched on my penlight. I was looking at Lynda's letter. My motive for killing Jullee. Pocketing it, I hung my shield from my neck and went looking for Cephas Purify.

LIII
Goodness Gracious

After Schiafino, another death. This time the deceased was none other than the almighty Ray Footman.

Twenty-four hours after Bobby Schemes checked out, Footman jumped or fell from his Gramercy Park penthouse.

A coroner ruled in favor of suicide, a lucky break for Mayor Tucker, since, I believed, Footman could have tied him to the Exchange Students. But that wasn't to be. There went my chance to see Tucker squirming in front of investigators and developing a memory or credibility problem. When told of Footman's blackmail plot to finance his reelection, Mr. T. managed to look baffled and mystified. His supporters, blacks and white liberals, bought his act. I didn't. And the reason I didn't is because, as the saying goes, there are no virgins in whorehouses.

What did Tucker know, and when did he know it? Good question. Too bad it wasn't raised by the NYPD or FBI, both of which treated him as though he were made of crystal. Mr. T. received no hard questions and no subpoenas. Nor did he suffer the indignity of damaging press leaks. Chalk that up to the politics of race. Mr. T. had White House connections and was expected to deliver New York City's black vote when the president ran for reelection. This plus the lack of a smoking gun prompted the department and the Feebs to back off. Our beloved mayor was home free.

Footman died without leaving a note. But then many suicides packed it in without saying good-bye. Footman's sudden passing shocked family and friends. All agreed he'd had no money or drug problems or any known physical or mental illnesses. Coworkers described him as hardworking, optimistic, and dedicated to Tucker. He'd been alone in his apartment at the time of his death, employed no live-in help, and his wife and two daughters had gone to Harvard to register the girls for the fall term. The only witnesses to his high-dive act had been three Persian cats.

A public show of grief was called for. No problem there. Tucker ordered city flags to be flown at half-mast, then issued a press release in which he praised Footman as an uncommon friend and a public servant of the highest order. There was no mention of Footman's involvement with the Exchange Students. Tucker also paid the obligatory consolation visit to Footman's widow. On the day of the funeral, he showed up with a long face, moist eyes, and a yarmulke on his nappy head. All of this just after he'd learned of his daughter's affair with Footman and had vowed to kill him for it.

Footman's death created a job opening. Actually, it created two. The city needed a new deputy mayor, and it needed a new police commissioner. Right after Footman took the big jump, Carl Dowd resigned as head of the NYPD. His replacement was none other than Con McGuigan. Dowd's being forced out was no surprise. The Exchange Students had operated on his watch, after all.

But then there was Tucker's promise in the last election. *As long as I'm mayor, New York will have a black police commissioner.* Like any politician's promise, this one was written on running water. The department did have a few qualified black candidates for the job—a deputy commissioner and a couple of experienced inspectors. My pick would have been the chief of detectives, a highly decorated black officer with plenty of street experience and my idea of a good cop. So why McGuigan.

The word that came to mind was *payoff. Ditto Head kills Footman, thereby erasing any connection between Tucker and the Exchange Students. In return, Ditto Head gets what he wants most in life.*

I decided I didn't care what Tucker and McGuigan were up to. When it came to power, these two had reached the point where there were no rules. I couldn't bring them down if I wanted to, and I didn't want to. Footman's death, murder or otherwise, was no great loss. He'd thought he could run with Bobby Schemes and that none of the shit would rub off on him. He'd been wrong. It had, and now he was dead. It was time for me to get on with my life.

Charges against Maurice Robichaux were dropped, prompting black activists to pack Baptist churches and entertain TV cameras by damning the white man's justice system. For once, I couldn't blame them.

Maurice had even more of a right to bitch. And a right to be compensated big time for what he'd gone through. Which is why shysters descended on him and his mother by the carload, crawling out from under rocks or from wherever lawyers holed up when they weren't dicking humanity. Each promised Maurice untold wealth from lawsuits, movie deals, and book deals. All he had to do was choose the best liar and let him go for it.

His mother sent me a nice thank-you note, handwritten on stationery the color of her Jackie Kennedy suit. With the note came an autographed copy of one of her books on black history. I couldn't be bothered reading it, so I gave the book to Dion. He couldn't be bothered either. He threw it in the back of the Henry J, where it lay for weeks until he gave it to the Mukerjees.

In any criminal case involving more than one perp, the first one to rat out his friends gets the best deal. The streetwise and calculating Jesus knew this to be a fact, which is why he was the first one through the prosecutor's door. He confessed to seven murders, asked for leniency, and offered to give up everyone from New York and D.C. cops to Harvey Rafaelson and my little friend Jullee Vulnavia. The prosecutor took him up on his offer. In return Jesus got five years in federal prison, to be followed by induction into the witness-protection program.

McGuigan's spin doctors, meanwhile, were working overtime. They let it be known that the idea of investigating the Exchange Students had been McGuigan's. Not Jack Hayden's, not mine, but that of Ditto Head, a two-fisted crime fighter if ever there was one. Hayden and I went along with this little scenario for our own reasons. Hayden was promised his captain's bars before the year was out. I played the game since McGuigan made it clear that in this matter my option tank was running on empty. He had questions about the Schiafino shooting, questions that could cause problems for me should our new commissioner decide he wanted answers.

And what were these questions? For openers, why hadn't I informed the department I was going to La Guardia. Why hadn't I called for backup. Why had I failed to inform motel security I was on the premises. And exactly how did I manage to kill Schiafino, since his gun appeared to have been drawn before he'd taken two bullets to the chest.

McGuigan could be hard-line, nasty, and vindictive. And then there was his bad side. Knowing all this, I paid close attention when he said his questions didn't necessarily call for answers, provided I behaved myself. He added he had no interest in pursuing the matter of Lynda's letter or Baby Cabrera's missing twenty-five K. Then he asked if I had any questions about Footman's suicide and did I feel inclined to go poking around this case as I'd done with Lynda's murder. I said I was satisfied with things the way they were. McGuigan said he was glad to hear that, then invited me to his formal swearing-in ceremony a few days hence. I said I'd try to make it.

As for the public, it was fed a wild tale about a handful of rogue cops working as contract killers, the few-bad-apples theory the department always fell back on whenever cops fucked up. Since it was a cop—me—who'd brought down the Exchange Students, the feds allowed McGuigan to put his own spin on events. In return, all trials were to be held in federal court. Harvey Rafaelson, Aldo, Big Red, Larry Aarons, and others in Schiafino's crew found themselves facing hard time in a federal prison, and since federal sentences don't carry parole, hard time would be hard indeed.

Aldo avoided trial by tucking a shotgun under his chin and blowing off most of his head. He'd probably been thinking about his cousin, the one doing time in Atlanta, and after thinking about him long enough he'd decided he couldn't do jail. As for those citizens who'd hired the Exchange Students, there were no arrests, indictments, or convictions.

F. Scott Fitzgerald said it best. *The rich are very different from you and me.*

Jullee Vulnavia, the well-known Vincent Price fan, found herself facing charges of accessory to murder and money laundering, among other things. But convicting her wasn't going to be easy. Jonathan Munro flew in a hotshot criminal lawyer from Texas to represent her, a guy who hadn't lost a case in over twenty years and who didn't get out of bed for anything less than a six-figure retainer. With that kind of talent calling the shots, Jullee could put up one hell of a defense, which is what Munro had in mind. And exactly what was he getting for his money? A guarantee that prosecutors would find it difficult, if not impossible, to link him to Schiafino and Footman via Jullee.

Munro's next move was to hire Lisa Watts as head of corporate security at three hundred thousand dollars a year. To me it appeared to be another case of money talks. Since McGuigan was boffing Lisa, her new job now obligated McGuigan to do the right thing. Which was to see that no evidence appeared linking Munro to the Exchange Students.

Ditto Head announced an upcoming series of cutbacks in the number of civilians employed by the NYPD. The cuts were for budgetary reasons, he said. Twenty people would be let go immediately, with another twenty to follow next month. The union didn't make a fuss, not after McGuigan explained the facts of life, which were that anyone who didn't leave quietly had another choice, which was to be charged as an accessory in a multiple murder case.

I visited Damaris Bauza in the hospital, where I gave Gavilan a couple of computer games. I also promised to take him to a Knicks play-off game even though the games were sold out. I knew an ex-cop working security at Madison Square Garden, and when a big game came up, he'd let me watch it from the tunnel leading to the players' dressing room. Gavilan was a Knicks fanatic. He couldn't have been happier. As for Shares, it was shut down and its liquor license revoked.

Eugene Elder decided the best way to survive was to cut and run. He fled the country and was said to be in Europe, traveling under a false passport and accompanied by a dancer from Shares.

"He called me the night before he left," Carlyle told me one evening over dinner not long after I'd shot Schiafino. We were in a small Italian restaurant across from her paper. The owner had her picture on the wall. When I said I was impressed, she beamed.

"Gene cried like a baby," she said. "He wanted me to come with him. He seemed to have forgotten that he already had a traveling companion."

"He's been doing a lot of crying lately. What did you tell him?"

"I told him good-bye. I wasn't comfortable talking to him. I remember him as strong, not the way he is now. In any case I can't see myself as a fugitive, especially in places where they don't have toilet paper. What do you think will happen to him?"

"He'll drink himself to sleep," I said. "Then he'll drink to get through the day. He'll feel homesick, and he'll drink to blot it out. He'll have to buy protection, which won't come cheap. Then one morning he'll wake up and find his lady's gone. That's probably when he'll get tired of running and allow himself to be caught. If he'd stayed here, he might have cut a deal. Nobody worked the system better than he did."

Carlyle said, "I did love him, you know. The first time, not this time. This time I think I was in love with something else. A memory. I don't know what's worse. Being with him and seeing him fall apart or not being there and imagining it happening."

I thought, *he's shit. Scrape him off your shoe, and get on with your life.* Then again, who was I to give advice? It would be a long time before I forgot Lynda. Growing older without her wasn't going to be easy. Would a thousand drinks be enough to kill the pain? I'd find out soon enough.

Carlyle smiled. "Won't be easy, but I do think it's time to forget Gene. Momma always told me, never let the same dog bite you twice."

I said, Momma was right.

Carlyle looked at her long manicured nails. "Speaking of

right, some people are saying the Schiafino shooting was anything but right. They're saying you shot him in cold blood."

"Really."

"Detective Bauza's saying that. He claims he never told you Schiafino would be at the motel."

"Who are you going to believe, me or a contract killer?"

Carlyle gave me a half smile. "I suspect you're smarter than the average contract killer. In fact, I know you are. Changing the subject, let's move along to Ray Footman's suicide. He wasn't the type to kill himself. I knew him. Knew him well. He's like you. Too smart to do something that dumb. What's your opinion? Did he or didn't he?"

"Only his hairdresser knows for sure."

"Don't be a wiseass."

I said, "Let's just say McGuigan's determined to be police commissioner. Meaning he's not going to investigate Footman's death. He doesn't want to. The mayor doesn't want him to either."

"Why do I get the feeling you're not being entirely forthcoming, as you police like to say? Interesting, by the way, that Tucker vowed to have a black commissioner for as long as he's in office. Suddenly, he's got a white one. What's your comment on that?"

"Nothing less than a supernatural occurrence." I poured more wine. "Sort of like you buying into McGuigan's spin on the Exchange Students when you know the truth. Which is that Tucker's dirty."

"I'm still a liberal," she said. "I think the city needs a black mayor and Tucker's the answer."

I thought, *If Tucker's the answer, it must have been a stupid question.*

Carlyle said, "I don't want to cost him the election. Which could happen if I ask too many questions. I have enough of the story to keep me happy."

She was silent, then said, "Maybe you're right. Maybe I'll wake up one day and find the price of black power is much too high. Until then . . ."

She drank more wine, then took a small envelope from her purse and handed it to me.

I said, What is it?

She smiled and waited.

I opened the envelope. She'd given me two tickets to Jerry Lee Lewis's show.

"Front row," she said. "If you like, I can also arrange for you to meet him."

For the second time tonight, she'd impressed me. Did I want to meet the Killer? Did a hobbyhorse have a hickory dickory? I asked how she'd gotten tickets when every show was sold out.

"New York's about power," she said. "In this town it comes down to who you know. And reporters know everybody."

She sang, *"You shake my nerves and you rattle my brain. Your kind of love drives a man insane."*

For the first time in a week, I smiled. "Where'd you learn that?"

"This afternoon," she said. "Bought one of his cassettes. I was pleasantly surprised. He can kick it. For a white boy, that is."

I looked at the tickets. Pure gold. And I had no one to go with.

And then I found myself asking Carlyle with the words coming easier than I'd imagine they ever would and just as easily she said yes.

THE BEST MEN'S FICTION
COMES FROM POCKET BOOKS

BOOMER Charles D. Taylor ❑ 74330-9/$5.50

THE 100TH KILL Charles W. Sasser ❑ 72713-3/$6.50

BRIGHT STAR Harold Coyle ❑ 68543 0/$6.50

DARK WING Richard Herman, Jr. ❑ 53493-9/$6.50

DEEP STING Charles D. Taylor ❑ 67631-8/$4.95

A TIME OF WAR Michael Peterson ❑ 56787-X/$6.50

FINAL ANSWERS Greg Dinallo ❑ 73312-5/$5.50

FLIGHT OF THE INTRUDER Stephen Coonts
❑ 70960-7/$6.99

RAISE THE RED DAWN Bart Davis ❑ 69663-7/$4.95

RED ARMY Ralph Peters ❑ 67669-5/$5.50

SWORD POINT Harold Coyle ❑ 73712-0/$6.99

THE TEN THOUSAND Harold Coyle ❑ 88565-0/$6.99

38 NORTH YANKEE Ed Ruggero ❑ 70022-7/$5.99

UNDER SIEGE Stephen Coonts ❑ 74294-9/$6.99

RED INK Greg Dinallo ❑ 73314-1/$6.50

AS SUMMERS DIE Winston Groom ❑ 52265-5/$6.50

IRON GATE Richard Herman, Jr. ❑ 87309-1/$6.99

GREAT FLYING STORIES Edited by Frederick Forsyth
❑ 00062-4/$6.50

I PLEDGE ALLEGIANCE 66717-3/$6.50
